MAGAZINE

Tin House

Volume 10, Number 4

"Real life, life at last laid bare and illuminated—the only life in consequence
which can be said to be really lived—is literature, and life thus defined is in
a sense all the time immanent in ordinary men no less than the artist."

—MARCEL PROUST, *Time Regained*

Available now or coming soon from

ASTA IN THE WINGS

"A cleverly constructed, beautifully written first novel . . ."

—*Booklist*, starred review

THE WRITER'S NOTEBOOK

"Entertaining"

—*The New York Times*

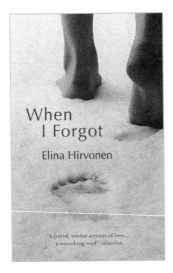

WHEN I FORGOT

"Potent, fragile and tender . . ."

—*The New York Times Book Review*

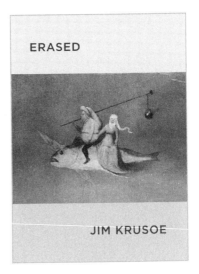

ERASED

"One of America's most sincere satirists . . ."

—Amy Gerstler, author of *Ghost Girl*

WE DID PORN: MEMOIR AND DRAWINGS

A memoir by Zak Smith

We Did Porn follows Zak Smith (aka Zak Sabbath) from the New York art scene to Los Angeles's seedy, yet colorful, underbelly—the world of alt porn. Through memoir and more than one hundred drawings, Smith narrates his foray into pornography and gives his readers a new understanding of the industry, its players, and its audience.

"Zak Smith's stylized portraits and acidic abstractions intimately capture stillness in an ever-encroaching world."—2004 Whitney Biennial

Available Now :: Paperback :: $24.95

THE CHILDREN'S DAY

A novel by Michiel Heyns

The Children's Day is a literary chronicle of a boy's coming of age in South Africa during the apartheid years of the sixties. Through a series of finely drawn and illuminating situations the novel captures the essence of what it is like to grow up in a world fraught with strange and sometimes violent contradictions of class, race, gender, and language.

"An important, lovely, and thoughtful book"
—A. L. Kennedy, *Bookforum*

Available August :: Paperback :: $14.95

"Writing isn't hard. It isn't any harder than ditch-digging."
Patrick Dennis

Michener Center for Writers
MFA in WRITING
FICTION   POETRY   SCREENWRITING   PLAYWRITING

A top ranked program. Dedicated and diverse resident faculty. Inspiring and distinguished visiting writers. $25,000 annual fellowships. Three years in Austin, Texas.

www.utexas.edu/academic/mcw   •   512-471-1601

THE UNIVERSITY OF TEXAS AT AUSTIN

DO SOMETHING SMART, READ THESE!

A Storm in the Blood
A Novel by Jon Stephen Fink

A wise and searching historical novel of political intrigue and terrorist action in turn-of-the-century London—based on a real-life story

Girl Trouble
Stories by Holly Goddard Jones

"A grand debut of a writer who is assured, sensitive, and wonderfully skillful.... A marvelous work of heart-breaking wisdom."
—Edward P. Jones, Pulitzer Prize-winning author of *The Known World*

How to Paint a Dead Man
A Novel by Sarah Hall

"One of the most significant and exciting of our younger novelists."
—*The Guardian*

More of This World or Maybe Another
Stories by Barb Johnson

"These are stunning stories. Barb Johnson is the kind of writer whose work I dream of finding and rarely do."
—Dorothy Allison, author of *Bastard Out of Carolina*

The Hidden
A Novel by Tobias Hill

"This dark and tense novel renders that experience of discovery and disillusionment with elegantly chilling skill."
—*Times Literary Supplement* (London)

Reasons for and Advantages of Breathing
Stories by Lydia Peelle

"Lydia Peelle has given us a collection of stories so artfully constructed and deeply imagined they read like classics."
—Ann Patchett, bestselling author of *Run*

the devil is a poet | a real doll | crying on the inside | psychedelic | lies!

all apologies | off the grid | give | fantastic women | the political future

ABOUT THE COVERS

quatters | trash | hollywood

Elissa Schappell

music

international obsession

the shock of the new

do not disturb

the dead of winter

Who doesn't like baby pictures?

Come on. There is something compelling, often amusing, and occasionally shocking about seeing an entire life laid out in pictures. So it seemed fitting that the cover of this, our tenth-birthday issue, display the full gamut of our covers from infancy to the cusp of, say, thirty. (And, yes, there is a very complex mathematical formula for converting human years into magazine years.)

Our very first cover, created by designer Jon Baird, resembled a handmade journal bound in warm, amber-colored leather and wrapped with a red and gold cigar band. At the center was a line drawing of the Tin House, as distinctive as a birthmark. Our early childhood issues were fanciful. Yes, the magazine was a magazine, and it was also an *objet*. Issue two resembled an antiqued tin box decorated with a surreal black and white self-portrait of Dare Wright, the eccentric and troubled author of the Lonely Doll book series, wearing nothing but a fisherman's net and a piece of driftwood. With issue six, we introduced themes, starting with "Hollywood." Issue seven, emblazoned as it was with a burning high-heeled shoe, appeared to be the perfect calling card for a dominatrix whose niche is pyromaniacs. In issue

thirteen, we got self-conscious and lost the bellyband, because, much like our gauchos, we realized the way it cut us in half wasn't flattering. Which doesn't mean we won't trot it out again when it becomes vintage. (Not so the gauchos.) We experimented in our twenties. The Music Issue was styled as a sixties-era space-age bachelor pad album, the Sex Issue a fifties pulp novel. Other covers, including one with a photo of John Ashcroft and one with a sad clown, reflected our fears. In our thirties, we reached out to artists we admired, such as graphic novelist and cartoonist cult hero Lynda Barry, whose surreal collage announced our Graphic Issue. The Fantastic Women issue was adorned with Neo-rococo painter Julie Heffernan's "Self portrait as Booty," and the notorious British graffiti artist Banksy's anti-war aerosol art tagged the Political Issue. The uproar over our last issue's "Tit Tot" cover—an apparently subversive image of a baby—a cheeky baby—nursing, has been gratifying. After all, art that provokes intense emotion, that enters through the eyes and lodges in the body, lives in us always. From our conception, that's what we striven for. To create covers that that feel alive. Because we are alive—and we are ten.

am I blue?

touch and go

graphic | evil | sex | monsters | work | hot and bothered

the willies

Tin House MAGAZINE

PUBLISHER / EDITOR IN CHIEF
Win McCormack

EDITOR
Rob Spillman

MANAGING EDITOR
Holly MacArthur

EXECUTIVE EDITOR
Lee Montgomery

SENIOR EDITOR
Michelle Wildgen

POETRY EDITOR
Brenda Shaughnessy

EDITOR AT LARGE
Elissa Schappell

ASSOCIATE EDITOR
Cheston Knapp

ASSOCIATE POETRY EDITOR
CJ Evans

ASSISTANT EDITORS
Brian DeLeeuw
Tonaya Thompson

PARIS EDITOR
Heather Hartley

ART DIRECTOR
Janet Parker

CIRCULATION DIRECTOR
Laura Howard

INTERNS
Helen Georgas
Rosalie Moffett
Patricia No
Emily Phillips
Danniel Schoonebeek

CONTRIBUTING EDITORS
Dorothy Allison
Nick Flynn
Alberto Fuguet
Jeanne McCulloch
Christopher Merrill
Rick Moody
Rachel Resnick
Helen Schulman
Tom Spanbauer
Bill Wadsworth
Irvine Welsh

READERS
Desiree Andrews
Sarah Bartlett
Gordon Buffonge
Billy Callis
Amber Clark
Lance Cleland
Emily Frey
Nicole Haroutunian
Jonathan Hunsberger
Caroline Keys
Ariana Lenarsky
Kimberly Meinert
Aaron Parrett
Kamala Puligandla
Peter Rawlings
Erika Recordon
Jordan Sayle
Kevin Stark
JoNelle Toriseva
Kyle von Hoetzendorff
Linda Woolman

Does the world really need another lit mag? A dozen years ago we asked ourselves this question and came up with a resounding *Yes!* The world really did need another literary magazine. Or, at least, we did. Our aim was to create a magazine that we wanted to read but also appealed to the man or woman on the subway platform. We wanted *Tin House* to be a haven for authors at the peak of their powers and also a jumping-off point for unpublished writers and anyone taking risks, pushing form and language. A magazine not identified with any one region (we ourselves are bi-coastal with offices in Brooklyn, New York, and Portland, Oregon) but international, drawing writers and contributing editors from all over the globe. A journal tantamount to being guest of honor at the greatest literary house party ever.

Along with poetry, fiction, and essays, we included our obsessions: food and drink, humor, pilgrimages, books that were loved and lost. We also knew, having personally shoveled mountains of slush, how hard it is for an unknown writer to break out, so we decided that in every issue we'd showcase two new voices, a fiction writer and a poet. And, we wanted the design to be a knockout, a magazine you'd see across the room and feel it was your destiny to own. A magazine that, like a great book, would warrant rereading. In the first year we took our show on the road, attending book festivals in Frankfurt, London, Miami, Los Angeles, and New York. We were determined to either make our mark immediately or flame out spectacularly. We are now publishing our fortieth issue and it is still just as thrilling to discover great writing as it was with our first.

In this special issue, some of our favorite writers from the past ten years contribute new work, including Ron Carlson, Rick Moody, and Stuart Dybek, who were in our very first issue. Our Premiere Issue also featured a story by David Foster Wallace, whom we miss. In the spirit of coming full circle, we present a story written at the budding stage of his brilliant career, previously seen only in his college literary magazine and published here with the blessing of Wallace's widow.

Over the past decade *Tin House* has not only grown as a magazine but now includes Tin House Books, which publishes ten books per year, and six years ago we built the Tin House Writers Workshop, held each summer in glorious Portland, Oregon. Along the way so many writers and artists have become like family to us. We offer our heartfelt thanks to all of you who have made these past ten years so meaningful, exciting, and gratifying. No amount of awards or accolades can compare. Of course, none of this would be possible without the initial courage and continuing enthusiasm and support of our unflagging publisher, Win McCormack. Lastly, we would like to thank our loyal readers, many of whom took the leap of faith early on and have seen us through renovations, floods, and small fires. Thank you for your enduring support.

CONTENTS

ISSUE #40 / SUMMER 2009

| |||||||||||||||||||||||||||| **Fiction** ||||||||||||||||||||||||||||||||||

Poetry

Poetry, continued

Interviews

COLSON WHITEHEAD

After the world of elevator operators, John Henry's battle with the steam engine, the warped world of branding, and a lyrical look at New York life, the MacArthur Genius finally tackles the autobiographical novel. He raps about Sag Harbor *and his previous work with Tin House editor Rob Spillman.* 53

BARRY HANNAH

A good funeral should make you horny, he believes. Novelist Tom Franklin extracts this and other bits of wisdom about writing and life from a Southern king of the short story. 214

Essays

Jean Nathan

MY DEAR LITTLE ANIMAL ← *The saga of Jean-Paul Sartre and his only known American lover.* 112

Tom Grimes

THE BLUE INSUPPORTABLE ← *Frank Conroy was attuned to the downbeats of life, its blue notes and moody rhythms. A former student recalls this maestro's career as a writer and teacher.* 158

Aimee Bender

Americca

When we came home from the movie that night, my sister went into the bathroom and then called out to our mother, asking if she'd bought another toothpaste as a hint.

I know I have major cavities, she said. But do we really need two?

Two what? asked my mother.

Two toothpastes, said Hannah.

My mother took off her sweater for the first time in hours and peered into the bathroom, where, next to the grungy blue cup that holds the toothbrushes, there were now two full toothpastes.

I only bought one, she said. I think. Unless for some reason it was on sale.

We all shrugged in unison. I brushed my teeth with extra paste and went to bed. This incident would've been filed away in non-memory and we would just have had clean teeth for longer, except that in the morning there was a new knickknack on the living room side table, a slim abstract circle made of silver, and no one had any idea where it came from.

Is it a present? asked our mother with motherly hope, but we children, all too honest, shook our heads.

I don't know what that is, I said, picking it up. It felt heavy and expensive. Cool to the touch. Nice, Hannah said.

My mother put it away in the top of the coat closet. It was nice, but it felt, she said, like charity. And I don't like too many knickknacks, she said, eyes elsewhere, wondering. She went to my grandmother and brought her a lukewarm cup of tea, which Grandma accepted and held, as if she no longer knew what to do with it.

Drink! my mother said, and Grandma took a sip and the peppermint pleased her and she smiled.

Happened again the next evening when, while setting up for a rare family dinner, my mother stood, arms crossed, in front of the pantry.

Lisa, she said, you didn't go to the market, did you?

Me?

Hannah?

No.

John?

No.

Grandma never shopped. She would get lost in the aisles. She would hide beneath the apple table like a little girl. Our mother, mouth twisted in puzzlement to the side, found soup flavors in the pantry she swore she never would've considered buying. She held up a can of lobster bisque. This is far too bourgeois for me, she said. Anyone else buy this? We all shook our heads. Wild rice and kidney bean? she said, What is this? I would never buy this—lemongrass corn chowder? They sell this stuff these days?

Yum, yelled Dad from the other room, where he was watching tennis.

Who put these here? asked Mom again.

Hannah paused, placing spoons on napkins. I don't really like soup, she said. I shook my head. Not me, I said. I definitely hate soup.

Our mother tapped her fingers against the counter, nervous.

What is going on? she said.

Hannah lined up the spoon with the knife. We've been backwards robbed, she said solemnly.

I laughed but her eyes were serious.

Alls I know is, she said, I did not buy that soup.

Neither did I, said Mom.

Neither did I, called Dad from the other room.

I could tell I was still the main suspect, just because I seemed the most interested in all of it, but as I explained repeatedly, why would a person lie about bringing food and new knickknacks into the house? That is nice. That is something to get credit for.

> Although being robbed would suck, there was nothing appealing about getting more items every day, and I felt a vague sense of claustrophia pick up in my lungs, like I might get smothered under extra throw pillows in the middle of the night.

Dad cooked up the corn chowder after he found an enormous piece of gristle in his mustard chicken. We all watched him closely for choking or poisoning but he smiled after each spoonful and said it was darned good and very unusual. Like Southwestern Thai, he said, wiping his mouth. Like . . . the Empress meets Kimosabe, he said. Like . . . silver meets turquoise, he said, laughing. Like . . . we all told him that was enough. Hannah checked the inside of the can for clues. After dinner, Dad collected water glasses from the rooms, singing.

That night, I kept a close eye on the back door but it stayed locked, and I even fixed a twig at its base to see if it got jigged during the night, but in the morning, the twig was just as before. I was walking to the bathroom to get ready for school when Mom cried out, and I ran over, and she was standing over the kitchen table, which held an extra folded newspaper. Hannah found a third pewter candlestick that matched the previous two, standing tall in the bookshelf. We ate our breakfasts in silence. Although being robbed would suck, there was nothing appealing about getting more items every day, and I felt a vague sense of claustrophia pick up in my lungs, like I might get smothered under extra throw pillows in the middle of the night. Like I might wake up dead under a pile of a thousand tiny wind-up toys. And we couldn't even sell the new stuff for extra cash because everything we got was just messed up enough to make it useless—the pewter candlestick was flaking into little slivers, and the silver circle thing had a subtle, creepy smell.

For the first time in my life, I cleaned my room after school. I threw out tons of old magazines and trash and dumb papers for school with the teacher in red pen stating: Lisa, we all know you can do better than this. I had the cleanest closet in years, which is why it was once again bad when I found, an hour later, a new mug on my side table of dancing cows holding balloons that said Happy Birthday! that ONLY could've been purchased by Hannah, but when I showed it to her she started to cry.

> Now the towel closet was full, not of anything fluffy, but of more thin and ugly towels. Tons of them.

They're trying to kill us! she sobbed, wiping her nose on her T-shirt.

Who? How? How are they trying to kill us?

The people bringing this stuff in.

But who's bringing it in? I asked. We've been home the whole time.

Ghosts, she said, eyes huge. She stared at the mug. It's not even your birthday, she said, not for months and months.

I stuck the mug in the outside trash can along with the extra newspaper. I kept my eyes carefully on all the doors. The twig stayed put.

We had a respite for a week, and everyone calmed down a bit and my mother went to the market and counted how many cans so she'd know. We ate the food we bought. We stared at the knickknacks that represented our personalities. All was getting back to normal until the next Sunday when Hannah opened the towel closet and screamed at the top of her lungs.

What? We all ran to her.

The towel closet had towels in it. Usually it had small, thin piles—we each had a towel and were expected to use it over four days for all towel purposes, and there'd be a big towel wash twice a week, one on Thursday, one on Sunday. We never stuck to the system and so usually I just used my towel as long as I possibly could until the murky smell of mildew and toothpaste started to pass from it onto me, undoing all the cleaning work of the previous shower.

Now the towel closet was full, not of anything fluffy, but of more thin and ugly towels. Tons of them. At least ten more towels, making the piles high. Countless piles of worn towels.

Well, I said. I guess we can cut the Thurs/Sun wash cycle.

My mother went off to breathe into a paper bag. Hannah straightened taller, and then put one towel around her hair and another around her body, a very foreign experience in our family.

I'm going to just appreciate the gifts, she said, even though her face looked scared. I've always wanted to use two at once, she said, even though her hair was dry and she was fully dressed in jeans and a T-shirt and the towel looked like she was getting a haircut.

At school the next week, it was past Halloween and we had to bring in our extra candies for the poor children of Glendora. Bags and bags came pouring in and, aside from candy, I brought in an extra bag of stuff for the poor children, full of soup cans and knickknacks I'd salvaged from the trash. Everyone in the family felt funny about it; maybe it was like passing on poison. But at the same time, throwing out whole unopened cans of lobster soup struck my mother as obscene. How often does a homeless woman who lives nowhere near saltwater get lobster? she asked, hands on hips, as I packed up the bag. We all shrugged. We liked how her guilt looked in this form of benevolence. I repeated it to my teacher. It's not a Snickers bar, I said, but it's got a lot more protein.

I think I saw my teacher take that soup can for herself. I watched her closely that week, but she seemed healthy enough, and my dad had never had a single negative symptom from his lemongrass corn chowder. I didn't eat any Halloween candy. I didn't want anything from anyone else.

I got a note from the shelter saying my bag was the best.

Hannah got a boyfriend. She didn't tell anyone but I could tell because she was using so many towels, making the bathroom a pile of towels, and for some reason I knew the towels were happening because of a boy. Why did she need to be so dry all the time? I asked her about it, when she came home for dinner and looked all pretty with her eyes bright like that. I had to set the table because she was late, and she apologized and said she'd take dish duty for two days.

It's okay, I said. Who is he?

She blushed, crazily. Who is who?

The reason you are late, I said.

I had to study.

Mom stood in the doorframe, but she wasn't listening. She wasn't out to bust Hannah.

How was your math test? Mom said, brushing the side of her hair with a soupspoon.

Okay, said Hannah, glaring at me. I got an A.

What did you hear? she asked, dragging me aside and cutting into my arm with her budding nails.

Nothing, I said. Ow. I just guessed.

How? she said.

No reason, I said. Towels. Who is it?

She said no one, but then she barely ate at dinner, which is rare for her, and usually I have to fight my way to the main dish to even get any because she is so hungry and that let me know she really liked him.

Dad lost his job. Then he got a new job. Then he got his old job back and went back to it. They were all in the same building.

We didn't get any more items for a few weeks. I started to miss them. I mean, I felt like I would die of claustrophobia and I had become paranoid about all things coming into the house including bath water and I had made a checklist for market items, shopping items, and all school items, but when I opened the refrigerator and saw all the same old stuff, I wanted to cry sometimes.

I left a few baits: I cleared my nightstand of all things so that it was ready for a deposit. Nothing. I bought a lobster soup with my own allowance, which made my mother shriek, but I assured her I'd bought it and I'd even saved the receipt to prove it. I brought it out of my bedroom, and she stared at the curling white paper and then looked at me, in the way she rarely did, eye to eye.

Are you okay, Lisa? she said. Ten-year-olds don't usually save receipts.

I'm trying to trap a ghost, I said.

Would you like to go to the mall? she asked. Her eyes were tired. She looked pretty with tired eyes, so I didn't mind so much.

We went to the nearest mall, over in Cerritos, which had been built twenty years ago and was ugly. I liked that about it. It was like a relative nobody liked but still had to be related to anyway. We went to the kids' store and she bought me two shirts, one orange, one red, and then I got very attached to a particular cap with an octopus on the cap part and I felt if I left it in the store I might dissolve. I didn't have much allowance left due to the spenditure of the lobster soup, and so I asked my mom as nicely as I could if I could have an advance and get the octopus cap because I loved it very much.

That? She was holding the store bag and trying to stop the salesperson from talking to her by staring out the door. Thanks, she was saying, thanks, thanks.

I love it, I said, putting it on my head. It was too big. I couldn't see well underneath it.

Please? I said.

We just got you two new shirts, she said. Do you really need a cap?

It's good for skin cancer, I said. Of the face.

She laughed. She was tired these days because she was having job trouble too; her job trouble meant she did not know how she could be useful in her life. Dad's job trouble was he had too much to do with his life. Sometimes I just wanted them to even

> Dot Meyers thought I looked dumb in a bad-fitting cap but she's dumb anyway and can't spell America right.

it out but I couldn't think of how. That afternoon, I didn't want to bother her more, but I wasn't certain I could leave the store with that cap still in it. If someone else bought it, I might tear in two.

I will pay you back, I said. I swear. Or we can exchange it for one of the shirts?

She got me the cap because I hardly ever asked for much, and at home, I slept with it on, and I wore my new orange shirt to school and back and I was ready to charge ahead when I noticed the octopus cap on my dresser.

I thought it was the one on my head except then I realized that one was already on my head. So this had to be a new one? I took the one on my head off and held them both side by side. Two octopus caps. I had two, now. One, two. They were both exactly the same but I kept saying right hand, right hand, in my head, so I'd remember which one I'd bought because that was the one I wanted. I didn't want another octopus cap. It was about this particular right-hand octopus cap; that was the one I had fallen in love with. Somehow, it made me feel so sad, to have two. So sad I thought I couldn't stand it.

I took the new one, left hand, to the trash, but then I thought my mom might see it and get mad that I'd thrown out the new cap she had especially bought for me, so I put the one I loved on my head and put the one I hated in the closet, behind several old sweatshirts. I went out to play wearing the first one. I played kickball with Dot Meyers next door but she kicks cockeyed and it was hard to see out of the cap and when I went inside, I scrounged in the closet for the second cap and it fit. That's what was so sad. It was the right size, and I put it on, and it was better. The ghosts had brought me the better cap. I put them both on, one after another, because at least by size now I could tell which was which, but it was just plain true that the one I loved did not fit and kept falling off and the one they brought did fit and looked better. Dot Meyers thought I looked dumb in a bad-fitting cap but she's dumb anyway and can't spell America right.

> It had no card, but it was really good wrapping, with those clean-cut triangular corners, and I opened it up and inside was a toy I had broken long ago.

I saw Hannah kissing a boy I'd never seen before outside our house in the bushes.

That night, I put a bunch of stuff in Hannah's bedroom to freak her out but she recognized it all as mine so it wasn't the same as the ghosts who came in with their own stuff, and I had no allowance to buy anything new.

I wore the good new cap to school.

I ate the lobster soup. I liked it. It had a neat texture. I liked it better than the usual plebeian chicken noodle my mom got. I liked the remaining wild rice one that hadn't made it into the Halloween bag; it was so hearty and different. I used the cow cup I'd salvaged from the trash, and the truth was, I liked the cow holding a balloon; it was cute. When I looked in the mirror, I sneered my upper lip and said, Benedict Arnold, Benedict Arnold, your head is on the block.

Mom came home from taking a class called Learning How to Focus your Mind, and she seemed kind of focused, more than usual at least, and she sat with Grandma on the sofa and talked about childhood.

After awhile I sat with them. There's nothing to do after homework and TV and creaming Dot Meyers.

You were a quiet child, said Grandma.

What did I like to do? asked Mom.

You liked to go with me to the store, said Grandma.

What else? asked Mom.

You liked to stir the batter, said Grandma.

What else?

I don't know, said Grandma. You liked to read.

Even as they were talking, I saw it happen on the dining room table.

Saw it as they were talking, but it wasn't like an invisible hand. Just one second there was a blank table, and I blinked, and then there was a gift on the table, a red-wrapped gift with a yellow bow. It was in a box, and I went to it and sat at the table. I knew it was for me. I didn't need to tell them, plus they were talking a lot, plus Dad was at work, plus Hannah was out kissing.

It had no card, but it was really good wrapping, with those clean-cut triangular corners, and I opened it up and inside was a toy I had broken long ago. Actually, I hadn't broken it; Hannah had. It was a mouse, made of glass, and Hannah had borrowed it without asking and dropped it in the toilet by accident—so she said—and broken off the red ball nose. I had been so mad at her I hadn't spoken to her for a week and I'd made a rule that she couldn't come in my room ever again and I asked Mom for a door lock but she didn't think I really meant it so I got one myself, at the hardware store, with a key, with money from my birthday, but I couldn't figure out how to put it on. Here was the mouse, with its nose.

What was next? Grandma?

Thanks? I said, to the air.

I took the mouse and put it on the shelf it used to be on, next to the mouse that had no nose, retrieved from the toilet. The mouse without the nose looked pathetic but a little charming, and the mouse with the nose, well. It had never been in the toilet.

When Hannah came home, I showed her. Mom's taking a new class, I said. That's good, she said. Her face was flushed. She seemed relieved, once she paid attention, that the new mouse had arrived. Sorry about the toilet thing, she said, for the fiftieth time. It's cute, she said, patting the new one.

Let's flush it down the toilet, I said.

What?

My eyes were pleading. I could feel them, pleading.

Please, Hannah.

Hang on, she said. She went to the bathroom and splashed her face and spent a minute in there with her crushiness, and then opened up. I brought both mice in.

Both, I said, the old and the new.

Fine, she said. Whatever.

How'd you do it?

I just dropped it in, she said.

On purpose?

Yeah.

I didn't blame her. Right now, it seemed like these mice were just made for the toilet. I sat next to her on the edge of the bathtub and dropped in the new guy. He floated around in the clean white toilet water.

Flush away, said Hannah, her eyes all shiny from kissing.

I flushed. He bobbed around and almost went down but didn't. He was slightly too big. The toilet almost overflowed. But still, the nose.

That's just what I did, she said. She was putting on lip gloss and smacking at herself in the mirror.

I picked up the wet new mouse and broke his nose right off. It took some pressure, me holding him good in one hand and then snapping it off. You can ruin anything, if you focus at it. There, I said.

I put both mice in the trash and washed my hands. Hannah broke up with her boyfriend a few weeks later because he'd started calling her honey, and I got picked for the kickball team, and we didn't get any more gifts. Not for years.

Mom found some work downtown as a filing clerk, and Dad almost got that promotion. Hannah went to college nearby but she lived at home because of the price of rent. Grandma got older and eventually died.

When I was about to graduate high school, I did notice a packet of yellow curry in the pantry while I was rummaging around, looking for a snack. It was in a plastic yellow envelope that just said Curry on it in red letters. I asked my mom if she'd bought it, and she said no. Hannah? No. Dad? No. I don't like curry, I said out loud, although I'd never tried it. As an afterthought, I brought it with me to college, where I had a scholarship, so I was the first one to leave home, it turned out, and it sat in the cupboard in the dorm for four years, alongside the oregano and the salt and my roommate's birth control pills. I took it with me to my first apartment that I shared with the utilities-shirker, and my second apartment with the toxic carpet, and in my third apartment, when I was twenty-seven, living alone across the country, I opened it up one night when I was hungry and made a delicious paste with butter and milk, and then I ate it over chicken and rice and cried the whole way through it. 🛡

Olena Kalytiak Davis and Rick Moody

Burning Man Haiku

wide awake again,
the night before traveling.
why the hell going?

every crumb I consume,
I think: this just might be it
for the next two days.

"Sit back, relax, and
enjoy the flight." It makes me
want to sit forward.

Leatherheads, starring
George Clooney. There is a charge
for headset rental.

gambling in Reno—
even here at the airport.
guys in bunny ears.

Burning Man, what a
homely name. Twenty years
and no replacement?

bad weed—can't get high
how will I survive the Man—
forgive me my sins

tall thing ahead—
nothing is supposed to be
taller than the Man.

here I am: nothing.
nothing is more terrifying.
nothing: here I am.

straighten up and fly
right, drunken man, the
cops are on the roof.

haiku period . . .
take your tampons out with you
leave no bloody trace

burning and looting
we the people of the Man
two hundred fifty

naked guy on bike—
are you really doing that?
comfort be damned.

"Is that Drum or is
it weed?" "I'm still subject to
piss tests." "Okay, thanks."

Jesus is the One—
women, yes; Somalis, yes;
casual sex, no.

bad jazz banged out on
an out-of-tune and muffled
spinet. gather round, kids.

you play "Low Spark of
High-heeled Boys" and I will have
to kill you, buddy.

Thunderdome! Burnouts
in cages bludgeoned
with foam bats. It's free!

"Who's ever heard of
Rumi? Ecstatic love is
an ocean? No one?"

just cover up the
nipples with some decoration.
you'll feel empowered.

is it Utopia
if the people believe that
it is Utopia?

if that's freedom, I'll
take dictatorship over
freedom any day.

go away chili-
eating man with the bad hair
I can't watch you eat!

one last haiku? I
thought I was done with this shit
infectious disease!

blood on the white sheets
just got back from Burning Man
still have not showered

THE PLANET TRILLAPHON
AS IT STANDS IN RELATION TO
THE BAD THING

FICTION

David Foster Wallace

I've been on antidepressants for, what, about a year now,

and I suppose I feel as if I'm pretty qualified to tell what they're like. They're fine, really, but they're fine in the same way that, say, living on another planet that was warm and comfortable and had food and fresh water would be fine: it would be fine, but it wouldn't be good old Earth, obviously. I haven't been on Earth now for almost a year, because I wasn't doing very well on Earth. I've been doing somewhat better here where I am now, on the planet Trillaphon, which I suppose is good news for everyone involved.

Antidepressants were prescribed for me by a very nice doctor named Dr. Kablumbus at a hospital to which I was sent ever so briefly following a really highly ridiculous incident involving electrical appliances in the bathtub about which I really don't wish to say a whole lot. I had to go to the hospital for physical care and treatment after this very silly incident, and then two days later I was moved to another floor of the hospital, a higher, whiter floor, where Dr. Kablumbus and his colleagues were. There was a certain amount of consideration given to the possibility of my undergoing E.C.T., which is short for "Electro-Convulsive Therapy," but E.C.T. wipes out bits of your memory sometimes—little details like your name and where you live, etc.—and it's also in other respects just a thoroughly scary thing, and we—my parents and I—decided against it. New Hampshire, which is the state where I live, has a law that says E.C.T. cannot be administered without the patient's knowledge and consent. I regard this as an extremely good law. So antidepressants were prescribed for me instead by Dr. Kablumbus, who can be said really to have had only my best interests at heart.

If someone tells about a trip he's taken, you expect at least some explanation of why he left on the trip in the first place. With this in mind perhaps I'll tell some things about why things weren't too good for me on Earth for quite a while. It was extremely weird, but, three years ago, when I was a senior in high school, I began to suffer from what I guess now was a hallucination. I thought that a huge wound, a really huge and deep wound, had opened on my face, on my cheek near my nose . . . that the skin had just split open like old fruit, that blood was seeping out, all dark and shiny, that veins and bits of yellow cheek-fat and red-gray muscle were plainly visible, even bright flashes of bone, in there. Whenever I'd look in the mirror, there it would be, that wound, and I could feel the twitch of the exposed muscle and the heat of the blood on my cheek, all the time. But when I'd say to a doctor or to Mom or to other people, "Hey, look at this open wound on my face, I'd better go to the hospital," they'd say, "Well, hey, there's no wound on your face, are your eyes OK?" And yet whenever I'd look in the mirror, there it would be, and I could always feel the heat of the blood on my cheek, and when I'd feel with my hand my fingers would sink in there really deep into what felt like a hot gelatin with bones and ropes and stuff in it. And it seemed like everyone was always looking at it. They'd seem to stare at me really funny, and I'd think "Oh God, I'm really making them sick, they see it, I've got to hide, get me out of here." But they were probably only staring because I looked all scared and in pain and kept my hand to my face and was staggering like I was drunk all over the place all the time. But at the time, it seemed so real.

> I took a needle and some thread and tried to sew up the wound myself. It hurt a lot to do this, because I didn't have any anesthetic, of course. It was also bad because, obviously, as I know now, there was really no wound to be sewn up at all, there.

Weird, weird, weird. Right before graduation—or maybe a month before, maybe—it got really bad, such that when I'd pull my hand away from my face I'd see blood on my fingers, and bits of tissue and stuff, and I'd be able to smell the blood, too, like hot rusty metal and copper. So one night when my parents were out somewhere I took a needle and some thread and tried to sew up the wound myself. It hurt a lot to do this, because I didn't have any anesthetic, of course. It was also bad because, obviously, as I know now, there was really no wound to be sewn up at all, there. Mom and Dad were less than pleased when they came home and found me all bloody for real and with a whole lot of jagged unprofessional stitches of lovely bright orange carpet-thread in my face. They were really upset. Also, I made the stitches too deep—I apparently pushed the needle incredibly deep—and some of the thread got stuck way down in there when they tried to pull the stitches out at the hospital and it got infected later and then they had to make a *real* wound back at the hospital to get it all out and drain it and clean it out. That was highly ironic. Also, when I was making the stitches too deep I guess I ran the needle into a few nerves in my cheek and destroyed them, so now sometimes bits of my face will get numb for no reason, and my mouth will sag on the left side a bit. I know it sags for sure and that I've got this cute scar, here, because it's not just a matter of looking in the mirror and seeing it and feeling it; other people tell me they see it too, though they do this very tactfully.

> I had little tricks I employed with regard to the "crying problem." When I was around other people and my eyes got all hot and full of burning salt-water I would pretend to sneeze . . .

Anyway, I think that year everyone began to see that I was a troubled little soldier, including me. Everybody talked and conferred and we all decided that it would probably be in my best interests if I deferred admission to Brown University in Rhode Island, where I was supposedly all set to go, and instead did a year of "Post-Graduate" schoolwork at a very good and prestigious and expensive prep school called Phillips Exeter Academy conveniently located right there in my home town. So that's what I did. And it was by all appearances a pretty successful period, except it was still on Earth, and things were increasingly non-good for me on Earth during this period, although my face had healed and I had more or less stopped having the hallucination about the gory wound, except for really short flashes when I saw mirrors out of the corners of my eyes and stuff.

But, yes, all in all things were going increasingly badly for me at that time, even though I was doing quite well in school in my little "Post-Grad" program and people were saying, "Holy cow, you're really a very good student, you should just go on to college right now, why don't you?" It was just pretty clear to me that I shouldn't go right on to college then, but I couldn't say that to the people at Exeter, because my reasons for saying I shouldn't had nothing to do with balancing equations in Chemistry or interpreting Keats poems in English. They had to do with the fact that I was a troubled little soldier. I'm not at this point really dying to give a long gory account of all the cute neuroses that more or less around that time began to pop up all over the inside of my brain, sort of like wrinkly gray boils, but I'll tell a few things. For one thing, I was throwing up a lot, feeling really nauseated all the time, especially when I'd wake up in the morning. But it could switch on anytime, the second I began to think about it: if I felt OK, all of a sudden I'd think, "Hey, I don't feel nauseated at all, here." And it would just switch on, like I had a big white plastic switch somewhere along the tube from my brain to my hot and weak stomach and intestines, and I would just throw up all over my plate at dinner or my desk at school or the seat of the car, or my bed, or wherever. It was really highly grotesque for everyone else, and intensely unpleasant for me, as anyone who has ever felt really sick to his stomach can appreciate. This went on for quite a while, and I lost a lot of weight, which was bad because I was quite thin and non-strong to begin with. Also, I had to have a lot of medical tests on my stomach, involving delicious barium-drinks and being hung upside down for X-rays, and so on, and once I even had to have a spinal tap, which hurt more than anything has ever hurt me in my life. I am never ever going to have another spinal tap.

Also, there was this business of crying for no reason, which wasn't painful but was very embarrassing and also quite scary because I couldn't control it. What would happen is that I'd cry for no reason, and then I'd get sort of scared that I'd cry or that once I started to cry I wouldn't be able to stop, and this state of being scared would very kindly activate this other white switch on the tube between my brain with its boils and my hot eyes, and off I'd go even worse, like a skateboard that you keep pushing along. It was very embarrassing at school, and incredibly embarrassing with my family, because they would think it was their fault, that they had done something bad. It would have been incredibly embarrassing with my friends, too, but by that time I really didn't have very many friends. So that was kind of an advantage, almost. But there was still everyone else. I had little tricks I employed with regard to the "crying problem." When I was around other people and my eyes got all hot and full of burning salt-water I would pretend to sneeze, or even more often to yawn, because both these things can explain someone's having tears in his eyes. People at school must have thought I was just about the sleepiest person in the world. But, really, yawning doesn't exactly explain the fact that tears are just running down your cheeks and raining down on your lap or your desk or making little wet star-puckers on your exam papers and stuff, and not too many people get super-red eyes just from yawning. So the tricks probably weren't too effective. It's weird but even now, here on the planet Trillaphon, when I think about it at all, I can hear the snap of the switch and my eyes more or less start to fill up, and my throat aches. That is bad. There was also the fact that back then I got so I couldn't stand silence, really couldn't stand it at all. This was because when there was no noise from outside the little hairs on my eardrums or wherever would manufacture a noise all by themselves, to keep in practice or something. This noise was sort of a high, glittery, metallic, spangly hum that really for some reason scared the living daylights out of me and just about drove me crazy when I heard it, the way a mosquito in your ear in bed at night in summer will just about drive you crazy when you hear it. I began to look for noise sort of the way a moth looks for light. I'd sleep with the radio on in my room, watch an incredible amount of loud television, keep my trusty Sony Walkman on at all times at school and walking around and on my bike (that Sony Walkman was far and away the best Christmas present I have ever received). I would even maybe sometimes talk to myself when I had just no other recourse to noise, which must have seemed very crazy to people who heard me, and I suppose *was* very crazy, but not in the way they supposed. It wasn't as if I thought I was two people who could have a dialogue, or as if I heard voices from Venus or anything. I knew I was just one person, but this one person, here, was a troubled little soldier who could withstand neither the substance nor the implications of the noise produced by the inside of his own head.

Anyway, all this extremely delightful stuff was going on while I was doing well and making my otherwise quite worried and less-than-pleased parents happy school-wise during the year, and then while I was working for Exeter Building and Grounds Department during the following summer, pruning bushes and crying and throwing up discreetly into them, and while I was packing and having billions of dollars of clothes and electrical appliances bought for me by my grandparents, getting all ready to go to

Brown University in Rhode Island in September, Mr. Film, who was more or less my boss at "B and G," had a riddle that he thought was unbelievably funny, and he told it to me a lot. He'd say, "What's the color of a bowel movement?" And when I didn't say anything he'd say, "Brown! har har har!" He'd laugh, and I'd smile, even after about the four-trillionth time, because Mr. Film was on the whole a fairly nice man, and he didn't even get mad when I threw up in his truck once. I told him my scar was from getting cut up with a knife in high school, which was essentially the truth.

So I went off to Brown University in the fall, and it turned out to be very much like "P.G." at Exeter; it was supposed to be all hard but it really wasn't, so I had plenty of time to do well in classes and have people say "Outstanding" and still be neurotic and weird as hell, so that my roommate, who was a very nice, squeakingly healthy guy from Illinois, understandably asked for a single instead and moved out in a few weeks and left me with a very big single all my very own. So it was just little old me and about nine billion dollars worth of electronic noise-making equipment, there in my room, after that. It was quite soon after my roommate moved out that the Bad Thing started. The Bad Thing is more or less the reason why I'm not on Earth anymore. Dr. Kablumbus told me after I told him as best I could about the Bad Thing that the Bad Thing was "severe clinical depression." I am sure that a doctor at Brown would have told me pretty much the same thing, but I didn't ever go to see anyone at Brown, mainly because I was afraid that if I ever opened my mouth in that context stuff would come out that would ensure that I'd be put in a place like the place I was put after the hilariously stupid business in the bathroom.

I really don't know if the Bad Thing is really depression. I had previously sort of always thought that depression was just sort of really intense sadness, like what you feel when your very good dog dies, or when Bambi's mother gets killed in *Bambi*. I thought that it was that you frowned or maybe even cried a little bit if you were a girl and said "Holy cow, I'm really depressed, here," and then your friends if you have any come and cheer you up or take you out and get you ploughed and in the morning it's like a faded color and

> It was quite soon after my roommate moved out that the Bad Thing started. The Bad Thing is more or less the reason why I'm not on Earth anymore.

in a couple days it's gone altogether. The Bad Thing—which I guess is what is really depression—is very different, and indescribably worse. I guess I should say rather sort of indescribably, because I've heard different people try to describe "real" depression over the last couple years. A very glib guy on the television said some people liken it to being underwater, under a body of water that has no surface, at least for you, so that no matter what direction you go, there will only be more water, no fresh air and freedom of movement, just restriction and suffocation, and no light. (I don't know how apt it is to say it's like being underwater, but maybe imagine the moment in which you realize, at which it hits you that there is *no surface for you*, that you're just going to drown in there no matter which way you swim; imagine how you'd feel at that exact moment, like Descartes at the start of his second thing, then imagine that feeling in all its really delightful choking intensity spread out over hours, days, months . . . that would maybe be more apt.) A really lovely poet named Sylvia Plath, who unfortunately isn't living anymore, said that it's like having a jar covering you and having all the air pumped out of the jar, so you can't breathe any good air (and imagine the moment when your movement is invisibly stopped by the glass and you realize you're under glass . . .). Some people say it's like having always before you and under you a huge black hole without a bottom, a black, black hole, maybe with vague teeth in it, and then your being part of the hole, so that you fall even when you stay where you are (. . . maybe when you realize *you're* the hole, nothing else . . .).

> And every proton and neutron in every atom . . . swollen and throbbing, off-color, sick, with just no chance of throwing up to relieve the feeling.

I'm not incredibly glib, but I'll tell what I think the Bad Thing is like. To me it's like being completely, totally, utterly sick. I will try to explain what I mean. Imagine feeling really sick to your stomach. Almost everyone has felt really sick to his or her stomach, so everyone knows what it's like: it's less than fun. OK. OK. But that feeling is localized: it's more or less just your stomach. Imagine your whole body being sick like that: your feet, the big muscles in your legs, your collarbone, your head, your hair, everything, all just as sick as a fluey stomach. Then, if you can imagine that, please imagine it even more spread out and total. Imagine that every cell in your body, every single cell in your body is as sick as that nauseated stomach. Not just your own cells, even, but the e. coli and lactobacilli in you, too, the mitochondria, basal bodies, all sick and boiling and hot like maggots in your neck, your brain, all over, everywhere, in everything. All just *sick* as hell. Now imagine that every single *atom* in every single cell in your body is sick like that, sick, intolerably sick. And every proton and neutron in every atom . . . swollen and throbbing, off-color, sick, with just no chance of throwing up to relieve the feeling. Every electron is sick, here, twirling off balance and all erratic in these funhouse orbitals that are just thick and swirling with mottled yellow and purple poison gases, everything off balance and woozy. Quarks and neutrinos out of their minds and bouncing sick all over the place, bouncing like crazy. Just imagine that, a sickness spread utterly through every bit of you, even the bits of the bits. So that your very . . . very *essence* is characterized by nothing other than the feature of sickness; you and the sickness are, as they say, "one."

That's kind of what the Bad Thing is like at its roots. Everything in you is sick and grotesque. And since your only acquaintance with the whole world is through parts of you—like your sense-organs and your mind, etc.—and since these parts are sick as hell, the whole world as you perceive it and know it and are in it comes at you through this filter of bad sickness and becomes bad. As everything becomes bad in you, all the good goes out of the world like air out of a big broken balloon. There's nothing in this world you know but horrible rotten smells, sad and grotesque and lurid pastel sights, raucous or deadly-sad sounds, intolerable open-ended situations lined on a continuum with just no end at all . . . . Incredibly stupid, hopeless ideas. And just the way when you're sick to your stomach you're kind of scared way down deep that it might maybe never go away, the Bad Thing scares you the same way, only worse, because the fear is itself filtered through the bad disease and becomes bigger and worse and hungrier than it started out. It tears you open and gets in there and squirms around.

Because the Bad Thing not only attacks you and makes you feel bad and puts you out of commission, it especially attacks and makes you feel bad and puts out of commission precisely those things that are necessary in order for you fight the Bad Thing, to maybe get better, to stay alive. This is hard to understand, but it's really true. Imagine a really painful disease that, say, attacked your legs and your throat and resulted in a really bad pain and paralysis and all-around agony in these areas. The disease would be bad enough, obviously, but the disease would also be open-ended; you wouldn't be able to do anything about it. Your legs would be all paralyzed and would hurt like hell . . . but you wouldn't be able to run for help for those poor legs, just exactly because your legs would be too sick for you to run anywhere at all. Your throat would burn like crazy and you'd think it was just going to explode . . . but you wouldn't be able to call out to any doctors or anyone for help, precisely because your throat would be too sick for you to do so. This is the way the Bad Thing works: it's especially good at attacking your defense mechanisms. The way to fight against or get away from the Bad Thing is clearly just to think differently, to reason and argue with yourself, just to change the way you're perceiving and sensing and processing stuff. But you need your mind to do this, your brain cells with their atoms and your mental powers and all that, your *self*, and that's exactly what the Bad Thing has made too sick to work right. That's exactly what it has made sick. It's made you sick in just such a way that you can't get better. And you start thinking about this pretty vicious situation, and you say to yourself, "Boy oh boy, how the heck is the Bad Thing able to do this?" You think about it—really hard, since it's in your best interests to do so—and then all of a sudden it sort of dawns on you . . . that the Bad Thing is able to do this to you because *you're* the Bad Thing yourself! The Bad Thing is you. Nothing else: no bacteriological infection or having gotten conked on the head with a board or a mallet when you were a little kid, or any other excuse; you are the sickness yourself. It is what "defines" you, especially after a little while has gone by. You realize all this, here. And that, I guess, is when if you're all glib you realize that there is no surface to the water, or when you bonk your nose on the jar's glass and realize you're trapped, or when you look at the black hole and it's wearing your face. That's when the Bad Thing just absolutely eats you up, or rather when you just eat yourself up. When you kill yourself. All this business about people committing suicide when they're "severely depressed;" we say, "Holy cow, we must do something to stop them from killing themselves!" That's wrong. Because all these people have, you see, by this time already killed themselves, where it really counts. By the time these people swallow entire medicine cabinets or take naps in the garage or whatever, they've *already* been killing themselves for ever so long. When they "commit suicide," they're just being orderly. They're just giving external form to an event the substance of which already exists and has existed in them over time. Once you realize what's going on, the event of self-destruction for all practical purposes exists. There's not much a person is apt to do in this situation, except "formalize" it, or, if you don't quite want to do that, maybe "E.C.T." or a trip away from the Earth to some other planet, or something.

Anyway, this is more than I intended to say about the Bad Thing. Even now, thinking about it a little bit and being introspective and all that, I can feel it reaching out for me, trying to mess with my electrons. But I'm not on Earth anymore.

I made it through my first little semester at Brown University and even got a prize for being a very good introductory Economics student, two hundred dollars, which I promptly spent on marijuana, because smoking marijuana keeps you from getting sick to your stomach and throwing up. It really does: they give it to people undergoing chemotherapy for cancer, sometimes. I had smoked a lot of marijuana ever since my year of "P.G." schoolwork to keep from throwing up, and it worked a lot of the time. It just bounced right off the sickness in my atoms, though. The Bad Thing just laughed at it. I was a very troubled little soldier by the end of the semester. I longed for the golden good old days when my face just bled.

In December the Bad Thing and I boarded a bus to go from Rhode Island to New Hampshire for the holiday season. Everything was extremely jolly. Except just coming out of Providence, Rhode Island, the bus driver didn't look carefully enough before he tried to make a left turn and a pickup truck hit our bus from the left side and smunched the left front part of the bus and knocked the driver out of his seat and down into the well where the stairs onto and off the bus are, where he broke his arm and I think his leg and cut his head fairly badly. So we had to stop and wait for an ambulance for the driver and a new bus for us. The driver was incredibly upset. He was sure he was going to lose his job, because he'd messed up the left turn and had had an accident, and also because he hadn't been wearing his seat belt—clear evidence of which was the fact that he had been knocked way out of his seat into the stairwell, which everybody saw and would say they saw—which is against the law if you're a bus driver in just about any state of the Union. He was almost crying, and me too, because he said he had about seventy kids and he really needed that job, and now he would be fired. A couple of passengers tried to soothe him and calm him down, but understandably no one came near me. Just me and the Bad Thing, there.

> I knew that the bus driver was probably going to lose his job, just as he had feared would happen. I felt unbelievably sorry for him, and of course the Bad Thing very kindly filtered this sadness for me and made it a lot worse.

Finally the bus driver just kind of passed out from his broken bones and that cut, and an ambulance came and they put him under a rust-colored blanket. A new bus came out of the sunset and a bus executive or something came too, and he was really mad when some of the incredibly helpful passengers told him what had happened. I knew that the bus driver was probably going to lose his job, just as he had feared would happen. I felt unbelievably sorry for him, and of course the Bad Thing very kindly filtered this sadness for me and made it a lot worse. It was weird and irrational but all of a sudden I felt really strongly as though the bus driver were really *me*. I really felt that way. So I felt just like he must have felt, and it was awful. I wasn't just sorry for him, I was sorry *as* him, or something like that. All courtesy of the Bad Thing. Suddenly I had to go somewhere, really fast, so I went to where the driver's stretcher was in the open ambulance and went in to look at him, there. He had a bus company ID badge with his picture, but I couldn't really see anything because it was covered by a streak of blood from his head. I took my roughly a hundred dollars and a bag of "sensemilla" marijuana and slipped it under his rusty blanket to help him feed all his kids and not get sick and throw up, then I left really fast again and got my stuff and got on the new bus. It wasn't until, what, about thirty minutes later on the nighttime highway that I realized that when they found that marijuana with the driver they'd think it was maybe his all along and he really *would* get fired, or maybe even sent to jail. It was kind of like I'd framed him, killed him, except he was also me, I thought, so it was really confusing. It was like I'd symbolically killed myself or something, because I felt he was me in some deep sense. I think at that moment I felt worse than I'd ever felt before, except for that spinal tap, and that was totally different. Dr. Kablumbus says that's when the Bad Thing really got me by the balls. Those were really his words. I'm really sorry for what I did and what the Bad Thing did to the bus driver. I really sincerely only meant to help him, as if he were me. But I sort of killed him, instead.

You could just say that I'd already more or less killed myself internally during the fall semester . . .

I got home and my parents said, "Hey, hello, we love you, congratulations," and I said, "Hello, hello, thank you, thank you." I didn't exactly have the "holiday spirit," I must confess, because of the Bad Thing, and because of the bus driver, and because of the fact that we were all three of us the same thing in the respects that mattered at all.

The highly ridiculous thing happened on Christmas Eve. It was very stupid, but I guess almost sort of inevitable given what had gone on up to then. You could just say that I'd already more or less killed myself internally during the fall semester, and symbolically with respect to that bus driver, and now like a tidy little soldier I had to "formalize" the whole thing, make it neat and right-angled and external; I had to fold down the corners and make hospital corners. While Mom and Dad and my sisters and Nanny and Pop-Pop and Uncle Michael and Aunt Sally were downstairs drinking cocktails and listening to a beautiful and deadly-sad record about a crippled boy and the three kings on Christmas night, I got undressed and got into a tub full of warm water and pulled about three thousand electrical appliances into that tub after me. However, the consummate silliness of the whole incident was made complete by the fact that most of the appliances were cleverly left unplugged by me in my irrational state. Only a couple were actually "live," but they were enough to blow out the power in the house and make a big noise and give me a nice little shock indeed, so that I had to be taken to the hospital for physical care. I don't know if I should say this, but what got shocked really the worst were my reproductive organs. I guess they were sort of out of the water part-way and formed a sort of bridge for the electricity between the water and my body and the air. Anyway, their getting shocked hurt a lot and also I am told had consequences that will become more significant if I ever want to have a family or anything. I am not overly concerned about this. My family was concerned about the whole incident, though; they were less than pleased, to say the least. I had sort of half passed out or gone to sleep, but I remember hearing the water sort of fizzing, and their coming in and saying "Oh my God, hey!" I remember they had a hard time because it was pitch-black in that bathroom, and they more or less only had me to see by. They had to be extremely careful getting me out of the tub, because they didn't want to get shocked themselves. I find this perfectly understandable.

Once a couple of days went by in the hospital and it became clear that boy and reproductive organs were pretty much going to survive, I made my little vertical move up to the White Floor. About the White Floor— the Troubled Little Soldier Floor—I really don't wish to go into a gigantic amount of detail. But I will tell some things. The White Floor was white, obviously, but it wasn't a bright, hurty white, like the burn ward. It was more of a soft almost grayish white, very bland and soothing. Now that I come to think back on it, just about everything about the White Floor was soft and unimposing and . . . *demure*, as if they tried really hard there not to make any big or strong impressions on any of their guests—sense-wise or mind-wise—because they knew that just about any real impression on the people who needed to go to the White Floor was probably going to be a bad impression, after being filtered through the Bad Thing.

The White Floor had soft white walls and soft light-brown carpeting, and the windows were sort of frosty and very thick. All the sharp corners on things like dressers and bedside tables and doors had been beveled-off and sanded round and smooth, so it all looked a little strange. I have never heard of anyone trying to kill himself on the sharp corner of a door, but I suppose it is wise to be prepared for all possibilities. With this in mind, I'm sure, they made certain that everything they gave you to eat was something you could eat without a knife or a fork. Pudding was a very big item on the White Floor. I had to wear a bit of a thing while I was a guest there, but I certainly wasn't strapped down in my bed, which some of my colleagues were. The thing I had to wear wasn't a straightjacket or anything, but it was certainly tighter than your average bathrobe, and I got the feeling they could make it even tighter if they felt it was in my best interests to do so. When someone wanted to smoke a tobacco cigarette, a psychiatric nurse had to light it, because no guest on the White Floor was allowed to have matches. I also remember that the White Floor smelled a lot nicer than the rest of the hospital, all feminine and kind of dreamy, like ether.

Dr. Kablumbus wanted to know what was up, and I more or less told him in about six minutes. I was a little too tired and torn up for the Bad Thing to be super bad right then, but I was pretty glib. I rather liked Dr. Kablumbus, although he sucked on very nasty-smelling candies all the time—to help him stop smoking, apparently—and he was a bit irritating in that he tried to talk like a kid—using a lot of curse words, etc.—when it was just quite clear that he wasn't a kid. He was very understanding, though, and it was awfully nice to see a doctor who didn't want to do stuff to my reproductive organs all the time. After he knew the general scoop, Dr. Kablumbus laid out the options to me, and then to my parents and me. After we all decided not to therapeutically convulse me with electricity, Dr. Kablumbus got ready to let me leave the Earth via antidepressants.

Before I say anything else about Dr. Kablumbus or my little trip, I want to tell very briefly about my meeting a colleague of mine on the White Floor who is unfortunately not living anymore, but not through any fault of her own whatsoever, rather through the fault of her boyfriend, who killed her in a car crash by driving drunk. My meeting and making the acquaintance of this girl, whose name is May, even now stands out in my memory as more or less the last good thing that happened to me on Earth. I happened to meet May one day in the TV room because of the fact that her turtleneck shirt was on inside out. I remember *The Little Rascals* was on and I saw the back of a blond head belonging to who knows what sex, there, because the hair was really short and ragged. And below that head there was the size and fabric-composition tag and the white stitching that indicates the fact that one's turtleneck shirt is on inside out. So I said, "Excuse me, did you know your shirt was on inside out?" And the person, who was May, turned around and said, "Yes I know that." When she turned I could not help noticing that she was unfortunately very pretty. I hadn't seen that this was a pretty girl, here, or else I almost certainly wouldn't have said anything whatsoever. I have always tried to avoid talking to pretty girls, because pretty girls have a vicious effect on me in which every part of my brain is shut down except for the part that says unbelievably stupid things and the part that is aware that I am saying unbelievably stupid things. But at this point I

> I have always tried to avoid talking to pretty girls, because pretty girls have a vicious effect on me in which every part of my brain is shut down except for the part that says unbelievably stupid things . . .

was still too tired and torn up to care much, and I was just getting ready to leave Earth, so I just said what I thought, even though May was disturbingly pretty. I said, "Why do you have it on inside out?" referring to the shirt. And May said, "Because the tag scratches my neck and I don't like that." Understandably, I said, " Well, hey, why don't you just cut the tag out?" To which I remember May replied, "Because then I couldn't tell the front of the shirt." "What?" I said, wittily. May said, "It doesn't have any pockets or writing on it or anything. The front is just exactly like the back. Except the back has the tag on it. So I wouldn't be able to tell." So I said, "Well, hey, if the front's just like the back, what difference does it make which way you wear it?" At which point May looked at me all seriously, for about eleven years, and then said, "It makes a difference to me." Then she broke into a big deadly-pretty smile and asked me tactfully where I got my scar. I told her I had had this annoying tag sticking out of my cheek . . .

So just more or less by accident May and I became friends, and we talked some. She wanted to write made-up stories for a living. I said I didn't know that could be done. She was killed by her boyfriend in his drunken car only ten days ago. I tried to call May's parents just to say that I was incredibly sorry yesterday, but their answering service informed me that Mr. and Mrs. Aculpa had gone out of town for an indefinite period. I can sympathize because I am "out of town," too.

> I think the air on the planet Trillaphon must not be as rich in oxygen or nutrition or something, because you get a lot tireder a lot faster there.

Dr. Kablumbus knew a lot about psychopharmaceuticals. He told my parents and me that there were two general kinds of antidepressants: tricyclics and M.A.O inhibitors (I can't remember what "M.A.O." stands for exactly, but I have my own thoughts with respect to the matter). Apparently both kinds worked well, but Mr. Kablumbus said that there were certain things you couldn't eat and drink with M.A.O. inhibitors, like beer, and certain kings of sausage. My Mom was afraid I would forget and maybe eat and drink some of these things, so we all conferred and decided to go with a tricyclic. Dr. Kablumbus thought this was a very good choice.

Just as with a long trip you don't reach your destination right away, so with antidepressants you have to "go up" on them; i.e., you start with a very tiny little dose and work your way up to a full-size dose in order to get your blood level accustomed and all that. So in one way my trip to the planet Trillaphon took over a week. But in another way, it was like being off Earth and on the planet Trillaphon right from the very first morning after I started. The big difference between the Earth and the planet Trillaphon, of course, is distance: the planet Trillaphon is very very far away. But there are other differences that are sort of more immediate and intrinsic. I think the air on the planet Trillaphon must not be as rich in oxygen or nutrition or something, because you get a lot tireder a lot faster there. Just shoveling snow off a sidewalk or running to catch a bus or shooting a couple baskets or walking up a hill to sled down gets you very, very tired. Another annoying thing is that the planet Trillaphon is tilted ever so slightly on its axis or something, so that the ground when you look at it isn't quite level; it lists a little to starboard. You get used to this fairly quickly, though, like getting your "sea legs" when you're on a ship.

Another thing is that the planet Trillaphon is a very sleepy planet. You have to take your antidepressants at night, and you better make sure there is a bed nearby, because it will be bedtime incredibly soon after you take them. Even during the day, the resident of the planet Trillaphon is a sleepy little soldier. Sleepy and tired, but too far away to be super-troubled.

This has nothing to do with the very ridiculous incident in the bathtub on Christmas Eve, but there is something electrical about the planet Trillaphon. On Trillaphon for me there isn't the old problem of my head making silence into a spangly glitter, because my tricyclic antidepressant—"Tofranil"—makes a sort of electrical noise of its own that drowns the spangle out completely. The new noise isn't incredibly pleasant, but it's better than the old noises, which I really couldn't stand at all. The new noise on my planet is kind of a high-tension electric trill. That's why for almost a year now I've somehow always gotten the name of my antidepressant wrong when I'm not looking right at the bottle: I've called it "Trillaphon" instead of "Tofranil," because "Trillaphon" is more trilly and electrical, and it just sounds more like what it's like to be there. But the electricalness of the planet Trillaphon is not just a noise. I guess if I were all glib like May is I'd say that "the planet Trillaphon is simply characterized by a more electrical way of life." It is, sort of. Sometimes on the planet Trillaphon the hairs on your arms will stand up and a chill will go through the big muscles in your legs and your teeth will vibrate when you close your mouth, as if you're under a high-tension line, or by a transformer. Sometimes you'll crackle for no reason and see blue things. And even the sound of your brain-voice when you think thoughts to yourself on the planet Trillaphon is different than it was on Earth; now it sound like it's coming form a sort of speaker connected to you only by miles and miles and miles of wire, like you're back listening to the "Golden Days of Radio."

It is very hard to read on the planet Trillaphon, but that is not too inconvenient, because I hardly ever read anymore, except for "Newsweek" magazine, a subscription which I got for my birthday. I am twenty-one years old.

May was seventeen years old. Now sometimes I'll sort of joke with myself and say that I need to switch to an M.A.O. inhibitor. May's initials are M.A., and when I think about her now I get so sad I go "O!" In a way, I would understandably like to inhibit the "M.A.:O." I'm sure Dr. Kablumbus would agree that it is in my own best interests to do so. If the bus driver I more or less killed had the initials M.A., that would be incredibly ironic.

Communications between Earth and the planet Trillaphon are hard, but they are very inexpensive, so I am definitely probably going to call the

Aculpas to say just how sorry I am about their daughter, and maybe even that I more or less loved her.

The big question is whether the Bad Thing is on the planet Trillaphon. I don't know if it is or not. Maybe it has a harder time in a thinner and less nutritious atmosphere. I certainly do, in some respects. Sometimes, when I don't think about it, I think I have just totally escaped the Bad Thing, and that I am going to be able to lead a Normal and Productive Life as a lawyer or something here on the planet Trillaphon, once I get so I can read again.

Being far away sort of helps with respect to the Bad Thing.

Except that is just highly silly when you think about what I said before concerning the fact that the Bad Thing is really

Low-Hanging Fruit

When I was twelve my father bought me

a sailboat—nothing America's Cup-ish, just something he thought even I couldn't get into trouble with—like a Sunfish, only tubbier and slower. The first day I owned it I dragged it to Long Island Sound in a thunderstorm. People were sprinting from the beach and here I was hauling this low trailer through the wet sand the other way. The rain was so heavy it knocked me to my knees. Lightning stripped the color away and left the afterimage of dune grasses and their individual shadows. It occurred to me that I should let go of the metal mast. When I did, it started this low keening, and my hair lifted, as if in celebration, and even I knew that something amazing was transpiring on a very fundamental level. My father appeared, in his raincoat, and dragged me off the beach by the collar. He wondered aloud then and

Jim Shepard

PHOTO: NASA AND STSCI

later if his son had the brains of a walking doorknob. He was at that point interrupting his son's first stirrings as a theorist. His son had been modeling something in his head, thinking that maybe there was *already* lightning *inside* the mast, and inside his *head*, trying to connect with some kind of energy in the air.

It wasn't the stupidest idea I've had. As my father and my wife would be the first to point out.

I'm a particle physicist. Most of us here could be dumped into that hopper, in terms of category, though of course there's the specialized-within-the-specialized: don't tell the accelerator physicists that they're particle physicists.

Here is in the general vicinity of the Large Hadron Collider, or in my case, this room with that screen, that chair, and that locker for my coat. My coat doesn't fit in it. It's not like they didn't warn me: when I'd wandered, stunned, out of grad school and into the job market, I'd been thinking mostly about Fermilab. And it's not like the CERN people gave me the hard sell. They told me: you come here, your office'll be a closet. *Everyone's* here.

Everyone is. Three thousand physicists, all roaming through how many little Swiss and French towns in their off-hours? Every one of them slopping food around and breaking things. Every one of them with a different idea of what constitutes collegiality. And as for all of the different project groups: well, let's just say that we've got some rivalries going. Even the engineers seem well-adjusted next to us. And they spend their every waking hour petrified of system failures.

What are they worried about? Well, what could go wrong? They've only cobbled together the most massive and expensive and complicated piece of scientific equipment ever built. Never mind the collider itself; some of these *detectors* are so big that working on them requires climbing gear. Everybody has triple and quadruple-checked everybody else's numbers, but so what? Tell that to the people on the *Challenger*. There've already been double-digit serious breakdowns.

But for us—the theory people—all that's neither here nor there. We're all like: C'mon, let's get this thing going. We only have so much data to work with. As far as we're concerned, an ideal world is a place where experiments happen faster.

All of us have kids and spouses and pets and hobbies but that's not where we live. Where we live is that part of the cortex where we do our model building: what my advisor liked to call Adventure Travel Through Concepts. And that's an ongoing whipsaw between exhilaration and despair. Welcome aboard, loved ones. Strap in. We call this the Widowmaker.

First you hope you come up with something. Then you hope that it leads to something else. Then that the something else doesn't bore you. Then that you're not just entertaining yourself. Theorist friends when they get uppity tell me they do *real* theory, not phenomenology. Me, I think: Whatever's in my intellectual playground *better* connect to the outside world. Because I'm not doing too well with that, otherwise. I've got the kind of life where even computational work makes me feel closer to the human race.

She complains that theorists say they have all the ambition, but really what they've got is vanity.

"You got *that* right," my wife said when I made that joke in her presence.

She was talking about my capacity for certain kinds of curiosities and my apparent incapacity for others. Did I *notice* that she barely came out of her room all weekend? Did it *seem* to me that dinners had been a little quieter those last few weeks before I left? Those questions and others hadn't seemed to have crossed my desk.

She claims I have a Dad thing going with my old advisor. She had some training in psychology and comes out with stuff like that every so often.

She complains that theorists say they have all the ambition, but really what they've got is vanity. But I say: when that curiosity's gone, what've you got?

Some stuff you come across and *bam*, you drop to your knees right there. You think: that's it—*that* shifts the paradigm. Other stuff, you're like: why is *this* taking up everybody's time? Some of the bigger-name theorists, they're just out there hustling. They're better salesmen.

The key is to go after the major stuff. Otherwise, you're one of those guys who's looking for what we call low-hanging fruit: the questions that are the easiest to answer.

I'm not the world's worst husband but there's a whole lot that I'd walk away from to be a part of something like this. To be a part of something one third as cool as this. The kind of collisions we're going to be generating should knock all sorts of stop-the-presses particles onto our screens, the way two torpedoes colliding head-on should knock some spray out of the Atlantic.

Imagine what it's like for us most of the time. We spend our days in front of chalkboards. Progress is slow. The tea gets cold. Our one idea of the last three weeks fizzles out.

Results that just confirm the standard model—as in, *Oh, look: there's a Higgs boson*—that'd be the most depressing result. We've been sleepwalking through the last thirty years waiting for what's going to shake us up.

My wife was crying next to me in bed the night before I flew to Geneva, and I put my hand on her forehead in the dark. She said, "Remember when you told me that the one thing physics teaches you is that the reality you think you observe doesn't have much to do with the reality that's out there?"

We're not entirely well-matched emotionally. My dad's way of putting it when I told him we were getting married was, "Well, it could work for a short while, if everything breaks right."

She had a miscarriage and felt like I wasn't entirely on board for the stunned-by-grief thing. She's also been blindsided by my refusal to try again.

I tell her: the overarching lesson from science in the last century is that *my* experience is not going to help all that much, in terms of providing a guide to *yours*.

It's like when she heard me sparring with an old friend who's a string theorist about the way some of the follow-up discoveries about the likelihood of the Higgs field were redefining the meaning of empty. She'd snorted. "What was *that*?" the string theorist asked, all the way from Berkeley.

They think this is even bigger for them than it is for us. This is the chance for what they do to make contact with observable physics and become an experimental science. If strings are as large as some of these people think—a billionth of a billionth of a meter—that's within reach of the LHC, and we'll see new particles whose masses line up like harmonics in a choral piece. We'll all be notes from the same melody, patterns from the same single kind of object: a string. They'll all go nuts with joy. As he puts it, they'll hear the shrieks over in the Humanities buildings.

Every time you turn a corner, something gets defamiliarized. This is the elevator that's going to take us to the next floor. Some of those nuts that have been too hard to crack are about to get pried open. What are you *really* looking for? my wife said to me, last thing, before I left. What we're *all* looking for. That saving thing, I think: that something that right now is beyond our ability to even imagine.

AN INTERVIEW WITH
COLSON WHITEHEAD

Rob Spillman

The arch cultural critic tackles comic timing, boomer nostalgia and computer games.

Colson Whitehead's novels *The Intuition-ist, John Henry Days,* and *Apex Hides the Hurt* reveal a uniquely jazzy prose stylist with a prodigious gift for invention and a killer satirical instinct. Gliding beneath the seemingly placid surface of everyday life, Whitehead attacks issues of race, class, and consumerism like a shark in a smoking jacket. For this Whitehead has earned an array of honors, most notably the MacArthur "Genius" Grant. The interviewer has seen Whitehead use his intimidating bona fides at the poker table, where he has turned some of us at *Tin House* (who shall go nameless) into gibbering losers.

It can then come as a surprise that in person and away from the poker table Whitehead is quick to laugh and has a wicked sense of humor. At the 2007 Tin House Summer Writers Workshop, Whitehead gave a reading from his then novel-in-progress, *Sag Harbor,* in which

he, complete with visual aids, gave an etymological breakdown of 1980s African-American teenage put-downs. In *Sag Harbor,* which is set over the summer of 1985, Whitehead follows fifteen-year-old Benji, an awkward kid with a dad-inflicted bad haircut, as he moves from his swanky, mostly white high school to the universe of childhood friends who congregate in the buppie enclave of Sag Harbor, on the East End of Long Island neighboring the Hamptons, where he tries to assert his identity as he straddles black and white cultures, moving from roller disco bat mitzvahs to the cult of Adidas. The overtly autobiographical novel doesn't shy away from familiar demons of race, class, gentrification, and the enormous influence of pop culture in America. His first novel, *The Intuitionist,* published in 1999, took on the world of elevator inspectors, and was followed by *John Henry Days* (2001), which dealt with the legacy of the man who battled the steam engine, and then *Apex Hides the Hurt* (2006), a look at the warped world of branding and the power of words to seduce, deceive, and comfort us. He has also written a collection of impressionistic essays, *The Colossus of New York* (2003), which can be read as a prose poem to his hometown. Before becoming a novelist, Whitehead was a culture critic for the *Village Voice*. The interview was conducted in a café near Whitehead's Brooklyn home.

ROB SPILLMAN: Was there a Proustian madeleine moment that triggered the writing of *Sag Harbor*?

COLSON WHITEHEAD: Not really. At first my research was going to iTunes and downloading a lot of eighties music. And bit-by-bit I was recreating mix tapes I had made twenty years before. The research was different because it was a lot of fun. I spent half the time thinking about it, staring off into space. And the whole summer would come back to me with these tiny little triggers.

RS: You mean aural triggers?

CW: Yeah.

RS: Was there any one song that brought it all back?

CW: Chapter six or seven is around [the band UTFO's song] "Roxanne, Roxanne." I went to YouTube, and finding their old video with their crazy leather pants

and haircuts and crappy production values brought back a certain flavor of 1984-'85. My agent is British and there is a lot of pop culture in the book and she had no idea what I was talking about. So I sent her a lot of videos. I sent her "The Message" by Grandmaster Flash, which was shot in the bombed-out Bronx, and she said, "This is what I thought New York looked like when I moved here in 1995."

RS: You once said that your ideal reader would be you at the age of sixteen. What would your sixteen-year-old self think of *Sag Harbor*?

CW: When I was sixteen I hated reading anything about teenagers. I found the whole thing excruciating, so anything repeating what I was going through at the time I would have to reject. So I'm not sure my sixteen-year-old self could get through this book.

And I also had a strong dislike for boomer nostalgia. So I'm basically my own boomer talking about the eighties with a certain kind of sentimentality that I would have abhorred, that I did abhor. I'm not sure this book is for me.

RS: The parents in the novel are always talking to the kids about what they should know, tsk-tsking the things they don't know—Marcus Garvey, etc. . . .

CW: Yeah, I just want to have fun.

RS: For me there is a clear moral throughline between your books regarding race,

class, and materialism. In this way, are all of your novels autobiographical?

CW: Yeah. Whenever I'm bringing a new character on the stage, the early animating force comes from me. Whether it's protagonist, antagonist, I'm using stuff that I have felt to some degree, or people I feel empathy for. In this book, there is a more direct analog between the setup and my life that is more autobiographical. But if you ask me, I am in there in all of my work. And, strangely, I think *Colossus* is my most autobiographical book because there's no filter, there's no story I have to tell, it's just my impressions of living in the city without any sort of mediating structure or story I have to get across.

RS: Did you approach this novel in a different way than the others? Your previous novels have many layers, with numerous cultural references both high and low. You've said in the past that "everything gets thrown in the hopper"—with *Sag Harbor*, did you feel limited in any way?

CW: Because I started as a culture critic for the *Voice*, writing music and TV reviews, and because pop music is so important to Benji and his friends, I was able to get my riffing in through the way they talk about music and pop culture of the time, so I did find that it was a relief not to have to invent a sub-culture. I didn't have to invent a slang for the junketeers or the elevator inspectors. It was really about recreating teenage speech and thought patterns. So when I was stumped at the end of the day it wasn't "how do these weirdoes see the world?" but more "how do I keep a through-line with Benji?"

RS: Do you think your years of writing first-person journalism at the *Village Voice* delayed your writing of an autobiographical novel?

CW: I think being super-aware of what people my age were writing at the time prevented me from writing that autobiographical first novel, or an overtly Gen-X-y first novel in 1996, or a novel about contemporary New York. My first job was opening packages for the books department at the *Voice*. They got forty books a day and it was my job to sort them. So I was painfully self-conscious of what people my age were supposed to put out, what publishers were publishing, and how they were received. So anything that was expected I found excruciating.

I think, also, being older and more comfortable with myself, I felt it was okay to write about adolescence, and to use a more direct approach to the events in my life. It isn't a cop-out. It is how you pull it off that's the most important thing.

RS: But did you set out to write against the grain of what the standard autobiographical novel is expected to be?

CW: Sure. The ones I can really name are *A Separate Peace*, *The Catcher in the Rye*, Stephen King's *The Body*, and in the traditional com-

> Whether it's protagonist, antagonist, I'm using stuff that I have felt to some degree, or people I feel empathy for.

ing of age story there is a *Big Event*—you find a body, a boy witnesses a lynching, the KKK is chasing you—and so I really wanted to be true to everyday experience, to the traditional route of the summer, which is you are .001 percent smarter than you were at the beginning of the summer, and you haven't had a big, life-changing moment or epiphany. It is more these small, incremental changes that add up to a new self over time. That creates its own set of problems: How do you make these small, every-day moments interesting? How do you make a fifteen-year-old interesting for three hundred pages when he is really just walking around being angst-y?

RS: You could read this almost as a collective novel, especially since you use the word "you" a lot at that beginning.

CW: I did want to capture a sense of the community, warts and all, and present him as part of this tradition, playing a role in this shifting array of generations. It isn't just his story, but all of their collective stories. An early title for the book was *The Replacements*. So they are all replacing each other in this dance. Sort of like your Labor Day self is replacing your Memorial Day

self. So this personal replacement is being enacted on the community at large.

RS: Are the characters in *Sag Harbor* like Tolstoy's in *War and Peace*—mash-ups of everyone he had ever known? Did you start with "real" characters in mind? Did you ever feel constricted by "reality"?

CW: I started with direct models, but each time they talked or moved or walked on stage, they did something different than the original model, then the story would play certain demands on them and so they would have to change. Now I'm at the point where I know my characters much better than the original people. I spent three and a half years thinking about the summer of 1985 and only three months living it.

RS: Was this a fun book to write? If "fun" is a word you can use when you're putting together a novel.

CW: When you have a good day at work it is fun. There's a small wave of exhilaration when you put a few competent sentences together. This book was more fun because the structure allowed me to use a lot more jokes. I wasn't sure other people would find the jokes funny, but I was definitely laughing.

RS: In your previous books, there is a lot of dark humor, but in those it was more dark situations that were extended. In *Sag Harbor* there is a lot more stand-up, like the etymological breakdown of slang, that are laugh-out-loud funny. To me it seemed like you were having a lot of fun.

CW: With *The Intuitionist* I am confined by the character of the book and [Lila] Mae's disposition—she's sour and repressed, so she's not going to be cracking a lot of jokes. The character of Benji and the situations allowed me to have a lot more fun.

RS: You use humor almost like a Trojan horse, as a means to sneak in more serious subject matter. Like in *Sag Harbor*, where Benji's Dominican boss pats his hair, a scene which is very funny, but it is right on the edge of turning into a serious situation, an absurd scene with potentially profound ramifications.

CW: My first response to Beckett, as a college kid, I was responding to that dynamic. Growing up we were a big TV-watching family, and at age seven, eight, watching George Carlin and Richard Pryor, they would have these sudden movements from the comedic to the tragic, these sudden sharp turns; that's something I learned from them. And then it becomes a way of pacing things, the push and pull between the two modes,

the way one cancels out the other. I was very conscious of pacing, of where the jokes fell, where the more gruesome stuff was coming in. How do you shift the mood, destabilize the reader, but also move things forward?

RS: Remember in the movie *The King of Comedy*, De Niro says, "You gotta kick 'em in the stomach when they're laughing."

CW: Yes, I agree.

RS: Johnny Lydon, aka Johnny Rotten, with Public Image Ltd., sang "Anger is an energy." And William Gass, when asked why he writes, replied, "I hate. A lot. Hard." Is anger an engine for you?

CW: Yeah. When I was writing *The Intuitionist*, I had previously written a novel that no one liked, I had twenty-five rejections, and I was so angry at Manhattan, where all of the publishers were. I was living in Brooklyn and I would walk across the bridge to save money and shake my fist and say, "You can't break me." So the whole time I was really angry and I was writing a book about elevator inspectors so I was shooting myself in the foot even more than before. So that was a useful fuel for sitting down and writing that book. With this book, it is down low. It is definitely in there.

RS: In *Sag Harbor*, Benji says, "Black boys with beach houses. It could mess with your head sometimes, if you were the susceptible sort." This book is set in the summer of 1985. Do you think that by the time your daughter,

> I was very conscious of pacing, of where the jokes fell, where the more gruesome stuff was coming in. How do you shift the mood, destabilize the reader, but also move things forward?

to whom this book is dedicated, is fifteen, she will be dealing with the same issues?

CW: It'll be there, but I'm not sure what form it will take, after four/eight years of Obama. It is all about authenticity. It takes all different forms. "I have a lot of money, so I'm not authentic." "I'm poor, and I aspire, so that makes me inauthentic." "I'm part of the new immigrant class coming to America, there's Americanness and my own culture that are battling." With her generation, there is still going be the common struggle of identity. "Who am I in the various cultural narratives of my community and the culture at large?" Lord knows she'll have her own problems, but hopefully they won't be the same as mine. At bottom it will be, "What does it mean to be a person at this time?"

RS: To ask a mundane question: How do you physically work? Computer, typewriter, longhand?

CW: Both. I take notes for months and months and months, getting the characters and the plot. "Chapter 2, Go to the beach, question mark." With this book, each time I started a chapter I would go through the three notebooks and transcribe it. There was a lot of organizing in notebooks, outlining, early character stuff. It isn't really in until it is on the computer, then I do a lot of revision.

RS: How much volition do your characters have? Do they fight you, or do you have control?

CW: I have it mapped out, but the story changes as I go along. With *John Henry Days*, I remember coming to a section and not knowing who the character was. The PR guy, I had to skip him and a year later I figured out who he was and wrote his chapter. And once I did find his voice it was fun and I let him do what he wanted to do. With this book, because it is a first person novel, and I'd never figured out how to do a first person for a whole book, once I had Benji's voice down, since everything was through his eyes, I didn't feel like the supporting characters could run amok; he was always keeping the action on track since he was in the center.

RS: For a lot of writers, the joy in writing comes in surprising yourself. With this novel, was it harder to surprise yourself?

CW: Because it doesn't have much of a plot, since it is a series of snapshots and vignettes of the summer, I was surprised by the end of a chapter by how much I was able to get in there, how much I was able to get out of so little.

RS: In *Sag Harbor*, there's a wonderful passage describing adolescence: "Keeping my eyes open, gathering data, more and more facts, because if I had enough information I might know how to be. Listening and watching, taking notes for something that might one day be a diagram for an invention, a working self with moving parts." This is also a perfect description for most writers I know. Do you still feel this way?

CW: Oh yeah, but for me the biggest thing that's happened to me is my daughter being born, and realizing there is a whole other way of living that involves a third person, and taking care of them, and taking care of their hopes and dreams and progress, and it isn't completely selfish, getting up really early in the morning, with no sleep. You figure out how to be a better writer, person, parent. And once you figure it out they're in college.

RS: When Elissa [Schappell] interviewed Toni Morrison for the *Paris Review,* Morrison said that she does not want to be referred to as a black writer or a woman writer, but simply as an American writer. Is there any way to for you to avoid these kinds of labels?

CW: The labels are by and for the people. When I was starting off I was very essentialist—I'm a black writer. I was very self-conscious about what a black writer was. Like I wasn't going to write about a shack in the South, walking down the road with your messed-up shoes. There are certain clichés about black literature that I rebelled against. I also identified with Ishmael Reid and Ralph Ellison and so I saw myself as wanting to live up to their example. Now I don't see that at all. I feel like I'm just a writer trying to figure out the next book. While I did identify myself as a black writer at the beginning of my "career," I think that was a holdover from growing up in the seventies with the nationalist idea of what my role was. I'm fine with whatever the first line of review says, i.e., "black writer," "African-American writer." Do people still say, "Philip Roth, Jewish-American writer?"

RS: You never hear "white writer" or "Caucasian writer."

CW: That's the nature of the review business. I have bigger fish to fry.

RS: When did you discover Ellison?

CW: In junior high. In a seventh-grade summer anthology, a collection of American short fiction. It was the first chapter of *Invisible Man,* the "battle royal" section. It was so new and startling. I had never encountered such rigorous metaphor work before. There's a blonde, and she has an American flag tattoo, they're wrestling on a gold coin on an electrified mat. I didn't read the whole book until college, but I remember being glad that there was another weirdo—a black weirdo—out there.

RS: When do you remember being conscious of wanting to be a writer?

CW: Sixth grade, seventh grade. Reading *Spiderman*, *X-Men,* thinking that would be a good gig. Reading *Carrie*, by Stephen King, which has an interesting formal structure, flashing back and forward. There were newspaper clippings and inserts.

RS: And it has the theme of the outsider.

CW: Right. I remember liking the structure of *Carrie*, and the fact that you could write about, say, telekinesis, or werewolves, or vampires, and keep it entertaining.

RS: Do you still retain that entertainment button?

CW: The stuff about the detective novel in *The Intuitionist*, I still have a love for it. I don't read a lot of science fiction or horror these days, but I have a lot of affection for the form. When I think of future projects, I often think of doing a riff on some aspect of fantasy fiction. There's nothing wrong with being entertaining. With the way I write, it would be fun to take an aspect of genre fiction and step on it, the way I stepped on detective fiction earlier.

RS: In *Sag Harbor*, Benji hides his love of the cheesy easy-listening radio station. Do you have any current guilty musical pleasures?

CW: I think they're all in the novel. I don't listen to "lite" FM, but there is that station, WLNG, in Sag Harbor, and they aggressively play these one-hit wonders. And you've heard them before. And after a while, you listen and start thinking, "This song makes a lot of sense. Burt Bacharach makes a lot of sense." It's embarrassing. All these naked, desperate declarations.

RS: My son wanted me to ask you if you play any video games.

CW: No, not any more. As a kid I played a lot of computer games. I'm a dork, so I had to reject all of my Apple II Plus games. Since I'm basically home alone all day, once I start playing a game, I'll play it compulsively and things will be lost. Someone recommended *Spore*.

RS: My son is way into *Spore*.

CW: Maybe I'll take that on book tour for the downtime.

RS: I'm warning you—it's easy to get sucked in and disappear forever. Leave breadcrumbs. 🏛

FICTION

Charles Baxter

The Cousins

My cousin Brantford was named for our

grandfather, who had made a fortune from a device used in aircraft navigation. I suppose it saved lives. A bad-tempered man with a scar above his cheekbone, my grandfather believed that the rich were rewarded for their merits and the poor deserved what they got. He did not care for his own grandchildren and referred to my cousin as "the little prince." In all fairness, he didn't like me either.

Brantford had roared through his college fund so rapidly that by the age of twenty-three he was down to pocket change. One bright spring day when I was visiting New York City and had called him up, he insisted on taking me to lunch at a midtown restaurant where the cost of the entrees was so high that a respectful noonday hush hung over its skeletal postmodern interior. Muttering oligarchs with monogrammed shirt cuffs gazed at entering patrons with a languid alertness. The maître d' wore one of those dark blue restaurant suits, and the wine list had been printed on velvety pages set in a stainless-steel three-ring binder.

By the time my cousin arrived, I had read the menu four times. He was late. You had to know Brantford to get used to him. A friend of mine said that my cousin looked like the mayor of a ruined city. Appearances mattered a great deal to Brantford, but his own were on a gradual slide. His face had a permanent alcoholic flush. His brownish-blond hair was parted on the right side and was too long by a few millimeters, trailing over his collar. Although he dressed well in flannel trousers and cordovan shoes, you could see the telltale food stains on his shirt, and the expression underneath his blond mustache had something subtly wrong with it—he smiled with a strangely discouraged and stale affability.

"Bunny," he said to me, sitting down with an audible expunging of air. He still used my childhood name. No one else did. He didn't give me a hug because we don't do that. "I see you've gotten started. You're having a martini?"

I nodded. "Morning tune-up," I said.

"Brave choice," Brantford grinned, simultaneously waving down the server. "Waitress," he said, pointing at my drink, "I'll have one of those. Very dry, please, no olive." The server nodded before giving Brantford a thin professional smile and gliding over to the bar.

We had a kind of solidarity, Brantford and I. I had two decades on him, but we were oddly similar, more like brothers than cousins. I had always seen in him some better qualities than those I actually possessed. For example, he was one of those people who always make you happier the moment you see them.

Before his drink arrived, we caught ourselves up. Brantford's mother, Aunt Margaret, had by that time been married to several different husbands, including a three-star Army general, and she currently resided in a small apartment cluttered with knickknacks near the corner of 92nd and Broadway.

Having spent herself in a wild youth and and at all times been given to manias, Brantford's mother had started taking a new medication called ElysiumMax, which seemed to be keeping her on a steady course where life was concerned. Brantford instructed me to please phone her while I was in town, and I said I would. As for Brantford's two half-sisters, they were doing fine.

With this information out of the way, I asked Brantford how he was.

"I don't know. It's strange. Sometimes at night I have the feeling that I've murdered somebody." He stopped and glanced down at the tableware. "Someone's dead. Only I don't know who or what, or when I did it. I must've killed somebody. I'm sure of it. Thank you," he said with his first real smile of the day, as the server placed a martini in front of him.

> We had a kind of solidarity, Brantford and I. I had two decades on him, but we were oddly similar, more like brothers than cousins.

"Well, that's just crazy," I said. "You haven't killed anyone."

"Doesn't matter if I have or haven't," he said, "if it feels that way. Maybe I should take a vacation."

"Brantford," I said. "You can't take a vacation. You don't work." I waited for a moment. "Do you?"

"Well," he said, "I'd like to. Besides, I work, in my way," he claimed, taking a sip of the martini. "And don't forget that I can be anything I want to be." This sentence was enunciated carefully and with precise despair, as if it had served as one of those lifelong mottoes that he no longer believed in.

What year was this? 1994? When someone begins to carry on as my cousin did, I'm never sure what to say. Tact is required. As a teenager, Brantford had told me that he aspired to be a concert pianist, and I was the one who had to remind him that he wasn't a musician and didn't play the piano. But Brantford had seen a fiery angel somewhere in the sky and thought it might descend on him. I hate those angels. I haven't always behaved well when people open their hearts to me.

"Well, what about the animals?" I asked. Brantford was always caring for damaged animals and had done so from the time he was a boy. He found them in streets and alleys and nursed them back to health and then let them go. But they tended to fall in with him and to get crushes on him. In whatever apartment or house he lived in, you would find recovering cats, mutts, and sparrows barking and chirping and mewling in response to him.

"No, not that," he said. "I would never make a living off those critters," he said. "That's a sideline. I love them too much."

"Veterinary school?" I asked.

"No, I couldn't. Absolutely not. I don't want to practice that kind of medicine with them," he said, as if he were speaking of family members. "If I made money off those little guys, I'd lose the gift. Besides, I don't have the discipline to get through another school. Willpower is not my strong suit. The world runs on willpower," he said, as if perplexed. He put his head back into his hands. "Willpower! Anyhow, would you please explain to me why it feels as if I've committed a murder?"

When I had first come to New York in the 1970s as an aspiring actor, I rode the subways everywhere, particularly the number 6, which in those days was still the Lexington IRT line. Sitting on that train one afternoon, squeezed between my fellow passengers as I helped one of them, a schoolboy, with a nosebleed, I felt pleased with myself. I had assimilated. Having come to New York from the Midwest, I was anticipating my big break and meanwhile waited tables at a little bistro near Astor Place. Mine was a familiar story, one of those drabby little tales of ideals and artistic high-mindedness that wouldn't bear repeating if it weren't for the woman with whom I was then involved.

She had a quietly insubstantial quality. When you looked away from her, you couldn't be sure that she'd still be there when you looked back again. She knew how to vanish quickly from scenes she didn't like. Her ability to dematerialize was purposeful and was complicated by her appearance: day and night, she wore dark glasses. She had a sensitivity to light, a photophobia, which she had acquired as a result of a corneal infection. In those days, her casual friends thought that the dark glasses constituted a praiseworthy affectation. "She looks very cool," they would say.

Even her name—Giulietta, spelled in the Italian manner—seemed like an affectation. But Giulietta it was, the name with which, as a Catholic, she had been baptized. We'd met at the bistro where I carried menus and trays laden with food back and forth. Dining alone, cornered under a light fixture, she was reading a book by Bruno Bettelheim, and I deliberately served her a risotto entree that she hadn't ordered. I wanted to provoke her to conversation, even if it was hostile. I couldn't see her eyes behind those dark glasses, but I wanted to. Self-possession in any form attracts me, especially at night, in cities. Anyway, my studied incompetence as a waiter amused her. Eventually she gave me her phone number.

She worked in Brooklyn at a special school for mildly autistic and emotionally impaired little kids. The first time we slept together we had to move the teddy bears and the copies of the *New Yorker* off her bed. Sophistication and a certain childlike guilelessness lived side-by-side in her behavior. On Sunday morning she watched cartoons and *Meet the Press*, and in the afternoon she listened to the Bartók quartets while smoking marijuana, which she claimed was good for her eyesight. In her bathtub was a rubber duck, and in the living room a copy of *Anna Karenina*, which she had read three times.

We were inventive and energetic in our lovemaking, Giulietta and I, but her eyes stayed hidden no matter how dark it was. From her, I knew nothing of the look of recognition a woman can give to a man. All the same, I was beginning to love her. She comforted me and sustained me by attaching me to ordinary things: reading the Sunday paper in bed, making bad jokes—the rewards of plain everyday life.

One night I took her uptown for a party, near Columbia, at the apartment of another actor—Freddy Avery, who also happened to be a poet. Like many actors, Freddy enjoyed performing and was good at mimicry, and his parties tended to be raucous. You could easily commit an error in tone at those parties. You'd expose yourself as a hayseed if you were too sincere about anything. There was an Iron Law of Irony at Freddy's parties, so I was worried that if Giulietta and I arrived too early, we'd be mocked. No one was ever prompt at Freddy's parties (they always began at their midpoint, if I could put it that way), so we ducked into a bar to waste a bit of time before going up.

Under a leaded-glass, greenish lamp hanging down over our booth, Giulietta took my hand. "We don't have to go to this . . . thing," she said. "We could just escape to a movie and then head home."

"No," I said. "We have to do this. Anyway, all the movies have started."

"What's the big deal with this party, Benjamin?" she asked me. I couldn't see her eyes behind her dark glasses, but I knew they were trained on me. She wore a dark blue blouse, and her hair had been pinned back with a rainbow-colored barrette. The fingers of her hands, now on the table, had a long, aristocratic delicacy, but she bit her nails; the tips of her fingers had a raggedy appearance.

> The fierce delicacy of Burroughs Hammond's poetry! On those nights when I had despaired and had waited for a god, any one of them, to arrive, his poetry had kept me sane.

"Oh, interesting people will be there," I said. "Other actors. And literary types, you know, and dancers. They'll make you laugh."

"No," she said. "They'll make *you* laugh." She took a sip of her beer. She lit up a cigarette and blew the smoke toward the ceiling. "Dancers can't converse anyway. They're all autoerotic. If we go to this, I'm only doing it because of you. I want you to know that."

"Thank you," I said. "Listen, could you do me a favor?"

"Anything," she nodded.

"Well, it's one of those parties where the guests . . ."

"What?"

"It's like this. Those people are clever. You know, it's one of those uptown crowds. So what I'm asking is . . . do you think you could be clever tonight, please? As a favor to me? I know you can be like that. You can be funny; I know you, Giulietta. I've seen you sparkle. So could you be amusing? That's really all I ask."

This was years ago. Men were still asking women—or telling them—how to behave in public. I flinch, now, thinking about that request, but it didn't seem like much of anything to me back then. Giulietta leaned back and took her hand away from mine. Then she cleared her throat.

"You are so funny." She wasn't smiling. She seemed to be evaluating me. "Yes," she said. "Yes, all right." She dug her right index fingernail into the wood of the table, as if making a calculation. "I can be clever if you want me to be."

After buzzing us up, Freddy Avery met us at the door of his apartment with an expression of jovial melancholy. "Hey hey hey," he said, ushering us in. "Ah. And this is Giulietta," he continued, staring at her dark glasses and her rainbow barrette. "Howdy do. You look like that character in the movie where the flowers started singing. Wasn't that sort of freaky and great?" He didn't wait for our answer. "It was a special effect. Flowers don't actually know how to sing. So it was sentimental. Well," he said, "now that you're both here, you brave kids should get something to drink. Help yourselves. Welcome, like I said." Even Freddy's bad grammar was between quotation marks.

Giulietta drifted away from me, and I found myself near the refrigerator listening to a tall, strikingly attractive brunette. She didn't introduce herself. With a vaguely French accent, she launched into a little speech. "I have something you must explain," she said. "I can't make good sense of who I am now. And so, what am I? First I am a candidate for one me, and then I am another. I am blown about. Just a little leaf—that is my self. What do you think I will be?" She didn't wait for me to answer. "I ask, 'Who am I, Renée?' I cannot sleep, wondering. Is life like this, in America? Full of such puzzles? Do you believe it is like this?"

I nodded. I said, "That's a very good accent you have there." She began to forage around in her purse as if she hadn't heard me. I hurried toward the living room and found myself in a corner next to another guest, the famous Pulitzer-Prize winning poet Burroughs Hammond, who was sitting in the only available chair. Freddy had befriended him, I had heard, at a literary gathering, and had taught the poet how to modulate his voice during readings. At the present moment, Burroughs Hammond was gripping a bottle of ginger ale and smoking an unfiltered mentholated cigarette. No one seemed to be engaging him in conversation. Apparently, he had intimidated the other guests, all of whom had wandered away from his corner.

I knew who he was. Everyone did. He was built like a linebacker—he had played high school football in Ohio—but he had a perpetually oversensitive expression on his wide face. "The hothouse flower inside the Mack Truck" was one phrase I had heard to describe him. He had survived bouts of alcoholism and two broken marriages, had lost custody of his children, and had finally moved to New York, where he had sobered up. His poems, some of which I knew by heart, typically dealt with the sudden explosion of the inner life in the midst of an almost fatal loneliness. I particularly liked the concluding lines of "Poem with Several Birds," about a moment of resigned spiritual radiance:

> Some god or other must be tracing, now,
> its way, _this_ way, and the blossoms
> like the god are suspended in midair,
> and seeing shivers in the face of all this brilliance.

I had repeated those lines to myself as I waited tables and took orders for salads. The fierce delicacy of Burroughs Hammond's poetry! On those nights when I had despaired and had waited for a god, any one of them, to arrive, his poetry had kept me sane. So when I spotted him at Freddy Avery's, I introduced myself and told him that I knew his poems and loved them. Gazing up at me through his thick horn-rim glasses, he asked politely what I did for a living. I said I waited tables, was an unemployed actor, and was working on a screenplay. He asked me what my screenplay was about and what it was called. I told him that it was a horror film and was entitled _Planet of Bugs_.

My screenplay had little chance of intriguing the poet, and at that moment I remembered something that Lorca had once said to Neruda. I thought it might get Burroughs Hammond's attention. "'The greatest poet of the age,'" I said, "to quote Lorca, 'is Mickey Mouse.' So my ambition is to get great poetry up on the screen, just as Walt Disney did. Comic poetry. And horror poetry, too. Horror has a kind of poetry up on the screen. But I think most poets just don't get it. But you do. I mean, Yeats didn't understand. He couldn't even write a single play with actual human speech in it. His Irish peasants—! And T. S. Eliot's plays! All those Christian zombies. Zombie poetry written for other zombies. They were both such rotten playwrights—they thought they knew the vernacular, but they didn't. That's a real failing. Their time is past. You're a better poet, and when critics in the future start to evaluate—"

"—You," he said. He lifted his right arm and pointed at me. Suddenly I felt that I was in the presence of an Old Testament prophet who wasn't kidding and had never been kidding about anything. "You are the scum of the Earth," he said calmly. I backed away from him. He continued to point at me. "You are the scum of the Earth," he repeated.

Everyone was looking at him, and when that job had been completed, everyone was looking at me. Some Charles Mingus riffs thudded out of the record player. Then the other guests started laughing at my embarrassment. I glanced around to see where Giulietta had gone to, because I needed to make a rapid escape from that party and I needed her to help me demonstrate a certain mindfulness. But she wasn't anywhere now that I needed her, not in the living room, not in the kitchen, or the hallway, or the bathroom. After searching for her, I descended the stairs from the apartment as quickly as I could and found myself back out on the street.

Now, years later, I no longer remember which one of the nearest subway stops I found that night. I can remember the consoling smell of New York City air, the feeling that perhaps anonymity might provide me with some relief. I shouted at a light pole. I walked a few blocks, brushed against several pedestrians, descended another set of stairs, reached into my pocket, and pulled out a subway token. In my right hand, I discovered that I was still holding on to a plastic cup with beer in it.

Only one other man stood on the subway platform that night. The express came speeding through on the middle tracks. The trains were all spray-painted with graffiti in those days, and they'd rattle into the stations looking like giant multicolored mechanical caterpillars—amusement park rides scrawled over with beautifully creepy hieroglyphs, preceded by a tornado-like racket and a blast of salty fetid air.

The other man standing on the platform looked like the winos that Burroughs Hammond had written about in his fragmentary hymns to life following those nights he had spent in the drunk tank. *No other life could be as precious to me/as this one*, he had written. If only I could experience some kindly feeling for a stranger, I thought, possibly I might find myself redeemed by the fates who were quietly ordering my humiliations, one after the other.

Therefore, I did what you never do on a subway platform. I exchanged a glance with the other man.

He approached me. On his face there appeared for a moment an expression of the deepest lucidity. He raised his eyelids as if flabbergasted by my very existence. I noticed that he was wearing over his torn shirt a leather vest stained with dark red blotches—blood or wine, I suppose now. He wore no socks. For the second time that evening, someone pointed at me. "That's a beer you have," he said, his voice burbling up as if through clogged plumbing. "Is there extra?"

I handed over the plastic cup to him. He took a swig. Then, his eyes deep in mad concentration, he yanked down his trouser's zipper and urinated into the beer. He handed the cup back to me.

I took the cup out of this poor madman's grasp and put it down on the subway platform, and then I hauled back and slugged him in the face. He fell immediately. My knuckles stung. He began to crawl toward the subway tracks, and I heard distantly the local train rumbling toward the station, approaching us. With the studied calm of an accomplished actor who has had one or two early successes, I left that subway station and ascended the stairs two at a time to the street. Then, conscience-crippled and heartsick, I went back. I couldn't see the man I had hit. Finally I returned to the street and flagged down a taxi and returned to my apartment.

> I took the cup out of this poor madman's grasp and put it down on the subway platform, and then I hauled back and slugged him in the face.

For the next few days, I checked the newspapers for reports of an accidental death in the subway of a drunk who had crawled into the path of a train, and when I didn't find any such story, I began to feel as if I had dreamed up the entire evening from start to finish, or, rather, that someone else had dreamed it up for me and put me as the lead actor into it—this cautionary tale whose moral was that I had no gift for the life I'd been leading. I took to bed the way you do when you have to think something out. My identity having overtaken me, I called in sick to the restaurant and didn't manage to get to an audition I had scheduled. A lethargy thrummed through me, and I dreamed that someone pointed at my body stretched out on the floor and said, "It's dead." What frightened me was not my death, but that pronoun: "I" had become an "it."

There's no profit in dwelling on the foolishness of one's youth. Everyone's past is a mess. And I wouldn't have thought of my days as an actor if it weren't for my cousin Brantford's having told me twenty years later over lunch in an expensive restaurant that he felt as if he had killed someone, and if my cousin and I hadn't had a kind of solidarity. By that time, Giulietta and I had children of our own, two boys, Elijah and Jacob, and the guttering seediness of New York in the 1970s was distant history, and I only came to the city to visit my cousin and my aunt. By then, I was a visitor from Minnesota, where we had moved and where I was a partner in the firm of Wilwersheid and Lampe. I was no longer an inhabitant of New York. I had become a family man and a tourist.

Do I need to prove that I love my wife and children, or that my existence has become terribly precious to me? They hold me to this earth. Once, back then in my twenties, all I wanted to do was to throw my life away. But then, somehow, usually by accident, you experience joy. And the problem with joy is that it binds you to life; it makes you greedy for more happiness. You experience avarice. You hope your life will go on forever.

———— ·◆· ————

A day or so after having lunch with Brantford, I went up to visit Aunt Margaret. She had started to bend over from the osteoporosis that would cripple her, or maybe it was the calcium-reducing effects of her antidepressant and the diet of Kung Pao chicken, vodka, and cigarettes she lived on. She was terrifyingly lucid, as always. The vodka merely seemed to have sharpened her wits. She was so unblurred, I hoped she wasn't about to go into one of her tailspins. Copies of *Foreign Affairs* lay around her apartment near the porcelain figurines. NPR drifted in from a radio on the windowsill. She had been reading Tacitus, she told me. "*The Annals of Imperial Rome.* Have you ever read it, Benjamin?"

"No," I said. I sank back on the sofa, irritating one of the cats, who leaped up away from me before taking up a position on the windowsill.

"You should. I can't read the Latin anymore, but I can read it in English. Frighteningly relevant. During the reign of Tiberius, Sejanus's daughter is arrested and led away. 'What did I do? Where are you taking me? I won't do it again,' this girl says. My God. Think of all the thousands who have said those very words in this century. I've said them myself. I used to say them to my father."

"Your father?"

"Of course. He could be cruel. He would lead me away, and he punished me. He probably had his reasons. He knew me. Well, I was a terrible girl," she said dreamily. "I was willful. Always getting into situations. I was . . . forward. *There's* an antiquated adjective. Well. These days, if I were young again, I could come into my own, no one would even be paying the slightest attention to me. I'd go from boy to boy like a bee sampling flowers, but in those days, they called us 'wild' and they hid us away. Thank god for progress. Have you seen Brantford, by the way?"

I told her I'd had lunch with him and that he'd said he felt as if he had killed somebody.

"Really. I wonder what he's thinking. He must be all worn out. Is he still drinking? Did he tell you about his girlfriend? That child of his?"

"What child? No, he didn't tell me. Who's this?"

"Funny that he didn't tell you." She stood up and went over to a miniature grandfather clock, only eight inches high, on the mantel. "Heavens," she said, "where are my manners? I should offer you some tea. Or maybe a sandwich." This customary politeness sounded odd coming from her.

"No, thank you." I shook my head. "Aunt Margaret, what child are you talking about?"

"It's not a baby, not yet. Don't misunderstand me. They haven't had a baby, those two. But Brantford's found a girlfriend, and she might as well be a baby, she's so young. Eighteen years old, for heaven's sake. He discovered her in a department store, selling clothes behind the counter. Shirts and things. She's another one of his strays. And of course he doesn't have a dime to his name anymore, and he takes her everywhere on his credit cards when he's not living off of her, and he still doesn't have a clue what to do with himself. Animals all over the place, but no job. He spends all day teaching dogs how to walk and birds how to fly. I suppose it's my fault. They'll blame me. They blame me for everything."

"What's her name? This girl?" I asked. "He didn't mention her to me."

"Camille," Aunt Margaret told me. "And of course she's beautiful—they all are, at that age—but so what? A nineteenth-century name and a beautiful face and figure and no personality at all and no money. They think love is everything, and they get sentimental, but love really isn't much. Just a little girl, this Camille. She likes the animals, of course, but she doesn't know what she's getting into with him." She looked at me slyly. "Do you still envy him? You mustn't envy or pity him, you know. And how is Giulietta?" Aunt Margaret had never approved of Giulietta and thought my marriage to her had been ill-advised. "And your darling children? Those boys? How are they, Benjamin?"

Aunt Margaret turned out to be wrong about Camille, who was not a sentimentalist after all. I met her for the first time at the memorial service five years after she and my cousin Brantford had become a couple. By then, she and Brantford had had a son, Robert, and my cousin had ended his life by stepping out into an intersection into the path of an oncoming taxi at the corner of Park Avenue and 82nd Street. If he couldn't live in that neighborhood, he could at least die there. He suffered a ruptured spleen, and his heart stopped before they admitted him to the ER. He had entered that intersection against a red light—it was unclear whether he had been careless or suicidal, but it was midday, and my cousin was accustomed to city traffic. Well. You always want to reserve judgment, but the blood analysis showed that he had been sober. I wish he had been drunk. We could have blamed it on that, and it would have been a kind of consolation, and we would have thought better of him.

One witness reported that Brantford had rushed onto Park Avenue to rescue a dog that had been running south. Maybe that was it.

In the months before his death, he had found a job working in the produce department at a grocery. When he couldn't manage the tasks that he considered beneath him—stacking the pears and lining up the tomatoes—he took a position as a clerk behind the counter at a pet food store on Avenue B. A name tag dangled from his shirt. He told me by telephone he hated that anyone coming into the store could find out his first name and then use it. It offended him. But he loved the store and could have worked there forever if it hadn't gone out of business. After that, he worked briefly at a collection agency making phone calls to deadbeats. He edited one issue of a humorous Web literary magazine entitled the *Potboiler*. What Brantford had expected from life and what it had actually given him must have been so distinct and so dissonant that he probably felt his dignity dropping away little by little until he simply wasn't himself anymore. He didn't seem to be anybody and he had no resources of humility to help turn that nothingness into a refuge. He and Camille lived in a cluttered little walkup in Brooklyn. I think he must have felt quietly panic-stricken, him and his animals. Time was going to run out on all of them. There would be no more fixes.

I wanted to help him—he was almost a model for me, but not quite—but I didn't know how to exercise compassion with him, or how to express

> What Brantford had expected from life and what it had actually given him must have been so distinct and so dissonant that he probably felt his dignity dropping away little by little until he simply wasn't himself anymore.

the pity that Aunt Margaret said I shouldn't feel. I think my example sometimes goaded him into despair, as did his furred and feathered patients, who couldn't stand life without him.

At the memorial service, Camille carried the baby in a front pack, and she walked through the doors of the church in a blast of sunlight that seemed to cascade around her and then to advance before her as she proceeded up the aisle. Sunlight from the stained glass windows caught her in momentary droplets and parallelograms of blues and reds. When she reached the first pew, she projected the tender, brave dignity of a woman on whom too many burdens have been placed too quickly.

> "Why didn't you ever come to see us?" she asked me, fixing me with a steady expression of wonderment as she nursed the baby.

Afterwards, following the eulogies and the hymns, Camille and I stood out on the lawn. Aunt Margaret, with whom I had been sitting, had gone back to Manhattan in a hired car. Camille had seemed surprised by me and had given me a astonished look when I approached her, my hand out.

"Ah, it's you," she said. "The cousin. I wondered if you'd come."

I gave her a hug.

"Sorry," she said, tearfully grinning. "You startled me. You're family, and your face is a little like Branty's. You have the same cheerful scowl, you two." She lifted baby Robert, who had been crying, out of the front pack, opened her blouse, drew back her bra and set the baby there to nurse. "Why didn't you ever come to see us?" she asked me, fixing me with a steady expression of wonderment as she nursed the baby. "He loved you. He said so. He called you 'Bunny.' Just like one of his animals."

"Yes. I didn't think . . . I don't think that Brantford wanted me to see him," I said. "And it was always like a zoo, wherever he was."

"That's unkind. We had to give the animals away, back to the official rescuers. It was *not* like a zoo. Zoos are noisy. The inmates don't want to be there. Brantford's creatures loved him and kept still if he wanted them to be. Why'd you say that? I'm sure he invited you over whenever you were in town."

She looked at me with an expression of honesty, solemn and accusing. I said, "Isn't it a beautiful day?"

"Yes. It's always a beautiful day. That's not the subject."

I had the feeling that I would never have a normal conversation with this woman. "You were so *good* for him," I blurted out, and her expression did not change. "But you should have seen through him. He must have wanted to keep you for himself and his birds and cats and dogs. You were his last precious possession. And, no, he really *didn't* invite me to meet you. Something happened to him," I said, a bit manically. "He turned into something he hadn't been. Maybe that was it. Being poor."

"Oh," she said, after turning back toward me and sizing me up, "*poor*. Well. We liked being poor. It was sort of Buddhist. It was harder for him than for me. We lived as a family, I'll say that. And I loved him. He was a sweetie, and very devoted to me and Robert and his animals." She hoisted the baby and burped him. "He had a very old soul. He wasn't a suicide, if that's what you're thinking. Are you all right?"

"Why?"

"You look like you're going to faint."

"Oh, I'm managing," I said. In truth, my head felt as if the late-afternoon sunlight were going right through the skull bones with ease, soaking the gray matter with photons. "Listen," I asked her, "do you want to go for a drink?"

"I can't drink," she said. "I'm nursing. And you're married, and you have children." How old-fashioned she was! I decided to press forward anyway.

"All right, then," I said. "Let's have coffee."

———— ·•· ————

There is a peculiar lull that takes over New York in early afternoon, around two-thirty. In the neighborhood coffee shops, the city's initial morning energy drains out and a pleasant tedium, a trance, holds sway for a few minutes. In any other civilized urban setting, the people would be taking siestas. Here, voices grow subdued and gestures remain incomplete. You lean back in your chair to watch the vapor trails aimed toward LaGuardia or Newark, and for once no one calls you, there is nothing to do. Radios are tuned to baseball, and conversations stop as you drift off to imagine the runner on second, edging toward third. Camille and I went into a little greasy spoon called Here to Eat and sat down at a table near the front window. The cook stared out at the blurring sidewalk, his eyelids heavy. He seemed massively indifferent to our presence and our general needs. The server barely noticed that we were there. She sat at one of the counter stools working on a crossword. No one even looked up.

Eventually the server brought us two cups of stale, burned coffee.

"At last," I said. "I thought it'd never come."

The baby was asleep in the crook of Camille's right arm. After a few minutes of pleasantries, Camille asked me, "So. Why are you here?"

"Why am I here? I'm here because of Brantford. For his memory. We were always close."

"You were?" she said.

"I thought so," I replied.

Her face, I now noticed, had the roundedness that women's faces acquire after childbirth. Errant bangs fell over her forehead, and she blew a stream of air upward toward them. She gave me a straight look. "He talked about you as his long-lost brother, the one who never came to see him."

"Please. I—"

She wasn't finished "You look alike," she said, "but that doesn't mean that you were alike. You could have been his identical twin and you wouldn't have been any closer to him than you are now. Anyway, what was I asking? Oh, yes. Why are you here? With me? Now."

"For coffee. To talk. To get to know you." I straightened my necktie. "After all, he was my cousin." I thought for a moment. "I loved him. He was better than me. I need to talk about him, and you didn't plan a reception. Isn't that unusual?"

"No, it isn't. You wanted to get to know me?" She leaned back and licked her chapped lips.

"Yes."

"Kind of belated, isn't it?" She sipped the hot coffee and then set it down.

"Belated?"

"Given the circumstances?" She gazed out the window, then lifted the baby to her shoulder again. "For the personal intimacies? For the details?" Her sudden modulation in tone was very pure. So was her irony. She had a kind of emotional Puritanism that despised the parade of shadows on the wall, of which I was the current one.

"Okay. Why do you think I'm here?" I asked her, taken aback by her behavior. The inside of my mouth had turned to cotton; rudeness does that to me.

"You're here to exercise your compassion," she said quickly. "And to serve up some awful belated charity. And, finally, to patronize me." She smiled at me. "*La belle pauvre*. How's that? Think that sounds about right?"

"You're a tough one," I said. "I wasn't going to patronize you at all."

She squirmed in the booth as if her physical discomfort could be shed from her skin and dropped on the floor. "Well, you probably weren't planning on it, I'll give you credit for that." She poured more cream into her coffee. My heart was thumping away in my chest. "Look at you," she said. "Goddamn it, you have a crush on me. I can tell. I can always tell about things like that." She started humming "In a Sentimental Mood." After a moment, she said, "You men. You're really something, you guys."

"Okay. Why do you think I'm here?" I asked her, taken aback by her behavior.

She bit at a fingernail. "At least Branty had his animals. They'll escort him into heaven."

"I don't know why you're talking this way to me," I said. "You're being unnecessarily cruel."

"It's my generation," she said. "We get to the point. But I went a bit too far. It's been a hard day. I was crying all morning. I can't think straight. My apologies."

"Actually," I said. "I don't get you at all." This wasn't quite true.

"Good. At last."

We sat there for a while.

"You're a lawyer, aren't you?"

"Yes," I said. She stirred her coffee. Her spoon clicked against the cup.

"Big firm?"

"Yeah." Outside the diner, traffic passed on Lexington. The moon was visible in the sky. I could see it.

"Well, do me a favor, all right? Don't ask me about Brantford's debts." She settled back in the booth, while the server came and poured more burned coffee into her cup. "I don't need any professional advice just now."

I stared at her.

"Actually," she said, "I could use some money. To tide me over, et cetera. Your Aunt Margaret said that you would generously donate something for the cause." She gave me a vague look. "'Benjamin will come to your aid,' she said. And, yes, I can see that you will." She smiled. "Think of me as a wounded bird."

"How much do you need?" I asked.

"You really love this, don't you?" She gave me another careless smile.

"You're in your element."

"No," I said. "I'm not sure I've ever had a conversation like this before."

"Well, you've had it now. Okay," she said. "I'll tell you what. You have my address. Send me a check. You'll enjoy sending the check, and then more checks after that. So that's your assignment. You're one of those guys who loves to exercise his pity, his empathy. You're one of those rare, sensitive men with a big bank account. Just send that check."

"And in return?"

"In return," she said, "I'll like you. I'll have a nice meal with you whenever you're in town. I'll give you a grateful little kiss on the cheek." She began to cry and then, abruptly, stopped. She pulled out a handkerchief from her purse and blew her nose.

> More than enough money resided in my wallet for purchases, but shoplifting apparently was called for.

"No, you won't. Why on earth do you say that?"

"You're absolutely right, I won't. I wanted to see how you'd react. I thought I'd rattle your cage. I'm grief-stricken. And I'm giddy." She laughed merrily, and the baby startled and lifted his little hands. "Poor guy, you'll never figure out any of this."

"Exactly right," I said. "You think I'm oblivious to things, don't you?"

"I have no idea, but if I do think so," she said thoughtfully, "I'll let you know. I didn't fifteen minutes ago."

"It seems," I said, "that you want to keep me in a posture of perpetual contrition." I was suddenly proud of that phrase. It summed everything up.

"Ha. 'Perpetual contrition.' Well, that'd be a start. You really don't know what Brantford thought of you, do you? Look: call your wife. Tell her about me. It'd be good for you, good for you both. Because you're. . ."

I reached out and took her hand before she could pronounce the condemning adjective or the noun she had picked out. It was a preemptive move. It was either that or slapping her. "That's quite enough," I said. I held on to her hand for dear life. The skin was warm and damp, and she didn't pull it away. For five minutes we sat there holding hands in silence. Then I dropped some money on the table for the coffee. Her baby began to cry. I identified with that sound. As I stood up, she said, "You shouldn't have been afraid."

She was capable of therapeutic misrepresentation. I knew I would indeed start sending her those checks before very long—thousands of dollars, every year. It would go on and on. I would be paying this particular bill forever. I owed them that.

"I'm a storm at sea," she said. "A basket case. Who knows? We might become friends after all." She laughed again, inappropriately (I thought), and I saw on her arm a tattoo of a chickadee, and on the other arm, a tattoo of a smiling dog.

Back in the hotel, I called Giulietta, and I told her everything that Camille had ordered me to say.

<hr />

That night, I walked down a few blocks to a small neighborhood market, where I stole a Gala apple—I put it into my jacket pocket—and a bunch of flowers, which I carried out onto the street, holding them ostentatiously in front of me. If you have the right expression on your face, you can shoplift anything. I had learned that from my acting classes. More than enough money resided in my wallet for purchases, but shoplifting apparently was called for. It was an emotional necessity. I packed the apple in my suitcase and took the flowers into the hotel bathroom and put them into the sink before filling the sink with water. But I realized belatedly that there was no way I would be able to get them back home before they wilted.

So after I had arrived in the Minneapolis airport the next day, I bought another spray of flowers from one of those airport florists. Out on the street, I found a cab.

The driver smiled at the flowers I was carrying. "Very nice. You are surely a gentleman," he said, with a clear, clipped accent. I asked him where he was from, and he said he was Ethiopian. I told him that at first I had thought perhaps he was a Somali, since so many cabdrivers in Minneapolis were from there.

He made an odd guttural noise. "Oh, no, not Somali," he said. "Extremely not. I am Ethiopian . . . very different," he said. "We do not look the same, either," he said crossly.

I complimented him on his excellent English. "Yes, yes," he said impatiently, wanting to get back to the subject of Ethiopians and Somalis. "We Ethiopians went into their country, you know. Americans do not always realize this. The Somalis should have been grateful to us, but they were not. They never are. We made an effort to stop their civil war. But they like war, the Somalis. And they do not respect the law, so it is all war, to them. A Somali does not respect the law. He does not have it in him."

I said I didn't know that.

"For who are those flowers?" he asked. "Your wife?"

"Yes," I told him.

"They are pretty except for the lilies." He drove onto the entry ramp of the freeway. The turn signal in the cab sounded like a heart monitor. "Myself, I do not care for lilies. Do you know what we say about Somalis, what we Ethiopians say? We say, 'The Somali has nine hearts.' This means: a Somali will not reveal his heart to you. He will reveal a false heart, not his true one. But you get past that, in time, and you get to the second heart. This heart is also and once again false. In repetition you will be shown and told the thing which is not. You will never get to the ninth heart, which is the true one, the door to the soul. The Somali keeps that heart to himself."

"The thing which is not?" I asked him. Outside, the sun had set.

"You do not understand this?" He looked at me in the rearview mirror. "This very important matter?"

"Well, maybe I do," I said. "You know, my wife works with Somali children."

The cab driver did not say anything, but he tugged at his ear.

"Somali children in Minneapolis have a very high rate of autism," I said. "It's strange. No one seems to knows why. Some say it's the diet, some say that they don't get enough sunlight. Anyway, my wife works with Somali children."

"Trying to make them normal?" the cab driver asked. "Oh, well. You are a good man, to give her flowers." He gazed out at the night. "Look at this dark air," he said. "It will snow soon."

———————

With my suitcase, my apple, and my flowers, I stood waiting on the front porch of our house. Instead of unlocking the door as I normally would have, I thought I would ring the bell just as a stranger might, a someone who hopes to be welcomed. I always enjoyed surprising Giulietta and the boys whenever I returned from trips, and with that male pride in homecoming from a battle, large or small, I was eager to tell them tales about where I had been and what I had done and whom I had defeated and the trophies with which I had returned. Standing on the welcome mat, I looked inside through the windows into the entryway and beyond into the living room, and I saw my son Jacob lying on the floor reading from his history textbook. His class had been studying the American Revolution. He ran his hand through his hair. He needed a haircut. He had a sweet, studious look on his face, and I felt proud of him beyond measure. I rang the bell. They would all rush to greet me.

The bell apparently wasn't working, and Jacob didn't move from his settled position. I would have to fix that bell. I released my grip on the suitcase and headed toward the side door, where we had another doorbell. Again I rang and again no one answered. If it had made a noise, I couldn't hear it. So I went around to the back, brushing past the hateful peonies, stepping over a broken sidewalk stone, and I took up a spot in the grassy yard, still carrying my spray of flowers. Behind me, I could smell a skunk, and I heard a car alarm in the distance. If I had been Brantford, all the yard animals would have approached me. But if I had been Brantford, I wouldn't be living in this house. I wouldn't be here.

Giulietta sat in the back den. I could see her through the windows. She was home-tutoring a little Somali girl, guiding her along a balance beam a few inches off the floor, and when that task was finished, they began to toss a beanbag back and forth to each other, practicing mid-line exercises. Her parents sat on two chairs by the wall, watching her, the mother dressed in a flowing robe.

I felt the presence of my cousin next to me out there in the yard, and in that contagious silence I was reminded of my beautiful wife and children who were stubbornly not coming to the door in response to my little joke with the doorbell. So I rapped on the window expecting to startle Giulietta, but when she looked up, I could not see through her dark glasses to where she was looking, nor could I tell whether she really intended to let me into the house ever again.

I have loved this life so much. I was prepared to wait out there forever.

Goo in the Void

Heidemarie Stefanyshyn-Piper: I can barely pronounce your name
but have been thinking of you ever since your grease gun
erupted into space. Causing your tool bag to slip

beyond the reach of your white glove
when you were attempting to repair the space station's
solar wing. Thanks

for that clump of language: *solar wing*. One of the clumps
of magick shat out by our errors. And thanks
to your helmet camera's not getting smeared,

in the inch between your glove and bag—irrevocable inch—
we see the blue Earth, glowing so lit-up'dly
despite the refuse we've dumped in its oceans,

the billion tons of plastic beads we use to make
the action figures that come with our Happy Meals.
Precursors to the modern Christmas tree and modern handle of the ax.

Precursors to the shoes and vinyl jackets of the vegans.
The clean-up crews call them mermaid's tears, as if a woman
living in the water would need to weep in polymer

so that her effort would not be lost,
as when riding in the front seat of the car
she emits a choking sob she fakes a little

to be heard above the engine, so the driver
glances sideways to take note of her wet cheeks. And makes
some show of contrition, or else stares down the orange spear

the sun throws out as it is overtaken
by the horizon of the sea. Which is filled also with plastic shoes
that show up so consistently alone

they cause disturbing dreams about one-legged tribes
such as described by Pliny
(e.g. the Monoscelli who hop *wondrous swiftly*)

before he sailed across the Bay of Naples, into
Mount Vesuvius's toxic vapor,
big mistake, though we understand the magnet

of volcanic spume. The mermaids are still weeping
from all the charcoal in their eyes,
and though we are not Romans, Heidemarie,

see how the myths keep being synthesized
by us who live 220 miles below you,
queasy from our spinning but still holding on

with no idea we are so brightly shining.

Freak-Out

1.

Mine have occurred in empty houses
down whose dark paneling I dragged my fingernails—

though big-box stores have also played their part,
as well as entrances to indistinct commercial buildings,

cubes of space between glass yellowing like onion skin,
making my freak-out obscure.

2.

Suddenly the head is being held between the hands
arranged in one of the conventional configurations:

hands on ears or hands on eyes
or both stacked on the forehead

as if to squeeze the wailing out,
as if the head were being juiced.

3.

The rules call for containment
even if the freak-out wants wide open space—

there are genuine cops to be considered,
which is why I recommend the empty vestibule

though there is something to be said for freaking out
if the meadow is willing to have you

face-down in it,
mouth open to the dry summer dirt.

4.

When my friend apologized for the one she was having in my car
I said she was sitting in the freak-out's throne—

as with love, so many fluids
from the body on display outside the body

until the chin gleams like the extended
shy head of a snail! Even without streetlamps, even

if the only light comes bouncing
off the wet needles of the firs.

5.

My friend was freaking out about her freak-outs
which came in the supermarket's produce aisle—

I said: oh yeah everybody freaks out with the produce
at night, it's definitely freak-inducing

when the fluorescent lights arrest you
to make their interrogation. Asking

why you can't be more like the cabbages, stacked
precariously, yet so calm and self-contained,

or like the peppers, who go through life
untroubled by their freakish whorls.

6.

What passes though the distillery of anguish
is the tear without its salt—drip-dropping
into the flask that's making not
the monster potion but the H Two...oh forget it

that comes when the self is spent.
Many battles would remain in the fetal pose

if the men who rule would rip
their wool suits from their chests like girls

in olden Greece. If the bomberesses stopped
to lay their brows down on a melon.

If the torturer would only
beat his pillow with his fists.

Fireball

The TV knob was made of resin, its gold skirt
like a kewpie doll's, but it was gone.
So we changed the channel
with a pair of pliers (on the flat spot
on the spindle): chunk chunk
and then lo, Jerry Lewis. Chunk chunk and lo,
the marionettes with giant hands. The song went:
my heart would be a fireball. And in the chunking
and the singing and the watching, lo, my heart became one.

Less pageantry in the now. Say *Sputnik*: no other word
climbs my throat with such majestic flames.
Gone, the marionettes in flightsuits made of foil
gone grainy on the boob tube. The tremulous way
their bodies moved, my fear for their well-being.
The comic stupidity of the child,
which is forgiven. Unlike the stupidities to come.

The boy had a guinea pig named Fireball, so I taught him
the song by way of mourning
when it died. He still possessed his sweetness,
unlike older sons who think you are a moron without big
subwoofers in your car. To that son I say:
you may think you are the nuts, just
because you drive around killing hookers
on a video screen that you will never have the Cuban missile crisis on,

you do not even really have the bomb, and how can anyone be cool
without the bomb, Sam Cooke, James Dean,
those boys lived kitty-corner to their annihilation.
But my son glazes—what's so special about the past
when everyone has one? And yours, ma,
is out of gas. Then he drives off, his speakers
booming with men who by no singing make
the heart throb just a hair short of the threshold of explosion.

Pioneer

Let's not forget The Naked Woman is still out there, etched
into her aluminum medallion
affixed to her rocket
slicing through the silk of space.
In black and white, in Time, we blast her

off to planets made of gases and canals,
so the hypotheses who lived there
would know we were demure and
largely made of hydrogen,
no angry afros or headdresses made of snakes.

We did not even dare to add, where her legs fork,
the little line to indicate she is an open vessel,
which might lead to myths about her
being lined with teeth,
knives, snakes, bees—an armament

flying through the firmament. Beside the man
who stands correctly inerect, his palm
raised to show he comes in peace, though you
globulous yet advanced beings
have surely taken a gander of our sizzling planet

and can see us even through our garments.
So you know about the little line—
how a soft animal cleaves from her
and how we swaddle it in fluff,
yet within twenty years we send it forth

with a shoulder mounted rocket-propelled grenade launcher:
you have probably worked out a theory
to explain the transformation. And you
have noticed how she looks a bit uncertain
as she balances on her right leg, her left

thrust out as if she's put her foot on top of something
to keep it hidden. Could be an equation
on a post-it, or could be a booby trap—
now comes time to admit we do not know her very well, she
who has slipped the noose of our command. Be careful

when you meet her: she could be silent like a stick
searching for another stick to make
some fire with as she slides through
her trajectory's silk sleeve. Or she could be silently
searching for a stick, like a piñata full of sleeping bees.

Amy Hempel

I Stay with Syd

I wasn't the only friend Syd's married

man hit on the time he came to see her at the beach. I could see he was going to adhere. So I did not want to talk to him. But then Syd had friends over the night before he was going home, and he invited me out west, said, "Why not this over here"—he meant me—"and that over there"—Syd—"not mingling, not taking anything away from each other?

"An amplitude!" he said.

After I turned down the married man, he brought Syd over, gave her a stagey kiss, then turned to me and said, "You're really something." I thought, What a hedge—why not just say you hate me. The striking part of his communication is what he doesn't say, when saying something would make a difference. A passivity.

Syd returns from the married man and wakes up in the night in tears and does not know why.

I went out onto the deck and examined a collection of shells. I like to say "conch" as much as I can. "Dumb conch." Then home to attend to the business end of a sleeping pill.

Between them it was always almost over, especially at the start. Start to finish, had they done all they might have, might have taken what—a month at most? But for Syd it was a romance like a movie by she couldn't think who. So they drew it out and one week each month I moved into the house at the beach.

I have lived here for so long. Here, and not here.

There's a storm blowing in from the south and I'm worried a tree will fall on the house. But I'm worried about that even when it isn't raining. Syd won't pay what the tree man wants to prune the old oak. "Then at least move your bed," the tree man said.

But it is not my bed to move. It is Syd's bed, Syd out west again to visit the married man who wants her to be faithful to him.

Syd returns from the married man and wakes up in the night in tears and does not know why.

"Because you are lonely and empty inside and nothing helps?" I said, and she said, "Yeah, that too."

I stay with Syd her first night back.

The storm makes landfall the night after she returns, and she says we might ride it out in a movie, so we drive to the old theater in the next town over, down the block from the good pizza place, and we sit too close to the screen. The air conditioning comes and goes. The lobby had already run out of Coke before Syd could place her order.

The preview was a sci-fi thriller, big on effects. Across the screen: "COMING IN SEPTEMBER!" Then the lights came up, and a police officer ushered everyone out of the theater, said there was a bomb threat.

Who bombs a movie theater?

We stood with a hundred other people across the street from the theater. We were not offered passes for another night, so we figured we might get back in. Only one police car showed up. Several people left to get beer and pizza. We could smell the ocean, even in the rain. My hair was thickened with salt water. Syd pressed a white spot into my sunburned shoulder and said, "Is there an SPF higher than fifty?"

The scent of fertilizer carried from the nursery down the road where you can spend time deciding among identical flats of annuals.

Thirty minutes, and the head of the unconvincing bomb squad, his bored partner returned to the patrol car, told us we could go inside.

Most of the original audience went in and found seats. We sat farther back this time. No reason.

The projectionist started over from the beginning with the same coming attraction, the sci-fi snooze. "Now we're getting nowhere," Syd said. She put an arm around my shoulder and we settled down to watch.

"COMING IN SEPTEMBER!"

Hurry up, summer, and end. 🛡

FICTION

Joshua Ferris

A Night Out

The city wasn't menacing. It was supposed

to be menacing. In all the movies and TV shows growing up there were muggings and stalkers and knife blades flashing under dim lights—that was the city. The usual targets were people just like them: a white couple with money moving blithely about as if the city were a field of poppies. But black, white, rich, poor—all the people catching them up in the city flux were going about their business with benign efficiency. They weren't bangers or crack addicts. They were annoyances. The city was at worst an irritation, and at best a place to have a drink, a meal, a night out, after which you went home and went to bed.

"Who was that?" Sophie asked.

She walked next to Tom with her arms folded just under her breasts, across her black fitted dress. Her purse straps dangled from one elbow. "Who?"

"The woman in the station."

"Clara?"

"Who is she?"

"Clara," he said. "I've told you about her. The analyst? Who they weren't going to fire but then they did?"

Sophie didn't reply. She continued with her arms folded and her head down as if walking underdressed into a winter wind, when in fact the night was intolerably hot. The flash of neon in the tailor's window, the blast of hot air from the subway grate and the acceleration of a bus pulling off the curb just made it worse. He was feeling these things bear down on him when, a few seconds later, he became aware that she was no longer beside him.

He stopped and turned. She was standing ten feet away. He could still make out her eyes. They weren't looking at him. They weren't looking at anything, really.

"Sophie?"

And that's when she turned and walked away.

"Sophie?"

He stood there a minute not understanding. It would be the lost minute, the hesitation that would cost him. Finally he started after her. He called out her name, louder each time. She picked up her pace and then broke into a run. He didn't want to run in the heat but he had no choice. She turned a corner. He reached it several seconds later. He looked for the back of her cotton shift, some bat-like flicker of her running through the crowd, but she was gone.

Sophie searched for the woman on the downtown platform. The riders were assembled thickly. No one wanted to move for the heat. A shirtless man made a commotion near a trash bin, cursing as he pulled a final leg from his sweatpants. He balled up the sweatpants and threw them down violently on the platform. "This is ignominy!" he cried. "Wouldn't happen in France. You cowards!" He slipped back into his high-tops, retrieved the sweatpants, and, leaving the platform, hitched up his loose boxers.

Clara looked away from the man and resumed waiting. She turned occasionally to peer down the tunnel, holding her little purse with both hands. Sophie stood behind her, at a rook's remove, two steps from touching her. She studied Clara's profile and her unruly black hair, her breasts, her thin legs running from skirt hem to leopard-print ballet flats, a brown bow on each toe.

Sophie didn't know how she knew this Clara was the one. She just knew. Tom had probably wanted to jump out of his skin when he saw her coming toward them, but some unfortunate scruple in him had forced a smile. Then Clara smiled, and Sophie saw them smile, and Tom must have known she would see, so to make everything aboveboard he stopped and said, "Clara?" and Clara said, "Oh, hi, Tom." Tom introduced the two women. Their handshake was broken by a descending stranger, which underscored the inconvenience of meeting on subway stairs. They said as much, and then they said goodbye. Clara continued down to the subway and Tom and Sophie joined the crowd on the street, and in their silence Sophie realized this too, even this, was just another thing she would have to assimilate into their reconciliation.

She stared at Clara standing on the edge of the platform with such fierce resolve that if Clara had fallen forward as the train was pulling in, Sophie would have felt responsible. But the train pulled in and she did not fall. Sophie turned away as the others started to cluster at the doors and the departing passengers threaded their way through. Clara disappeared inside the train and Sophie drifted down the platform, trying for one last look through the window. She didn't know what she had just gained. A better understanding? The continuing right to come unhinged?

They were having dinner with her parents. Stupid to have run away from Tom. They would be late now.

The doors began to close and without thinking Sophie ran for them. They opened again and she stepped on. She started to pick her way toward Clara.

Tom ran out of options quickly enough. Her phone was going straight to voice mail; he swiped his MetroCard and peered down the vacant, desultory platforms; he came out again and found no message waiting for him. He circled the block a few times but met only the faces of strangers, in an endless procession, each in the midst of pursuing a different life.

He couldn't hail a cab to take him to the place where the problem could be solved, that place didn't exist. He couldn't call Dr. Stopes back from Chicago, where she was hand-feeding her dying mother, in order to conduct an emergency session about containing rage and the proper way to apologize. He couldn't go up to a cop and report her missing because they required twenty-four hours. He could only offer more apologies, make more promises and disavowals, and dedicate more nights and mornings and weekends to convincing her where his heart was. But then only if he could find her.

One stop in, Sophie had moved close enough to reach out and touch Clara. They both gripped the same overhead bar as the train jerked into motion. A guy in a porkpie hat and T-shirt, talking to his girlfriend in the middle seat, stood between them. Sophie used him to shield her while she scrutinized Clara. Her hair was astonishing, and her face was button cute. Sophie could imagine a continuum of photographs from infanthood to present day in which the pinch-cheeked Clara looked the same, adorably the same. So she was prettier than Sophie—that was settled. She continued to stare until the man in the hat glanced her way and she was forced to avert her eyes.

She was in a moving train heading downtown, away from Tom, away from her parents. No one knew where she was. Someone always knew where she was. She was either on call or at the hospital or with Tom. She stared down at her feet. If she chose, she could continue to ride the train, to the last stop on the line, and then focus all her attention on the most fundamental things, like where to sleep that night. That there were alternatives to the apartment had never really occurred to her before. She could go home with a stranger. There were any number of them on the train with her. And they were only a fraction of how many in the city itself. She could lean around the guy with the porkpie hat and ask Clara if she felt special. That was all. "Do you feel special?"

The train made three more stops and Clara got out. Sophie stood frozen. The doors hung open after the last passengers departed. She wanted Clara to come back. The conductor told them to stand clear of the closing doors. Without Clara there was no reason to be on the train. She hurried to catch the doors in time, thrusting a hand between them. They opened again reluctantly and she stepped out. She saw Clara's black nest of hair in the distance. She followed her out of the station and onto the street.

———————— ◆ ————————

The adrenaline coursing through Tom after Sophie's disappearance brought back memories of the recklessness he had courted during that period of time when he was carrying on behind her back. He had found it both delicious and terrifying to disappear from his life. It was as if he had plunged through a portal to arrive suddenly in a stranger's bedroom in Queens, illicit thrill engorging his heart as he took Melissa from behind on rumpled bedsheets, and then plunged back through the portal to arrive home before Sophie returned from the hospital. Again through the portal he found himself in a bar with Melissa on the Lower East Side getting drunk in the afternoon, engineering the logistics of a quickie in the men's room. And the portal would once again plop him down heavily on the bed he shared with Sophie and place a magazine in his hands, and when she came in, she would wake him with a kiss and ask if he'd been drinking, and an excuse always came quickly to him, as if whispered into his ear by one of the voices living on the other side of the portal.

> Her hair was astonishing, and her face was button cute. Sophie could imagine a continuum of photographs from infanthood to present day in which the pinch-cheeked Clara looked the same, adorably the same.

He did it because he was restless and because he had never done it before. It was a capricious desire, the most cruel, and also the most innocent. Going back and forth through the portal, he had thought he could envision the eventual reckoning. She would be sad, angry, hateful, and leave him. Or he would manage to convince her that it was stupid and temporary, which he'd always meant it to be, and she would stick around and they would work things out. He never imagined it could somehow be both.

After he confessed, he was willing to tell her everything, every detail, but she wasn't interested. She didn't want to know a thing, only that he'd broken it off. Which he had, but Melissa kept calling and sending him texts until he was forced to change phones. The two of them as a thing just went dead. She was one waitress in a city of how many. He'd met her at a firm function when she'd served his table, and after he parted with clients and colleagues he returned to the restaurant and got her number. He thanked God they had never exchanged e-mails.

He stepped into a bar and ordered a beer, waiting, worried, hoping she would call. The name and address of the bar were printed on the cover of a matchbook and he texted them to Sophie and also left them on another straight-to-voice-mail message. He walked out of the bar to stand in the excoriating heat because she might be somewhere within spotting distance now and the uncertainty was becoming intolerable. He was even tempted to call Dr. Stopes, her dying mother be damned, to ask for some prescription of what to do in this particular circumstance. He noticed a small chalkboard sign sponsored by Carlsberg Beer standing upright just outside the bar, its slate surfaces advertising in both directions three-dollar well drinks until 9:00 PM. He went back inside.

It was important for him to give her the name and location of the bar not only so that she could find him after she had walked off her anger but also for all the names of bars he had never given her, all the times he had hidden in plain sight in the unfathomable city. That evening he had called her before leaving work, took the subway home, and called her again from their landline—a chain of calls meant to reestablish the links of his whereabouts. He wanted no dropout, no unaccountable gaps. If she would just once again jump with him, he promised to move from link to link without falling through, staying on the surface where he belonged. He had suggested her parents' visit, a visit he foresaw as a weekend full of strong, transparent links. No portal in sight, not even a memory of Melissa's mouth. But she hadn't jumped, she had fled, and the unaccountable gap was now his to suffer.

He still hadn't touched his beer when he left the bar fifteen minutes later. He bent down in front of the Carlsberg sign and smeared the specials into a white cloud with the cuff of his shirt. He had taken a small piece of chalk off the bar when the bartender wasn't looking and now he addressed a note to Sophie in large capital letters, first on one side and then on the other. It said he would wait for her at the restaurant where they were meeting her parents.

She followed Clara down the street. They passed a tree in a grate, a bus stop, a bench-press machine dragged to the curb as trash. Her phone continued to ring. She had silenced it but even on silence it vibrated with every new message. It was like being on call when she wasn't on call. She had the sudden urge to be rid of it. She tossed it into a green metal bin at the corner. Now she had only her identification and access to money.

She followed Clara into a bar. It was a small place, air-conditioned, with music playing just at the level of burden. The bar took up the far wall, with room for a black sectional sofa in the corner. Opposite the bar, against the wall with the windows, ran a long wooden booth that seated those at the tables. Sophie watched Clara walk to the last table and, in the shadowy distance, thought she saw her shake hands tentatively with the man across from her. She sat down at the bar and observed them, ordered her first and then her second martini, and noticed their effortful smiles, their eager postures and strained muscles.

So this is what Tom had wanted and what he'd gotten: meeting in a dark bar with a woman who was not his wife, flirting over drinks just as this newest man was doing now. Reasonably certain no one would recognize him. Phone off those times she'd tried to call from the hospital: out of reach, giddily lost in the city. Anonymous, nameless, up for anything. No rules, no vows. A new person altogether. The city was without censure. For the first time, she thought she understood its allure.

Clara stood. She touched her purse and said something to the man, who nodded as she walked off. He took a drink of his beer and followed her with his eyes to the door of the women's room. Sophie stood and steadied herself. She took her martini from the bar and started walking toward the man. She wasn't at all sure of what she was about to do.

Tom's affair had given Sophie a belated, private glimpse at the stupefying reality of a world conducting, in discreet doses, one enormous continuous orgy. Behind a wall of exacting precedent and false decorum people were apparently going around fucking each other all the time. When, on occasion, Sophie got word that one of the doctors in her group was having an affair with a pharmaceutical rep, or a nurse was screwing one of the doctors, she expressed a sincere shock. How naive she had been! How naive anyone was to express a sincere shock at news of two copulating bodies. It was as if this particular type of scandal contained, alongside its other comorbidities, like herpes and bastards, a very specific sort of amnesia in which the scandalized forgot with every new instance that this activity was not only confined to abstractions like politicians and celebrities, but happily indulged in by their own mortal colleagues and friends, their wives, their loving husbands. She would never have considered Tom a candidate, and yet he had confessed, and after the initial and total collapse of her illusions, she had vowed to give him six months, only to find herself looking at everyone differently, wondering if her situation was an aberration of bad taste and terrible fortune, or if this was, in fact, how the adult world worked. When she set her drink on the table and sat down across from Clara's companion, she still didn't know which it was.

> Tom's affair had given Sophie a belated, private glimpse at the stupefying reality of a world conducting, in discreet doses, one enormous continuous orgy.

"Hello," she said, extending her hand. "My name is Monica."

She was surprised and impressed by how fluidly the lie had issued forth. The man took her hand.

"I'm David."

"Hi, David. David, would you mind if I asked you a question?"

"Do I know you?"

She guessed him to be in his early thirties, a shock of auburn hair receding in a widow's peak but thick where it counted, as if painted there with an artful stroke. Despite the heat he wore a brown corduroy jacket over a green T-shirt. On the shirt, an animated slice of pizza said something she couldn't read inside a thought balloon. His two days of stubble and pretentious block-frame glasses indicated he could probably differentiate between cheeses and knew the names of underground bands.

"No, you don't know me. I've been watching you from the bar. Your girlfriend just went into the restroom."

"She's not my girlfriend."

"No? Who is she?"

"She's . . . well, she's . . ."

"Will you come outside with me?"

"What for?"

"So I can ask you a question."

"You can't ask it in here?"

"I would rather ask it outside," she said.

———————— ·•· ————————

They would have been early if they'd remained on track; as it was, Tom arrived at the restaurant only twenty minutes late. The hostess led him down the narrow passageway that opened into the spacious dining room and he saw Sophie's parents sitting at a table for four.

Tom needed the evening to go well. Vid and Emily looked in good health and greeted him with enthusiasm. He sat down and the hostess handed him a menu. Soon there was a man filling his glass with water. Tom began to drink and found the water wonderfully refreshing under the circumstances, the hot walk and so forth. He was still drinking when Emily said, "You have something on your cuff. What's on your cuff?"

"Where's Sophie?" asked Vid.

"Oh, that's chalk."

"She go to the restroom?"

"Vid, sit down," said Emily. She craned her neck around. "Is she coming, Tom?"

"She is coming. She is coming."

Vid sat down. "Is she in the restroom?"

"She's up front putting her credit card down in advance so you guys don't pay for dinner."

"Oh no she's not."

"Vid, sit down. Let her pay if she wants."

"Actually," said Tom. "That's not where she is. But we do want to pay for dinner. You guys pay for dinner all the time and it's only fair that we pay for it once in a while."

"When we retire, you can pay."

"When do you think you'll retire, Vid?" asked Tom.

Vid began to talk about his job. He was a contractor who could retire whenever he wanted but his 401k had taken a beating lately and he still enjoyed the work. Emily craned around again but when she turned back she listened to Vid talk and didn't interrupt. They were nice people. They trusted him. They didn't need to know right away why Sophie hadn't walked in beside him because Tom was family, too. He was who they had at the moment. The rest of the family would be along shortly. That's how it was with family. He had jumped on a very firm link joining Vid and Emily at dinner here and he didn't care to consider how much farther he'd fall through the portal than some dive bar on the Lower East Side if they knew the truth. That dive bar, with its hard-earned associations of exhausted drunkenness, vulgar sex, and ricocheting consequence would be a toehold in heaven.

"Hello," she said.

They all turned. He couldn't believe it. He was staring at Melissa, who had evidently gotten a new job.

"Dylan?" she said.

Tom looked at Emily and then Vid.

"Dylan?"

When he turned back she was breathing heavily, staring at him with a commanding, closed-lipped silence. He could almost see her little heart pounding.

"Hi, Melissa."

She lashed out, striking him hard on the shoulder with her fist.

"Oh," said Emily, jerking back.

———— ✦ ————

Monica was the type of girl who did this sort of thing. She was shrewd and manipulative and she knew hard truths about men that other women were too faint to admit. She was without a phone at the moment and had no definite place to sleep but those things were opportunities, not weaknesses.

David hesitated at the door, looking one last time in the direction of the restroom. Monica knew it was not the sort of hesitation that expressed doubt about what he was doing. It was courtesy—if his companion were coming out just then, he could signal to her that he would be right back. All the same it was a fragile moment, and Monica didn't hesitate. "If you really want," she said, "you can be back before she is. I promise."

He let the door shut. The heat was as fast and consuming as a virus. His attention was pulled away by the frightening speed at which an unmarked cop car tore past them. It lifted into the air at an irregularity in the road and nearly scraped across the cars at the curb. It was gone as fast as it came. David turned away from it to find Monica staring at him. He looked neither as slight nor as bookish as he'd seemed sitting in the darkness.

"Why did you agree to come outside with me?"

"Why did I agree? Is that your question?"

"No."

"I don't know. I was being polite."

"Are you on a first date with that woman?"

David put his hands in his pockets and rocked back on his feet. "Why do you ask?"

"It seems that way."

"It's the first time we've met in person but we've exchanged e-mails."

"Did you meet online?"

"That's more than one question."

"What's your goal? That's my question."

"My goal?"

"Is it long-term, short-term? Do you want to get married, or do you want something else?"

"It's just a first date."

"She's attractive. More attractive than I am, don't you think?"

David glanced down at her breasts. Men were always looking at Monica's breasts, always quickly and inadvertently, and then trying to recover. "You're both attractive," he said.

"I want you to fuck me, David," she said, with a steady voice and unflinching gaze. "I want you to take me home and fuck me and I don't think that girl in there will do that for you tonight."

David suddenly looked like a very small boy.

"You can invite her along if you want, although she might not be game. She is prettier," said Monica, "but I'm game."

David had stopped rocking. A boisterous departure from the bar turned Monica's head. When she looked back, David was still staring at her.

———— ◆ ————

Out on the street, in the polluted vapors of the night, Tom tried to rally. He had suggestions for other restaurants. Emily and Vid wanted to know why that waitress had struck him. "Her?" Tom replied, a casual thumb thrown back at the restaurant. Someone he had dated before he met Sophie. Sophie had caused him to break her heart. The fact that she still had so much anger was something to puzzle over, almost laugh at. Tom almost laughed. The human condition was a mystery. Why do we do the things we do? He suggested that perhaps she was a psychopath. She had had many cats. He suggested they return to that French place where they'd eaten on the night they'd first met, the one everyone loved. Emily and Vid wanted to know why that waitress had called him Dylan. Because Dylan was his middle name. He would call Sophie now and tell her to meet them at that French placed they all loved. His middle name wasn't Dylan, it was Andrew, said Emily. His name was Thomas Andrew Oakenfield and his initials were TAO. He should have known she'd remember that, from all those wedding invitations. Emily and Vid wanted to know where their daughter was. On her way. Got held up at the hospital. But they had spent the day with Sophie and knew she wasn't working and had promised not to be on call that weekend. What the hell was going on? Tom just wanted everything restored. There was a safe decorous cohesion when everything wasn't spiraling out of control. Emily declared she was calling Sophie. Vid looked at his son-in-law with an expression he'd never seen before, slit-eyed and unwavering. It really brought out his resemblance to a professional football coach. Tom cautiously moved away from him. He felt sure that Emily would have no luck getting Sophie on the phone. There would be the need for a lot of explaining. Next he knew he was squatting down on the begrimed sidewalk among the glittering shards and blobs of gum tar, letting his body fall back against the sliding gate of a closed boutique, watching in his periphery his in-laws circle, stand still, look over at him, worry taking them away, intimations of deep trouble placing them beyond his reach, and Tom could not summon any reason that might incline him to rise again. He had reentered the portal, and, wow, wow, this at last was where it had set him down.

———— ·◆· ————

She waited while he went back inside the bar. He reappeared in no time. Swinging from door to sidewalk he spoke without seeming to address her. "Okay, let's get out of here kind of fast," he said.

He walked ahead of her at a distance of plausible deniability until they were safely beyond the bar, and Clara. He slowed down on the next block, so now they walked side by side, though subtly she felt him leading.

"What did you say to her?" she asked.

"Her?" he said, gesturing behind them in the direction of the bar. "I just told her I was being called away."

"Are you someone who gets called away ordinarily?"

"Not ordinarily," he said.

She felt no compunction, but also no sense of victory. She hadn't been motivated by spite or the desire for vengeance but by something more urgent, and the ramifications were only now setting in. Either he, too, was an aberration, another poor choice on her part, or the truth laid bare. He should have chosen differently. He had looked to her like someone who might have chosen differently.

"I just realized something," she said. "I haven't eaten."

He smiled. "Would you like to eat?"

"Yes, but I don't have any money."

She'd left her purse in the bar. She'd failed to take it with her when they had gone outside.

"I can buy you something to eat."

"I also don't have any money to get home."

"Wait a minute," he said. He stopped. "Is this something . . . ?"

"What?"

"Something professional?"

"Professional?"

She shook her head. It must have put him at ease, because after a little time had passed, they resumed walking. They kept silent, though. She still had no idea where in the city she was and no memory of how to return to the subway. And there was something else she had forgotten. Melinda? Melissa?

"Hey," she said.

He stopped and turned.

"What's my name?"

They stood in front of an empty bank. The paneled window was broad as a billboard. Sodium brightness fell on empty teller windows and three smiling links of a velvet rope. He bit his lower lip and returned an embarrassed gaze from the place in the distance where he'd sought the answer.

"Give me a hint?"

"You don't remember?"

He shook his head. Without thinking, she launched herself forward, pushing him with everything she had. His solid frame took most of the impact but he was thrown off balance. She came at him a second time and he grabbed her wrists.

"You don't deserve to fuck me," she said.

Their struggle was backlit by the glaring bank. "Do you know what I just did for you?" he asked in disbelief.

"Let go of me."

"You owe me."

"Let go or I'll scream."

He let go. "Whore," he said.

She turned and screamed up and down the street. "Help me!" she cried. "Help me! Rape!"

He backed away.

"Rape! Help me!"

He turned and, walking quickly in the direction of the bar, almost ran right into Clara. He juked past her and disappeared around the first corner.

Sophie backed up. She slid down the window of the bank and sat on the pavement with her legs together bent to one side. She leaned over and heaved audibly, gasping to hold back tears, and pushed away the offered hand of the worried passerby hovering over her.

"Are you okay?" he asked. "Is everything okay?"

She looked up and saw the man and Clara gathered around her. They wanted to help her, stand her on her feet, guide her to the subway, see her home. No, everything's not okay, she thought, everything's not okay. And your kind little gesture, your concern for my well-being, what a fucking charade.

arf

CLARISSA DIAUGEIA

Stuart Dybek

You ever had a boyfriend kissing your booty?

Girl, I never had no boyfriend who wasn't kissing my butt.

No, girl, I mean really kissing it.

Yeah, well, men are dogs. They want a sniff.

Kissing it all over.

Pass me that ketchup.

All over. French kissing, soul kissing, you know what I'm saying? I got to spell it out for you, girl?

You the one bringing it up. At the dinner table.

I'm just curious to know you ever had a boyfriend like that? And this is coffee break, not no dinner, for some of us at least.

Was a manner of speaking. We at a table. How's your ketchup technique? I hate when it's a new bottle. One good splat and your food is like road-killed.

I got to go make a call. See you, girl. Them nasty fries gonna give you a big booty.

———— ◦ ————

Toujours pour la première fois
C'est à peine si je te connais de vue . . .

Martin has written on a napkin: Always for the first time, I scarcely know you when I see you. The lines are by a French poet, but, Martin thinks, Cole Porter might have written them. It is Martin's practice when traveling to a foreign country to bring a book of poems and a dictionary in the language of that place. He sits in an orange plastic booth, drinking black coffee, still three more hours to kill before a flight to Paris. He's eaten the one Big Mac he'll eat this year, while imagining the bistro food to come—rabbit with green olives, Belon oysters, champagne—and thinking about the woman with whom he hopes to share those meals. They're supposed to meet at a hotel on the river in Saint-Germain, and he can't help worrying whether, even though it's a hotel she's chosen, she'll be there. He can't help wondering, though it is none of his business, what excuse she's made for the trip to her husband, whom she refers to by profession rather than name—the Geologist.

Why stay with him, Martin once asked.

Why do you think, she asked back, knowing he wouldn't answer.

Ma femme à la chevelure de feu de bois
Aux pensees d'éclairs de chaleur . . .

My woman—or is the "femme" there "wife"?—whose hair is a wood fire, Whose thoughts are heat lightning . . .

Ma femme aux cils de bâtons d'écriture d'enfant . . .

My woman—or wife or is it my love?—whose eyelashes are a child's writing . . .

Cole Porter wouldn't have come up with that.

The Geologist is an executive with Standard Oil who, she says, drank himself into a coronary before he became a cycling fanatic. He cycles on a recumbent bike before a wide-screen television while watching classic boxing and at the end of his ride is soaked in sweat and panting like a dog.

> *A l'heure de l'amore et des paupières bleues*
> *Je me vois brûler à mon tour je vois cette cachette solennelle*
> *de riens*
> *Qui fut mon corps . . .*

At the hour of love and blue eyelids, I see myself burning, I see the solemn hidden place of nothings, which was my body . . .

Panting like a dog, giving me those cocker-spaniel eyes, sniffing around me like a dog in heat are ways she's described the Geologist. And, while Martin has never heard her say men are dogs, when he catches the phrase from the booth behind him, he has an urge to turn, but doesn't. He never gets a look at the woman whose boyfriend likes to root around, but after she leaves, Martin hears her friend, the woman with the fries, shake the crushed ice in her cup and take a slurp of her drink, then whisper aloud, "whore."

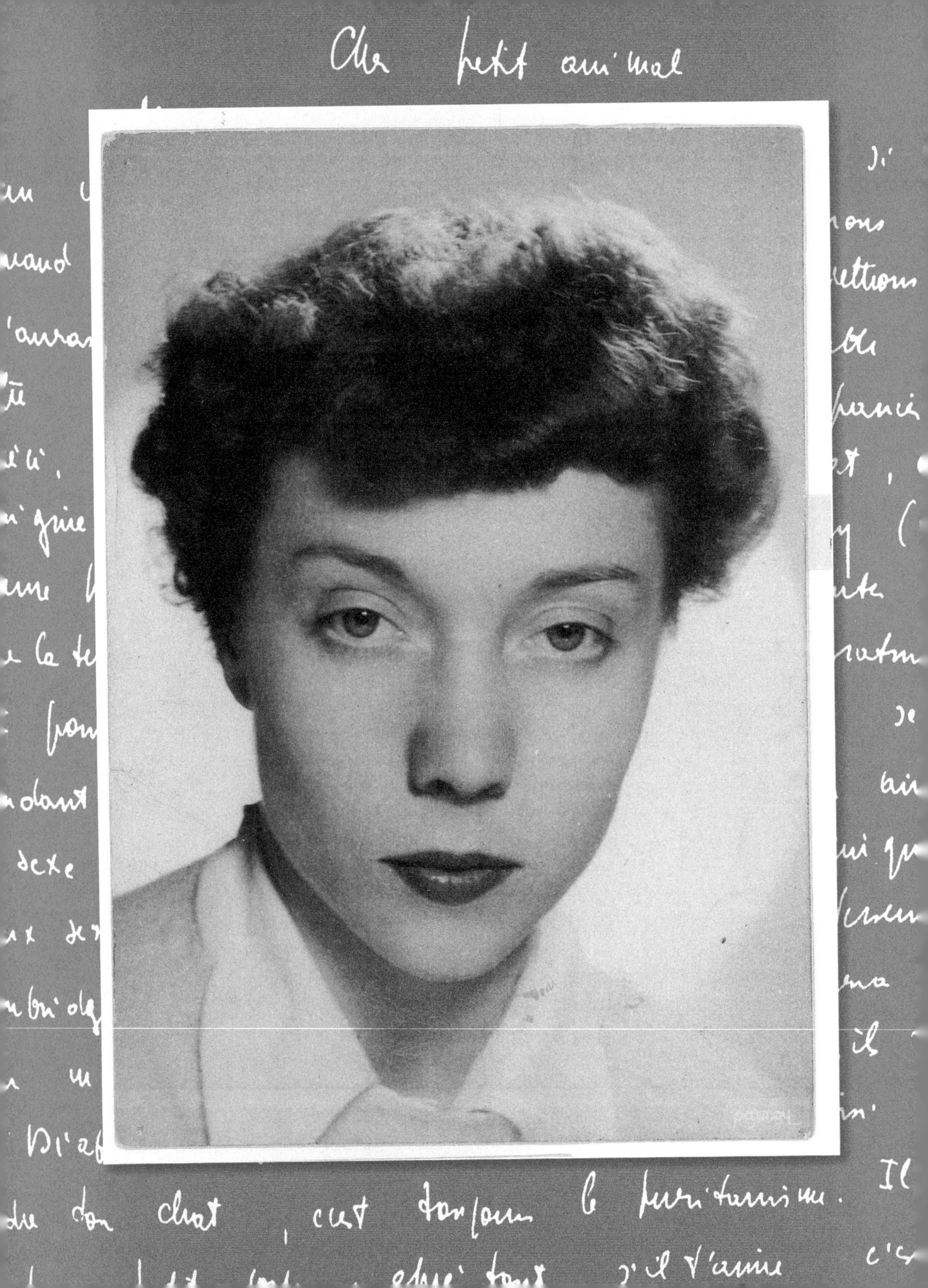
Cher petit animal
du son chat, c'est toujours le puritanisme. Il

"MY DEAR LITTLE ANIMAL"

Jean Nathan

The Affair, Epistolary and Otherwise, of Jean-Paul Sartre and Sally Swing

Despite an obsession with all things Sartrean, I had never heard of Jean-Paul Sartre's only American mistress until she came up in a monthly seminar on biography at New York University. A biographer friend of the mistress mentioned her in the context of a case of "Whose Life Is It Anyway?" The mistress had tried to write a memoir about the affair, including Sartre's fifty-eight love letters to her, but this plan was quashed when his executor refused her permission to publish the letters. She tried to rewrite the memoir without the letters, but died before its completion.

The discussion moved on but I could not stop thinking about the unfinished memoir. When the seminar was over, I cornered the friend. What was the mistress's name? Where were the letters? Where was the memoir? Her name was Sally Swing Shelley. The letters had been given to a library. She did not know what had become of the memoir.

I had once written an article for the *New York Times* about an artist with the surname Swing. I called to ask him if he'd ever heard of Sally Swing. It turned out she was his aunt. "Sally was a fabulist," he said. "She worked at the United Nations, but if you had asked her she would have told you she invented the United Nations." If I wanted to know more, he suggested I contact his father, John Swing, Sally's younger brother, and gave me his phone number.

Sally had not invented the letters. When I tracked them down at New York's Morgan Library, they were not only real, they were exquisite, and I was spellbound. Judging from the span of dates—they were not in chronological order—the relationship had gone on for three years; clearly, it

Left: Portrait of Sally Swing in Paris, undated

had been substantial. How Sally Swing was viewed in the Sartre scholarship, I did not know, yet, but he had certainly spilled a lot of ink on her. Now I was even more curious to see her memoir.

I contacted Sally's executor, her second husband, Jim Shelley, who was well aware of Sally's affair with Sartre and her attempts to write about it. Neither he nor John had any objection to my seeing the unfinished memoir; they seemed to welcome the idea. I viewed their gallantry in my regard as a sort of sweetly displaced version of the love and supportiveness they had felt for Sally. She had wanted her story out and perhaps they viewed me as someone who could do that for her, as if by proxy, and thereby give her her due. If anything, her brother seemed invested in the idea of the affair's importance. Along the way, when I asked him about some information I had gleaned, he sounded very much like the lawyer he is when he said, "I think it strengthens the case that they indeed had shared an uncommonly close and important relationship. It certainly was far more than a one-night stand." Still, no matter how cooperative they were, no one seemed to be able to produce the memoir. Did it even exist?

The search had been delegated to Sally's stepson, Ward Shelley. His discoveries would span several years. Finally, six months after this began, Ward called to say he had found the memoir materials and photocopies of the Sartre letters, in French and in translation in the Shelleys' house in Manasota Key, Florida. Later, he found more in her two computers in their New York City apartment and copied this onto disks for me. Later still, at the Easton, Connecticut house that Sally had inherited from her parents, Raymond and Betty Gram Swing, Ward found about forty letters that Sally had written to her mother in the Sartre years. There were twenty such letters in the library's collection, which she had clearly relied upon to jog her memory as she wrote. There's every reason to believe she had forgotten this other batch even existed.

I don't know what I had expected, but it was certainly not what I had before me now. It was all as messy and frenzied as the affair it described and would take months to wrestle down into something resembling order, even after I had separated out the bank statements, phone bills, and all other manner of detritus that had landed in it.

The memoir itself turned out to be a chaotic jumble of thousands of pages of myriad drafts in the form of multiple photocopies and computer printouts. Sally despised the computer, I later learned, and could neither master its proper use nor trust it to maintain its contents, hence, I gathered, the mania to print hard copies and replicate them incessantly.

"My God, what letters!!!" Sally once wrote to her mother, rightly considering Sartre's letters to her "some of the most beautiful love letters imaginable." Her photocopied collection, however, was its own fresh hell, at least to organize into page and chronological order. There were originally 178 pages in all, in French, in tiny, neat, yet difficult to read handwriting, some translated by her, some by others she hired to help. The count of her duplicates in both languages was easily ten times that, all of it almost hopelessly scrambled, every page of every letter having become separated from its companions.

Sally's letters to her mother, however, were remarkable both for the coherent information they contain and as the record of an astonishingly intimate mother-daughter bond. I thought of these letters as a latter-day version of the epistolary relationship between Marie de Sevigne and her daughter—if Françoise had written of how "wowwy" her figure looked in a certain dress, discussed her sex life freely, signed off "I remain your little Bohemian girl," and sealed her letters with a red lipstick kiss.

When I first heard about Sally's unfinished memoir, it seemed that her chief obstacle was her inability to publish Sartre's letters. Now, as I did my best to reconstruct her work, I realized the writing itself was also problematic. Despite an exceptional intelligence and her experience as a print and radio journalist, matters of organization and structure stymied her, as did the very basic questions of what she wanted to say and how she wanted to say it.

Along with her inexperience with long-form writing, she seemed unsure whether she was writing a Sartre biography, an existentialism primer, a psychological case study—she had a field day analyzing Sartre's various complexes, ranging from Napoleon (he, like she, was 5 feet 2 inches tall) to Narcissus to Oedipus—a juicy tell-all, or a disquisition on world politics of the time. As with the tone—speaking of Sartre it can shift from bitter to adoring and back in the space of a paragraph—her objective changes constantly. Perhaps none of this would have been such a problem had she not been seventy-four when she embarked on this venture.

Even she must have sensed the degree to which she was having trouble finding her way, as evidenced by notes to herself and many, many attempts at outlines. She tried naming it, but even that eluded her. For a time she favored *Sartre's Secret Love*, but later considered *Sartre's Fourth Woman*; *Footnote to a Life*; *A Question of Choice*; *PADES*, an allusion to his nickname for her, an acronym of "little wild and difficult animal" in French; *Sartre Through the Prism of Time*; *Sartre and I*; and *Amid a Crowd of Stars*, a line borrowed from the William Butler Yeats poem *When You Are Old*.

There were as many false starts as titles, including this especially awful one: "Where does my story begin? In the moment of such intense pressure that a tiny lump contained the entire universe, and then in a

> Despite an exceptional intelligence and her experience as a print and radio journalist, matters of organization and structure stymied her.

A page from Sally's Paris scrapbook, clockwise from left: Sally and her mother, Betty Gram Swing; Sally, unidentified man and her mother; Sally; unidentified man on a ski weekend; Sally. Center: Jean-Paul Sartre.

Left: "Pour Sally"—A drawing of Sally by Jean-Paul Sartre scrawled on his notes for his future obituary, 1947. Right: From a letter from Jean-Paul Sartre to Sally from the Côte d'Azur written just after the consummation of their relationship, May 1948. He writes of their upcoming trip to Tunisia. "Tunis will be a thousand and one nights for a little American...You know you have to have two pairs of eyes and two pairs of hands in the local marketplace. Otherwise you miss a lot of what's going on."

millisecond of soaring relief the universe shot out to the end of time? In the moment of conception when deep in Betty's womb, Raymond's sperm fertilized the waiting egg? Or the night I came home from the Associated Press office in Boston, and said to Betty 'I want to go to Paris!'"

After meeting with Arlette Elkaïm-Sartre, a later Sartre mistress who became his adopted daughter and executor, Sally wrote yet another beginning, this one raging and nonsensical. "Sartre! Sometimes you make me so angry that I would like to iron you out flat, fold you up and mail you back to Simone de Beauvoir's grave. There you are buried, grave next to grave. Shouldn't we all be buried there eventually? All the women you have loved, so you could coddle them and sympathize over their broken hearts? Perhaps they would have to empty the Montparnasse cemetery to make room for us all."

In the end, it was possible to piece together something resembling eight chapters, by turns lucid and poignant, incoherent and preposterously self-aggrandizing. For every promising, if underdeveloped, set piece—her trip to the Dior showroom to be squeezed into a borrowed gown to wear to the 1947 Cannes Film Festival, where she would first meet Sartre; going along on a visit to Colette's apartment with him—there's an off-the-wall passage, as when she lengthily cites scientific evidence that she and he were meant to be together based on their partially Alsatian ancestry and DNA links.

Still, by editing and splicing the elements together—and letting a good amount fall to the cutting room floor—an engrossing and intriguing story from multiple points of view does emerge. I came to see the unfinished memoir, the letters to her mother, and Sartre's letters to her and to Beauvoir about her as voices or characters in a gripping drama. Speaking of his relationship with Sally, Sartre had written to Beauvoir in the spring of 1948: "There's a play in it . . . don't you think?"

Sally Swing arrived in Paris in the fall of 1945, after her graduation from Smith College in Northampton, Massachusetts. Even as a student, she had worked for the Boston Globe and the Boston bureau of the Associated Press. Her most memorable extracurricular achievement, though, had been to commandeer a bus from Boston to bring a group of medical students, deferred from wartime military service, to the man-starved women's school. Her professors accused her of being "boy crazy." Unapologetically, she told them she did it because she found men more interesting to talk to than her classmates, whose conversation revolved around future wedding plans and silver patterns. She wanted no part of what she called "the marriage racket." She was going to become a journalist—in Paris.

Armed with a letter of recommendation from her AP boss ("Miss Sally Gram Swing . . . has a natural flair for this business. And to use an inelegant word has plenty of guts . . ."), a crash course in French, a diaphragm in her purse, and a jaunty new chartreuse huntsman's style hat that she thought would make her look older—but still wearing the bobby socks and loafers de rigueur among college girls of the day—Sally set off to seize her dream.

If the Paris Post, a short-lived affiliate of the New York Post, where she had first wangled a job, was "a puny show," her new life was "grand." Breathless letters home describe "dashing out articles by the carload," raucous parties, men—and propositions—galore ("My god these Frenchmen are as unfaithful as rabbits"), "overhung" mornings, weekend ski trips, even a burgeoning acquaintance with the "terribly amusing" Gertrude Stein. ("Never fear," she assured her mother, "I shall NEVER go queer on you.")

Her mother seemed most interested to know when she'd be coming home. Sally implied she wasn't when she wrote: "I really have the perfect life, darling."

Eighteen months after the Allied victory in Europe, Paris was still contending with the war's aftershocks, food and fuel shortages among them. But these, along with Sally's momentary bouts of homesickness and various personal setbacks, were all met with her characteristic resiliency. "Oh, well. Might as well have the bumps early in life," she wrote her mother after breaking up with a boyfriend. "We were not suited sexually, he not liking it as much as me and you know how that changes everything."

On a particularly bad week, the used car she had just bought was rear-ended and she left the valuable violin a friend had loaned her in a taxi. Then came the *Paris Post's* demise, but she quickly found an entry level job at CBS Radio—arranged through family connections to Edward R. Murrow— and then a better job at the Paris bureau of United Press covering fashion, politics, and anything else that came up.

It was in September 1947 that Sally, twenty-three, was given an assignment that would change her life. Her UP bureau chief was sending her to Cannes to cover the film festival and to interview Jean-Paul Sartre for an advance obituary, if she could arrange it. Sartre was to be at the festival for the debut of his film *Les Jeux Sont Faits* (The Chips are Down).

However excited she was by the idea of Cannes, Sally was less than thrilled to meet Sartre, by then already a major celebrity in France. What her editor called "all that existentialism stuff" would be a headache to write about, let alone spell—she wrote it as "existensialism" at first—and living in the shadow of her well-known journalist father had left her "fed up with famous men." (During the war, Raymond Gram Swing broadcast a nightly fifteen-minute radio program of news and commentary providing some seven million households with analysis of what was going on in Europe.)

"Being the offspring of a well-known person is a pain," she wrote. "If you perform well, your father gets the credit. If you perform poorly, he is brought into the conversation in such a way that by comparison your stature shrivels even further."

Still, no one shaped Sally more than her father, unless it was her "rock-ribbed feminist" mother. Betty Gram Swing had been arrested five times while demonstrating for women's right to vote, most notably in 1917 for setting fire to an effigy of President Wilson in front of the White House. In jail, she had endured solitary confinement and an eight-day hunger strike.

"Betty," as her three children called her, would also prove a rock-ribbed wife. When they married, she insisted her husband add her name to his—he had begun as Raymond Edwards Swing. And during their marriage, when Raymond was "off the preserves," as Betty referred to his affairs, she matched her husband lover for lover.

By the early 1940s, Raymond had gone off the preserves for good, and in Sally's junior year at college, the Gram Swings divorced. "The crisis," as Sally termed the unraveling of her parents' union, may have inspired her longing "to be free of Raymond, to be free of Betty" and the idea of living an ocean away.

However fed up she may have been, Sally idolized her father, always wanting

> Sally wrote yet another beginning, this one raging and nonsensical. "Sartre! Sometimes you make me so angry that I would like to iron you out flat, fold you up and mail you back to Simone de Beauvoir's grave."

to be a newsman like him. And she adored and revered her mother, who had instilled in her only daughter a strong belief in the power of her own agency and an extraordinary sense of freedom. She took to heart Betty's admonishments never to learn to cook—Betty's mother had emigrated from Denmark and worked as a cook—or type, lest she end up doing either as a profession. Also taken to heart was her mother's belief in the importance of "a regular sex life," a subject about which the entire family spoke openly. When Sally's older brother wrote that he was considering marriage, Sally counseled him: "As to the gal sitch. Should suggest again that you hold fire. Find a good bed mate if you can and wait for a while." A diaphragm, she advised, was critical. Sally was having a friend send her "goo" from London as it was impossible to find in Paris.

She found her philosopher prey on her third night in Cannes, when Maurice Chevalier, a previous interview subject, invited her to join him and an entourage of starlets for dinner. It was Chevalier who first spotted Sartre sitting at a table on the restaurant's outdoor terrace. "I recognized him immediately from press photos but was not prepared for how ugly he really was," she wrote later. "His right wall-eye was covered with a milky membrane through which one could see the pupil wandering about, but mostly pointing way up in the corner to the upper right. It was not in sync with his good left eye. His hair was dyed red-blond, his snaggle teeth were covered with tobacco stains as were his fingers." She thought he looked "toadlike."

If not exactly a princess herself—she had recently adopted a masculine hairstyle, "permed and shortish," and weighed, at 130, "a bit much"—on this evening she was certainly decked out like one. Wearing an evening gown she had confected herself, having jettisoned the Dior gown as its tightness allowed her to neither breathe nor eat, the intrepid reporter marched over to his table to request an interview.

Beholding this blond, blue-eyed, franglais-spouting apparition, Sartre said he'd be delighted. He suggested they meet for lunch when they returned to Paris and gave her his phone number. She could hear him chuckling as she walked away. He later told her that his dinner companions, an American movie producer and his wife, were aghast when he let it be known that his intentions were purely salacious.

Back in Paris, Sally waited a few days before dialing DANton 16-13. When she did, Sartre, at work on his play *Les Mains Sales*, said he remembered her well. He suggested she meet him at Cavanaugh, a quiet second-floor restaurant on the Boulevard Saint-Germain where they wouldn't be disturbed.

To his dismay, she arrived "all business," paper and pen in hand, firing off questions even before she sat down. He cooperated long enough for her to scribble "Mobilized in '39, long golden hair at six, 'the pope of Existentialists,'" until his impatience overtook him. This was exactly *not* what he had in mind. But if she was going to insist on sticking to her agenda—to gather the facts for his future obituary, then she was writing far too slowly. He grabbed the paper from her hands, a pen from his pocket, and began composing the notes himself, in French, speaking it aloud as he went along. "One wall eye, a front tooth broken in 1915, never replaced, never wears a hat or suspenders, smokes a pipe, born 21 June 1905, stayed 10 months in his mother's belly, lost his father at 18 months, his right eye at 25 months."

Continuing in this playful vein, he stopped to draw a caricature of his hapless interviewer, writing "Pour Sally" above it. Amused and flattered, she decided maybe he wasn't really as physically repellent as he had struck her at first. After he finished interviewing himself, more seriously after the drawing, he interviewed Sally. Five hours later, he knew her life story and she had not only her notes for his future obituary but an invitation to lunch the next week.

"He is extremely wise, witty and nice, slightly malicious, ugly as sin, but utterly charming," she reported to her mother after the second lunch. "We are now buddies . . . Of course I need not stoop to tell you he is the father of existentialism . . ." After lunch, which began at 1 P.M., they moved on to a café, where they stayed until 7 P.M. "So you can see the conversation was mutually interesting and he passed up two dates to stay. (With me) . . . [He] has me figured out to a 'T' which is sometimes rather startling."

> She wrote later [of Sartre] (upon first sight) "His right walleye was covered with a milky membrane through which one could see the pupil wandering about."

The actual seduction would take eight more months. Over this time, the forty-four-year-old philosopher courted Sally Swing with flowers and chocolates, letters, phone calls, lunches and dinners, gifts of books and philosophy tutorials.

It wasn't as if she didn't have him figured out quite close to a *T*, as well. After reading, at his suggestion, a passage in *Being and Nothingness* on bad faith between men and women, she scolded him: "So all this talk about loving to talk to me and take me out is just because you want to get into my pants!"

Still, she wrote, he waited "patiently like a spider with a particularly juicy fly," although there were periodic attempts at a more direct approach. One took place on a day that Sally was home sick from work. "He appeared with a bouquet of flowers and sat at the edge of my bed. We had a friendly chat for awhile, when suddenly he said, 'Petite, why won't you go to bed with me?' 'Well, for one thing, you remind me of my father,' I said. 'But I am not your father,' he said in his low sensuous voice as he patted my leg ever so gently. Not willing to give an inch, I added, 'Besides, I don't have affairs with married men.' 'But I'm not married,' he said emphatically. 'What about Simone de Beauvoir?' 'I am not married to Simone de Beauvoir or anybody else.' I held fast and told him that he didn't interest me that way."

By May 1948, he was sending her an addendum to the advance obituary that had started it all. "47-48: met a young American journalist in Cannes called Sally Swing—taken with her at first glance . . . becomes more and more attached to her and ends up leaving with her for Tunis." This letter, sent from the Côte d'Azur, where he had gone with Beauvoir, ends: "I care for you, my darling, I care very much for you. I kiss you on your mouth which I love. Love [in English] J P Sartre."

Days earlier, a lunch at Chez Allard had concluded in Sartre's bedroom in the apartment where he was then living with his mother. The two-part seduction began in her car as she was driving them to lunch. "Sartre suddenly grabbed my chin in his hand and . . . planted a kiss on my mouth with such force that I almost drove the car off the road. . .that kiss was like a lightning bolt. It released in me a desire for him so intense which had perhaps been latent for a long time . . ."

After lunch, he directed her to a parking place near his apartment at 42 rue Bonaparte and led her upstairs by the hand. "He . . . started to undress me slowly, kissing my shoulders tenderly as he undid my blouse, pulling it down and when he had removed my brassiere with a flip, he kissed my breasts as the tip of his tongue rubbed back and forth on the tip of my nipples, making me more and more excited . . ."

'Petite, why won't you go to bed with me?'

Greatly impressed with his sexual prowess, and by their physical compatibility, a "deliriously happy" Sally wrote: "I had fallen deeply in love with him, and visa versa [sic]."

The picture, however, was far less rosy—and far more crowded and complex—than she at first imagined. There was, of course, Beauvoir, whom Sally viewed benignly, at that point, as Sartre's "sister and companion and vice president of existentialism." But there were others as well. And because he was "a stickler on loyalty," he told her he could not give up any of these "previous" women for her. A strict schedule would be necessary. When he was not traveling, her "days" would be Wednesday evenings (including dinner and a sleepover) and Saturday nights (an after-dinner sleepover) until Sunday afternoon (including lunch).

"Still giddy after my first romantic experience with him," she wrote, "I told him I didn't care, as long as he was faithful to me." He had assured her that his relations with Beauvoir were no longer sexual. She wanted to assume the same was true of the others. "Nothing disturbed the pattern," she wrote, "unless it was a rather deep conflict that I had in my mind and heart about his behavior."

She resented his other liaisons, even if they were platonic, and wept profusely when

Newspaper feature on Sally Swing, an American journalist covering the Paris Peace Conference at the Luxembourg Palace, from an unidentified French newspaper in 1946, the year before Sally met Sartre.

SALLYS SWING
DONNE A 40 MILLIONS D'AMÉRICAINS LA TEMPÉRATURE DU LUXEMBOURG

A NEUF HEURES, CHAQUE MATIN, Miss Sallys Swing gravit l'escalier qui mène à la salle réservée aux journalistes, située au rez-de-chaussée du palais du Luxembourg. Un autobus spécial l'a amenée du Grand-Hôtel, où elle occupe une des trois cents chambres réquisitionnées pour la presse.

LA machine à fabriquer la paix du monde est entrée dans son troisième mois d'existence. Pour les 1.500 délégués qui représentent vingt et une nations admises à la rédaction des traités, les séances quotidiennes du Luxembourg sont devenues presque une routine, que réveillent de temps en temps les éclats de voix de M. Evatt, ou les interventions de M. Vichinsky. Les journalistes, qui étaient plus d'un millier à l'ouverture de la conférence, se sont progressivement lassés de cette monotonie, et bon nombre d'entre eux, trouvant que les travaux n'avançaient pas assez vite, ont regagné leurs pays respectifs. Seules les grandes agences internationales et quelques quotidiens à gros tirage ont maintenu sur place leurs correspondants dont l'effectif ne dépasse pas aujourd'hui 200. Représentant les yeux et les oreilles du monde, ils ont pour mission de renseigner des millions de lecteurs sur les débats compliqués des 21. Miss Sallys Swing, correspondante de l'agence United Press, est parmi ces trois cents journalistes qui resteront à leur poste jusqu'à ce que le dernier mot du dernier discours ait été prononcé. Grâce à elle, quarante millions d'Américains lisent chaque jour dans leur journal, en prenant leur petit déjeuner, les dernières nouvelles diplomatiques de Paris. Voici, prise au hasard, une journée au Luxembourg de Miss Sallys Swing, informatrice accréditée auprès de la Conférence de la Paix.

MISS SWING TAPE ELLE-MÊME SES ARTICLES, qui sont ensuite câblés par fil spécial au bureau new-yorkais de l'agence United Press.

AU RESTAURANT DU PALAIS DU LUXEMBOURG, on mange à la carte pour 75 et 125 francs. Voici un menu-type : sardines à l'huile, plat de viande, légumes, fromages, entremets. Vin en supplément. Ce sont les repas les plus copieux et les moins chers que l'on puisse trouver à Paris.

he left her for another. (Sartre, who had been a meteorologist in the war, likened her constant emotional outbursts to the weather, going from sun to rain, in this case, laughter to tears, "ten times in the day, squared.")

In calmer moments, she voiced conditions, too—that he *tutoie* her (he always used the more formal address of "vous" with Beauvoir), that he shave everyday, dye his red hair—an idea of another woman—back to its natural color, and get a new overcoat so he wouldn't look "so slovenly." He complied.

On other matters, Sally seems not to have batted an eye, including Sartre's predilection for sex with role play. In what would come to be their favorite scenario, she played "The Little Orphan," while he played the orphan's nanny, a part he gave an English name, "The Patronizing Dame." She also raised no objection when he told her he liked to make love within earshot of his mother.

Sally in Paris, undated.

On the entrance to the new apartment she took to be closer to his was a plaque that read, "Here Louis Pasteur visited his grandchildren." He suggested a second plaque might someday be added: "Here Sartre visited his American mistress." She laughed and stuck out her tongue at him. "Over time," she wrote, "Sartre and I were increasingly in love and happy as two children with a new toy."

The plan to go to Tunisia together hadn't worked out—annoyingly, Beauvoir claimed that trip. But their lives did mesh in countless other ways that pleased her. Gradually, her "days" and hours increased. "The schedule," she wrote her mother, "is out the window . . . We see each other constantly. I am really very very happy. He is wonderful in bed, tender and adorable and full of humor and life and happiness. We have such a harmonious life together . . . he finds me pretty and passionate, as I am with him as he is the first man I have ever slept with whom I respect as a man, as a mind, and as a human being. I love him with my heart and soul."

Sartre would take her to Rome for nine days; back home they cruised around Paris and the countryside in "Rosalie," the name they gave to her beat-up four-horsepower Fiat. (When it eventually died, Sartre wrote her a condolence letter.) She accompanied him on visits to Albert Camus, Colette, Alberto Giacometti, André Gide, and Tristan Tzara, among others. (Tzara expressed his envy of Sartre's paramour and asked Sally if she didn't have a sister for him.) She met and was well-liked by his mother. At Sally's place, they prepared little dinners; at his, they played Beethoven and Schubert together—he on the piano, she on the violin.

When she left Paris, in blizzard conditions, to fly home to Connecticut to visit her mother for Christmas, he wrote that he had passed a sleepless night worrying that she might be "lost in the Atlantic." When the next day's newspapers carried no news of a plane crash he wrote of his vast relief. (He had seen her off at the airport and would pick her up on her return. The elaborate reunion celebration he'd planned lasted two days.)

When Sartre offered to support her financially, she refused. She told him she was proud of her ability to earn her own living and enjoyed her work, for the most part.

She did accept his gift of a cat, but to her immediate regret. The cat turned out to have been mistreated by its previous owner and had a monstrous disposition. Before leaping to its death from her fifth-floor window, it destroyed her apartment, clawed, bit, and upset her, but not nearly as much as the information that was dawning on her only gradually. Sartre presided over what was in fact an intensely sexually active harem, with Beauvoir at its head and, in that period, several women of higher ranking. As she would calculate, she clocked in at number four. (She was actually number five.) She sobbed; he held her in his arms, wiped her tears, stroked her hair, and suggested she arrange a similar setup for herself.

Distressed and confused, she tested out these developments in a letter to her mother, sounding almost brainwashed in her attempt to come across as neutral: "As you know, he is a man that is worth all these women . . . He wants me to have other affairs because he says he cannot satisfy me sexually with [the others] in the picture, which is understandable . . ." She sounds more like herself when she adds: "I can't get excited about the prospect as I am still very much in love with JPS and there you are."

The gift of the cat was to keep her company when Sartre visited or traveled with the other women, leaving Sally, consumed by anger and jealousy, to rage as wildly as the cat. It was for that reason and for her sexual voraciousness that Sartre nicknamed her PADES, an acronym for *petit animal difficile et sauvage*.

Beauvoir, whom Sartre also called by a nickname with an animal reference—*Castor*, meaning beaver in English—usually managed to remain at least outwardly composed in the face of all Sartre's affairs. She did lose her cool over Sally at one point. Having coerced her into a café rendezvous, Beauvoir refused to sit down with Sally or allow her to order her a drink. Instead she stayed standing, gripping the chair back so tightly that her knuckles turned white, and spat out, "You're not going to get pregnant, are you?" Sally, who was in fact thinking of it, assured her she was not.

". . . He wants me to have other affairs because he says he cannot satisfy me sexually with [the others] in the picture, which is understandable . . ."

By now, considering "the beaver" as "a thorn in my side" and "humorless and frumpy," Sally wrote Sartre to complain of their nasty encounter. He wrote back: "Tell me, why was the lady so scared of you?"

Meanwhile, Sartre was busy reassuring "the lady" there was no reason to feel threatened by Sally and downplaying their involvement. He wrote to Beauvoir in Chicago in the spring of 1948—where she was visiting Nelson Algren, *her* American lover at the time— that despite his "warm and cordial feelings" for Sally, he admired her only as a working journalist. (He did admire that she worked for a living; the work she did was another matter. Throughout their relationship, he urged her to write a book about Paris or to turn her painting, a hobby, into a true profession. Her assignment of the moment particularly enraged him. The Paris media was paying more attention to the royal visit of the then-Princess Elizabeth than they were to the British blocking Jewish war survivors from settling in Palestine. He favored the creation of a Jewish state.)

In his descriptions of Sally to Beauvoir, he mocks her constant mishaps, whether losing her hat or a handbag containing thirty thousand francs on an evening out— or the story she's after. He tells of Sally, sent to cover the Princess's lunch at the Trianon Palace, sneaking onto the palace grounds, suffering scratches and blisters while fighting her way over eight kilometers of bramble-covered terrain, only to arrive, her clothes in tatters, to find fifty journalists at the scene, all unscathed, all of whom had entered by the front door.

He also makes fun of her voracious appetites for food and for sex, and complains how put-upon he feels by the latter. "I mount and I perform," he writes, giving Beauvoir the impression that sex with Sally is an onerous duty.

The letter's conclusion, though, is most chilling: "She has become attached, of course, but spares herself my assurances of a future detachment. I think it will cause her pain but she will work it out. There will still be a painful parting, but for you my little sweet, there will be no painful return [from Chicago] . . . I am waiting for you, I would love to see you and tell you everything."

But if parting was near, Sally had no inkling. "Glad you were glad about JPS. I adore him," she wrote her mother that same week. "He is a saint, a clown, a kind delightful and adorable human being . . . . I see him every night . . . . I rush over to his apartment in Saint-Germain des Prés and if he is still working on his novel I lie down on the bed in the corner of his light green study littered with books and take a nap.

He is so wonderful, so tender and loves to make love as much as I—if anything we overdo it and both have slight difficulties and have to stop for a day which is awful!"

Then we play a bit of piano and violin . . . then woop-off into a cab to some glorious restaurant . . . then we pack off to my bare and funny apartment which he hated at first and now loves. He is so wonderful, so tender and loves to make love as much as I—if anything we overdo it and both have slight difficulties and have to stop for a day which is <u>awful</u>!"

When Beauvoir did return and she and Sartre took off for a vacation, his letters to his PADES include nary a hint of a future detachment. "I love you very much, my little one," he writes. "I think of you; when you feel lonely you can tell yourself that there is an excellent chance that I am thinking of you and my thoughts are only tenderness, sweetness, esteem, and respect for you, and desire for your beautiful body."

He writes of worshipping every inch of that body—"I kiss your body all over, your mouth, your armpits and the orange tips of your breasts" and its smell—"I believe that it's the smell of warm bread, well-baked, with a light after-smell of vanilla and also a smell of herbs, I think." Over and over, he offers evidence of his affection: "I love you my sweet little animal, I think of you, I am charmed by you—I am faithful to you, and I long so very very much to hold you in my arms." He recounts his sleepless nights without her, expresses worry for her well-being, his desire for her happiness, his pain at causing her suffering. On a lighter note, he chides her for her mistakes in French—she became near-fluent under his tutelage—and playfully sticks in difficult words he knows she'll be forced to look up.

Playful turns cruel, though, especially when in response to her letters railing against his infidelities or expressing her sense of being mistreated. In one instance, after she's berated him for taking Beauvoir on the trip instead of her and accused him of taking enjoyment in hurting women, he baits her: "There's my little animal with its tail caught . . . difficult animal come close to me—beat and scratch me."

He tries to calm her with intellectual gobbledygook—"Even when I don't have a direct and precise thought concerning you, you are part of the foundation from which everything rises"—or with tales of the wholesome life he leads in her absence—"I work ten hours a day. At philosophy (what is the truth) and the novel (2nd volume of the third part), I read an hour or two and the rest of the time I eat, sleep and walk in the mountains."

At other times, Sartre seems genuinely to fear losing her, describing himself as "worried stiff" when he doesn't hear from her. "Don't add to our sadness by becoming my enemy," he implores her. "Let's stay together in all the ill that befalls us, it's the best way and it's less unhappy." He deploys all manner of psychological manipulation and his considerable force of reason.

Sally and her mother frequently conferred on strategies for keeping him. At one point, she writes to Betty: "Now don't think I'm not being foxy with the old boy, every once in a while I go out with some attractive so and so . . . or I don't call him up one day, or I don't appear until late, and the poor dear is in a panic. So I am not being too eager about it all although a day like yesterday, which was so harmonious . . . makes it hard to play hard to get if you see what I mean. JPS says that each day we have together he becomes more attached to me."

Although the relationship would never settle into anything like the stability for which Sally yearned, for most of 1948 and into early 1949 her assessment that the "affair with Sartre is still going great guns" is borne out by how much of his time is devoted to her. She describes romantic walks by the Seine, picnics in Montmartre, weekends in Fontainebleau, evenings socializing or attending plays, operas, and ballets, and nights making love.

On the eve of one of Sartre's trips with Beauvoir, she writes that "he actually burst into tears the other night when I said I was sad to leave him. He lost his temper this morning when I asked if he would think of me today, saying he would like to know what the hell I thought he thought about all day long if it wasn't me."

For a time, Sartre even went along as Sally steered the conversation to the subject of the future. She told her mother that the trip to Rome in July, 1948, had "clinched . . . the mutual affection and tender love we have the one for the other . . . He is deeply in love with me and says he banks his future happiness, all his happiness on the continuation of our relationship . . ." It was on that trip that he went so far as to bring up marriage and children, even if he would spend the rest of the relationship backpedaling.

Although Sally warned her mother he might have been "carried away by the moment," and she well knew "he hates the institution of marriage," Sartre "said he would like nothing better than to marry me and have some children (one or two) and that if this could ever be worked out you would come into the picture, and we would raise the two in the United States until five years old and then bring them back to France."

Even several weeks after their return from Rome, on the eve of yet another of his departures, marriage talk was still in the air. "He said he would insist that if we ever did get married that I keep a career and paint as well. Ah me . . . He took me in his arms all night and rocked me back and forth and there were tears in his eyes too. He said that I must think that ours is only the beginning of a great love, not the end. So you see parting was not so bad as I had thought these last few days."

On his return, the backpedaling began in earnest. He told her, and she told her mother: ". . . he didn't think he could ever marry me, which was a blow to my heart." Now, she explored with him, her mother, and even the medical doctor that attended both Sally and Sartre, whether she should have a baby out of wedlock. "Despite the fact that JPS can't marry me," she writes Betty, "what you say about having a child anyway gives me hope. I know he wants one very much . . . It is a big step and one which would take enormous thought and courage. I love you so much, not only because I do, but also because you above all would be the first to give me your confidence if such a thing did happen. It might not be a bad idea. And then we could be together for long periods of time and have my child (and his!) with us. Would you like that, darling?"

This plan slowly erodes for all sorts of reasons, including Sally's concern that her financially strapped mother might not be available for child rearing. "Especially if you are working you will not want an illegitimate stranger dawdling around the house. Or would you???????")

Soon, her doctor and her mother were recommending that she back-pedal, too, and consider Sartre "a casual lover." The doctor, who was undoubtedly riveted to be privy to such intimate information regarding Sartre's private life, opened Sally's eyes to the possibility that "JPS, as so many intelligent men, was really in love with himself." The doctor told her that "the need for all the women showed that he was incapable of loving any one of them, but only sought self love in the reflection of their love for him." Rationalizing away, she writes Betty, "Well, darling, you see [Sartre] as all geniuses is far from balanced in his personal life. First I didn't realize what it quite was. When he is with me he is . . . perfect in every way. I wracked my brains and then the doctor told me. It was exactly in the fact that he was so sweet when he saw me, but didn't want or

couldn't want to find his satisfaction completely in one person. This makes sense to me. It could be much worse. He is as tender as ever, and as darling, and I am COMPLETELY RESIGNED TO TAKING HIM WHEN HE WANTS TO and not making a constant fuss about it as I did at first to no avail."

But she is clearly shaken. One minute she is feeling "rather like a high-wire artist, happy as a loon balancing along," the next she is "terribly blue about him." She questions, doubts, and suffers. "Perhaps I am a fool (surely) I should say, but right now I am still so much in love with him that every minute he is away hurts and hurts."

Counting on his return to make the hurt go away, she now learns that there will be "regime" changes when he is back. Sartre blames this necessity on Beauvoir, who was always a convenient excuse. Beauvoir, she writes Betty, is "jealous of me. (naturally.) He is gone on me 100 percent." But she is demanding "the lion's share [of his time] because of 20 years' lead on me and the fact that they have made their lives together." Sartre, claiming to be exhausted by the struggle, is giving in. "He feels like a piece of pie"—she means the pie itself—"with everybody griping because they did not get big enough pieces."

> "JPS, as so many intelligent men, was really in love with himself." The doctor told her that "the need for all the women showed that he was incapable of loving any one of them, but only sought self love in the reflection of their love for him."

For her part, Sally is "fit to be tied," refusing "to be put into second place, if you know what I mean. He writes me beautiful letters as always, but you know how men are. They want their cakes and eat them too. Simone de Beauvoir feels that she has the right to lots of his time, which I suppose she has, but I'm damned if I'm going to be the victim of it. I wrote him a stinking letter . . . saying that he was selfish which I think he is . . . . I have some hopes that the situation can be arranged for the best . . . he wrote and said that the 3 or 4 last days he realized that he loved me more than ever before . . . Anyway, dearest heart, realize that I am alright now in good health and not sad at all, rather slightly irritated and bewildered."

The mixed signals were indeed bewildering. Just as he was pushing her away he was pulling her closer. Knowing that Betty was having trouble continuing to pay John Swing's Harvard tuition, Sartre offered to step in; he also offered to pay Betty's airfare and provide spending money for a visit to Paris. Although touched, her mother declined these offers. Sally, impressed by the generosity extended to her family, told her mother of her struggles to accept the situation and do better at controlling her emotions. "He will give me the money, the knowledge, and the love, but not the time. He loves me, that I know. That makes the whole affair so much bigger you see. And when I revert to the little girl bourgeois and cry because he won't marry me and have children . . . well, darling . . . I say that I am intelligent at least to see my mistakes two weeks or three after they are blindly made."

Despite her efforts, by the spring of 1949 more storm clouds were gathering. Dolores Vanetti, a French woman living in America whom Sartre had met and taken up with on a solo visit to the United States in 1945, had announced plans to divorce her American husband and move to Paris to be with him. "The bitch in America," Sally wrote her mother, was "kicking up all sorts of fuss." Sartre had not counted on this and Sally understood that if Dolores were to follow through with her plan, "that would be the end of us. (JPS and me.)"

Sartre, she wrote, "is distraught, and at his nerves' end. He is fighting to do right by this old bag (I'd like to poison her) and yet his heart is with mine, and we are so happy . . ." But after a "specially difficult whining barrage from me," Sartre "proposed that we stop 'living together,' i.e., stop all sexual relations." After more discussion and much argument, they decided neither liked this idea and continued on, although she does acknowledge, "With all this folderol most women would have given him the air a long time ago, but I love him too much to give him up."

> "With all this folderol most women would have given him the air a long time ago, but I love him too much to give him up."

As masterful and efficient as he was at his game, by summer 1949 Sartre could no longer manage this particular harem configuration. Someone had to go. What one Sartre biographer called his "pattern of scheduled promiscuity" worked best when no one balked at the setup. Dolores was not just acting out, she was threatening suicide. Plus, he needed a free slot to make room for Michelle Vian, Boris Vian's soon-to-be-ex-wife. They had spent time together the previous spring and he had plans to launch a serious courtship in the fall.

On Sally's twenty-fifth birthday, August 3, 1949, a month short of two years after they first met, Sartre wrote from Panama, where he was traveling with Dolores. "My sweet little one, this will change our way of life. I cannot be 'your man' any more."

After hearing of Sally's state—she was devastated, and by now quite ill—an alarmed Betty flew to France to be with her. If buoyed by her mother's presence, her true recovery did not begin until Sartre contacted her on his return and sought out visits both alone with her and together with her mother. But after Betty's departure in October and not seeing Sartre for a few days, Sally wrote her mother that she was, yet again, "in serious dumps." That letter had not even reached its destination before Sally, "walking on air," was firing off another.

Letter from Sally to her mother, 1949.

"Hold your breath for BIG NEWS: YESTERDAY JPS CAPITULATED!!!!! Ah, oui. It was so wonderful you can't imagine . . . Well, yesterday he said, 'I will come and wake you up in bed . . .' So I got all dolled up at seven A.M. after a sleepless night . . . and then pretended to go back to sleep. He walked straight in and 'woke me up' and the relationship between us was so electric nothing could be done about it. I was shaking, literally with joy and feeling for him and sensual desire. He took me in his arms, and well, obviously he felt much as I did . . . He told me Dolores arrives on the 7th of November, [She had gone to America to be with her husband] and I said, well, if we could only have this once things would be different for me, and I wouldn't

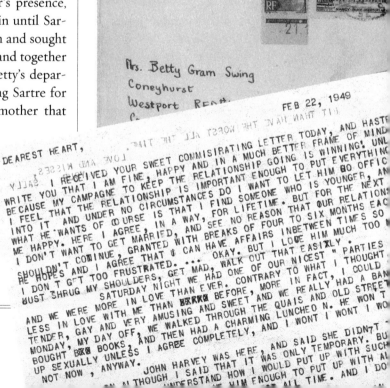

feel so bad. . .So he made up his mind on the spot, although he said maybe we'd better wait a week. I said fine with me, then being the typical male he is he said the hell with waiting a week, and we went right on from there. Of course it won't be a regular affair, it can't be, and even if we don't have that terrible joy we had yesterday (I don't think I could take it too often and I remember your warning only too well about overdoing it), it means that his feelings for me are very far from platonic, which he explained long and intellectually.

"He also said that even when Dolores came he would skip out and see me a couple mornings . . . He also said that he would try and spend some of Christmas day with me, so as you see, my situation though extremely difficult is very, very far from being lost. Hooray hooray . . . Isn't it darling of him to give over his morning work hours to making me happy . . . I know this will make you happy, darling, and somehow the intensity of the moment yesterday made all the suffering of this summer worthwhile. He told me yesterday the thing most important to him in the world was his work, and I said I agreed, because I do. And that will come first with me, too, as mine is important."

But when Dolores did return, work was the last thing on Sally's mind. Although there is evidence he did "skip out" on Dolores on at least one morning, alerting Sally in a quick note, "My Sweet PADES, I'll be with you tomorrow, Sunday, around 9:15 A.M. and I'll stay with you until 12:45 P.M.," Sally became so desperate for Sartre's attention that she managed to have herself checked into the American Hospital with only a slight cold.

"Well guess who came to get me out of the hospital at noon today?" she gushes in the next letter to her mother. "None other than old JPS himself who was désolé about my being there (desired effect) and said Dolores was leaving in a week's time and that all was arranged so that I would see him just as before. He was so affectionate and so warm and sweet . . . I received yr. letter about leaving my heart open to other adventures . . . Of course I agree with you! And I will try very hard—But the fact is that he promised me I was in his life to stay; plus the fact that . . . he will send D. back to America in 2 years if she doesn't behave."

Ten days later, she writes Betty: "Dearest heart . . . the morale is excellent. Mostly since Dolores has left for Cannes where she will sit on her can without JPS for the next six months. He will remain in Paris . . . and we will resume as before our close friendship. He is so cute. He said that half of him was on my side, and the other half made him realize that our affair couldn't work out and that there was a perpetual battle . . . anyway, so far, right now, my side is on the up, and anyway, I am more or less resigned to the idea that I must look for someone else . . . . but of course I still spend my off days with him, and this week we are going to Chartres to look at the stained glass which has just been completely put back in."

But perpetual battle had taken its toll on their status quo, such as it was. Perhaps the tenets of the president of existentialism had rubbed off. She was in charge of her own life and if she was "sick of these emotional crises every few months," she had better act. Perhaps having met Marcello Maria Benvenuto Spaccarelli, a dashing young Italian journalist working in Paris, had something to do with strengthening her resolve. After announcing, "The next time I fall in love it will be for keeps and no mistake about it," she began seeing Marcello, whose architect father had been hired by Mussolini to design the Via della Conciliazione in Rome. By Easter of 1950, they were living together and discussing marriage.

In the ensuing six years, Sartre and Sally exchanged only a few letters. She wrote to tell of her move to the United States in 1950, her marriage to Marcello in 1951, her pregnancy in 1954, and, shortly after the birth of their son, Sidney, their Mexican divorce in 1955. In his replies, Sartre sounds as tender as ever, persisting in addressing her as his "sweet PADES" or his "little orphan," and to himself as "The Patronizing Dame." He tells her things with Dolores are "about over," talks of his work, and expresses his sympathies regarding Marcello, whom he refers to as "the crooked Italian." But he had clearly moved on.

A December 1955 letter he wrote in response to the news that she was planning to come to Paris—shades of Dolores—the following March, in which he suggests two weeks would be plenty, would be his last to her. On this trip, the newly-divorced Sally, then working for Voice of America, seems to have harbored hopes of resuscitating the relationship. Although they met for lunch frequently during her visit—Beauvoir even joined them once—Sally wrote to Betty, "No romance there I'm afraid, for me."

In 1960, Sally married James Shelley, an electrical engineer with whom she would live happily and prosperously for the next forty-six years. She had a successful career as a public information officer for UNESCO, then as chief of public information for the Non-Governmental Section of the United Nations, and later as a United Nations radio correspondent doing interview programs for AP Radio and Deutsche Welle. She was also a women's rights activist.

When she wrote to Sartre in 1971 to announce another trip to Paris, it was Beauvoir who replied—long after the fact. In 1974, Sally wrote Sartre for what would be the last time, probably because it was again Beauvoir who responded. (Sartre had had strokes in 1971 and 1973; perhaps that explains why Beauvoir had taken over his correspondence.) The very last contact would be Sally's condolence letter to Beauvoir when Sartre died, in 1980, and Beauvoir's reply thanking her.

When an English translation of Sartre's letters to Beauvoir came out in 1992, Sally was stunned to learn how cruelly he spoke of her behind her back.

Sally did keep an eye on the Sartre world, reading the spate of Sartre and Beauvoir biographies that were published in this country from the late 1980s on. These blew the lid off Sartre and Beauvoir's amorous games, but if she was mentioned at all, it was as little more than a footnote. When an English translation of Sartre's letters to Beauvoir came out in 1992, Sally was stunned to learn how cruelly he spoke of her behind her back. She also felt somehow vindicated to come across Sartre's admission to Beauvoir in a letter years before Sally met him: "I quite profoundly and sincerely consider myself to be a bastard—a sickening sort of academic sadist, a wage-earning Don Juan." But she knew he was being disingenuous and she knew he was much more than that.

> One of Sartre's lovers did commit suicide, Dolores threatened it and Michelle Vian would later attempt it; still another went mad.

Thinking she might somehow set the record straight where she was concerned, and presuming anyone cared, she toyed with the idea of writing a memoir of their time together. She never did more than attempt a translation of his letters, which she kept stored in a green leatherette jewelry box.

In 1995, at the age of seventy, Sally gave the epistolary record of her affair with Sartre, as well as twenty letters written to her mother during that period, to the Morgan Library through a gift-purchase arrangement. She asked that the materials be restricted. She told Christine Nelson, a curator of literary and historical manuscripts there, that she was planning to write a memoir and asked for photocopies of them all.

But it was not until 1999, just after the seventy-five-year-old Sally suffered a transient ischemic attack (TIA), a stroke-like event but with no lasting damage, that she began the memoir in earnest. Two weeks after the attack, she had consulted a Freudian analyst. (After leaving Paris, she had studied psychoanalysis in the hopes of becoming an analyst herself.) She came away convinced that the TIA was due to her unresolved anger at Sartre and that writing the memoir might save her life. Jim Shelley was supportive, agreeing that she needed to "get the Sartre thing off her chest." When friends asked him if it wasn't awkward for him to have his wife writing about a former lover, he told them, "Come on, we're all adults."

In 2002, having been advised that she would need permission from the Sartre estate to publish the letters, she and Jim paid a visit to Arlette Elkaïm-Sartre in Paris. She was cruel and dismissive, coolly informing Sally there had been even more mistresses than Sally had thought and maliciously suggesting that he had written identical love letters to many of them. But the biggest bomb that Elkaïm-Sartre dropped that day was to inform Sally of her intention to block publication of the letters until 2050. As a courtesy, she would approve the publication of four of the fifty-eight. It would not be until December 2004 that they agreed on which four those would be.

Sally's plan to make Sartre's letters her memoir's cornerstone was effectively sabotaged. All she had so far—annotations and a bit of connective material—would have to be fleshed out at much greater length if it would amount to a book. Sartre would have recognized his PADES's reaction: until she suffered a cerebral hemorrhage in December 2005, she raged, wrote and re-wrote wildly. She died the following May.

What propelled her? Clearly, she took pride in having occupied the attentions of a great—and difficult—man and in living to tell the tale. (She knew of the casualties. One of Sartre's lovers did commit suicide, Dolores threatened it and Michelle Vian would later attempt it; still another went mad.) Unlike Sartre's other "other women"—he described those that attracted him as "drowning women"—she may have gone under a few times, but she always fought her way back up.

Her story, though, was drowned—not by Sartre, but by his executor. Sally may have been less important to Sartre than she wished, but based on the record, she was much more to him than has been acknowledged. It was certainly far more than a one-night stand. 🕯

mostl old mer

In 1000 turnpike rest areas, 1000 old men
are walking 1000 dogs.
Most of the dogs are small, which makes them easier
to tuck into Fords and Toyotas and carry along.
Dogs are luggage, too,
but they can't be packed.

Sometimes kids walk dogs, and
old women, but mostly it's old men.
1000 old men, coast to coast. Often
the dogs themselves are old; white muzzles
and puzzled eyes caked with that stuff that says,
"Sorry, pal, must die soon."

An old man on 80 outside of Lincoln
wears a golf-cap in the rain.
An old man just north of Savannah
on 95 wears shorts with a hanging seat.
There is a sore on one ashen leg that's been there
awhile, awhile, oh yes, awhile.
A sneering old man under the Tucson sun with
his pipe turned upside down in his

bald and gleaming dentures.
These are 3 of 1000. The leashes they hold
bind them in a crosscountry web, 1000
old men in fellowship along the highways
and so many of them totter as they do
their duty, tugged along by 1000 dogs
(mostly old) sniffing the yellow tattoos
on the grass—scents of other old dogs
and old men, here where nobody knows anybody
and the traffic never ends.

Steve
Almond

Donkey Greedy, Donkey Gets Punched

Dr. Raymond Oss had become, in the

restless leisure of his late middle age, a poker player. He had a weakness for the game and the ruthless depressives it attracted, one of which he probably was, fair enough, though it wasn't something he wanted known. Oss was a psychoanalyst in private practice and the head of two committees at the San Francisco Institute. He was a short man with a meticulous Trotsky beard and a flair for hats that did not suit him. He cured souls, very expensively, from an office near his home in Redwood City.

On Saturday mornings, Oss put on a sweat suit and orthotic tennis shoes and told Sharon he was off to his tai chi class. Then he shot up 101 straight to Artichoke Joe's in San Bruno, where he played Texas Hold 'em at the $3/6 table for five hours straight. He mucked 80 percent of his hands, bluffed only on the button, and lost a little more than he won.

He didn't mind losing, either, if the cards were to blame. It was only when he screwed up—when he failed to see a flush developing or got slow-played by some grinning Chinese maniac—that he felt the pinch of genuine rage. And even these hands offered a certain masochistic pleasure, a mortification that was swift and public.

It was an inconvenient arrangement, tawdry from certain angles, but Oss couldn't help himself. The moment he spotted the dismal pink stucco of the casino's facade, the sea of bent cigarettes rising from the giant ashtray under the awning, he felt a squirt of brainless adrenaline. He had become addicted to the garlic-and-ginger prawns, too, a dish so richly infiltrated with MSG that it made his tongue go numb. Sometimes, toward the end of a session, having made his third and final promise to cash in after the next hand, Oss would sit back and let the sensations wash over him: the clack of Pai Gow tiles being stirred, the nimble flicking of the cards, the confusion of colognes and nicotine, the monstrous lonely twitch of the place. He loved Artichoke Joe's, especially while hating it.

———— •◦• ————

One day, Oss arrived home to find Sharon waiting in his den. She pulled out a green eyeshade and a deck of cards and began dealing them onto his oriental rug. She'd done theater in college.

"How long have you known?"

Sharon frowned.

Jacob (age eleven) had tipped her off, the little shit. "He hacked into your computer," Sharon said.

"I didn't hack into anything," Jacob yelled from the hallway. "I just clicked the History tab for, like, one second."

Sharon began speaking in her calm social-worker tone. Oss glanced at the scattered cards—a cluster of four hearts, queen high—and thought of his henpecked father. "You could have told me," Sharon said. "I would have understood."

He didn't want his wife's understanding. He had enough of that already. He wanted her indignation, her censure, the stain of his moral insufficiencies tossed between them like a bet. But she saw his Duplicity and raised her Forgiveness.

So he bid Artichoke Joe's farewell—farewell green felt! Farewell ginger prawns!—and began playing in a weekly game with fellow analysts. The twenty-dollar buy-in, the non-alcoholic beer, the arthritic dithering over a seventy-five-cent raise; it was his penance.

Overall, he felt himself vaguely improved. He began to hike the Stanford Hills and re-read Dostoevsky and brought Sharon to the Swiss Alps for a month. His older son, Ike,

> "I play cards," he said. "I take money from people who don't want it anymore."

insisted on calling him Cisco, it being his impression that the Cisco Kid had been a famous gambler. Jacob continued to sneak into his office in the hopes of catching him playing online. "Check it before you wreck it, daddy-o," he warned. Oss wanted very much to strike the boy, just once, near the eye.

———— ·•· ————

Gary Sharpe appeared in his office that fall. Oss would recall this coincidence later with an odd blend of pride and shame. Sharpe was tall and pale, handsome in a sneering way. He sat miserably and squinted. "So how's this work? Do I hand you my checkbook now, or wait till the end of the session?"

"This is a consultation," Oss said. "We're merely trying—"

"Or maybe I should just dump the cash at your feet?"

Oss sighed without appearing to. It was one of his tricks. "Small, unmarked bills work best. Now why don't you tell me why you're here."

Sharpe shook his head. "My wife."

"She suggested you come?"

"Suggested. You could say that. She's a shrink, too. Her supervisor is some pal of yours. Doctor Penn. I'm not sure how it works with you people. She feels I'm depressed owing to unresolved issues with my father, who, by the way, died when I was seventeen. So technically I have issues with my dead father."

"And you feel?"

Sharpe inspected his fingernails. "I'm in a volatile business. I've explained this to her a few thousand times."

"So you're not depressed?"

"Depressed. Christ. Whatever happened to 'sad'? I guess there's no dough in sadness. As for your next question, yeah, I've done the drugs. Paxil, Wellbutrin, some new one they've got called Kweezlemonkey. That one goes up your ass as a minty fresh gel."

Oss laughed. "Sounds refreshing."

"Right. I get the funny shrink. Perfect." Sharpe fake yawned. He looked like he hadn't slept in a few weeks.

"Are you aware of what an analysis entails?"

"My wife filled me in. I lie on my back and complain about what an asshole everyone is. Then, when you've made enough to pay for your new deck, the angels blow a trumpet and I'm cured. What a fucking racket. You people should carry guns."

"I do," Oss said.

Sharpe would be back, the bluster said as much. He'd blame it on his wife for a few weeks, then they could begin the work. "What is it exactly you do, Mr. Sharpe?"

"I play cards," he said. "I take money from people who don't want it anymore."

— ◆ —

So this was his new patient: Gary "Card" Sharpe, winner of the 2003 World Series of Poker, enfant terrible of the World Poker Tour, notorious for his table talk, his braying laugh, his signature line of poker-themed clothing and paraphernalia (Look Sharpe™).

On Friday, Oss spotted Penn in the parking garage.

"Thanks for the referral."

Penn smiled. "One greedy prick deserves another." He zapped his trunk open and began removing stuffed animals. Penn was always doing things like this, things that made no sense. "His wife's a real sweetheart. She'll leave him if he doesn't shape up."

"No pressure, though."

"Take it as a compliment. You'll know what he's talking about, anyway. All the lingo. Down and dirty. Double down."

Oss took off his derby and inspected the rim. "I wasn't aware you considered me such an expert at poker."

"I wasn't aware you considered me such an idiot." Penn tapped his brow with a yellow monkey. "Come on, Ray. Tai chi? How long have I known you?"

"He's going to hassle me about the fee nonstop."

"Of course he is," Penn replied. "He's a gambler. That's how he keeps score. Speaking of which, you in Friday?"

Penn played in the weekly game. He held his cards as if the ink were still wet and studied them like runes. Then he lost cheerfully. Everyone loved Penn, in the same way they sort of hated Oss.

———— —•— ————

For the most part, Sharpe talked poker. His disquisitions inevitably began, *You know what I fucking hate?* He fucking hated the Internet. He fucking hated the TV coverage. He fucking hated the travel.

"You ever been in the Reno airport before dawn, Oss?"

"Can't say I've have the pleasure."

"I fucking hate that place. It's like hell with slot machines. Even the air smells sad. Care to guess why I was there so early? So I could get back from a tournament in time for this shit-ass session."

"How'd you do?"

Sharpe shrugged. "Twelve K, plus sponsor money. We wound up chopping the pot at the final table. You know what that means? It means we got rid of all the donkeys, the shit players, then split the prize money."

"Sounds like easy money," Oss said.

Sharpe bristled. "Easy?" he said.

"I just meant—"

"I know what you meant," Sharpe said. "I'm sure a guy in your position—you don't think playing poker takes much brainpower, do you? It's just a bunch of cigar smoke and dumb luck. What's your game anyway, doc? Bridge? You probably sit around on Saturday night playing penny-a-point, creaming your fucking chinos because somebody made small slam in hearts." Sharpe's upper lip curled. "You know who you fucking remind me of? My fucking dad."

Now we're getting somewhere, Oss thought. He waited a moment before asking, "How so?"

"Oh, you'd like that, wouldn't you?"

Oss sighed his silent sigh. "This isn't a poker game, Gary. You don't win by hiding your cards."

"I don't win at all," Sharpe said. "I just give all the chips to you."

"I can only help if you're forthcoming with me."

Sharpe exhaled through his nose. "So now you're Dr. Phil? Dr. Phil: the midget version with the stupid hats." He sneered. "What the fuck is up with these hats anyways? You're bald, doc. Deal with it."

———— –•– ————

Oss was secretly thrilled to be treating Sharpe. The depth of his rage was refreshing. It returned Oss to his adolescence, to the loathing he so lavishly apportioned to his own father, who sold hardware, who developed pathetic infatuations with his prominent customers. (My good friend Dr. Lindell. My good friend Magistrate Johns.) The old man, with his Brooklyn brogue and small-time dreams. *A man who gambles, he liked to say, is a man who doesn't want his shoit.*

Sharpe could be tender, too. He was terrified of losing his wife. "Back in college, she figured I'd go to some hedge fund. I told her as much. Look: she's not thrilled with the choices I've made. But she's got a better heart than me, doc. That's more or less the basis of our marriage."

Oss was stunned to discover that Sharpe had a child as well, a boy named Doyle. "Sharp little bastard," Sharpe said. "He slaughters me at everything. Concentration. Go Fish."

"A born card counter, eh?"

"No no no," Sharpe said. "He's not going to wind up rotting in some casino. He's got a real imagination."

"Poker doesn't require imagination?"

"Donkey greedy. Donkey gets punched. The rest is just math. He gets the creative stuff from Kate, these crazy little comic books he draws, he does all the plots himself. Seven years old! Every dad says this shit, I guess. But you know, sometimes he looks at me and I'll realize for a second how fragile he is. It makes me want to cry." Sharpe swallowed hard; his ear flushed for a moment. "I have no idea why. It's like I want to protect him from some terrible thing and I don't even know what."

———— –•– ————

Oss urged Sharpe to think about what that thing might be, but by the next session, he'd retreated to the old troughs of grievance. "You know what

I fucking hate," he said. "All these guys from Google, with their mirror shades and their goatees. Chin pussies, I call them. You can't swing a dead cat in Artichoke Joe's without hitting Google trash."

Oss froze for a moment.

"What?" Sharpe said. "Why'd you stop taking notes?"

Oss sat back and scratched out Did-not-Did-not-Did-not. "You were saying?" he said.

"Wait a second." Sharpe smiled. "I just said something that threw you off. Don't bullshit a bullshitter, doc."

Oss's tongue tingled. He could taste the ginger prawns. "I suppose I was surprised you'd play at a local casino. Wouldn't people recognize you?"

"Of course they fucking recognize me."

"But wouldn't that make it tough? Why would anyone play against you?"

> That's not gambling, it's Disneyland. Gambling is about people ruining their fucking lives."

Sharpe did his full-throated bray. "You're kidding, right, doc? Everyone in that place wants to play me. For fuck's sake. I'm like Barry Bonds to these donks. Only they can play against me. They can even beat me. Shit. It's mostly up to the cards."

"I see," Oss said. For a moment he imagined what it might be like to sit across the table from Sharpe, the sort of irrational hatred a guy like him could generate.

"That's what I hate about these Google guys. They've got all this dumb money, more than they know how to squander. So they throw it at me for a few hours and brag about that one gut-shot they hit for the next ten years. That's not gambling, it's Disneyland. Gambling is about people ruining their fucking lives."

"So that's your goal? To ruin your life?"

Sharpe's brow crimped and Oss, studying his face from behind, noticed for the first time that the sneer on his lip was in fact the result of a small scar.

"You have to realize what you are," Sharpe said. "If you're a gambler, you're a gambler. That's how your nerves fire. I wake up every morning thinking about that next great bet. You can get all high and mighty and call that an addiction. Or you can call it what it is: fucking desire. I'll tell you this, there's nothing sadder than a gambler in denial. I should know. My dad was one."

Oss waited for Sharpe to elaborate. It was a lot of what he did. The silence dragged on.

"What?" Sharpe said finally. "What the fuck do you want from me?"

In August, Sharpe returned from the World Series of Poker in a black mood. He'd been knocked out of the tournament on the third day, a humiliation Oss had witnessed (with some relish) on ESPN2.

"I've got a tell," Sharpe said to Oss now. "I fucking know it. There's no other way to explain it. You know what a tell is, right? That's like something that gives away how you feel. Like that swallowed sigh thing you do when you're frustrated. That's a tell."

Oss sat back in his chair.

"Don't act so surprised," Sharpe said. "This is what I do for a living, okay, doc? I read people. We're in the same business that way, only I look them in the eye before I take their money. Now I need some fucking help from you, for once, because obviously I'm doing something I'm not aware of."

"What happened?"

Sharpe threw up his hands as if he were tossing a salad, a salad at which he was furious. "Bad cards. Bad beats. That I can handle. I'll scrape by with shit luck. But this was different. I let it get personal, which is, rule one: it's never fucking personal. Because how else does a puke like Bill Tandy sniff out three bluffs in a row?"

"Who's Bill Tandy?"

"My exact fucking point, doc." Sharpe closed his eyes. "This guy, Mr. Retired Real Estate Puke from Tucson, he sits there eyeballing me for ten seconds and suddenly he pops his tongue under his lip, which is what he does when he knows he's got a guy beat—it's his tell."

From where he was sitting, Oss could see the cuff of Sharpe's right ear redden again. "Couldn't he have just been guessing?" Oss said.

"He had jack-high crap," Sharpe muttered. "You don't guess against me with jack-high crap. Even an old donkey knows that. No, he saw something. This fucker saw something. And I want you to tell me what."

"Me?"

"I've been paying you a grand a week. You're supposed to be so observant, so wise to my subconscious. It's about time you offered some return on my fucking investment."

"I didn't realize it was my job to make you a better poker player," Oss said.

Sharpe glared at the ceiling. "It's your job to make me a happier person, you little shit."

"Winning doesn't seem to make you a happier person, Gary."

"Meaning what?"

Oss remained silent.

"You are a complete french-fried asshole, Oss. I pity your fucking wife and the disfigured dwarf children that sprung from her loins. Honestly. You're worse than my old man."

"I take it he didn't approve of your career."

Sharpe grinned. "No, he didn't. And he spanked me on my little bum in front of all my friends and I cried and cried. Wah-wah-wah. Then I tried to kill him, but I went blind instead and stumbled into a giant cave that smelled like my mother's snatch. God you're obvious."

Sharpe closed his eyes. "I'm not angry," he said. The cuff of his ear flushed. "He had a shitty hand and he lost. The end."

As a younger analyst, Oss would have laughed and let Sharpe jump the hook. But he had come to recognize disgust as the first form of disclosure. "You said earlier that your father was a gambler in denial. What did you mean?"

Sharpe let out an exasperated sigh. "He worked in the financial sector. He played the market. That's all I meant. All those guys are gamblers. The whole fucking thing's a big bet."

"What happened to him?"

"He made a bad bet."

"And?"

"And he hung himself."

Was this another bluff? It was hard to tell with Sharpe.

When he finally spoke again his voice had lost its belligerence. It wasn't soft so much as deflated. "My dad made his nut off something called 'portfolio insurance.' The idea was that you paid a premium to limit your losses. Then came the crash of eighty-seven and the whole thing blew up." Sharpe shook his head. "And the reason it blew up is simple: he was selling the fantasy of risk-free gambling—which doesn't exist. So he lost everything and took some rope out to the garage and my mom and me were left to scrounge through his estate for rent money." Sharpe smiled his sneering smile. "This is the guy who lectured me about responsibility, about doing the right thing."

Oss didn't say anything for a time. He thought, oddly, of his own father, the way he fingered each coin from his palm onto the counter when making a purchase. Pop was a child of the Depression. He had tasted poverty. And still, Oss found his elaborate caution around money shameful.

"I can see why you might be angry at him," Oss said.

Sharpe closed his eyes. "I'm not angry," he said. The cuff of his ear flushed. "He had a shitty hand and he lost. The end."

———————— ·◦· ————————

It wasn't as if the discoloration was obvious. You'd really have to be looking to spot it. But then, that was what pros did. They looked for signs.

Oss's first impulse was to drop a hint, maybe suggest a longer hairstyle. But the more he pondered the matter, the more misguided this seemed. His role was to help the patient come to terms with the unbearable facts and feelings of his history. In fact, it was the loss at poker that had induced Sharpe (finally) to discuss his father. Was it also true that Oss derived a certain pleasure from withholding? That it served as a form of revenge against an equally withholding and, at times, emotionally abusive patient? It was possible.

One thing was clear: the closer Sharpe drew to the sources of his depression, the more recalcitrant he grew. One sweltering June afternoon, he showed up in an obvious state of inebriation. "I've had a few," was how he put it.

"Any particular reason?" Oss said.

"A few works better than one." Sharpe belched. "Anyways, I've decided you want me to lose. The sadder and more fucked up I become, the more dough you make."

"You're my bread and butter?"

"You said it, Ossipoo." Sharpe shuffled an invisible stack of chips. "You also get off on looking down on me. You think I'm some cretin. Like I should read more books or something."

Oss thought of Dostoevsky's gambler, Alexei. He had always imagined the character in a green velvet waistcoat, watching the roulette wheel spin. Freud argued that Dostoevsky—like most gamblers—subconsciously wanted to lose. He sought to punish himself for the death of his parents. His father had been a vicious drunk, murdered by his serfs, supposedly. The novelist had done that one better, letting the Karamazov boys do the deed themselves. Was there no love so disastrous as that between a son and father? Oss himself was still a wreck when it came to his pop, whose gentle hand he had held even as death took him under.

"Are you fucking listening to me?" Sharpe said.

"Of course," Oss said.

"What was I just talking about?"

Oss stared down at his notes. Absurdly, his eyes were stinging. "You were asking me, for perhaps the hundredth time, why you should keep coming here."

"And?"

"We are trying to understand your discontent. This is not easy work," Oss said.

"Oh for fuck's sake."

———— ·◆· ————

Sharpe began traveling overseas on what he called "the sheik circuit." Dubai, the Emirates. "Hey," he said, when Oss complained about missed sessions, "the price is right. You want I should ask any of them if they need a nice Jewy analyst?" He continued to appear for sessions drunk. He flew into paranoid rages. He celebrated his year anniversary as a patient by presenting Oss with a bill for forty-eight thousand dollars, requesting a full refund "for failure to deliver the contracted services."

Oss prescribed medications intended to ameliorate the bipolar symptoms. He urged Sharpe to cut back on alcohol and poker. Sharpe responded by flouting his bills.

A week before Thanksgiving, he shambled into the office and nodded at Oss's hat rack. "Tell me you didn't wear the fucking beret outside this office. Christ. You're like a one-man stupid-looking contest." He plopped down on his back. His unlaced sneakers thwacked the couch.

"We've discussed payment at length. That discussion is now over. You either pay your outstanding fees or we terminate."

"Would you accept chips?" Sharpe reached into his pocket. "No? Ooooh, the silent treatment. I must be in trouble."

"You're not a child, Gary."

"I love it when you get all stern, doc. I really do. It makes me think of me dear old da!" Sharpe rubbed at his eyes dramatically. "He was a lot like you, Ossipoo, a little donkey who thought he was a big shark. And look how that turned out. You know what he was wearing when I found him swinging from the rafters?"

"Hold on a moment," Oss said.

"A silk ascot. Right under the rope. I shit you not, doc. He's got the fat blue face, his tongue's hanging out, his eyes are about to pop from their sockets, there's shit dripping from his pants, and the stupid fuck—"

"Is this true?" Oss said. "If this is true—"

But Sharpe had said too much. They both knew it. "You think I need this shit? You think I ever needed this shit?" He brayed, but his voice cracked around the sound. "Fuck you, doc. No, seriously. We're done here."

It was a sad moment for Oss, because he loved his patients, even the difficult ones, for the weaknesses they laid before him, for their courage, and because it had been Sharpe, after all, who looked like an animal, a beast of burden, charging blindly from his office, off into a world that could bring him no peace.

"You did what you had to do," said Penn, to whom Oss inevitably and resentfully confided. "Some patients can't be saved."

Sharon was less sympathetic. "He sounds like a royal asshole," she said that evening.

"Mom said a-hole," Jacob shrieked.

"Shut up," Oss roared. "Shut your mouth until further notice."

Jacob held his cheek as if he'd been slapped. Sharon stared at him in horror.

"The kid has to learn not to be a tattletale," Oss said. "Alright, look. I apologize. It's been a long day."

Oss tried to put Gary Sharpe out of mind. But he kept turning up: on the poker shows, loud and unhappy, with bloodshot eyes. Oss missed him. While his other patients murmured their soft complaints, his mind drifted to desirable poker hands. Ace/jack suited. Pocket queens. He found himself volunteering to do weekend Costco runs, knowing these would lead him past Artichoke Joe's. He limited himself to one game per month, then two.

It was nearly a year later, on a sleepy Tuesday afternoon, that Oss looked up from his seat and saw his former patient striding across the casino floor. He wore a tracksuit the same color as his stubble. Oss knew he should muck his hand and slip out quietly. But he hesitated just long enough to allow Sharpe to spot him.

There was a buzz in place by now, several folks at his elbow. Sharpe made straight for Oss. "Don't I know you?" he said.

Oss looked up and smiled.

"How the hell are you?" Sharpe seemed genuinely glad to see him. "I didn't realize you played here."

"I don't, really," Oss said. "Occasionally."

The other players at the table stared at him in astonishment. You, their eyes said. Really?

The manager of the poker section hurried over and began genuflecting. Sharpe stepped away from the table so they could finish up the hand. He did some backslapping, signed one of his hats for a trembling Indian kid, posed for photos. Then he smiled and nodded at an empty seat across from Oss. "Mind if I join you gents?"

> His eyes flicked from face to face on the flop. It was something like watching a shark—the grace and efficiency of his aggression.

"We're happy to start a no-limit table," the manager said.

"No no," Sharpe said. "Just want to play a few hands. No big deal."

"You can have my seat," Oss said. "I was just about to cash out."

"Come on now," Sharpe said. "You're going to hurt my feelings, doc." He dropped into the empty seat. "I was hoping you might teach me a few things."

The dealer glanced at Oss. Staying at the table was clearly the wrong thing to do on about six levels. But the air around him was crackling with a strange electricity. He shrugged and nodded.

It was immediately obvious the speed with which Sharpe processed information: table position, pot odds. His eyes flicked from face to face on the flop. It was something like watching a shark—the grace and efficiency of his aggression. His outbursts, so petulant on TV, came off as charming in person, a way of relieving the essential tedium of the game. When Oss took a pot with two small pairs, Sharpe applauded. "Thattaboy," he said.

For his part, Oss avoided looking at Sharpe, and in particular at his ears.

"How you two know each other?" the dealer said.

"Doc was an advisor of mine for a time." Sharpe grinned. "He has, despite that idiotic Greek fisherman's cap, a keen financial sense."

Everyone laughed.

"What kind of advice you give?" the dealer said.

"The expensive kind," Sharpe roared.

Oss waited for the laughter to subside. "How are things going?" he asked.

"My wife's going to take 50 percent of everything." Sharpe downed the rest of his beer and gestured for another. "Aside from that it's jim-fucking-dandy."

"I'm so sorry," Oss said.

Sharpe sneered. "It's not like I'm going to kill myself."

Oss wanted to pull him aside, to talk to him privately. But they were at the poker table, a place where the only intimacy permitted was between a man and his own fortune. It was time for Oss to go.

The problem—and it really was a problem—was that he'd been dealt two cards by now. Good cards.

These were, in fact, the best cards he'd gotten all day. The bet came to him and he raised. Everyone folded except Sharpe, who was the big blind. "Alone at last," he said.

Oss laughed uncomfortably.

The flop came:

This gave Oss two pair, aces and kings, an exceptional hand. He thought briefly about checking. Perhaps it was best to get through the hand and get out. Instead, he bet the limit.

Sharpe glanced at Oss. "Mighty proud of that pair, are you? I'd be, too. But you shouldn't tell the whole table, doc." He inhaled loudly through his nose. Oss realized, with a start, that Sharpe was imitating him.

"That's just cruel," someone murmured.

"No, that's poker," Sharpe snapped. "I just did the good doctor a big favor. Saved him a good deal of money down the line. More than he ever did for me." He finished his beer. "I raise."

Oss could feel the room start to thrum. He looked at the flop again and did some quick math. The chances that Sharpe had three of a kind were one in 2500. He might be playing for the club flush, but that was a dumb bet. "Reraise," Oss said.

Sharpe smiled. "Oh for fuck's sake, doc. You already cost me fifty grand. What's a little more?"

The turn card was the two of clubs.

If Sharpe was a looking for a flush, he'd just made it. He might also have a three/four, which would give him a straight, though that would mean he'd drawn to an inside straight, something he would never do. No, if anything, Sharpe had the flush. But the odds on that were one in five. Two pair still made Oss a heavy favorite. "I'll bet," he said. "I don't think you have the flush."

"You're right," Sharpe said unhappily. "But I'll raise anyway."

Oss looked up. A small crowd had begun to form. Or maybe it had been there all along, to watch the great Gary Sharpe clobber some poor donkey. That's what he was to these folks: a donkey. A dilettante with a nasty little mid-week habit. They were just waiting for him to fold.

"Reraise."

Sharpe sat back. Another beer had disappeared down his throat. "Well now, doc, I hope those oats feel good. But do me a favor, since you're so confident: let's at least stop playing kiddie poker." He turned to the manager. "Can we make this a no-limit game?"

The crowd let out a murmur.

The manager said, "It's a limit table, Gary. I really can't do that."

"A little side wager then? How about that?"

The manager regarded Sharpe in bureaucratic despair. "The casino cannot be party to any such arrangement. That'd be between you gentlemen."

"Excellent," Sharpe said. "I'd say we've got enough witnesses. So what if we say I see your six, and raise you ten thousand dollars on the side."

Oss cleared his throat. "You're kidding, I assume."

"No sir."

"I think it's best if we just stick to the table limits."

Sharpe began nodding. "Oh I see, little man. You just want to play the safe game, nothing that could get you hurt. Does your wife even know you're here? How fucking sad."

> Oss realized, with a twinge of pity, that Sharpe was trapped. He'd gotten himself in too deep, allowed it to become personal.

Oss glanced at Sharpe's ears, just for a second. He knew it was some kind of violation—of analytic trust, of basic decency—but he couldn't restrain himself. They were as pale as the rest of him.

"What's the matter, doc? You don't look so hot." Sharpe brayed. "Alright. Listen. I'm gonna do you another favor, for old time's sake. In front of all these nice folks and God himself, I'm gonna tell you to fold. Just throw your cards in the middle of the table and be done with it, little man. Go home and tell your wife a good lie."

It was an astonishing display. A few people in the crowd whistled. Someone said, "Classic Sharpe."

Oss reached for his cards. He certainly meant to fold, to put an end to this foolishness. But he paused for a moment first.

Sharpe gulped at his beer. "Okay, we're all done here, folks. The good doctor is all done pretending. That's okay, doc. Just walk away. There's no shame when you're beat." The cuff of his right ear flushed. "You want to see the hand you lost to? Would that help?" Sharpe made as if to reach for his cards. His ear had gone crimson now.

Oss felt his chest start to fizz. His hands, which had been hovering over his cards, trembled. He clasped them together and nearly burst into laughter. "I appreciate all your kind advice," he said. "But I guess I'll have to call anyway."

"Okay," Sharpe said loudly. "I tried. I honestly tried. I'm no longer responsible for what happens next. That's on you, doc."

Oss realized, with a twinge of pity, that Sharpe was trapped. He'd gotten himself in too deep, allowed it to become personal.

The dealer turned over the river card. It was the ace of spades.

The board now looked like this:

Oss couldn't quite believe his eyes. He had hit a full house on the river, aces over kings. Even if Sharpe wasn't bluffing, even if he'd made his flush, Oss had him beat. It seemed almost cruel.

Sharpe glanced at the fifth card, as if it was of no great concern to him. "One more round of betting," he said. "You feeling lucky?"

"Check," Oss said.

"Ten thousand," Sharpe said. He was plainly out of his mind.

Oss cleared his throat again. "Listen," he said, "I think this has gone far enough."

Sharpe turned to the crowd and brayed. "I'm not sure if you're entirely familiar with your options here, doc. You've got three: call, raise, or fold."

"Okay," Oss said. "I get it."

But Sharpe wasn't done. He was never done. "More than a year of my life you wasted with your overpriced psychobabble bullshit," he murmured. "And here's the funny part: you actually think that shit matters, that you're saving people with your little spells and incantations. Are you starting to get it, doc? This is what matters, right here." He gestured to the cards that lay between them, then to crowd. "So don't disappoint all these nice folks, doc. They came here to see what happens next."

Oss closed his eyes and considered how he had arrived at this point. He knew some of it was his fault. But was it his fault that he'd been dealt a monster hand? Was it his fault that his opponent was a psychotic asshole? Hell, if anything, he'd tried to help the psychotic asshole.

Sharpe was now leering at him (psychotically) and blowing beer fumes across the table. "Be a good boy," he bellowed. "Save your shirt. Remember: guys like me always beat guys like you."

"Double it," Oss said.

He couldn't quite believe the words had come out of his mouth. He honestly hadn't meant to say them. But the moment he did, his body surged with joy. He felt as if he might be floating. "Double it," he said again.

The crowd let out a whoop.

The manager drew a cell phone from his pocket and began dialing frantically.

"Let's make it an even forty," Sharpe shot back. He was slurring now. "That's right. Forty thousand, you greedy bastard. You want to hang yourself in public, here's your chance. I can't save you."

A great calm descended on Oss. He had seen patients for more than half his life. Whatever tumult they created in the present, it all traced back to the past. Whatever wrath they aimed at him, he was merely a hired stand-in. And so here was the famous Gary Sharpe, face to face at last with his father. He wanted to destroy the old man, but deep down he wanted to destroy himself more.

He'd been unable to convince Sharpe on the analytic couch. But perhaps here, at the poker table, which had become his refuge, his final hiding place, the lesson might stick. "Let's make it an even fifty thousand dollars," Oss said.

"Okay now," said the manager, "now that, that's the final raise, okay? Okay guys? I don't care what the private arrangement is."

The crowd hissed, but Sharpe held up his hands for silence. He looked remarkably serene, resigned to his fate. "Fair enough," he said. "I call. Now do what you came here to do, doc. No hard feelings." He leered again and Oss saw not the garish smile but the faint scar on his lip. It made him want to weep, to see how far human beings would go to hide from the truth of themselves.

There was nothing else for him to do, though, so Oss turned over his cards. He could hear the crowd roar. "I'm sorry," he said. "I truly am. I didn't want it to come to this."

"Sure you did," Sharpe said. He smiled gently. Then he turned over his cards:

STEVE ALMOND

There was a moment of confused silence, then the crowd let out a collective gasp. "Take a good look," Sharpe said.

Oss inspected the community cards again. The green felt took on a queasy shimmer. He saw Sharpe's hand now:

A straight flush.

The shock hit Oss in waves. He felt the nerves in his neck constrict. He was having trouble breathing. All around him was noise and jostling. Two or three people reached to comfort him. Sharpe rose from his seat and walked around the table. He squatted down and gestured for the others to step back.

Oss stared at his ears, which seemed now to be blazing.

"Yeah, my wife was kind enough to tip me off, just before she gave me the boot. And you know the crazy thing? Alcohol has the exact same physiological effect on me. Imagine that! What are the odds, doc?"

Oss found that his hands were still clasped, but there was no feeling in either of them. It was as if he were dead now, as if he were holding the hand of his own dead father.

"Now don't go worrying about the dough. We can set up a payment plan, something weekly." Sharpe tried for a grin, but it wouldn't hold.

"What in God's name have I done?" Oss whispered. He suspected he was weeping. His cheeks certainly felt wet.

"Settle down now, doc." Oss felt a hand laid upon his shoulder with unbearable tenderness. The room was a bright blur, at the center of which hovered Sharpe's face; the sneer was gone, replaced by a familiar sorrow. Already his triumph was slipping away, into the unbending shadows of vengeance. "The man who can't lose always does," he said softly. "Did you learn nothing from our work?"

THE BLUE
INSUPPORTABLE

Tom Grimes

Remembering Frank Conroy

When I was young, we owned very few books. My father had dropped out of school after finishing the eighth grade; my mother barely graduated from high school. Working for Firestone Tire & Rubber in the 1960s, my father earned Bob Cratchit-like wages. Meanwhile, my mother raised my brother, sister, and me, which largely entailed driving us to and from grammar school, feeding us mustard or Miracle Whip sandwiches—only when I became a soda jerk in high school did I discover that meat or cheese belonged between the two spongy slices of white bread—and forcing us to do our homework. In my parents' minds, their children's destinies had been preordained. I would become a dentist. Predictably, my sister would become a nurse in order to quickly meet, bed, and marry a doctor. As for my younger brother, he would avoid the completely illiterate, mentally retarded life each of us

blithely expected him to lead by emerging from his chrysalis of childhood idiocy in an oil-stained jump suit with his name stitched above one breast as an auto mechanic. In short, we were urchins, and books were a luxury because, as my parents repeatedly explained to us, money did not grow on trees, money did not burn holes in their pockets, they were not made of money, and, unintentionally admitting to their failings as breadwinners, they did not make money hand over fist.

Still, books fascinated me, and, gradually, I built my library. In the 1960s, I bought new pocket-sized paperbacks that sold for as little as seventy-five cents; hardbacks were beyond my means. When I reached college in 1972, I could walk into a bookstore with twenty dollars and walk out with twenty tomes, from the classic to the contemporary. Like all bibliophiles, I bought more books than I could read. At some point, Frank Conroy's memoir, *Stop-Time*, appeared, like an unanticipated supernova, in my literary galaxy. Since its author's childhood in some ways mirrored my own, the book (I'm now about to switch astrological metaphors) drew me toward it the way gravity draws a planet toward the sun. As a boy, Frank had lived in Manhattan in a small Upper-East-Side apartment, where his bedroom's bookshelves held eight hundred paperbacks. His dipsomaniac, and largely absent, father, who died when Frank was twelve, had left the books to him. They

New York Times 1967 ad for the original edition of *Stop-Time*.

outnumbered my growing collection. But I saw myself in Frank, who wrote, "I read very fast, uncritically, and without retention, seeking only to escape from my own life through the imaginative plunge into another." And, "It was around this time that I first thought of becoming a writer. In a cheap novel the hero was asked his profession at a cocktail party. 'I'm a novelist,' he said, and I remember putting the book down and thinking, my God what a beautiful thing to be able to say."

While attending Haverford, a small liberal arts college "founded on the Quaker values of dignity, academic strength, and tolerance," Frank sold his first story. After graduation, he did what most fiction writers in their twenties do: over the course of four years he completed a novel that he later described as "flat-out dead, like a stillborn baby." In the same essay, entitled "My Teacher," written when Frank was fifty-eight, he admitted that the experience devastated him. "My God, how desperately

I wanted to be a writer." At Haverford, a man Frank called "Professor Cipher" had been his mentor. He line-edited Frank's work, instructed him to think of the reader, not himself, when composing a story, and advised him to write with unambiguous clarity. (As Camus said, "Those who write clearly have readers, those who write obscurely have commentators.") At the time Frank's apprenticeship ended, perhaps a dozen creative writing programs existed. Today, more than three hundred do. Had Frank attended Stanford or Iowa, his writing may not have improved, but he may have seen his mistakes more quickly and saved himself a year or two's work on his novel. Instead, Frank worked in solitude. Books guided him. Yet his isolation may have been his salvation. Had Frank sat in workshops and listened to others, he may not have developed his unique style.

As a literary genre, the memoir barely existed before Frank published *Stop-Time*. He once told me that "the book was completely out of synch with the era." To write it he disregarded Nixon, LBJ, Vietnam, acid trips, political protests, the space race, the Cold War, and the Pill. He didn't attempt to mimic Pynchon, Vonnegut, or Heller's black humor, or imitate Mailer, Capote, and Wolfe's New Journalism. Instead, he created note-perfect, crystal clear prose, through which he distilled his adolescence into such intellectual and emotional purity that it seemed eternal. In 1969, *Stop-Time* was nominated for the National Book Award for non-fiction, and despite its modest sales—seven thousand copies in

hardcover—Frank's accomplishment made him a literary celebrity. Norman Mailer described *Stop-Time* as "an autobiography with the intimate unprotected candor of a novel." William Styron praised "its freshness, its wisdom, and, above all, in this day of youthful indulgence, its almost total lack of self-pity." At twenty-nine, Frank had achieved what Susan Sontag considered to be the sole responsibility of a writer—to write a masterpiece.

At Elaine's, a chic Upper-East-Side restaurant where Woody Allen had a reserved table, Frank began to swig bourbon with the literati. *Esquire* and the *New Yorker* commissioned articles and essays. Hollywood mailed him five-figure checks for doctoring screenplays. With his wife and two young sons, he moved from Manhattan to Brooklyn Heights. Then, on Nantucket Island, he reconstructed, with the help of a crew of hippies, an unheated barn, which became his family's summerhouse. As a boy, Frank had been rootless and poor; now he had two homes and, given his wife's trust fund and his earnings from writing, he had money as well. Success intoxicated him: "music, movies, my favorite bar, the excitement of meeting new people after my first book came out. There was a kind of forward momentum I never questioned, but simply rode, night after night, a continuous social stimulation to which I became addicted." But, shortly, fame reversed his life's trajectory and he crashed. In his 1995 essay, "Leaving New York," he confesses, "the more my marriage weakened, the more desperately

> "It was the most important night of my musical life, because I no longer had to think of myself as an impostor. If Charles Mingus got up to play with me, I must have been doing something right.

I tore around town. Much deeply foolish behavior, and I blame no one but myself for that. Years of hysteria." At thirty-five, he had "no job, an unpredictable income as a pianist and freelance magazine writer, no savings, and . . . no plan." After his divorce, Frank's time with his sons—one five, one seven—was limited to three months each summer. Beyond that, he was absent from their lives, mimicking his own fatherless childhood.

He retreated to Nantucket, where he tried working on a lobster boat, but found he wasn't strong enough to keep up. Soon, screenwriting assignments dwindled to nothing, and magazines no longer commissioned him to write essays. ("New Yorkers tend to think of anyone who's left as having died.") Every winter, he had to crawl under his barn to de-ice the frozen aluminum pipes with a blowtorch. He was alone and had only one means of rescuing himself: the piano. As a boy, he'd taught himself how to play the blues, "moving slowly into easy variations and complications . . . inching along like a typical autodidact, leaving great gaping holes in my training."

Yet he assembled a repertoire. And, in his twenties, while he still lived in New York, he played nightly gigs at a bar. One evening, between sets, his bass player vanished. Having no choice, Frank nervously took the stage.

I sat down and began to play midrange chords with my left hand and an improvised line with my right. The tune was 'Autumn Leaves.' Sometime in the third chorus a large black man got up from his dinner table and moved forward . . . As he approached, I recognized Charles Mingus—the foremost jazz bassist in the world—and I was afraid. Mingus, a manic-depressive, was famous for sudden onsets of rage.

But he simply grabbed Frank's AWOL partner's base and began to play. Frank had no choice: he joined him. "It was the most important night of my musical life, because I no longer had to think of myself as an impostor. If Charles Mingus got up to play with me, I must have been doing something right. I was no genius, but I was a musician." Isolated on Nantucket, Frank put together

He had written a legendary memoir.
Whatever he published would be seen
through the lens of *Stop-Time* and judged
in comparison to it.

a jazz quintet, which played at a club named the Roadhouse. Summer crowds filled the band's coffers, and during the winter local patrons provided enough business to allow Frank to pay his mortgage and buy groceries. He'd survived without any help from New York. As he'd said, once you leave, "they simply forget about you."

But literature hadn't. "Forty, broke, unemployed and in debt," Frank wrote near the end of his life, "I accepted an offer to come to Iowa and the well-known Writers' Workshop more from a sense of desperation than any deep conviction that I'd know what to do when faced with a roomful of young writers. I was, in fact, apprehensive." But that phase passed. Over time, Frank became comfortably authoritative. Like a character out of Dickens, his literary touchstone, he had risen from debtor to Workshop director. *Stop-Time* had survived, too. Twenty years after its publication, the book was still in print. Its 1985 paperback edition now bore the subtitle *The Classic Memoir of Adolescence.* On the cover, above Frank's name, an Andrew Wyeth-like illustration depicts a black-haired boy. His age is indeterminate—he might be twelve, he might be fifteen. He leans against a building's outer wall, its color a washed-out tan, duskier than a strip of white pine. In the distance stand two leafless trees. A wintry sun casts no shadows. The boy wears a dark green zippered jacket, visible from its collar to mid-arm. His head tilts toward the reader, who notices the boy's partially closed eyelids, his straight but somewhat thick nose, his graceful lips. It's a somber portrait, the boy's expression guarded, his vulnerability unmistakable.

That, too, had changed. In 1989, when I met him, Frank had a slight overbite. A lick of his silver hair continually fell across his right eye and he had to brush it back. His hands were large, his fingers long, ideal for a piano player, and he smiled more than he laughed, as if he always held something back. Yet despite his success, I detected in him a quality (which I knew to be not entirely true) of a boy who had leapt from adolescence straight into accomplished adulthood. By the time I arrived in Iowa City—I had submitted a novel excerpt and Frank admitted me to the Workshop based on it—Frank wore a literary halo. The first chapter of his novel, *Body & Soul*, had been published in the September issue of GQ magazine. Famed editor Seymour Lawrence had given him a six-figure advance to write the book and Frank's agent, Candida Donadio, (I later learned) told Frank, "When Sam Lawrence pays you to sit down and write a novel, you sit down and write a novel," although I believe Frank was intimidated by the idea of writing one. In October, his essay "Think About It" appeared in *The Best American Essays of 1989*. Frank's new publications resurrected his reputation and (I'm speculating here) put him at ease. He no longer had to worry about directing the program with a relatively thin body of work. Sixteen years had passed between the appearance of *Stop-Time* and the publication of his second book, *Midair*, a slim short story collection. But if Frank did lack confidence, he hid it. The day preceding our first class, students gathered in a large classroom, many of us sitting lotus style on the floor, others with our knees pulled to our chest, once all the seats were taken. Frank stood at a podium and introduced himself. Finally, he mentioned the year's visiting writers, concluding with "and Norman Mailer is coming," his voice rising to convey our good fortune, although Mailer's strongest work was a decade old and younger students considered him a relic. If Frank had promised Raymond Carver, a buzz would have engulfed the room. But Carver had died a year earlier, in 1988, leaving many of us with the feeling that his work had been incomplete. Most writers die with their work unfinished, their masterpieces never written. Illness, jobs, family obligations, laziness, loneliness, dwindling talent, drunkenness, fear, and star-crossed events

can overwhelm us. Our lives pass, yet the book's absence remains a mystery. Once, it had been as palpable as a heartbeat. And then what might have been dies with us.

Nevertheless, I was electrified by hope. I'd anticipated a grand setting for the workshop: green, freshly-clipped lawns, ivy-covered walls. Instead, the English-Philosophy Building, which housed it, was a square brick structure with few windows surrounded by a busy road, the muddy Iowa River, a parking lot, and a set of train tracks. EPB's halls were dim and box-car straight, its tile floors scuff-marked, its plaster ceiling low. Light fixtures were scarce. Room 457, which sounded like a torture cell out of Orwell's *1984*, was where Frank held his workshop. I reached it by climbing four flights of thick metal stairs. Six or seven students loitered outside its doors. Feeling out of my depths, and by nature prone to solitude, I wandered past them. Fifty feet away, a short hallway intersected with the main one and I slid into it. Then I saw Frank appear in his office doorway, holding a set of keys. He glanced up. A moment later he said, "Are you Tom?"

"Yes."

"Come on in here." Once we were in his office he said, "Close the door." He sat behind a wide desk. Manuscripts were everywhere. An *Oxford American Dictionary* was propped open on a stand behind his chair, its fine print visible from where he'd told me to take a seat. He didn't ask about me at all. To him, I was a novel incarnate. All he saw was literary promise. And yet, gradually, we became friends. As I wrote my novel, he wrote his.

Now whether or not it's true, Tolstoy said we have to write as if all of history is looking over our shoulder. I tried to keep this in mind. But Frank had an additional problem. He had written a legendary memoir. Whatever he published would be seen through the lens of *Stop-Time* and judged in comparison to it. Also, another seventeen years of silence between books would raise questions and start rumors. "When I published *Midair*," he said to me, "reporters asked where I'd been. They wanted stories about madness and being locked in psych wards. Alcoholism, drug abuse. Sensationalism! Where had I been? I'd been earning a living! But what do they know? They're journalists." However, if Frank felt any anxiety, he disguised it. In fact, he radiated confidence, publicly anyway. After *Body & Soul*'s first chapter appeared in GQ, foreign rights to the novel began to sell. Before the novel had been written it seemed destined for success, although selling a book based on a partial manuscript drew a smaller advance, Frank once told me. "If a book's done, it's done. If it isn't, who knows? You could get hit by a bus. Then the publisher's out a hundred grand."

Still, despite his good fortune, Frank did his homework. *Body & Soul*'s protagonist, Claude, rises from poverty to stardom (Dickens again) by virtue of his exceptional talent as a classical pianist. For his debut, Claude would "be performing Mozart's Double Piano Concerto in E-Flat Major, with Charles Fredericks [Claude's musical benefactor] at the Longmeadow Music Festival in Longmeadow, Massachu-setts." Claude announces this in a letter to Catherine, the rich young woman he loves without being loved in return, just as Pip loves, but is largely abused by, Estella Havisham in *Great Expectations*. Frank flew to New York to visit Peter Serkin, one of the world's foremost classical pianists, to learn how Claude's part of the Concerto should be played. Seated at his grand piano, Mr. Serkin said to Frank, "Claude should emphasize this note." Then he struck a key in the lower register and allowed it to reverberate. "Mozart wanted an unmistakably deep sound here. We're certain of this for a simple reason. This was the lowest note and final key on Mozart's piano."

Like his *Stop-Time*, *Body & Soul* was completely out of synch with its era. Frank didn't imitate Carver's quote-unquote minimalism. He didn't mimic DeLillo's substitution of cultural criticism for plot. And his characters didn't nail babies to trees, as Cormac McCarthy's do in *Blood Meridian*. No, in terms of narrative structure and aesthetic sensibility, *Body & Soul* is Victorian. To Frank, nineteenth-century novelists had mastered the genre, and in *Body & Soul* he paid homage to the works through which he escaped his adolescent fears and his family's unstable life. *Body & Soul* is a bildungsroman, and its concerns are strictly bourgeois: success, money, and, to a certain extent, virtue. Claude is an innocent, and the characters surrounding him are generally decent and generous, except for his mother, an alcoholic cab driver who, early in the novel, abuses Claude physically, when she isn't locking

Mr. [Artie] Shaw had tracked Frank down to tell him no one had written a better book about how it felt to play music.

him in their basement apartment. Like Frank in *Stop-Time*, Claude is often terrified and alone. Whenever he has the chance he sneaks into a theater where he watches movies with "total attention, so captivated that it was a shock when the movies ended, as if his soul had been flying around in the dark and had now slammed back into his body. Outside, the unnaturally still street and the implacable heat seemed to claim him, to smother the quicksilver emotions of the films and flatten him in his contemplation of the meaningless, eternal, disinterested reality of the street, of its enduring drabness and familiarity. To come out of the RKO was to come down, and he rushed home to the safety and company of the piano." Above all, what sets *Body & Soul* apart from contemporary novels is its absolute lack of irony. It isn't cynical, it doesn't indulge in postmodern gameplaying, and, for the most part, it avoids lyrical flourishes. Instead, the novel's first half radiates an Olympian calm. The second half, however, surrenders the restraint that made the novel's beginning sublime.

I idolized Frank and wanted *Body & Soul* to be an unqualified success. It wasn't. But over the years, the novel found a wide audience, and it's beloved by musicians. Being abstract and writing about music with authority and precision and without sentimentality is nearly impossible. But Frank does it in *Body & Soul*. In this regard, the novel stands as a singular achievement, and musicians recognize this. When the novel was published, Frank embarked on a reading tour. One evening, his hotel telephone rang; the operator said Frank had a call from a Mr. Shaw. "I thought, okay," Frank told me, "he's the local auto mechanic." But it was Artie Shaw, one of the great jazz clarinet players. "When I realized who it was," Frank said, "I was like, 'Maestro!'" Mr. Shaw had tracked Frank down to tell him no one had written a better book about how it felt to play music. Although I was never much of a musician (I had some piano and guitar lessons when I was a boy), I didn't doubt him. Frank's description of Claude's debut is detailed and radiant. "After the staccato chords of the tutti, after the heartbeat rest of silence, when he and Fredericks laid in their double trills as one, together shaped the grace notes and announced the unison E-flat with the same firm touch, after the bar and a half of descending sixteenths flowing like grains of sand in an hourglass, Claude removed his hands from the keyboard and listened to Fredericks play the next eleven bars. It was clear, spirited, and apparently effortless." The novel's musical passages are unmatched.

The romantic passages would have benefitted from a slightly ironic touch. More Hemingway, and less Dickens. By coincidence, which is a nineteenth-century novelistic convention, Claude is reunited with Catherine. It's here that the pitch of Frank's sentences relies a bit too indiscriminately on his idol's lack of restraint. Speaking about Estella in *Great Expectations*, Mrs. Havisham advises Pip to "Love her, love her, love her! If she favors you, love her. If she wounds you, love her. If she tears your heart to pieces—and as it gets older and stronger—it will tear deeper—love her, love her, love her! I'll tell you what real love is. It is blind devotion, unquestioning self-humiliation, utter submission, trust and belief against yourself and against the whole world, giving up your whole heart and soul to the smiter—as I did!" Similarly, when he and Catherine make love, Claude imagines that "Passion was a force to be fed, eagerly and gratefully fed like some hungry angel with them in the room possessed of the power to lift them out of themselves. Out of the body, out of the world to some deep blue otherness where their souls would join, in and with the blue. Sailing along together in the blue, the blue insupportable to a soul alone."

Typing the above passage was difficult for me, and I confess to feeling that, in a way, I've betrayed Frank. But, intellectually, I don't believe I have. For Frank, the text, not the writer, is sacrosanct, and I'm (perhaps mistakenly) confident that he would appreciate my honoring his work by dissecting it closely, delicately, and, yes, lovingly. He wrote in memory of his own teacher, Professor Cipher, "I wholeheartedly offer these memories and these words as a prayer." Here, I do the same.

Shortly before he died, Frank assembled a collection of his essays, entitled *Dogs Bark, but the Caravan Rolls On: Observations from Then and Now*. Frank's skill as an essayist is not alluded to often enough. True, *Stop-Time* eclipses most of Frank's work, but his essays are models of precision, clarity, and compression. Frank loved tricks and the trick of a good essay is to say much more than what appears on the page. Great essays resonate. Like music, they have overtones; sounds echo sounds; they layer and enrich the original note. When you read a great essay you shouldn't notice that the writer began at a seemingly random point in time but by the essay's end an entire life has passed and, as an aftershock, the reader is reminded of the miracle of being alive. For each of us, one-day time will stop forever. Frank died three and a half years ago. I miss him immensely. But I can hear his voice whenever I want to. All I have to do is remove one of his books from my shelves and open it. 🜶

A poem by D. A. Powell

Backstage Pass

The rigging has come down again. Just last week
you fed on the free candy from the bank's candy dish.
Now you will be everywhere: Toronto, Ithaca,
Chicopee Falls. It's a bigger job than you expected.

So many components to the trap drum set: pedals,
wingnuts, hi-hat, snare. Be gentle with the heads. Yes,
that's what they're really called—check the package.

Just keep the bandmates happy, mister, just bring them
fudge, the Bud they asked for, the Amstel Light.

Whatever you have to do to keep yourself: in the back
of the bus, on a bumpy road, the stink of the guys' pits,
their bobbing heads, patting the back of your hand.

Did you remember to pack extra sticks, the strings
and picks. Did you check. One, two. Did you check.

What, of this Goldfish,

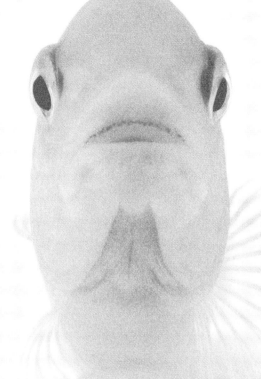

FICTION

Etgar Keret

Translated by Nathan Englander

Would You Wish?

Yonatan had a brilliant idea for a docu-

mentary. He'd knock on doors. Just him. No camera crew, no nonsense. Just Yonatan alone, a little camera in his hand, asking, "If you found a talking gold-fish that granted you three wishes, what, of this goldfish, would you wish?"

Folks would give their answers, and Yoni would edit them down, make clips of the more surprising responses. Before every set of answers, you'd see the person standing stock still in the entrance to his house. Onto this shot he'd superimpose the subject's name, his family situation, his monthly income, and maybe even the party he'd voted for in the last election. That, together with the wishes, and maybe he'd end up with some real social commentary, a testament to the massive rift between all our dreams and the often unpromising realities in which we live.

It was genius, Yoni was sure. And, if not, at least it was cheap. All he needed was a door to knock on and a heart beating on the other side. With a little decent footage, he was sure he'd be able to sell it to Channel 8 or Discovery in a flash. Either as a film or as a bunch of vignettes, little cine-matic corners, each with that singular soul standing in a doorway, followed by three killer wishes, precious, every one.

Even better, maybe he'd cash out, package it with a slogan and sell it to a bank or cellular phone company. Maybe tag it with something like, "Different dreams, different wishes, one bank." Or, "The bank that makes dreams come true."

———— · ————

No prep, no plotting, natural as can be, Yoni grabbed his camera and went out knocking on doors. In the first neighborhood, the kindly folk that took part generally requested the foreseeable things: health, money, bigger apartments, either to shave off a couple of years or a couple of pounds. But there were also the powerful moments, the big truths. There was one drawn, wizened old lady that asked simply for a child. There was a Holocaust survivor, a number on his arm, who asked very slowly, and in a quiet voice—as if he'd been waiting for Yoni to come; as if it wasn't an exercise at all: he'd been wondering (if this fish didn't mind), would it be possible for all the Nazis left living in the world to be held accountable for their crimes? There was a cocky, broad-shouldered lady-killer who put out his cigarette and, as if the camera wasn't there, wished he were a girl. "Just for a night," he added, holding a single finger right up to the lens.

And these wishes were just from one short block in one small, sleepy suburb of Tel Aviv. Yonatan could hardly imagine what people were dreaming of in the development towns and the collectives along the northern border, in the West Bank settlements and Arab villages, the immigrant absorption centers full of broken trailers and tired people left to broil out in the desert sun.

Yonatan knew if the project was going to have any weight, he'd have to get to everyone, to the unemployed, to the ultra-religious, to the Arabs and Ethiopians and American ex-pats. He began to plan a shooting schedule for the coming days: Yaffo, Dimona, Ashdod, Sderot, Taibe, Talpiot. Maybe Hebron even. If he could sneak past the wall, Hebron would be great. Maybe somewhere in that city some beleaguered Arab man would stand in his doorway and, looking through Yonatan and his camera, looking out into nothingness, just pause for a minute, nod his head, and wish for peace—that would be something to see.

———— ·•· ————

Sergei Goralick doesn't much like strangers banging on his door. Less so is he amenable to it when those strangers are asking him questions. In Russia, when Sergei was young, it happened plenty. The KGB felt right at home knocking on his door. His father had been a Zionist, which was pretty much an invitation for them to drop by any old time.

When Sergei got to Israel and then moved to Yaffo, his family couldn't wrap their heads around it. They'd ask him, What are you looking to find in a place like that? There's no one there but addicts and Arabs and pensioners. But what is most excellent about addicts and Arabs and pensioners is that they don't come around knocking on Sergei's door. Like that, Sergei can get his sleep, and get up when it's still dark. He can take his little boat out into the sea and fish until he's done fishing. By himself. In silence. The way it should be. The way it was.

Until one day some kid with an earring in his ear, looking a little bit homosexual, comes knocking. Hard like that—rapping at his door. Just the way Sergei doesn't like. And he says, this kid, that he has some questions he wants to put on the TV.

Sergei tells the boy, tells him in what he thinks is a straightforward manner, that he doesn't want it. Not interested. Sergei gives the camera a shove, to help make it clear. But the earring boy is stubborn. He says all kinds of things, fast things. And it's a bit hard for Sergei to follow; his Hebrew isn't so good.

The boy slows it down, tells Sergei he's got a strong face, a nice face, and that he simply has to have him for this movie picture. Sergei can also slow down, he can also make clear. He tells the kid to fuck off. But the kid is slippery and somehow between saying no and pushing the door closed, Sergei finds that the kid is in his house. He's already making his movie, running his camera without any permission, and from behind the camera still telling Sergei about his face, that it's full of feeling, that it's tender. Suddenly the kids spots Sergei's goldfish flitting around in its big glass jar in his kitchen.

The kid with the earring starts screaming "Goldfish, goldfish," he's so excited. And this, this really pressures Sergei, who tells the kid, it's nothing, just a regular goldfish, stop filming it. Just a goldfish, Sergei tells him, just something he found flapping around in the net, a deep-sea goldfish. But the boy isn't listening. He's still filming and getting closer and saying something about talking and fish and a magic wish.

Sergei doesn't like this, doesn't like that the boy is almost at it, already reaching for the jar. In this instant Sergei understands the boy didn't come for television, what he came for, specifically, is to snatch Sergei's fish, to steal it away. Before the mind of Sergei Goralick really understands what it is his body has done, he seems to have taken the burner off the stove and hit the boy in the head. The boy falls. The camera falls with him. The camera breaks open on the floor, along with the boy's skull. There's a lot of blood coming out of that head, and Sergei really doesn't know what to do.

That is, he knows exactly what to do, but it really would complicate things. Because if he brings this kid to the hospital, people are going to ask what happened, and it would take things in a direction Sergei doesn't want to go.

"No reason to take him to the hospital anyway," says the goldfish, in Russian. "That one's already dead."

"He can't be dead," Sergei says, with a moan. "I barely popped him. It's only a burner. Only a little thing." Sergei holds it up to the fish, taps it against his own skull to prove it. "It's not even that hard."

"Maybe not," says the fish. "But, apparently, it's harder than that kid's head."

"He wanted to take you from me," Sergei says, almost crying.

"Nonsense," the fish says. "He was only here to make a little nothing for TV."

"But he said . . ."

"He said," says the fish, interrupting, "exactly what he was doing. But you didn't get it. Honestly, your Hebrew, it's terrible."

"Yours is better?" Sergei says. "Yours is so great?"

"Yes. Mine's super-great," the goldfish says, sounding impatient. "I'm a magic fish. I'm fluent in everything."

All the while the puddle of blood from the earring kid's head is getting bigger and bigger and Sergei is on his toes, up against the kitchen wall, desperate not to step in it, to get blood on his feet.

"You do have one wish left," the fish reminds Sergei. He says it easy like that, as if Sergei doesn't know—as if either of them ever loses count.

"No," Sergei says. He's shaking his head from side to side. "I can't," he says. "I've been saving it. Saving it for something."

"For what?" the fish says.

But Sergei won't answer.

———————— –•– ————————

That first wish, Sergei used up when they discovered a cancer in his sister. A lung cancer, the kind you don't get better from. The fish undid it in an instant—the words barely out of Sergei's mouth. The second wish Sergei used up five years before, on Sveta's boy. The kid was still small then, barely three, but the doctors already knew. Something in her son's head wasn't right. He was going to grow big but not in the brain. Three was about as smart as he'd get. Sveta cried to Sergei in bed all night. Sergei walked home along the beach when the sun came up, and he called to the fish, asked the goldfish to fix it as soon as he'd crossed through the door. He never told Sveta. And a few months later she left him for some cop, a Moroccan with a shiny Honda. In his heart, Sergei kept telling himself it wasn't for Sveta that he'd done it, that he'd wished his wish purely for the boy. In his mind, he was less sure, and all kinds of thoughts about other things he could have done with that wish continued to gnaw at him, half driving him mad. The third wish, Sergei hadn't yet wished for.

"I can restore him," says the goldfish. "I can bring him back to life."

"No one's asking," Sergei says.

"I can bring him back to the moment before," the goldfish says. "To before he knocks on your door. I can put him back to right there. I can do it. All you need to do is ask."

"To wish my wish," Sergei says. "My last."

The fish swishes his fish tail back and forth in the water, the way he does, Sergei knows, when he's truly excited. The goldfish can already taste freedom. Sergei can see it on him.

After the last wish, Sergei won't have a choice. He'll have to let the goldfish go. His magic goldfish. His friend.

"Fixable," Sergei says. "I'll just mop up the blood. A good *sponga* and it'll be like it never was."

That tail just goes back and forth, the fish's head steady.

Sergei takes a deep breath. He steps out into the middle of the kitchen, out into that puddle. "When I'm fishing, while it's dark and the world's asleep," he says, half to himself and half to the fish, "I'll tie the kid to a rock and dump him in the sea. Not a chance, not in a million years, will anyone ever find him."

"You killed him, Sergei," the goldfish says. "You murdered someone— but you're not a murderer." The goldfish stops swishing his tail. "If, on this, you won't waste a wish, then tell me, Sergei, what is it good for?"

It was in Bethlehem, actually, that Yonatan found his Arab, a handsome man who used his first wish for peace. His name was Munir; he was fat with a big white mustache. Super photogenic. It was moving, the way he said it. Perfect, the way in which Munir wished his wish. Yoni knew, right while he was filming, that this guy would be his promo for sure.

Either him or that Russian. The one with the faded tattoos that Yoni had met in Yaffo. The one that looked straight into the camera and said, if he ever found a talking goldfish he wouldn't ask of it a single thing. He'd just stick it on a shelf in a big glass jar and talk to him all day, it didn't matter about what. Maybe sports, maybe politics, whatever a goldfish was interested in chatting about.

Anything, the Russian said, not to be alone. 🐟

Where Nothing

FICTION

David Gates

Ever Happens

Lily has figured out this much: open the downstairs windows at night to let the cool air in, then close them in the morning and the house stays cool all day. Didn't her father always say she had a splendid mind? While Portia, her older sister, only had a good head on her shoulders. The upstairs windows you always keep open, because of the axiom that heat rises. No, higher than an axiom: a law. No, higher still than a law: a truth. Unless truth and law rule side by side. Upon a throne of adamant. Is this not a splendid thought? A Miltonic thought? She should really be writing these things down.

She'd shared a taxi back to Brooklyn with Portia's married boyfriend—Portia being otherwise occupied—whom she kissed when he dropped her at her building, tongues involved.

She's in Connecticut, house-sitting for the Hagertys the first three weeks of August, with the use of their second car, and sleeping in their dead daughter's bedroom. This is their weekend-and-summer getaway, but Marian Hagerty hates the look of air conditioners in the windows, so in August they fly to Main-à-Dieu, on the easternmost coast of Cape Breton, in a chartered seaplane, to watch the fishing-boat races. Joe Hagerty had hired Lily's father straight out of Harvard Law—a charity case, he liked to say. This got a laugh at her father's memorial. Everyone there knew Skip Kiernan had turned down Harry Blackmun's offer of a clerkship.

The Hagertys' daughter, Elena, had gone to Dalton while Lily was at Brearley, but the summer Lily turned nine, the Kiernans rented a house near Joe and Marian's place—they hadn't yet bought their own getaway—and her father drove her over one day to play tennis with Elena on the Hagertys' clay court. (Portia, who was twelve, chose to go to the lake with her mother.) Elena, long hair flying, had Lily panting and sweating in the first few volleys. Lily remembers, years later, doing coke with Elena in the bathroom at Portia's wedding, and Elena, now *très gamine* with her boy-length hair, possibly coming on to her. A kiss on the lips? With just the most petite dart of the tip of Elena's tongue? Elena had on an electric blue dress with spaghetti straps, and when she leaned forward over the countertop, Lily saw the nipples of small breasts. Elena has been dead for five years now, and Lily's found not a trace of her in her old room: nothing in the dresser drawers but flowered paper lining the bottoms, nothing in the closet but satin-padded hangers. Are the Hagertys really so sure the dead don't mind?

In these three weeks, she will swim every day; the Hagertys' Subaru Forester has a sticker for the recreation area at the lake. She will eat better, keep her cell phone off, go online only once a day—just in case anybody responds to the résumés she sent out—and not smoke the weed she's brought. She will read *The Custom of the Country* (the others were so good), reread *Mansfield Park* (the only one that's still not too girly), try again to push beyond the first six books of *Paradise Lost*, and leaven all this with whatever she may choose, on a whim, from the Hagertys' shelves. Won't *that* be something, to have a whim. As distinct from an impulse. And every night will be movie night: 11 P.M. sharp, in bed, lights out, with her laptop and a glass of something. She's brought only a half-dozen of the old usuals along, since Marian told her the video store in town is owned by "film buffs." This got Lily picturing gay boys with toned bodies, whom she could go look at every day in their tight T-shirts. Who says the pastoral is dead?

Portia had tried to talk her out of coming here—a bad time to isolate, she'd said. Portia has confided that when she's alone she'll sometimes hear her father speaking to her. But Lily needed to get away from her one-bedroom in Brooklyn Heights, which she'd rented on the now-exploded theory that neighborhood trumps space. And also to get away from Dagon, let's admit, whom she'd lately been feeding on Rice Krispies, and whose litter box she'd been finding herself unable to clean and refill. Renaldo, the intern she's kept in touch with since being laid off, agreed to stay with him in return for the three weeks of air-conditioning and a shorter subway ride. On the morning she gave Renaldo her keys, she finally bought cat food and changed the litter, which proved she could do it, strictly speaking.

And then there was this. On the Fourth of July, after a party where the revelers got high to watch the fireworks from a roof garden in Tribeca, she'd shared a taxi back to Brooklyn with Portia's married boyfriend—Portia being otherwise occupied—whom she kissed when he dropped her at her building, tongues involved, then hands under the clothes, and who's been e-mailing her ever since, and whom she's been e-mailing back. So really, doesn't this speak well of her, taking herself out of harm's way? Although—and here *is* a Miltonic thought—*Which way I fly is Hell; my self am Hell.*

-------- --•-- --------

It's after midnight when she gets here: a bus to Torrington, then a taxi along miles of unlighted country roads. Inside, the house is hot and stuffy; she sets her bags down in the kitchen and goes around opening windows. On the counter, weighted down by the keys to the Subaru, she finds a note from Marian Hagerty that goes to the tune of *You may go down the lane*, whatever whatever, but don't go into Mr. McGregor's garden. Lily is not to drink the wines in the cellar, each laid down by Joe to be opened at such and such a time. ("Not that you would, of course.") She is not to have parties—"a friend or two is perfectly fine"—or overnight guests. If she uses the court, she is to wear only tennis shoes—i.e. bare-assed and breasts bouncing? Oh well, poor Marian. The once-scandalous second wife, suddenly in her sixties, bereft of her child and having to deal with Joe, now eighty-four and still playing doubles, with neighbors' young wives as his partners.

Up in Elena's bedroom, thank God, there's a three-foot-square floor fan; Lily puts it on the highest speed and goes back downstairs for her duffel and her wheeled suitcase. She takes her orange plastic box of weed out of the zippered compartment and puts it in the freezer, between a pint of Häagen-Dazs vanilla and a bottle of Stoli. Any one of these three things could lead to the other two. But she goes to bed without. Isn't that what she's *been* doing?

In the morning, she makes coffee in the Hagertys' French press and takes it out to the shady porch ("Please do not leave food on the veranda—we get the occasional raccoon") along with a bowl of the muesli she found in the cupboard. The box says both "no sugar added" and "not a low calorie food": mixed signals, as if from a man!

Driving into town along the shore of the lake, she spots a farm stand: a rustic wagon that holds an array of tomatoes, squashes, ears of corn. Then a bar called Tony's, with a green canvas awning. The town is a two-block main street without parking meters; she finds the video place, the organic market, and the wine shop, where she is to ask for "Victor." A tiny hair salon, so wittily called Delilah's. In the wine shop, she buys a seventy-five-dollar bottle of sherry—sherry! inspired!—for movie time. The younger, more handsome of the two men, the one with the curly hair, must be Victor. Oh, just a guess.

On the way back she slows down for a better look at this Tony's, although bars are *not* in the plan, then stops at the farm stand and buys zucchini, yellow summer squash, and a fat tomato. It's when she opens the kitchen door that she makes her discovery: she'd closed the downstairs windows so nobody could get in, and now it's actually cool in here. Not a word of *this* in Marian Hagerty's note!

She puts on her black bikini and checks herself: today is a good day. She and Portia had been issued the wrong bodies, back in the antelife. Lily has the ectomorphic mind—even the ectomorphic name—while portly-sounding Portia stole the show, slinky-limbed, in the one ballet recital they did together. After that, Lily begged to take tap instead—all those old musicals their father made them watch—then refused to go when she learned the students had to wear tights: you could see the flesh shaking even on *Ruby Keeler*'s thighs, for Pete's sake, when she tapped in *42nd Street*.

At the lake, she spreads one of the Hagertys' towels on the grass and takes her sweet time unbuttoning her shirt, sliding her jeans off, arching her back. From behind her sunglasses, she looks around, but it's all moms and kids. Just as well. Truly. The water's warm at the surface, icy when you dive down. When she comes out, her body feels cool at the core, and she lies down in the sun, so calmed it's disturbing.

She eats a dinner of brown rice with zucchini and garlic, sliced tomato on the side. Then she goes up to Elena's room, pulls down the shade, slips panties off one leg and thinks up Richard in the taxi, her hand down the front of his jeans, her other hand down the back, then thinks up reaching into Elena's blue dress—it's vacation!—then touches her own breast with her free hand, then brings Richard back in, to play with her and Elena: even alone, you can't know who's watching. She makes herself come, twice, in Elena's bed. Outside it's still daylight.

When they went through her father's things, Lily took a white shirt with a Brooks Brothers label and his razor, with which she now shaves her legs. In the back of his closet, she found the Doré print that used to hang above the desk in his study; when he got sober, he'd replaced it with a photo of their cottage in Dennisport. ("What's your favorite sport?" her father would ask them, turning his head to the backseat, and they would shout back, "Dennisport!") When she was little, she would go into the study to look at it: a man with bat wings, clawing at his head with one hand; his chest seemed to have bosoms and he wore a skirt that came up above his knees. Underneath it was written, *Me miserable! Which way shall I fly/Infinite wrath and infinite despair?* Neither her mother nor Portia had wanted the print, so Lily hung it over her non-working fireplace in Brooklyn Heights. Sometimes she thinks it's bringing her bad luck. But didn't she have bad luck before?

Except during the couple of years before he went to Silver Hill, Skip Kiernan had continually reread Shakespeare, Milton, and Johnson; their subliminally channeled cadences, he believed, had saved some corporate criminals from doing serious time. He used to pay Portia and Lily ten cents a line to memorize poems and recite them while he sat in his leather armchair with his drink. Portia stopped because it was babyish, but one night Lily made five dollars on Emily Dickinson. When Lily finally found a full-time job, fact-checking and copyediting at an upmarket bridal magazine, her father offered her ten thousand dollars, on top of her tuition, to quit and go get what he called "your PhD." Behind Matt's back. So now Matt's out of the picture, she's lost the job anyway, and she's just turned thirty-three. *Me miserable!*

Lily was in Amsterdam with Matt when Elena was shot by bandits in Malaysia, where she'd gone to work with Catholic Charities. "They had all that trouble with her," Lily's father said, "then finally she gets her act together, then this. Don't *you* go doing good in the world."

"Yeah, what are the odds," Lily said.

The next morning she goes into the video store on the chance they might have *Gold Diggers of 1933*, which she was stupid not to have brought.

"I knew it," the man at the counter says. "No. I'm sorry, we should." His short blond hair's just starting to go gray, and he's got lines at the corners of his eyes and the beginnings of man breasts under the knit shirt.

"Oh, it was just a whim," she says. "I'm afraid if I start browsing, I'll never get out of here." Already she's spotted *Carnival of Souls*.

"That wouldn't break my heart," he says. Straight for sure, just unappealing. "If you find yourself jonesing for something, here's the number." He hands her a card. "Ask for Evan."

Well, it's a day for whims, isn't it? Walking past the hair salon, she sees that both chairs are empty—and there's your gay boy. Maybe. He's got a shaved head, and he's wearing a Hawaiian shirt. "Don't be bashful," he says when she sticks her head in. "Come. Sit." A boom box on the glass shelf is playing the Robert Plant-Alison Kraus CD that everybody's sick of back in the city. "First let me get a look at the lay of the land, and then we'll shampoo you."

He's got strong fingers—she can feel her scalp move on her skull—and he's rough with the towel. She's still not sure about him. "So," he says, walking her back to the chair, "what are we doing today?"

"Something we may end up regretting," she says.

On the way home—why *not* call it that?—she keeps pulling down the visor to check herself in the makeup mirror. The sky's getting dark to the west; when she gets out of the car she hears faraway thunder. Excuse enough to bag the swim. She allows herself a few minutes in the bathroom to turn her head from side to side in front of the mirror; she hadn't realized her ears were so big. She takes a shower, puts on her father's big white shirt, then goes out to the porch, lies in the hammock, and tries to stop touching her hair and get serious about *Mansfield Park*. Maria has fled with Henry Crawford—and Mary Crawford has proved so deficient in moral sense that she merely calls it "folly"! When the storm hits, she closes the book to watch: hailstones bouncing off the lawn, big trees waving like feather dusters. Isn't that good? Better write that one down.

> "Don't you get enough action with my sister?" she says. "*And* your wife?"

After eating dinner she turns her cell phone on and finds a new message, from Richard. *You're not answering your e-mail. Call me. Contact me.* What time is it, eight o'clock? A couple of hits now and it'll wear off in time for movie night. She goes to the freezer and pinches just that much off a bud. It's cool in the living room, where the original wood paneling has been cured in a couple of centuries of smoke from the original walk-in fireplace. She presses her nose into the wall, wishing to exchange molecules with that aroma, then lies back on the long leather sofa with her head propped up and starts her iPod—a mix Renaldo made for her, which sounds cold and clattery. The second song takes a much longer time to go by than the first, and when she's somewhere in the middle of the next one she can't remember back to the first song—oh, good, this is good. If you could be this way all the time, you'd never worry about the years flying by, because even an hour is just so full, too full actually.

She wakes up on the sofa in full morning light. She'd considered going up to the bedroom, but it would've been hot and she would've had to deal with the fan, and let's admit, she had been afraid Elena might be up there. One of the big buds is gone, and half the bottle of sherry. She starts coffee; that and Advil should take care of the headache, though Satan's whispering, *How's about a little drinkie?* She eats a handful of raisins and—though it's way off-schedule—goes upstairs to get into her bikini.

The lake water feels so cold she just stands there up to her knees, hugging herself. She looks around: at this time of morning there's nobody here to see her punk out. Just a thin little girl whose fat mommy is yelling, "*That doesn't work for me!*" What has the little girl done?

Back at the house, she finds rackets and some cans of balls in the mudroom and goes out to the tennis court. She hits six balls over the net, then walks over, barefoot on the hot clay, and hits them back. Okay, clearly, she can't put this off any longer. She goes back inside and turns on her cell.

"Hey, I was about to give up on you," Richard says. "Listen, some friends of mine invited me up to Kent this weekend. That's not too far from you, right?"

"Don't you get enough action with my sister?" she says. "*And* your wife?"

"Correct me if I'm wrong, but, somehow I got the idea that you and I both sort of take things on a case-by-case basis."

"You're making me wet," she says.

"Okay, you're pissed at me. I'll give you a call when I get up there tomorrow night."

"You really like yourself, don't you?"

"I'll pass on that one," he says. "How about you?"

Lily's thing with Matt had broken up a year before Portia's marriage did—which was counterintuitive, because shouldn't the less traditional couple be revealed to have the stronger foundation, or was this counter-counterintuitive? She'd moved into Matt's low-tide-smelling factory loft in Greenpoint, where he'd lived with Melissa, his previous girlfriend. One night the bass player in his band said, "Thanks, Liss," as Lily passed him a platter of couscous and lamb; when she brought it up later, Matt said it wasn't his fault. That was when she got the idea to fuck the bass player.

He was a tall, lanky specimen, like all bass players, named Rob. *Called* Rob, strictly speaking. This would be a one-shot deal, off in its own space: wear a halter top to a gig, brush the girls against his arm, e-mail him to consult about a gift for Matt's birthday, meet him at Sam Ash, go for a drink afterwards. Portia herself couldn't have done it more efficiently.

When Lily refused to go to his place a second time, Rob quit the band and moved back to Chapel Hill, which wasn't at all the spirit of the thing. And then she began to e-mail him—not only men were allowed to send mixed signals!—and of course Matt got into her e-mail, and whatnot.

By the time Portia found out about her husband's girlfriend in Barcelona, Lily was able to give her refuge in Brooklyn Heights, on the foldout she'd been so prescient to buy. Every night Lily and Portia drank a bottle of Sancerre apiece and watched one of the old movies their father had loved; Portia always sobbed at the happy endings, then kept sobbing, even after Lily had clicked over to CNN.

"I felt like Daddy was watching with us," she said one night, when *Swing Time* was over and Larry King had Ed Asner on, talking about his autistic son.

"I'm curious," Lily said. "What kind of stuff does he say? You know, when he's speaking to you?"

"He just says—I don't want to say." She began to cry again. "He says, 'I'm taking care of you now.'"

"I wish he'd spread it around a little," Lily said.

"I don't know," Portia said. "He's not doing *that* good of a job."

Portia had never liked getting high when they were teenagers, but Lily asked around and found some weed sneaky enough not to panic her at first. But they overdid anyway, and after vomiting (Lily used the sink and let Portia have the toilet), they lay spooned on the bathroom floor the rest of the night. "Don't take this the wrong way, okay?" Portia said in the morning, when they finally felt okay to go to bed. "But that was the most fun I've ever had with you."

Portia had met Richard when some of her friends brought some of their friends to the housewarming at her new apartment. Lily had disliked him—the leather jacket plus the soul patch *plus* the wedding ring—and where was the wife? She overheard him telling Portia that he'd rather read Edith Wharton than Henry James—clever fellow—and then he whispered something and touched the tip of his index finger to the tip of her nose.

"But what's in it for you?" Lily asked her a couple of weeks later.

"Nothing," Portia said. "I mean, the obvious. What you used to call it—uninhabited sex? I just don't really trust him."

"Why would you possibly trust him?"

"I don't mean that way. I mean, of course not. I mean, I think he could get really angry?"

"Oh, honey," Lily said. "So does the wife know?"

Portia refilled her glass and passed the bottle to Lily. "Who knows what that's about. Why are you trying to make me feel bad? I don't go off on *you*. And *your* weird stuff. Actually he reminds me of you."

Portia had promised to drive up with Lily to spend the Fourth with their mother in Dennisport, just the three of them, and they would take the Hobie Cat out and scatter the ashes. Lily had already reserved a rental car. Then Portia called to say that Richard had invited them both to watch fireworks.

"Great, so Mom's going to be alone on the Fourth."

"This can't wait one day? Anyhow, the Rosenmans are going to be having their big thing. She'll be fine with it."

"Are you going to be fine with it?"

"Listen, I just need to do this, okay?" Portia said. "I thought you were supposed to be the great mind."

But surely only the mind of Omniscience could have foreseen that Portia would go into the bedroom with the host, a lean man in his sixties with a trimmed white beard, and his plump young wife. And that she herself would let this Richard tell her that these were "cool people," that Portia would be okay, and did she want to share a cab back to Brooklyn. And that she would touch a finger to the tip of his nose.

———— · ————

Thursday night the parking lot at Tony's is full—weekenders getting an early start. She's chosen her black tank top, nothing under it, and taken out her contacts in favor of her black-rimmed glasses, to make herself look more violable. There's a lone pool table with a faux-Tiffany lamp above it, and three televisions over the bar, the sound off, playing what look to be two different baseball games. Lily takes a stool at the end of the bar with an empty stool next to it. The bartender looks like—it takes her a second—the gink who sings "Shuffle Off to Buffalo" with Ruby Keeler! Whose name she happens to know is Clarence Nordstrom.

She orders a gin and tonic and begins watching the Red Sox and Cleveland. The batter in the whiter uniform has pants that come down to his feet like pajama bottoms, but so tight you can see his kneecaps. When she was thirteen and had hit a home run in softball at summer camp, her father took her to Shea, where the Mets lost a doubleheader to Atlanta. He'd said, "Only the Braves deserve the pair," and refused to tell her why that was funny. She can't really taste the gin, which is either why you should never order gin and tonic, or why you should always. She turns to check out the room—these stools swivel! The best!—and some guy's already coming her way, as if she's the drop of blood in a cubic mile of ocean. "I almost didn't recognize you with the hair," he says. "Looks good actually." His eyes go to her breasts. "Evan."

"Evan, right." The video store. "Lily. Actually it should be Portia." Oh my: Clarence Nordstrom does pour a good one. "At least it's not Elena, right?"

His eyebrows come in toward his nose. "What's wrong with Elena?"

"Now that," she says, "is genuinely funny. I'm liking you already." She leans forward—so embarrassing, but—and fiddles with the hem of her jeans long enough for him to see what there is to see. Then she straightens up and looks him in the eyes, which is easier than you'd think: you look at the eyes. "What are you drinking, *Evan*?"

> Some guy's already coming her way, as if she's the drop of blood in a cubic mile of ocean.

"Let me." He raises a finger and Clarence Nordstrom is there. "Another one for the young lady," he says, "and I'll have." He looks at the bottles behind the bar. "Knob Creek rocks?"

"*Grazie*," she says. "So *Evan*. Is this a place where nothing ever happens?"

"Apparently not," he says. Oh now surely he's in the right age demographic to have listened to Talking Heads. She thinks to check his ring finger. No. But he's been married, you can just tell. The bartender sets the drinks down. "So tell me, is that what you do?" she says. "Work at the video store?"

"Actually, during the year I teach media studies." He raises his glass. "Success to crime. So what do you do?"

"Work for a magazine nobody's ever heard of," she says. "I mean I used to."

He does his eyebrow thing again; it's imaginable that someone might find it fetching. "So you live in the city?"

"You're remarkable," she says.

"I'm not." He takes a sip and she sees he's already down to ice cubes.

"Oh. Well maybe I'm just setting the bar low tonight."

"So you're just up here visiting?"

"Tell you what," she says. "Why don't we finish up the due diligence, and then I have some very expensive sherry back at the house." She'll decide later if weed will scandalize him.

"Really," he says. "Whatever the catch is, it must be a doozy."

"Oh, I *like* a man who says 'doozy.'" She fishes out her lime wedge, sets it on the bar, and rocks it with her fingertip. "Do you know 'Wynken, Blynken, and Nod'? I mean, why would you?" She leans forward again—those pesky jeans! "What's the trouble, do you not want to?"

"Oh no, believe me," he says. "Just, I should probably tell you I've been sort of seeing somebody. Does that bother you?"

"Ah," she says. "So *you're* the one with the doozy. No, actually this makes me very happy. I mean, as long as she's not waiting outside with a gun." She drains her glass, the rim hitting her nose. "It *is* a she?"

His mouth comes open. "Hey, what the fuck?"

"That's better." She touches her index finger to the tip of his nose. "You were starting to lose me when you were being so nice. I have to go use the doozy." She gets off her stool and stands up just fine.

———————— ·•· ————————

"Daddy used to say he was a high-functioning workaholic," Portia said at the memorial. (Got the laugh). "But today I wanted to tell you some things you *didn't* know." Their father had asked them both to speak, along with Joe Hagerty, but Lily froze while trying to write something and had to settle for reading the second-to-last stanza of "Lycidas." It was Portia who'd dealt with the Harvard Club, pulled herself together enough to say something of her own, even hired the fucking bagpiper.

Lily had been waiting in the cottage when they brought him home to die. They'd taken him off the plane on a stretcher, but her mother said he'd sat up straight in his seat all the way from New York. She'd had to force herself to hold the hand with the needle taped to the back. High on the morphine and the five-hundred-dollar-an-ounce hydroponic Lily found for him—a last-minute appeal to Matt—he asked Lily to read him "Wynken, Blynken, and Nod," probably for some drifty Rosebud reason. She had to go online to find the thing, and now she can remember only something about rocking in the misty sea, and that the original title was "Dutch Lullaby."

And then she'd missed the main event because she had to be at work. She'd run through her vacation time—a stupid trip down to Chapel Hill in the summer—and the magazine would give her only two weeks of family leave, plus her personal day. And they must have been planning to lay her off then! That Tuesday night, while her car was warming up in the driveway, she promised her father she'd be back Friday, very late. According to Portia, he'd tried to wait for her—he'd made it till three that afternoon—but the fact remained.

"Daddy," Portia told his friends and colleagues, "had taken them to see Dexter Gordon at the Blue Note and Pavarotti at the Met and Nureyev at ABT, taught them to sail and to drive stick. Every Wednesday had been movie night, eight o'clock sharp. "When I was little," Portia said, "I believed that Fred Astaire could actually dance on the ceiling. I believed my father could too. And Daddy, I always will." Well: after that, one hardly needed "Amazing Grace."

———— ·—· ————

When she finally gets poor Evan out of Tony's bar, Lily keeps his headlights in her rearview mirror, though what's she going to do if he takes it into his head to peel off? He pulls up next to her in the driveway, and she sees him turn his cell off before getting out of his car.

"You know I drive by here all the time?" he says. "I always wondered what it was like inside. How old is this house?"

"Old." She takes him by the hand. "Come."

She has to put the candle over on the dresser so the fan doesn't blow it out, and in this light he's really not unthinkable. After he gets off the first time she has to persuade him that no, she *likes* getting (as he puts it) turned over, and then she has to talk him through it. So it was smart to have said nothing about weed. This time he groans as if wounded. Sweet man. The due diligence had revealed that he *was* divorced and that, surprise surprise, the wife got the house.

After his breathing smoothes out, with a growl at the end of every out-breath, she gets out of bed and goes down to the kitchen. She takes one hit—just one, or she'll never get to sleep—settles onto the sofa, gets to work with her fingers, then has a superstitious thought: she mustn't come while thinking up Elena—or in that white instant when she's bodiless she'll find Elena there, waiting to snatch her through into the world of the dead! Okay well now she *has* to, just to prove the thought wrong. When she returns to herself, still breathing hard, she understands what a crazy risk she's just taken.

She goes back upstairs, lies down so they're not touching, feels herself start to drift. Poor, sweet man. But then it's daylight and he's all over her again.

"What time is it, baby?" She rolls out from under him. Maybe she can get out of this one with hands and the Astroglide she was so prescient to pack—how about her hands cupped around his hands? This always got Matt.

When he catches his breath again, he says, "You're pretty incredible."

She's wiping up with last night's tank top, a lost cause anyway. "So are you going to have some 'splainin' to do?"

"Do we have to talk about it right this second?"

"I'm not trying to *steal* you." She lies back down, pressing the girls into his arm. "Just borrow you a little more."

"Shit," he says, "I forgot I have to open up this morning."

"Haven't you already?" She remembers he did that same little thing last night, with the eyebrows. "I'll make us some coffee."

She gets out of bed and puts on a T-shirt, which comes down just far enough to cover and still give him glimpses, and goes down to the kitchen. Spooning coffee into the French press, she hears the toilet flush upstairs. She puts water on to boil and goes into the half-bath off the living room.

> "If you don't come back tonight," she says, "you're going to jerk off to me the rest of your life."

When she comes out, he's sitting on an arm of the sofa, fully dressed, even his loafers. "So we have to talk about tonight," she says. "What time can you come over?"

"I actually can't tonight."

"Oh," she says. "Now let me guess."

He's turning red—sweet to see. "I could see you Sunday night."

"That's going to be way too late," she says. "Why don't we have our coffee out on the porch."

"You going back to the city?"

"Oh, you sound so hopeful," she says. "Has something happened to my incredibleness?"

"I told you the situation," he says.

She moves over to the front door and leans her back against it. "What if I don't move?"

"Please don't fuck with me," he says.

Clearly he means the *please* to sound ominous, but she can hear the *please* beneath it. He doesn't seem like a hitter, much as she might like to get hit. "If you don't come back tonight," she says, "you're going to jerk off to me the rest of your life."

"Shit," he says. "I fuckin' *knew* you were crazy. Let's not make this a big drag for both of us, okay?"

So he has some wit after all. And some woman, surely, has loved him. Maybe his wife, for a while. And maybe his new lady is beginning to love him too, the one she's gotten him to betray.

———— –•– ————

When Lily came by to pick her up in the rented Ford Explorer on July 6, Portia opened the passenger door, stuck her suitcase in and said, "I don't really want to talk, okay?" She made her seat go back like a dentist's chair and slept most of the way to Dennisport. Lily set the cruise control between seventy and seventy-five—the golden mean!—and they passed from one public radio listening area to another, like Venn diagrams. Lily learned that since the solstice they'd been losing two minutes of sunlight every day, and that seven people had been killed in two suicide bombings—she didn't catch where—and that Terry Gross's nervous fake laugh was getting worse. As they were going over the Bourne Bridge, Portia opened her eyes and said, "I can feel you over there judging me. So what did Richard have to say?"

"Why would he get to say anything?" Lily said. "Me either, for that matter."

"Oh, you're so Zen," Portia said. "Fuck you. Fuck *me*, actually. So who did he go off with?"

"Nobody," Lily said. "Actually, he was nice enough to drop me at my place."

"Really. Are we talking about the same person?" Portia looked over at Lily. "Oh. And were you nice enough to invite him up?"

"Come on, I have *some* boundaries," Lily said. "So does he, apparently."

Portia settled back in her seat. "I have to get my head around this."

They found their mother out on the deck with a canvas on her easel. "No, don't look," Janet said. "How was the traffic? I always hated the drive up here." Their father's favorite car game had been for them all to take turns improvising verses to "I Know an Old Lady Who Swallowed a Fly"; once he'd rhymed *swallowed your father* and *Why did she bother?* Their mother hadn't spoken the rest of the way. "Listen, I've got tuna steaks marinating. What do you think, should we just go out and do this while we've still got some daylight?"

"How far out are we going?" Portia said. "I don't like those clouds."

"As far as I'm concerned, we can *wade* out and do it," Janet said. "I doubt he's going to know the difference."

"You don't know what he knows," Lily said.

"Do you think he's *hovering*? You're not back on pot, are you?"

"Mom, we have to respect his wishes," Portia said.

"Oh, well far be it from me," Janet said. "I know how much *my* wishes always counted."

"I think you did all right for yourself, mother," Lily said.

"Can we not get into this now?" Portia said.

"No, I like it that she thinks," Janet said. "It's a very attractive quality. Or would it be an *attribute*? Whatever it was your father had."

"Can we not get into this now?" Portia said.

"I'm sorry, am I ruining the occasion?" Janet walked back over behind her canvas. "This is vile." She took it off the easel and dropped it face-down on the decking. "I hope he *is* hovering, actually. Just to sweeten up his eternal reward."

———— • ————

So how's this for prescience? Of course Lily will turn her cell phone on, and of course Richard will call, and of course she will give him directions. And again she will fuck a man in a dead girl's bed. Two in two days? She's unstoppable!

She rolls back over against Richard, fingers creeping around in his chest hair; you always come when it's the bad boy. The fan's still roaring, drying her sweat, giving her chills. "So," she says. "I think I'm going to go for sixteen men on a dead man's chest. Or is the pirate thing over with?"

"Hmm, I'm picturing that," he says. "Looks a little gay."

"Have you ever done two women?"

"Why? Is that a thing that interests you?"

"Did you and Portia do that?"

He takes her hand away and sits up against the headboard. "I don't think I need to answer these questions."

"Oh that's right," she says. "You go case by case. So is it hot to fuck sisters?"

"What about you? Is it hot to fuck somebody that fucked your sister?"

She puts her legs over the side and stands up. "Do you really have to leave so soon?"

He grabs her arm and yanks her back onto the bed.

"What are you going to do?" she says. "Rape me?"

He lets go of her arm. He reaches down, finds his T-shirt, and pulls it over his head. Stands up and steps into his briefs. "So." Picks up his shirt. "Is Portia going to know about this?"

Lily makes no move to get up again. "Come on, wouldn't you rather just freestyle it?" she says. "It should be more exciting for you. Test your little"—she flitters her fingers—"*ganglions*. You can watch her face for signs. If you're looking for your pants, they're over by the door."

From the bedroom window, she looks down and watches his car back out of the driveway; her arm still hurts where he grabbed. It's eight o'clock and getting dark. Two minutes of light a day. She's got three hours to fill just to get to movie time—and she's already run through everything she's brought except *Royal Wedding*, which she really doesn't want to watch. And then? And after that? She hasn't had her swim today, could that be what's wrong? The recreation area closes at sunset, but that shouldn't stop a girl who's already figured out so much.

She leaves her underwear on the floor, pulls on her jeans and gets her father's white shirt out of the closet, goes downstairs and tucks the one-hitter and her lighter into the pocket. She's halfway to the lake before she looks down and sees she's driving barefoot. The gate is closed, so she passes on to the far side, where it's privately owned, and narrow paved drives have signs arching above them: Lochbrae, Breezy Shores, Pinewoods. She turns into a lane with a small sign simply reading *Private*, and parks on the dirt, out of sight of the road. Reaches into her pocket.

When she gets out of the car, the white shirt seems to glow in the dimness, so she takes it off, her jeans too, and steps, naked, through the trees on merciful pine needles, to where she can see water, a wooden dock, a cottage with lights on. She looks both ways, then leaves the cover of the pines and walks toward the grassy bank. These people can't see: she's been gifted with invisibility. Only the dead can see her nakedness, and haven't they been watching all along? She steps onto the moss at the edge of the bank—its softness feels green—and into weeds and water. Her feet sink to the ankles in muck. It'll feel warmer once she gets in. She wades till the water's up to mid-thigh, leans forward, and launches herself.

It's as close to flying as we get in this world: breast-stroking through this uncanny element midway between earth and air, your legs out behind you, your feet touching nothing. She swims out until she's breathing hard, turns, treads water and looks back. The lights are on in the cottages, and here and there on the shore she can see tiny people clustering around the flames of outdoor grills. She looks up at the sky; the stars are coming out, and the voices from far across the water are pinpricks in the silence. Her heart's slowing again, she's getting her breath. She treads water, floats awhile on her back, then treads water, then floats awhile. You could do this forever—in fact, you are to do this until you see the way leading on from here, or until the dead speak to you at last. 🛡

FIVE FICTIONS FROM THE MIDDLE OF THE NIGHT

Lydia Davis

Swimming in Egypt

We are in Egypt. We are about to go deep-sea diving. They have erected a vast tank of water on land next to the Mediterranean Sea. We strap oxygen to our backs and descend into this tank. We go all the way to the bottom. Here, there is a cluster of blue lights shining on the entrance to a tunnel. We enter the tunnel. We swim and swim. At the far end of the tunnel, we see more lights, white ones. When we have passed through the lights, we come out of the tunnel, suddenly, into the open sea, which drops away beneath us a full kilometer or more. There are fish all around and above us, and reefs on all sides. We think we are flying, over the deep. We forget, for now, that we must be careful not to get lost, but must find our way back to the mouth of the tunnel.

The Schoolchildren in the Large Building

I live in a very large building, the size of a warehouse or an opera house. I am there alone. Now some schoolchildren arrive. I see their quick little legs coming through the front door and I ask, in some fear, "Who is it, who is it?" but they don't answer. The class is very numerous—all boys, with two teachers. They pour into the painting studio at the back of the building. The ceiling of this studio is two or even three stories high. On one wall is a huge mural of dark-complexioned faces. The schoolboys crowd in front of the painting, fascinated, pointing and talking. On the opposite wall is another mural, of green and blue flowers. Only a handful of schoolboys is looking at this one.

The class would like to spend the night here because they do not have funds for a hotel. Wouldn't their hometown raise the money for this field trip? I ask one of the teachers. No, he says sadly, with a smile, they wouldn't, because of the fact that he, the teacher, is homosexual. After saying this, he turns and gently puts his arms around the other teacher.

Later, I am in the same building with the schoolchildren, but it is no longer my home, or I am not familiar with it. I ask a boy where the bathrooms are, and he shows me one—it's a nice bathroom, with old fixtures and paneled in wood. As I sit on the toilet, the room rises--because it is also an elevator. I wonder briefly, as I flush, how the plumbing works in that case, and then assume it has been figured out.

In the Gallery

A woman I know, a visual artist, is trying to hang her work for a show. Her work is a single line of text pasted on the wall, with a transparent curtain suspended in front of it.

She is at the top of a ladder and cannot get down. She is facing out instead of in. The people down below tell her to turn around, but she does not know how.

When I see her next, she is down from the ladder. She is going from one person to the next, asking for help in hanging her artwork. But no one will help her. They say she is such a difficult woman.

The Piano

We are about to buy a new piano. Our old upright has a crack all the way through its sounding board, and other problems. We would like the piano shop to take it and resell it, but they tell us it is too badly damaged and cannot be resold to anyone else. They say it will have to be pushed over a cliff. This is how they will do it: two truck drivers take it to a remote spot. One driver walks away down the lane with his back turned while the other shoves it over the cliff.

The Piano Lesson

I am with my friend Christine. I have not seen her for a long time, perhaps seventeen years. We talk about music and we agree that when we meet again she will give me a piano lesson. In preparation for the lesson, she says, I must select, and then study, one Baroque piece, one Classical, one Romantic, and one Modern. I am impressed by her seriousness and by the difficulty of the assignment. I am ready to do it. We will have the lesson in one year, she says. She will come to my house. But then, later, she says she is not sure she will be returning to this country. Maybe, instead, we will have the lesson in Italy. Or if not Italy, then, of course, Casablanca. 🏛

Semi Semi Dash

The last time I saw Big Logos he was walking
to the Quantum Physics Store to buy magnets.
He told me his intentions. He was wearing

a jumpsuit with frayed cuffs. I thought the cuffs
got that way from him rubbing them against
his lips but he said they got that way

with age. We had two more blocks to walk.
"Once I do this, what are you going to do?"
he asked. "I wish you wouldn't do it," I said.

Big Logos bought the magnets & a crane
delivered them to his house. After he built
the 900-megahertz superconductor, I couldn't go

to his house anymore because I have all kinds
of metal in my body. I think if you love someone,
you shouldn't do that, build something like that,

on purpose, right in front of them.

Nicholas Hughes Is Dead

Tonight I went looking for the Mohawk
to tell him something, it was going to be
brilliant, whatever it was, in his language.

My Spanish teacher suggested I say—
"Do you want to come over & take something?"
but *take something* seemed vulgar

& I had already made love to him to myself
twice, so I was feeling nostalgic when
the taxi arrived & drove past the harbor

where the Norwegian Sun was no longer
docked, having given its passengers
to Ushuaia & having taken them back

to the Sun Club & the Body Waves Spa.
The driver recognized me, how nice,
from the weekend before. I am still here,

still drinking, still moored. At the bar,
I looked in the usual places for the Mohawk
& couldn't find him & there was no tonic

I wanted to drink without him. I went home
to read the headlines, hoping to find
the Mohawk's face in some other face,

& found Nicholas Hughes, fisherman
of the Alaskan seas, took his life
& dammit I'm at the wrong pole

I knew it! I meant to be at the north one
with Nick where I would've asked him
to take something from me instead.

AROUSED AT THE
FUNERAL

Books of the decade our editors don't want to see laid to rest.

Ravelstein

BY SAUL BELLOW

JON RAYMOND

It's perhaps no big surprise that Chicago, America's meatpacking town, is also America's great abattoir of politics. In the last decade alone the city has spit out not only a chief executive in its liberal Saul Alinsky mold but an entire administration packed with goons from its Leo Straussian neoconservative wing. One could almost define a national political dialectic by way of the Windy City alone, with its opposing poles of populism and snobbery fighting for primacy, though who'd be the populist and who the elitist would probably be subject to debate.

In any case, the community-organizing side of the equation is currently in ascendance, leaving those of us still puzzling over the reign of Greenspan and co.—indeed, over the soul life of neoconservatism in general—to keep the candle of memory alive. For this, we turn to Saul Bellow's final novel, *Ravelstein* (2000), in search of lingering clues. Published the very year George W. Bush was first elected, the book's fictionalized subject is none other than University of Chicago culture warrior, mentor of Paul Wolfowitz and Norman Podhoretz, among others, and decades-long Bellow confrere Allan Bloom, most famous as the author of *The Closing of the American Mind*—a jeremiad against multiculturalism, feminism, and all things non-canonical—and as a grandee at the center of a veritable fraternity of Republican power-mongers. Bellow, a neocon fellow traveler himself, paints a portrait of his dear friend in vivid colors, offering the reader insight, one hopes, not only into a daring conservative thinker, but also, perhaps, into a whole intellectual movement as well.

The book opens, ironically enough, in France, with Bellow surrogate Chick sharing coffee and brioche with Bloom surrogate Ravelstein in the Hôtel de Crillon. Ravelstein is in an effulgent mood, having recently published a gigantic bestseller and thus finally coming into the money he has always spent so profligately anyway. He registers immediately as a creature of large and eccentric habits, splayed out in his kimono, smoking his Dunhills, holding forth on Keynes and the Bloomsbury group. "Nobody in the days before he struck it rich had ever questioned Ravelstein's need for Armani suits or Vuitton luggage," the demure Chick observes, "for Cuban cigars, unobtainable in the U.S., for the Dunhill accessories, for solid-gold Mont Blanc pens or Baccarat or Lalique crystal to serve wine in—or have it served. Ravelstein was one of those large men—large, not stout—whose hands shake when there are small chores to perform. The cause was not weakness but a tremendous eager energy that shook him when it was discharged."

The two friends proceed to talk. The first seventy pages or so of the book are mostly pure, high-minded Bellowian conversation, delivered, as usual, with a gusto bordering on ADD. We're treated to heavy-duty philosophizing cut with American concreteness of thinking, aggressively painted sketches of faces and backstories, anthropological non sequiturs, and learned political analysis. Along the way we find ourselves caught up in the genuinely affectionate rapport between two great lovers of ideas, eagerly glimpsing the intellectual world they inhabit, a world thick with big ideas, sure, but also lewd gossip, psychoanalytic speculation, and risible Borscht-belt jokes. It's a world not so different from the one seen in Bellow's long short stories, "Cousins" and "What Kind of Day Did You Have?" or even *Hertzog* in a way—a place that no one, barring perhaps Bellow himself, has ever actually lived in, but a powerful fantasy region nonetheless, at least as much so as the Left's dingier, more bohemian version. In Bellow's world, belletristic Jews jet-set between Chicago, New York, and Europe, parsing geopolitics with world leaders, making snap judgments of foreign academics, wearing Hermès ties, drinking wine from fine crystal. It's a heady scene, a veritable theater of masculine power, and in the male conversation one starts to make out the shape not only of Bellow's imagination, but the imaginations of his and Bloom's student offspring as well. Wolfowitz et al gain some color and scent in this well-appointed milieu, their postures and mental tics cohering into something like an overall weltanschauung. One hopes that, on the day this junta returns to power, as it most definitely will, this book remains near the top of the Bellow reading list, waiting to shed light onto the extra-ideological facets, the aesthetics, if you will, of the neocon lifestyle.

In the second half of the book, however, the tone shifts considerably, as Ravelstein, a gay man of decidedly pre-Stonewall vintage (he prefers the term "invert"), is stricken with AIDS, and here the book vaults far beyond any simple political reading. As Chick's friend deteriorates, and as Chick himself ponders the breakup of his marriage and the beginning of another, the specter of death falls all around. A man with a transplanted heart visits Ravelstein's deathbed, as does an elderly couple contemplating suicide. Chick debates the ethics of his acquaintance with a man named Grielescu, a former Romanian fascist most likely responsible, in some fashion, for mass murder. And then, in the book's final third, our portraitist himself undergoes a near-death experience following food poisoning in the Caribbean, and the book's ruminations on nihilism, Judaism, and the afterlife take on a harrowing, even hallucinatory aspect. *What happens when death arrives?* Chick is pressed to contemplate. "The pictures will stop" is the best he can come up with, though he approaches the question from many angles.

John Updike said that an author's successful late works are often characterized by a "translucent thinness." Relatively speaking, *Ravelstein* would be a decent example of that thesis. In it, we're no longer dished up the thick, rich liver pâté of Bellow's heartiest writing, but rather something smoother, a little less heart-clogging. The Bellow that emerges here is a surprisingly mellow guy, almost chastened with age, still disinterested to the point of subtle racism and misogyny in the world outside his class, but capacious within the folds of twentieth-century Jewish experience. In other words, he comes across as a pretty circumspect fellow, quite unlike the neocons we have come to know on TV and in the *American Spectator*, with their self-serving hawkishness, their highly selective consciences, their pseudo-Nietzschean contempt for human weakness of any kind.

The one thing we do learn from the book about that ilk is how they came to love their University of Chicago teachers so much. Ravelstein/Bloom is presented in a fiercely loving light, irascible, buoyant, charismatic to the end, and Chick/Bellow, his dutiful biographer, is at his most tender. But then again, the problem was never Bellow or Bloom themselves anyway, great writers and devoted teachers both. The problem was their students, who have so gladly adopted the teachers' poses—the Turnbull and Asser shirts, the Maria Callas recordings—as well as their prejudices, but so rarely their passionate practice of self-analysis.

Other Electricities

BY ANDER MONSON

CHESTON KNAPP

Ander Monson's *Other Electricities* (2005) is set on the Upper Peninsula of Michigan, that weird, jutting, northern claw part of the state that isn't the glove. The book's concerned, for the most part, with the penumbral place where the physical meets the emotional; how weather—our environment—bears on and mirrors our inner lives. I guess it'd be called a "novel in stories," but like so much else when we talk about this book, that deserves an asterisk, because many of the stories aren't stories, at least not in the way we typically understand them; they're lists, impressionistic riffs, flashes of poetry, and diagrams of radio schematics. The characters swirl in and out of these "stories" like something meteorological—a chart at the beginning helps us follow their relations and intertwined arcs and, further, a "Helpful Guide to the Characters" summarizes their importance to the narrative. After all that, though, it's probably snow and its consequences that can be said to be the book's main character. One consequence especially, death, hangs over the book like a heavily pregnant ceiling of cindery clouds; that of Liz, the "love interest / conundrum," does so in particular.

Let's look at the first actual sentence of the book, from a story where a young policeman, no more than nineteen, must relate to Liz's parents the news of her fatal car crash through the ice on prom night: "The snow is on everybody tonight—on upturned faces, reflected back in the irises of children in the window; on the hot back of your wife's neck as you know she's shoveling the snow at home; on the men chopping wood for the stove, warming themselves (as the Finnish proverb goes) twice." He's invoking Joyce's "The Dead" so intently here that Michael Furey might well have risen from that lonely churchyard on the hill to dance some kind of jig. Such transparent ambition would surely verge on hubris in a lesser writer's hands, but it becomes quickly clear that Monson's echoing Joyce here not to say, "Look at me, I'm like Joyce," but rather, "Isn't it still true that snow and death and loss and sadness and just plain-old psychic pain are all indissolubly bound up like the cords of some fantastic rope?"

And it's with this very rope that Monson ensnares and binds us as we read, rapt and saddened by such a mysterious place, a place haunted by so much demise and decay, so much ice and snow. People are constantly going "through the ice," either as the result of their own stupidity, as in the cases of the countless snowmobilers who try to race across it (a warning: "Never Snowmobile Drunk. Just Don't Do It."), or by chance, accident, or fate, as is the case with Liz. There are other deaths, too, the results of emphysema, car crash, even a murder.

In "Subtraction is the Only Worthwhile Operation," Monson writes, "This story is a reflex against grief." And while that may be true for the author during the process of creation, the resulting story distills for the reader this grief and presents it as new and raw, as something for us to breathe in and savor. Monson's stories do just that, they let grief breathe—and for those of us left behind, either after a death or after a story's creation, isn't that the sweetly bitter something sad we end up with after all?

Here's a little something from "Residue": "In the years since his brother's death, Christer has collected Christmas trees . . . He has a particular spot in the woods where he brings and suspends them, tied up by heavy twine, in oak trees. There is one old oak in the forest where sixteen desiccated pine trees dangle from its upper branches. . . . The trunks swing back and forth, and creak quietly in the wind. He hears one tiny silver berry bell tinkling, buried forgotten and deep." Residue means, of course, that which is left. After Christmas, the trees. After a storm, the snow, ice. After death, grief, distance.

In fact, the radio schematics that act as a kind of refrain throughout the book are paired with meditations on distance, addressed to some unidentified loved one, presumably Liz: "Dear, distance is the center of the world, unbearable like magma, untouchable like gas"; "Dear, some distances are accidental."

These deaths seem, to a certain degree, unavoidable, to be bearing down on the inhabitants of the Upper Peninsula like the imminent collision of a couple of titanic pressure systems. "Forecast" chronicles the weeks before the murder that "happens" in the book, the asterisk here being that we experience only the affects of the murder; with his certain narrative grace, Monson gives us only the residue of the act, which is all the more powerful. He writes, "All this will end in ink on newsprint, ink that bleeds off onto the hands under too much use. All this will end in ink in accidental overprinting on the press—the superimposition of the crime on the weather forecast page." And there you have it, what you could call a controlling image, among hundreds of images that demand to be considered a controlling image. A palimpsest of loss and weather, both vying to be called the prime text.

In his essay "Man and the Sea Shell," Paul Valéry wrote, "Common language is ill suited to describing forms, and I despair of expressing their whirling grace." And I feel a similar anxiety about diluting the power this book achieves through its strange, organic manner of accretion like—I can't help it—snow piling up on our brains. I could go on and on about how, through its manifold formal and structural innovations, *Other Electricities* achieves its intricate resonances, about how it's always tidally hurling you back into its world, how it's self-conscious without being annoyingly clever or coy—that it, in fact, displays a pointed and devastating vulnerability through that very self-consciousness. I could quote you image after image, line after line all the way to some Borgesian end—for nothing short of that could fully mine its complexly rich lode. It's a true shame that such a book would fly just enough under the radar to allow me to write about it here, but maybe the reading public can only handle so many formally innovative, challenging works at a time. Anyway, wasn't it Eliot who wrote, "Human kind / Cannot bear very much reality"? So I'll stop now and fulfill my contractual obligation by saying, in my best blurb-ese, "This is a damn fine piece of literary art, a real impressive achievement, especially considering it's a debut."

DAVID MARKSON

ROB SPILLMAN

David Markson is going down fighting, and he's not giving an inch to convention, zeitgeist, or potential sales. Born in 1927, Markson found success early with a series of genre novels; it helped that he was friends with Malcolm Lowry (about whom he wrote his Columbia dissertation, in 1952), Dylan Thomas, Conrad Aiken, and Jack Kerouac. One of his early novels, *The Ballad of Dingus Magee*, a parody of a Western, was turned into a mostly forgettable movie starring Frank Sinatra. At the time it would have been hard to imagine that his prose style would evolve, à la Mondrian, from crowd-pleasing genre fiction to spare, postmodern blocks of text, first with *Springer's Progress*, a nasty little novel about a middle-aged novelist, then to *Wittgenstein's Mistress*, an apocalyptic meta-novel featuring one- or two-sentence thought blasts, a book that David Foster Wallace called "pretty much the high point of experimental fiction in this country" and upon which Markson could have built a po-mo empire. Instead, he refined his pointillism into a quartet of "novels," *Reader's Block, This Is Not a Novel, Vanishing Point*, and *The Last Novel*, which feature a near total abandonment of narrative.

Published in paperback by three small presses (god bless you Counterpoint, Dalkey Archive, and Shoemaker & Hoard), each of these end-game novels is made up of one- or two-sentence blocks regarding various intellectual subjects, including:

- Facts about famous writers and artists—"Berlioz read every Fenimore Cooper novel as quickly as it appeared. And admitted that fully four hours after he finished *The Prairie* he was weeping over the death of Natty Bumppo."

- Anti-Semitism—"Knut Hamsun was an anti-Semite. And was so blatantly sympathetic with the Germans in both world wars that thousands of Norwegians mailed him back copies of his novels in contempt."

- The nature of narrative—"Stories happen only to people who know how to tell them. Said Thucydides."

- The Classics—"*Andromache. Alcestis. Helen. Medea. The Bacchae.* Each of which Euripides ends with his chorus

speaking an identical verse—to the effect that the ways of the gods are unpredictable."

- Big ideas, mainly in the form of unattributed quotes, many of which are not in English—"*Dormir nonchalamment à l'ombre de ses seins.*"

- Morality—"I am become death, the shatterer of worlds. Recited J. Robert Oppenheimer from the *Bhagavad-Gita* at Alamogordo."

- And, always, the starving artist and his legacy—"Raphael, Caravaggio, Watteau, Van Gogh, and Toulouse-Lautrec each died at thirty-seven."

- With occasional nods to the "author" and "reader"—"Should he give him children, if he is still being autobiographical?"

Reading these novels is like spending hours with a crazy uncle who happens to have an encyclopedic knowledge of every book ever written, every painting ever painted, and every piece of music ever composed. And who disgorges bits of knowledge in an endless, unfathomable pattern. And yet! Yet, somehow, Markson spins this erudition and intelligence into self-conscious webs, narratives without narratives, micro-poems that miraculously accrue and cohere into meditations on the creative life, art, and intellectualism.

What emerges is a portrait of sickly, lonely, deviant genius, with "nothing now, but my books." These novels are a remarkable achievement, what should be required reading for anyone aspiring to create.

Here is how *Reader's Block* ends:

> And Reader? And Reader?
>
> In the end one experiences only one's self.
> Said Nietzsche.
>
> Nonlinear. Discontinuous. Collage-like. An assemblage.
>
> Wastebasket.

The Big House: A Century in the Life of an American Summer Home

BY GEORGE HOWE COLT

JEANNE MCCULLOCH

When I was young, probably about eight or nine years old, I confused being "home sick" with the term "homesick." This was around the same time that I was first being invited to spend the night at the houses of friends. At nearly every sleepover, my mother would send me off with her favorite admonishment in houseguest politesse—don't use too many of their towels—and I was off. Yet deep into the night, it would hit me that the bed I was in was not my bed; the sliver of light through the window did not take on the familiar slant across the floor, and the very smell of the sheets, the almost spookily static sounds of someone else's family sleeping in the dark, was so different than my own that a strange sensation would well up inside and I'd believe that I was sick and needed to go home. After my tearful phone call, my father would come to get me, coat thrown over his pajamas, cuffs hastily tucked into his galoshes, hair uncombed, and bring me home. We were silent, but for our quiet yawns, during the cab ride through the streets of Manhattan in the early Sunday morning before dawn. I believed homesickness was an ailment, for which the only cure was the comfort of my own bed. But perhaps really the cure was getting a little older, when leaving home was an adventure and "home" was—to borrow an Elvis Costello line—not where it used to be, but anywhere you hang your head—in other words, in the comfort you take with you; that emotional, psychological region we call—for lack of a better term—true homeland security.

George Howe Colt's 2003 memoir, *The Big House*, has the subtitle *A Century in the Life of an American Summer Home*. In essence, it is one man's account of a love affair with a house. It is also a multi-textured inquiry into the questions: How does a house become a home? And what, exactly, is a home?

Over the years, I've asked many people to tell me the first thing they imagine when they think of home. A man who grew up on army bases told me it was the image of a pie on the table, the pie being the only constant in a childhood on the road. For another it's the smell of a linen closet, or a nursery song, or in one case the sound of a car siren screeching down Madison Avenue in the night. In Colt's case, the home

in question is an early-twentieth-century shingled "cottage," so called because of the style of architecture, not the size, which in many cases was considerable—the Colt house being a sixteen-bedroom example. Colt's family home was built in 1902 on Buzzards Bay, in Cape Cod, by his ancestor Ned Atkinson; it became the one common gathering area for five generations of Atkinsons (the "Ats," as they were known) and Colts—all of whose voices echo, like benevolent ghosts, through the pages of his book.

As Colt's Aunt Ellen says of trifle, the family dessert, *The Big House* has many layers. On one layer, it is a history of the seaside summer home through the ages, long before the word "summer" was used as a verb. But *The Big House* is also, and primarily, a paean to the timeless ways of the WASP.

Colt, along with his wife, the writer Anne Fadiman, and two children, is spending a final summer in the house before it is sold. This is a world where houses have names (the "*Big House*" was originally the "*Rooftree*"); the rooms have names too: "Grandma's Dressing Room" remains the room originally occupied by Grandma, even if she's long dead. Volumes of leatherbound guest books are lovingly placed and replenished in the hallway throughout generations. In the milieu of the Brahmin WASP, Colt writes, the only thing more vulgar than talking about money is spending it, and tennis balls are recycled as often as names; both are believed to be in short supply (though one assumes balls are not replaced with the same WASP iconic flair—Dunlap Jr., Dunlap the Third, Uncle Dunny, Little Dun-Dun, etc.). Family tennis itself is less a game than a reenactment of politesse and revenge, better taken place over the slightly more courteous proceedings of the court than in the barbs subtly and obliquely exchanged—because WASPS are never overt—over many cocktails at sundown.

These things would be easy to parody, but, distinctively, *The Big House* is a brave celebration of family. I want to say brave, because, speaking as one myself, it's hard not to sound clichéd and satirical about that particular brand of American, the Northeast WASP. Though as a breed they've had their day in the literary sun, at the hands of such masters as John Cheever and Robert Lowell (who famously coined the term "Mayflower screwballs" in one of his poems), their struggles often appear as those of loafers in loafers, a repressed gang of lock-jawed yacht-clubbers with drinking problems and names like Buffy. It is hard to do what Colt does, which is to somehow speak of people like Aunt Buffy (yes, he has one) without irony, and to give an honest, respectful portrayal of their struggles with issues of health and wealth, and in so doing imbue the house, or, more accurately, the "home,"—that basic yet elusive concept—with its double-edged reality: it is both an anchor and a constriction, which, as Colt perceives it, ties us to the past, but also ties us down.

Having loved and lost a family seaside home myself, I was relieved—as I hope Colt was—that for reasons of economics it was impossible for *his* family to hang onto their beloved house. In the long run, the resonance is in something Colt's mother told him: "It isn't how much money you have, it's how much love you have." It's the love that is the home, not the house.

When I first came upon *The Big House*, I remember underlining one passage: "How long does it take to say good-bye to a room?" On the surface, it's a strange question, but when the house is the family home, the answer is that, ideally, one never has to. "I have always thought of it as home," Colt writes, "if home is the one place that will be in your bones forever." It is in his good-bye to the house that the true beauty of his prose becomes most buoyant. The house, like an old family member, is laid to rest in an elegiac passage about the wind:

> When the wind races up Buzzards Bay, as it does almost every afternoon, it plays the Big House like a flute . . . By now the house is so worn that even the gentlest breeze can produce a sigh . . . . 'Oh, if only these walls could talk,' guests in the Big House often say. I've always felt the walls do talk, and the sound they make is sometimes a wail, sometimes a sigh, and sometimes a joyous hullabaloo. The wind seems to come not from outside but from inside. To me it's the house's song, a blend of the voices of all the people who have lived here over the last hundred years. Now that we are selling the house, the

voices sound more urgent than ever, trying to make themselves heard. And as I lie here, Anne sleeping beside me, Susannah in Grandma's Dressing Room, Henry in the Little Nursery, I wonder: When the house is sold, what will happen to the wind?

In my garden in New York City, there is a forty-year old tortoise who has lived there much longer than the recent residents. In the winter, she (we have no idea who decided she was a she, much less who named her Sister Martha) hibernates somewhere underground. In the spring she reappears, miraculously, it seems to us, to soak up the sun until Thanksgiving, when she quietly disappears again. Sister Martha has always seemed to me a testimony of the value of learning to carry your home with you—in her case on her back, for us ideally in our heads, or as Colt would have it, in our bones. But golden summers, like golden families, often shine most brightly in our memories—or, in the case of *The Big House*, in a fine, elegiac memoir—of the place we all long to return to, if only in concept, and if only because, in concept, they have to take us in.

Let's Talk About Love: A Journey to the End of Taste

BY CARL WILSON

BRIAN DeLEEUW

People like me who spend much of their time reading and proselytizing for literature are almost inevitably, at some point, forced to confront the possibility that they are perhaps elitist assholes. I could maybe avoid this if I surrounded myself exclusively with other writers and publishing types (or plunged my head, ostrich-like, into the deep sands of reclusion or super-specialized academia), but that's both implausible and, in its homogeneity at the very least, undesirable. If I'm going to be an engaged member of contemporary urban America, my preoccupation with literature is going to be implicitly questioned simply by the fact that I spend a lot of time on something that the culture at large does not. The impulse is to answer in the negative: I read books because I don't care about

CSI or Iron Man or *Us Weekly*. After all, "Tastes are composed of a thousand distastes," or so said Paul Valéry. Which is of course a not-so-implicit judgment on the people who do care about those things. And even if, instead, I choose to argue in the positive and clamber upon my rickety soap-box to declaim those beloved virtues of literature—depth, subtlety, some squirrelly notion of truth—I am asserting the primacy of a particular value system, my value system: these things I care about are more important than the things you care about. Append an apologetic "to me" to this statement, and I slide into a relativistic morass; leave the statement as is, and I am the aforementioned asshole.

Which brings me to Céline Dion.

When Canadian music journalist Carl Wilson decided to investigate the construction of taste in his excellent contribution to Continuum's 33 ^{1}/$_3$ series, *Let's Talk About Love: A Journey to the End of Taste*, "by looking closely at a very popular artist I really, really can't stand, Dion was waiting at the front of the line." And why not? Who likes Céline Dion anyway? Well, it turns out, aside from the stereotypical soccer moms and gay-diva enthusiasts, Céline's biggest fans apparently include war-weary Iraqis, Ghanaian taxi drivers, China's minister of culture, and Jamaica's roughest roughnecks, one of whom explained, "Bad man have fi play love tune fi show 'dat them a lova too." So what's Wilson's problem? And is it a problem he should care about solving?

His approach is to delve into the histories of two equally unfathomable concepts: that of a universal, disinterested hierarchy of taste and that of Céline Dion herself. For the investigation of the latter, we get sharp and lucidly-written précis on Québécoise culture and politics, the history of schmaltz, and the global hybridization of pop music; for the former, discussions of Hume and Kant, the Russian-American artist duo Vitaly Komar and Alexandir Melamid, and the French sociologist Pierre Bourdieu. (Bourdieu, for his part, declared much like Valéry that "tastes are perhaps first and foremost distastes, disgusts provoked by horror or visceral intolerance of the tastes of others;" he also appeared to believe the whole enterprise of culture was to, in Wilson's words, "perpetuate and reproduce the class structure" through the strategic deployment of "distinction.") Wilson also looks closely at his own aesthetic prejudices and what affirming or denying them might mean; it was, after all, his experience as an authenticity-obsessed music journalist now mellowing into more tolerant middle-age that prompted the writing of this book in the first place.

While the Céline trivia is fascinating—her manager and now-husband René Angélil mortgaged his house to pay for her debut album; her first big international break came when she won the 1982 World Popular Song Festival in Tokyo; she has thirteen siblings—what makes this book compulsory reading for anybody invested in the arts are its conclusions about aesthetics and democracy. Wilson begins by wondering if he could possibly learn to love Céline's music; he concludes, "perhaps my experiment was too tyrannical. It would be no solution to say we have to love everything, the equivalent of loving nothing." Instead, it is important to give Céline's album *Let's Talk About Love* "a sympathetic hearing, to credit that others find it lovable and ask what that can tell me about music (or globalism, or sentimentality) in general." For Wilson, the end result of such sympathy on a mass scale is democracy itself, by which he means "not a limp open-mindedness, but actively grappling with people and things not like me, which brings with it the perilous question of what I am like." He continues: "Democracy, that dangerous, paradoxical and mostly unattempted ideal, sees that the self is insufficient, dependent for definition on otherness, and chooses not only to accept that but to celebrate it, to stake everything on it." Since the lover of literature in America today exists in a more or less constant state of "grappling with people and things not like me," it seems important to realize that such an oppositional stance can be mined

for both knowledge of others (but not in a condescending way) and self-knowledge (but not in a narcissistic way), rather than just the usual—for me, at least—cocktail of irritation and self-righteousness.

Wilson's book was released in December 2007 to review coverage of moderate volume and positive bent; in the very month of this writing—March 2009—he appeared on Comedy Central's *The Colbert Report*, which gave his book a delayed bump in publicity and sales. All of which would suggest this particular piece of writing is not exactly "lost;" yet I suspect the book, filed as music criticism or pop-cultural studies, may still be unknown to many people concerned with the role of literature in contemporary American society. This would be unfortunate at any time, but today, when it finally seems as though all the ritualized talk of publishing's impending implosion may be for once warranted, books such as Wilson's—able to address the knottiness of cultural value without elitist hyperventilation or populist schadenfreude—are more valuable than ever.

Essence and Alchemy: A Natural History of Perfume

BY MANDY AFTEL

ELISSA SCHAPPELL

And in the beginning there was smell, our most primal sense, that which draws the infant to the breast, the lover to her quarry in the dark. Scent is our most profound trigger of emotion and memory, and yet an author who yearns to enrich her writing with olfactory details is at a loss. One can cast back to Proust, who found his muse in the madeleine, or Dickens, who wallowed in the stench of London's alleyways, or Shakespeare, who waxed romantic at the smell of a rose, but where is the contemporary writer at whose knee one can learn after thoroughly exhausting Patrick Süskind's novel *Perfume*? Where can she find the language, the courage to describe the smell of a new Apple computer still in the box, the aroma of an unwashed tween with a spray tan cruising the mall?

Look no further than the pages of Mandy Aftel's enchanting book, *Essence and Alchemy: A Natural History of Perfume*, which was published in 2001. At turns charming and erotic, scientific and scholarly, Aftel's illustrated compendium delves into the history, science, and mystery of scent, while guiding those aspirants eager to learn the ancient and esoteric art of perfumery. A more passionate or learned mentor would be hard to find, for Aftel, founder of Aftelier Perfumes, is, in the age-old tradition of perfumers before her, a true seeker, on a quest to extract the "quinta essentia, the spark of divinity at the heart of living things."

In *Essence and Alchemy* this quest leads readers deep into the past, to the ritual anointing of the dead by the Egyptians, the aromatizing of the Roman baths, and the followers of Mohammad, who imbued the mortar they used to erect their mosques with a musk that, with the sun's heat, infused their worship with scent.

Unlike the majority of modern perfumers, Aftel, a pioneer in the natural perfume world, preaches the use of traditional methods—beakers and Bunsen burners—and purely natural elements. While synthetic perfumes are capable of mimicking the essence of a scent, they are incapable of reproducing the spirit, soulfulness, and energy that exists only in a living thing's natural state, in the way that one can copy Anna Pavlova's arabesques or imitate the distinctive style of pianist Glenn Gould, but never possess the magic. A night-blooming Jasmine born on the vine hardly resembles that born in a test-tube.

The body can't be fooled. Even while beauty conglomerates market pheromone-laced cologne engineered to spark desire, it is, Aftel (the mistress of aphrodisiacs) confides, the rank odor of animal musk and sweat that really gets our rocks off.

It is the same with books on scent. While others exist, it's a tragedy that this enchanting little tome—which garnered bouquets of praise when published nearly a decade ago—has, sadly, faded away. It is nearly as rare, it seems, as ambergris.

Essence and Alchemy is in a class of its own because Aftel is not simply a perfume aficionado or a "Nose" trained to discern the subtle complexities of fragrance (laying waste to the adage a rose is a rose is a rose), but one blessed with the gift. In the way that a composer who hears a symphony is able to mentally transcribe the notes, or an artist to draw out the soul of a landscape with a piece of charcoal, Aftel not only distills the ineffable, the beauty and voluptuousness of a budding English rose, but intoxicates us with heady descriptions of its procurement.

If that's not enough, Aftel also assumes the role of teacher.

Aftel's vision of scent is as a mode of artistic expression drawing on a palette of scents, an orchestration of olfactory chords, capable of capturing place and time in memory and transforming consciousness in unexpected ways. In the spirit of passing along her craft, Aftel leads the apprentice alchemist step-by-step through the composition of his or her own unique eau de moi.

Essence and Alchemy will inspire you to stop and, yes, smell the roses. It will open a window into your imagination and, whether you are inventing a world in a beaker or on the page, let in the scent of something exotic and divine.

BARRY
HANNAH

Tom Franklin

Interview, with Handgun

"Suicide lurks in almost anyone intelligent."
—BARRY HANNAH

Oxford, Mississippi, is a famously literary town—the mayor owns the bookstore and rides a bicycle to work. Apprentice writers fumble in the dark at Faulkner's grave, pouring bourbon over the stone or leaving pencils erected in the dirt. Local fireman Larry Brown and lawyer John Grisham have become famous novelists. Bartenders read. Menus have items named after books. Writers are always touring through, and the night I'm remembering now, George Singleton had given a brilliant reading at Square Books. Now we were all upstairs in the City Grocery Bar, spilled out onto its ivied balcony with our drinks and cigarettes, laughing, a spice of fall chill in the air. Charged with finding someplace to eat, I'd made reservations for six people at eight o'clock at the crowded,

chic new restaurant down the street. I'd already called to up our number to ten, but when, at seven-thirty, Barry Hannah unexpectedly walked up the stairs, unwrapping his scarf from around his neck, I knew I'd have to call again.

Sad truth is, Barry rarely goes to bars any more. His health keeps him away, or his current work-in-progress, *The Sick Soldier at your Door*. He's been dry for so long that most of the bars have different names now than when he drank in them; Murff's was Ireland's then and City Grocery was Syd & Harry's. Still, every bartender in town knows him. They have stories.

But now, tonight, here he was. He smiled at the applause that met him as he reached the top of the stairs, his name called not just from students and literary types, but from the lawyers, chemists, and construction workers lining the bar and even the bouncer, looking up from his

Larry McMurtry. Barry hung his scarf and then his coat on the rack and waited for Chip, the bartender, to bring him his Coke and ask if he'd been fishing lately.

"Not anywhere good, baby," he said, smiling.

He shook everyone's hand but in a moment he was on the balcony, sitting across from Singleton, tracing lines in the air with his cigarette, drinking his Coke and telling stories, his laugh crackling in the high eaves of the old buildings. I called the restaurant and upped us to twelve and pushed our reservation back another half an hour. Because usually, if Barry stops by a bar, it won't be for long. But that night, in the fall air, he blessed us with his company and stories and stayed and talked and laughed and smoked. I kept moving the reservation and adding people until the hostess told me that even if they had a table that big we couldn't have it because they were closing. I hung up and went back outside with a new Bud Light and soon was laughing with everyone else.

At some point Barry disappeared. We looked around, then someone pointed below us, in the street. He was down by his motorcycle in his leather jacket, rewrapping his neck, and, without a helmet, he mounted the bike and kicked it to life. We called our goodnights from the balcony, not yet aware how hungry and drunk we were, that we needed a captain, a plan—we didn't know that in a moment filmmakers Joey Lauren Adams and Joe York would kick open the balcony doors with Popeye's chicken

and biscuits for all—we simply watched as Barry gunned his Kawasaki and began his slow circle of the town square, raising, in my memory at least, a triumphant fist.

———— · ————

Oxford writer Neil White, who used to play tennis with Barry Hannah, says that despite being taller, twenty years younger, a nonsmoker, and a player with better form, he could never beat Barry. Not once.

"Why?" I asked.

Neil couldn't say. "There's just . . . something about him."

It's true. There is.

In the last several years, he's beat cancer twice and had heart surgery. He kept writing, oxygen-bound, weak, the whole time.

"Oh, he's scrappy," says Susan, his wife, herself battling a recurrence of breast cancer. He met her in the early eighties, drunk, at the Hoka Theater in Oxford. He was wearing a sports jacket and swimming trunks, and he asked her to marry him—that very day—because she had a carport where he could park his boat (that she was gorgeous and tough didn't hurt). Now Susan and Barry have seven full-time dogs. Barry lounges in the backyard in their aboveground pool, hooked to his oxygen, and tries not to smoke. He rarely drinks these days. An occasional beer. A vodka and tonic. "He's the best teacher ever," Neil says. "He can talk about the art of writing like nobody I've ever heard."

Yes, he was wild when he was younger. Stories abound in Oxford. Knives thrown at ceilings. Firearms, bows and arrows, drugs, police, and always the drinking. But that was two decades ago.

Due to the illnesses of himself and his wife, Barry and I postponed this interview a few times. But at last, on the day he was coming over, I cleared the house of children and shut off the phone. He was prompt, as he always is, and we sat outside, on the porch of my little office facing our backyard and, over the fence, the neighbors' yard. It was nippy but sunny. We'd hoped to talk while shooting some guns, planned to go out to our pal writer Ace Atkins's pond in rural Paris, Mississippi, and fire pistols and rifles and shotguns at cans and clay pigeons. Because that didn't happen, perhaps as a consolation, Barry produced, at the beginning of the interview, a derringer. He passed it over and it was heavier than it looked; they always are. I unclicked it to watch the butts of the two cartridges rise, then snapped it shut and aimed it at a Bradford pear tree, the swing set, a redbird. Then gave it back.

At some point we started to talk about fishing, and I remembered to turn on my tape recorder.

BARRY HANNAH: You've got to be good and lucky too, to catch a good fish. I've been neither in the five years that we've tried. You're talking two charmed fishermen here, and we cancel it out of each other.

TOM FRANKLIN: I used to be a good fisherman, until you came along.

BH: Yeah. That was my story.

TF: A couple of the times we've fished, at Wall Doxey State Park, I noticed our different styles, approaches. I'd go to one corner of the dock and put a cork out there, or two corks out there, and just watch them the whole time, moving one here or there, a few feet maybe. And you're wandering all over the docks and around the banks, climbing onto limbs.

BH: Probably trying for the big bass.

TF: You're not going to let me make this a metaphor, are you? How most of the rest of us find our little spot and sit there safely on the dock. And you're on the other side of the lake, on a log, about to fall in, casting some lubed-up space-age lure?

BH: [Laughs.] As the writer, I'm always the last to know. I'm just doing what I can at the time.

TF: You've had at least one fishing story in each of your collections. What is it about fishing that draws you to that subject in your writing?

BH: The pull of the unknown, underwater. That tug, that tug. Ever since I was old enough to hold a cane pole, fishing's been a joyful, natural sport and feast, you know. And you also gotta be crafty to catch a good fish, one you want to eat. We ate largemouth bass here in those days. Nowadays I let them go because I don't need them.

TF: [pointing his pencil at the pistol on the table]: You're a collector of firearms—pistols, rifles, shotguns. Does shooting get you closer to your characters?

BH [looks stricken]: No, no. Shooting is just a hobby, a target hobby. Now I shoot beer cans, not mammals. I get a peckerwood thrill out of seeing this thing in my hand lurch and blow something up in the air. That's all.

It may get me closer to history if I hold a weapon of an era, so you would know how heavy the weapon was, say the derringer in the 1880s. Or up to the 1920s. But you don't really need to own it, all you need to do is see it. But lately I'm horrified by guns. The wholesale shooting has become so awful in America. Not only are guns cheap and used by cowards but they're also just too convenient to end things or give you tension in stories.

TF: Can you talk about how your short stories, as you see them, have progressed? How, say, are the stories in *High Lonesome* different from the ones in *Airships*?

BH: I know my *Bats Out of Hell* stories are longer. I just had a fit of writing after my father's death. And it was almost like glossololia or something, I couldn't quit writing stories, they just kept coming. Short, long. I'm typing like a fiend, or writing by hand. Which is something I trust. And *Airships* was edited beautifully by Gordon Lish. He was getting me the most out of every sentence. He would have probably pared down the stories of *High Lone-*

some a good deal. I became my own short story editor after learning from Gordon, in workshop. I like a long story, but nobody wants to publish a long story unless you're, say, Richard Ford. It's just a mode that's unfortunately not hot now.

The short story was what it absolutely was when I was in college: Hemingway, Cheever, J. D. Salinger, Flannery O'Connor, Eudora Welty, and Faulkner. Their short works were, I guess, the best to teach in the classroom. I mean, I'm like most dudes, I didn't read much in college that wasn't assigned. I thought I was doing plenty. I'd read the things that were assigned in other courses and just hated them—what I didn't want to know, I didn't learn.

TF: You mentioned Gordon Lish, and I wanted to ask, in a little more detail, about your own editing process.

BH: *The Sick Soldier at Your Door* has come back from my editor at Grove—

TF: This is the new book.

BH: Yeah. And I was in such despair. I love the voice so much, but I'd forgotten what I try to teach students, and what I love myself. I had done the book in monologues and forgotten the tension a book needs all the way through. Monologues were the wrong way to do it . . .

TF: Can you describe your process of working on *The Sick Soldier At Your Door?*

> I'm in remission, but there's still some pain, some depression. But there are no excuses, finally; you don't lose a minute, if you're alive.

BH: The overview took a long time on this book. Now, after seven years of dither, *Sick Soldier* will be short stories. It was never a novel. I just couldn't find this simple truth and punished myself needlessly by thinking too much, gathering too much. I've done this for three years before so this was a record and hell to live. However, I'm excited by the stories. Now, I can jump to with zeal and purpose every morning.

TF: I've heard it was a sequel to *Ray*.

BH: The book will be no sequel. A possible son of Ray, El Burden, appears in one story as a lay preacher on a yellow Triumph motorcycle. He has fallen on hard times. His alcoholic nephew is an arsonist holding Burden's last forty thousand dollars.

TF: So how will you go about putting the tension in, or—

BH: Well, it's there already, just buried. I need to cut it down to a nub, I hope, about like *Ray*. The original *Ray*, where I started with about seven hundred pages. And now it [*The Sick Soldier*] is around three hundred pages. In the end I'll probably get it down to a 130-page book. I hope. That's what it needs. A reason to read it.

TF: Is that typical for your process, to write a lot more than you use? With both novels and stories?

BH: Yep. I can't bear to revise. I want to give it away to an editor. "Please, do it for me!" I can't revise myself very well. [Richard] Bausch, a very fine writer, he hates the first draft. But me? I love the first draft. It's just different with us. Richard Ford, I asked his wife, does he ever sit down and dash off a story? She says, "Absolutely not." He's very meticulous. For Tim O'Brien, a paragraph a day is a miracle. He works slowly, like a gem cutter, to see if this is true—if this is true, if it's natural, if it's right. And that's the way, that's the measure of a writer.

TF: Can you talk about the autobiographical aspects of *Ray* and *Sick Soldier*?

BH: I've fought autobiography because, in my sick days, it's kind of shut-in literature I don't like. My work always requires me in the world, living and trying. Otherwise I might end up writing self-conscious meditative poetry, for God's sake.

TF: What's it like when you're on fire with a story? Like the ones in *Bats Out of Hell*?

BH: I'm typing like a fiend. Or writing longhand in a number of school journals.

———— ·•· ————

TF: How has illness affected your work?

BH: Lately, I think medication has gotten in my way. I'm in remission, but there's still some pain, some depression. But there are no excuses, finally; you don't lose a minute, if you're alive. It'll all count. Every sentence. If you become one of the suffering, you're apt to become more tender in your stories. The illnesses, having been lived, do not invite me as a subject. Sickness stops my creativity. I'm no Proust. I must feel a mild ecstasy for my writing to be any good. You don't get this with catheters, depressive trips to the doctor's offices, chemotherapy—believe me.

I mean, finally I got of an age where age was interfering with my work. I don't have the energy for everything. And I don't think I was born to be more than a lieutenant. Possibly. I don't like responsibility for everybody, I don't want to know everybody, I don't want to micromanage, I don't have these—I don't need power.

TF: Obviously you have less time and energy, but has it affected your writing process?

BH: I've become a major movie buff. I used to scorn people like me. But now I have all kinds of videos, DVDs, and I passively sit back and watch them. Even a bad movie can teach you something. They are the art of our day.

[William] Harrison taught me that back in the sixties. But for a writer the Hollywood experience is so stupid and devastating. Harrison's spent much time out there. And had a little success, finally, one or two financial bonanzas.

TF: Does becoming a movie buff make you want to go back and start writing movies again?

BH: No. I made the mistake of trying—well, it wasn't a mistake, it was a financial necessity—of wanting to be a screenplay writer, with [Robert] Altman getting me some jobs. There was a writers' strike going on out there then, and I wasn't a member of the union. We were just pitching back and forth at each other and being pleasant. But I was no good at it because I depend on everything else that a screenplay does not do. None of my good stuff is in a screenplay, nothing of it.

TF: And your work would be very hard to adapt, for obvious reasons.

BH: See, things are so simple. I think Altman won an Oscar once for a screenplay he did overnight. See? The great smash *Aliens*, Tom McGuane told me, was written by a couple of guys on speed in about two days. I don't doubt it, but it's so simple, I might not be able to do it. And I think that's what writers often realize—that is so simple, so true, what have I been thinking man, this guy is on it, he's on the bean. It's the simplicity we're after, isn't it?

TF: Yeah. Why is it so hard to achieve?

BH: Noise. You allow the world to get in. When I was young, I drank socially, in revelry, but I got into trouble with booze because it closed things out beautifully for me. It was a medication, and you even get physically deaf—I didn't know that until a few years ago—through beer. That's why people at bars are just screaming, it seems. See, if you're straight and you go in there, everybody's screaming at each other, even if there's not a band. You actually go deaf, and it's not just because you're hard of hearing; the alcohol numbs the hearing. So, it was getting in that zone, the quietness where I could find my own voice, and alcohol helped. It's a crying shame that it's bad for you, or that you must increase the quantity if you've got a disease, you know, you must increase until you're ill.

TF: And people worried that you wouldn't be able to write more when you stopped drinking.

BH: I did, hugely. That was one of the major problems I had stopping. I was in great fear that I would lose all of my stuff.

TF: But then, *Bats Out of Hell*.

BH: Yeah. I really put more effort or was more on fire with natural juice for *Bats Out*

Some lines, collected by Jake Rubin, a former student of Barry's, from Barry's classes:

Hug a tree. Get in there with the dogs. Save a dog. Or take the leap of absurdity and love your wife.

....

It's common wisdom: funerals make you horny.

....

Writing is a lonely business. You've got to be your own party.

....

I've been sick of irony for forty years.

....

I'm sick of reading about dysfunctional families. I've been married three times. It's like a marine reading about Vietnam.

....

You want to write what the camera can't get. I've never seen a reality TV show worth a shit. I'm sorry. Adverbial, adjectival writing—that's for old blue-haired women.

....

If we have any more preachers in Southern lit, I'm gonna vomit. Just as a comment.

....

Like rap music and rock and roll, you don't have to be able to write to be a writer.

> I've never been interested in intellectual experiments. I prefer to thrill people in their guts rather than in their heads.

of Hell, so I like that book probably a little better than *Airships*, because *Airships* was thirty years ago. I love it that *Airships* has gotten fame and notoriety now that it is being taught.

TF: You know, you've had some famous students over the years. I thought you might just talk about Larry Brown a little bit, you know—what's it been like seeing him start, and then seeing his entire career?

BH: Okay, number one, Larry was never my student in a class. But it's like my relationship to Jim Whitehead up at Arkansas—he's a beautiful poet but he never taught me. Except he taught me everything, he taught me when we shot pool, he taught me in the bar at Roger's Recreation [in Fayetteville, Arkansas]. Big, tall man, passionate about poetry, quoted Yeats, you know. He was a bad pool shot, though. [Laughs] But I said, "My God, you know, that's a good life." If you're that big and athletic and feel that much for poems, I mean, they gave me a shot in the arm and I'm a smaller guy, but I never had any interest in being ultra-sensitive. But I wanted to write—so did Larry.

Larry started out wanting to be Stephen King, wanting to entertain so hugely, that

he wrote for vast financial success, which is a really wonderful motive. Except he hadn't found the voice yet. He took a course here at Ole Miss under Josephine Haxton—whose nom de plume is Ellen Douglas—and that's the only college course he had as far as I know, ever. But he started reading Conrad and Flannery O'Connor, and he found his own voice, that natural Mississippi hill country voice, after a hundred failures. All of his early stories were deeply bad, and I didn't want to hurt his feelings because he was so sincere. So I looked them over, and I don't remember teaching him anything, but maybe he learned something. He learned that he wanted a little pain and that he wanted out of that fire station [Brown was a fireman for nineteen years], didn't want to be trapped there anymore, that was part of his life that he'd like to quit. But his financial motivation was right honest, and the fact that he finally learned all the craft he needed in one class is not surprising. Because he was a brilliant learner, a fast learner. At the firehouse, you don't get to be a captain just for showing up. And he was in his thirties when he was captain. That's pretty good, I think.

TF: How has your teaching changed over the years?

BH: It's gotten a lot simpler. The things that I do well in my own work, I didn't ever think about, because I'd been trained on good storytelling and helped by a few good teachers. But outside of beginning, middle, and end and "thrill us," what else is there to teach? There's no theory, there's nothing that guarantees publication. I've never been interested in intellectual experiments. I prefer to thrill people in their guts rather than in their heads. With some of the MFA writing I read now, I wonder, "My God, didn't anybody get it across that you've got to entertain?" You're fortunate if what entertains you entertains the crowd also.

It's impossible for me to behave as if I were thirty-five when I was writing *Airships*—it's impossible. And I must say you don't necessarily gain a lot by age; you sometimes are in danger of becoming the old hack plagiarizing his own former work. That's probably why the old often bore people, they just say the same damn things over and over, and they just deal in truisms. That's the mass of America, one truism after another. For instance, the word motherfucker is a truism now. It's just empty. It used to be an exciting word because it's the worst thing you can imagine, you know? But now it's just a weak flat noun.

It may be just my time of life, but I've been teaching better, I hope. My essays have gotten a lot better. But what I want is what I had in *Airships* and *High Lonesome* and *Bats Out of Hell* and *Captain Maximus:* joy. Joy, just joy, just jump in there because you're onto it. You've gotta write it. You feel it deep in the pit of your stomach.

The River Nemunas

FICTION

Anthony Doerr

I'm fifteen years old. My parents are dead.

I have a poodle named Mishap in a pet carrier between my ankles and a biography of Emily Dickinson in my lap. The flight attendant keeps refilling my apple juice. I'm thirty-six thousand feet over the Atlantic Ocean. Out my little smudgy window the whole world has turned to water.

I'm moving to Lithuania. Lithuania is in the upper right corner of Europe. Over by Russia. On the world map at school, Lithuania is pink.

Grandpa Z is waiting for me outside baggage claim. His belly looks big enough to fit a baby inside. He hugs me for a long time. Then he lifts Mishap out of his carrier and hugs Mishap, too.

Lithuania doesn't look pink. More like gray. Grandpa Z's little Peugeot is green and smells like rock dust. The sky sits low over the highway. We drive for a long time, past hundreds of half-finished concrete apartment buildings that look like they've been set here by the retreat of a huge flood. There are big Nokia signs and bigger Aquafresh signs.

Grandpa Z says, Aquafresh is good toothpaste. You have Aquafresh in Kansas?

I tell him we used Colgate.

He says, I find you Colgate.

We merge onto on a four-lane divided highway. The land on both sides is broken into pastures that look awfully muddy for early July. It starts to rain. The Peugeot has no windshield wipers. Mishap dozes in my lap. Lithuania turns a steamy green. Grandpa Z drives with his head out the window.

Eventually we stop at a house with a peaked wooden roof and a central chimney. It looks exactly like the twenty other houses crowded in around it.

Home, says Grandpa Z, and Mishap jumps out.

The house is long and narrow, like a train car. Grandpa Z has three rooms: a kitchen in front, a bedroom in the middle, and a bathroom in the back. Outside there's a shed. He unfolds a card table. He brings me a little stack of Pringles on a plate. Then a steak. No green beans, no dinner rolls, nothing like that. We sit on the edge of his bed to eat. Grandpa Z doesn't say grace so I whisper it to myself. Bless us O Lord and these thy gifts. Mishap sniffs around skeptically between my feet.

Halfway through his steak Grandpa Z looks up at me and there are tears on his cheeks.

It's okay, I say. I've been saying it's okay a lot lately. I've said it to church ladies and flight attendants and counselors. I say, I'm fine, it's okay. I don't know if I'm fine or if it's okay, or if saying it makes anyone feel better. Mostly it's just something to say.

———————— ◆ ————————

It was cancer. In case you were wondering. First they found it in Mom and she got her breasts cut off and her ovaries cut out but it was still in her, and then Dad got tested and it was in his lungs. I imagined cancer as a tree: a big, black, leafless tree inside Mom and another inside Dad. Mom's tree killed her in May. Dad's killed him three weeks later.

I'm an only child and have no other relatives so the lawyers sent me to live with Grandpa Z. The Z is for Zydrunas.

Grandpa Z's bed is in the kitchen because he's giving me the bedroom. The walls are bare plaster and the bed groans and the sheets smell like dust on a hot bulb. There's no shade on the window. On the dresser is a brand-new pink panda, which is sort of for babies, but also sort of cute. A price tag is still pinned to its ear: 39.99 L. The L is for Litas. I don't know if 39.99 is a lot or a little.

> Dear God, please watch over Mom in Heaven and please watch over Dad in Heaven and please watch over me in Lithuania.

After I turn off the lamp, all I see is black. Something goes tap tap tap against the ceiling. I can hear Mishap panting at the foot of the bed. My three duffel bags, stacked against the wall, contain everything I own in the world.

Do I sound faraway? Do I sound lost? Probably I am. I whisper: Dear God, please watch over Mom in Heaven and please watch over Dad in Heaven and please watch over me in Lithuania. And please watch over Mishap, too. And Grandpa Z.

And then I feel the Big Sadness coming on, like there's a shiny and sharp ax blade buried inside my chest. The only way I can stay alive is to remain absolutely motionless so instead of whispering Dear God how could you do this to me, I only whisper Amen which Pastor Jenks back home told me means I believe, and I lay with my eyelids closed clutching Mishap and inhaling his smell, which always smells to me like corn chips, and practice breathing in light and breathing out a color—light, green, light, yellow—like the counselor told me to do when the panic comes.

At 4 A.M. the sun is already up. I sit in a lawn chair beside Grandpa's shed and watch Mishap sniff around in Lithuania. The sky is silver and big scarves of mist drag through the fields. A hundred little black birds land on the roof of Grandpa's shed, then take off again.

Each house in Grandpa Z's little cluster of houses has lace curtains in the windows. The houses are all the same but the lace is different in each one. One has a floral pattern, one a linear pattern, and another has circles butted up against each other. As I look, an old woman pushes aside a zig-zag-patterned curtain in one of the windows. She puts on a pair of huge glasses and waves me over and I can see there are tubes hooked through her nose.

> He says this means that just because you can't see something doesn't mean you shouldn't believe in it. I can't tell if he means Jesus or gravity.

Her house is twenty feet away from Grandpa Z's and it's full of Virgin Mary statues and herbs and smells like carrot peels. A man in a track suit in the back room is asleep on a bed. The old lady unhooks herself from a machine that looks like two scuba tanks hung on a wheeled rack, and she pats the couch and says a bunch of words to me in Russian. Her mouth is full of gold. She has a marble-sized mole under her right eye. Her calves are like bowling pins and her toes look beaten and crushed.

She nods at something I don't say and turns on a massive flat-screen television propped up on two cinderblocks, and together we watch a pastor give mass on TV. The colors are skewed and the audio is garbled. In his church there are maybe twenty-five people in folding chairs. When I was a baby Mom talked to me in Lithuanian so I can understand some of the pastor's sermon. There's something about his daddy falling off his roof. He says this means that just because you can't see something doesn't mean you shouldn't believe in it. I can't tell if he means Jesus or gravity.

Afterward the old lady brings me a big hot stuffed potato covered with bacon bits. She watches me eat through her huge, steamy eyeglasses.

Thanks, I say in Lithuanian, which sounds like achoo. She stares off into oblivion.

When I get back to Grandpa Z's house he has a magazine open in his lap with space diagrams in it.

You are at Mrs. Sabo's?

I was. Past tense, Grandpa.

Grandpa Z circles a finger beside his ear. Mrs. Sabo no more remember things, he says. You understand?

I nod.

I read here, Grandpa Z says, clearing his throat, that Earth has three moons. He bites his lower lip, thinking through the English. No, it used to has three moons. Earth used to has three moons. Long time ago. What do you think of this?

————————— ·—· —————————

You want to know? What it's like? To prop up the dam? To keep your fingers plugged in its cracks? To feel like every single breath that passes is another betrayal, another step farther away from what you were and where you were and who you were, another step deeper into the darkness? Grandpa Z came to Kansas twice this spring. He sat in the rooms and smelled the smells. Now he leans forward till I can see the little red lightning bolts of veins in his eyes. You want to speak?

No thanks, Grandpa Z.

I mean talk, he says. Talk, Allie?

No. Thanks.

No? But to talk is good, no?

Grandpa Z makes gravestones. Gravestones in Lithuania aren't quite like the ones in America. They're glossy and smooth and made of granite, but most of them are etched with likenesses of the people buried underneath them. They're like black-and-white photos carved right into the stones. They're expensive and everyone spends money on them. Poor people, Grandpa Z says, spend the most. Some times he etches faces while other times he does the deceased's whole body, like a tall man standing in a leather jacket, life-size, very realistic, buttons on the cuffs and freckles on the cheeks. Grandpa Z shows me a Polaroid of a tombstone he made of a famous mobster. The stone is seven feet tall and has a life-size portrait of a suited man with his hands in his pockets sitting on the hood of a Mercedes. He says the family paid extra to have a halo added around the man's head.

Monday morning Grandpa Z goes to his workshop and school doesn't start for two months so I'm left alone in the house. By noon I've looked through all of Grandpa Z's drawers and his one closet. In the shed I find two fishing rods and an old aluminum boat under a tarp and eight jars of Lithuanian pennies and thousands of mouse-chewed British magazines: *Popular Science* and *Science Now* and *British Association for the Advancement of Physics*. There are magazines on polar bears and Mayan calendars and cell biology and lots of things I don't understand. Inside are faded cosmonauts and gorillas hooked up to machines and cartoon cars driving around on Mars.

Then Mrs. Sabo shows up. She shouts something in her derelict Russian and goes over to a chest of drawers and pulls open a cigarette box and inside are photographs.

Motina, she says, and points at me.

I say, I thought you couldn't remember things.

But she is sticking the photos under my nose like she has just remembered something and wants to get it out before she forgets it. Motina means Mom. All of the photos contain Mom when she was a girl. Here she is in a polar bear costume and here she is frowning over what might be an upturned lawnmower and here she is tramping barefoot through mud.

Mrs. Sabo and I lay out the pictures in a grid on Grandpa Z's card table. There are sixty-eight of them. Five-year-old Mom scowls in front of a rusted-out Soviet tank. Six-year-old Mom peels an orange. Nine-year-old Mom stands in the weeds. Looking at the photos starts a feeling in my gut like maybe I want to dig a shallow hole in the yard and lie down in it.

I separate out twelve of the pictures. In each of them, my mom—my Subaru-driving, cashew-eating, Barry-Manilow-listening, Lithuanian-immigrant, dead-because-of-cancer Mom—is either standing in murky water or leaning over the side of a junky-looking boat, helping to hold up some part of a creepy and gigantic shark.

Erketas, Mrs. Sabo says, and nods gravely. Then she coughs for about two minutes straight.

Erketas?

But by now the coughing has shaken all the comprehension of out her. The man in the track suit comes over and says something and Mrs. Sabo stares at the lower part of his face for a while and eventually the man coaxes her back to her house. Grandpa Z comes home from his job at 2:31.

Grandpa, I say, your toilet paper might as well be made out of gravel.

He nods thoughtfully.

And is this my mom, I ask, with all these great whites?

Grandpa looks at the pictures and blinks and puts a knuckle between his teeth. For maybe thirty seconds he doesn't answer. He looks like he's standing outside an elevator waiting for the doors to open.

Finally he says, Erketas. He goes to a book in a box on the floor and opens it and pages through it and looks up and looks back down and says, Sturgeon.

Sturgeon. Erketas means sturgeon?

River fish. From the river.

We eat sausage for dinner. No bread, no salad. All through the meal the photos of Mom stare up at us.

I rinse the dishes. Grandpa Z says, You walk with me, Allie?

He leads me and Mishap across the field behind the colony of houses. There are neat little vegetable gardens and goats staked here and there. Grasshoppers skitter out in front of us. We clamber over a fence and pick our way around cow dung and nettles. The little trail heads toward some willows and on the other side of the willows is a river: quiet and brown, surprisingly far across. At first the river looks motionless, like a lake, but the more I look, the more I see it's moving very slowly.

> She has lived through the first Lithuanian independence and the second one, too. She fought with the Russians the first time, against them the second time.

Mishap sneezes. I don't think he's ever seen a river before. A line of cows saunters along on the far bank.

Grandpa Z says, Fishing. Is where your mother goes. Used to go. Past tense. He laughs an unsmiling laugh. Sometimes with her grandpa. Sometimes with Mrs. Sabo.

What's it called?

The River Nemunas. It is called the River Nemunas.

———— ◆ ————

Every hour the thought floats to the surface: If we're all going to end up happy together in Heaven then why does anyone wait? Every hour the Big Sadness hangs behind my ribs, sharp and gleaming, and it's all I can do to keep breathing.

Mrs. Sabo, Grandpa Z says, is either ninety years old or ninety-four years old. Not even her son knows for sure. She has lived through the first Lithuanian independence and the second one, too. She fought with the Russians the first time, against them the second time. Back when all these houses were a communal farm under the Soviets, she used to take a rowboat every day for thirty-five years and row six miles up the river to work in a chemical plant. She went fishing when no women went fishing, he says.

Nowadays Mrs. Sabo has to be hooked up to her oxygen machine every night. She doesn't seem to mind if I come over to watch TV. We turn the volume up really high to hear over the wheezing and banging of her pump. Sometimes we watch the Lithuanian pastor, sometimes we watch cartoons. Sometimes it's so late we only watch a channel that shows a satellite map of the world, rotating forever across the screen.

———— • ————

I've been in Lithuania two weeks when Counselor Mike calls on Grandpa Z's cell phone. Counselor Mike, a lawyer who chews bubblegum and wears basketball shorts. It's two in the morning in Kansas. He asks how I'm adjusting. Hearing his wide-open American voice calls up for me, in a sudden rush, summertime Kansas. It's like it's right there on the other end of the phone, the air silky, the last porch lights switched off, a fog of gnats hovering above Brown's pond, the moon coming to earth through sheets and layers and curtains of moisture, streetlights sending soft columns of light onto grocery store parking lots. And somewhere in that sleepy darkness Counselor Mike sits at his clunky kitchen table in his socks and asks an orphan in Lithuania how she's adjusting.

It takes me a full ten seconds to say, I'm fine, it's okay.

He says he needs to talk to Grandpa. We got an offer on the house, he says. Grown-up stuff.

Is the offer good?

Any offer is good.

I don't know what to say to that. I can hear music coming from his end, faraway and full of static. What does Counselor Mike listen to, deep in the Kansas night?

We're praying for you, Allie, he says.

Who's we?

Us at the office. And at church. Everyone. Everyone is praying for you.

Grandpa's at work, I say.

Then I walk Mishap across the field and over the fence and through the rocks to the river. The cows are still on the far side, eating whatever cows eat and whipping their tails back and forth.

Five thousand miles away Counselor Mike is staying up late to plan the sale of the orange plastic tiles Dad glued to the basement floor and the dent I put in the dining room wall and the raspberry bushes Mom planted in the backyard. He's going to sell our warped baking sheets and half-used shampoos and the six Jedi drinking glasses we got from Pizza Hut that Dad said we could keep only after asking our pastor if Star Wars would have been "endorsed by Jesus." Everything, all of it, our junk, our detritus, our memories. And I've got the family poodle and three duffel bags of too-small clothes and four photo albums, but no one left who can flesh out any of the photos. I'm five thousand miles and four weeks away and every minute that ratchets past is another minute that the world has kept on turning without Mom and Dad in it. And I'm supposed to live with Grandpa Z in Lithuania, what, for the rest of my life?

Thinking about the house sitting there empty back in Kansas starts the Big Sadness swinging in my chest like a pendulum and soon a blue nothingness is creeping around the edges of my vision. It comes on fast this time and the ax blade is slicing up organs willy-nilly and all of the sudden it feels like I'm looking into a very blue bag and someone's yanking the drawstring closed. I fall over into the willows.

I lie there for who knows how long. Up in the sky I see Dad emptying his pockets after work, dumping coins and breath mints and business cards onto the kitchen counter. I see Mom cutting a fried chicken breast into tiny white triangles and dunking each piece in ketchup. I see the Virgin Mary walk out onto a little balcony between the clouds and look around and take ahold of French doors, one on either side of her, and slam them shut.

I can hear Mishap sniffing around nearby. I can hear the river sliding past and grasshoppers chewing the leaves and the sad, dreamy clanking of faraway cowbells. The sun is tiny and flame-blue. When I finally sit up, Mrs. Sabo is standing beside me. I didn't know she could walk so far. Little white butterflies are looping through the willows. The river glides past. She says something in machine-gun Russian and I sit up and she sets her frozen hand on my forehead. Then we watch the river, Mrs. Sabo and Mishap and me, in the grass in the sun. And as we watch the water, and breathe, and I come back into myself—I swear—a fish as big as a nuclear missile leaps out of the river. Its belly is spotless white and its back is gray and it curls up in mid-air and flaps its tail and stretches like it's thinking, This time gravity will let me go.

When it comes back down, water explodes far enough across the river that some drops land on my feet.

Mishap raises his ears, cocks his head. The river heals itself over. Mrs. Sabo looks at me from behind her huge eyeglasses and blinks her milky eyes a dozen times.

Did you see that? Please tell me you saw that.

Mrs. Sabo only blinks.

Grandpa Z gets home at 3:29.

I bought you a surprise, he says. He opens the hatchback of the Peugeot and inside is a crate of American toilet paper.

Grandpa, I say. I want to go fishing.

———————— ·-· ————————

Dad used to say God made the world and everything in it and Grandpa Z would say if God made the world and everything in it, then why isn't everything perfect? Why do we get backaches and why do beautiful healthy daughters get cancer? Then Dad would say well, God was a mystery and Grandpa Z would say God was a, what's the word, a security blanket for babies, and Dad would stomp off and Mom would throw down her napkin and blast some Lithuanian words at Grandpa and go jogging after Dad and I'd look at the plates on the table.

Grandpa Z crossed the ocean twice this spring to watch his daughter and son-in-law die. Did God have explanations for that? Now I stand in Grandpa Z's kitchen and listen to him say that there aren't any sturgeon anymore in the River Nemunas. There might be some left in the Baltic Sea, he says, but there aren't any in the river. He says his dad used to take Mom sturgeon fishing every Sunday for years and Mrs. Sabo probably caught a few in the old days but then there was overfishing and pesticides and the Kaunas dam and black-market caviar and his dad died and the last sturgeon died and the Soviet Union broke up and Mom grew up and went to university in the United States and married a creationist and no one has caught a sturgeon in the Nemunas River for twenty-five years.

Grandpa, I say, Mrs. Sabo and I saw a sturgeon. Today. Right over there. And I point out the window across the field to the line of willows.

It is photos, he says. You see the photos of your mother.

I saw a sturgeon, I say. Not in a picture. In the river.

Grandpa Z closes his eyelids and opens them. Then he holds me by the shoulders and looks me in the eyes and says, We see things. Sometimes they there. Sometimes they not there. We see them the same either way. You understand?

———— ·—· ————

I saw a sturgeon. So did Mrs. Sabo. I go to bed mad and wake up mad. I throw the stuffed panda against the wall and stomp around on the porch and kick gravel in the driveway. Mishap barks at me.

In the morning I watch Grandpa Z drive off to work, big and potbellied and confused, and I can hear Mrs. Sabo's machine whirring and thunking in her house next door and I think: I should have told Grandpa Z to trust me. I should have told him about the pastor's old daddy and the stepladder and Jesus and gravity and how just because you don't see something doesn't mean you shouldn't believe in it.

Instead I wade into Grandpa Z's shed and start pulling out boxes and granite samples and chisels and rock saws and it takes me a half hour to clear a path and another half hour to drag the old aluminum boat into the driveway. It's flat-bottomed and has three bench seats and there are maybe a thousand spiders living beneath each one. I blast them out with a hose. I find a bottle of some toxic Lithuanian cleaner and I pour it all over the hull.

> After a while Mrs. Sabo comes tottering out in her big eyeglasses and her little arms and looks at me like a praying mantis.

After a while Mrs. Sabo comes tottering out in her big eyeglasses and her little arms and looks at me like a praying mantis. She lets off a chain of coughs. Her son comes out in his track suit with a cigarette between his lips and he watches me work for ten minutes or so and then he leads his mother back inside.

Grandpa Z gets home at 3:27. There are boxes and hoses and rakes and tools all over the driveway. The bottle of solvent has left bright, silver streaks across the hull of the boat. I say, Mrs. Sabo and I saw a sturgeon in the river yesterday, Grandpa.

Grandpa Z blinks at me. He looks like maybe he's looking into the past at something he thought had ended a long time ago.

He says, No more sturgeon in the Nemunas.

I say, I want to try to catch one.

They not here, Grandpa Z says. They endangered species. It means—

I know what it means.

He looks from me to the boat to Mishap to me. He takes off his hat and drags his hand through his hair and puts his hat back on. Then he nudges the boat with the toe of his sneaker and shakes his head and Mishap wags his tail and a cloud blows out of the way. Sunlight explodes off of everything.

<hr />

I use an ancient, flat-tired dolly to drag the boat through the field and over the fence to the river. It takes me three hours. Then I lug the oars and the fishing poles down. Then I walk back and tell Mrs. Sabo's son I'm taking her out on the river and guide Mrs. Sabo by the arm and lead her across the field and sit her in the bow of the boat. In the sunlight her skin looks like old candle wax.

We fish with blunt, seven-foot rods and ancient hooks that are as big as my hand. We use worms. Mrs. Sabo's face stays completely expressionless. The current is very slow and it's easy to paddle once in a while and keep the boat in the center of the river.

> I tell her a bald eagle's feathers weigh twice as much as its bones. I tell her aardvarks drink their water by eating cucumbers.

Mishap sits on the bench beside Mrs. Sabo and shivers with excitement. The river slips along. We see a whole herd of feral cats sleeping on a boulder in the sun. We see a deer twitching its ears in the shallows. Black and gray and green walls of trees slide past.

In the late afternoon I pull onto what turns out to be an island and Mrs. Sabo steps out of the boat and lifts up her housedress and has a long pee in the willows. I open a can of Pringles and we share it.

Did you know my mother? I ask Mrs. Sabo but she only glances over at me and gives me a dreamy look. As if she knows everything but I wouldn't understand. Her eyes are a thousand miles away. I like to think she's remembering other trips down the river, other afternoons in the sun. I read to her from one of Grandpa Z's nature magazines. I tell her a bald eagle's feathers weigh twice as much as its bones. I tell her aardvarks drink their water by eating cucumbers. I tell her that male emperor moths can smell female emperor moths flapping along six miles away.

It takes me a couple of hours of rowing to get back home. We watch big pivot sprinklers spray rainbows over a field of potatoes and we watch a thousand boxcars go rattling along behind a train. It's beautiful out here, I say.

Mrs. Sabo looks up. Remember? she asks in Lithuanian. But she doesn't say anything else.

We don't catch any fish. Mishap falls asleep. Mrs. Sabo's knees get sunburned.

———————— ·–· ————————

That one day is all it takes. Every morning Grandpa Z leaves to go carve dead people's faces into granite, and as soon as he's gone I take Mrs. Sabo out in the boat. An old-timer six houses down tells me I should be using rotten hamburger meat, not worms, and that I should stuff it inside the toes of pantyhose and tie the pantyhose to the hooks with elastic thread. So I get some hamburger and put it in a bucket in the sun until it smells like hell, but the pantyhose won't stay on the hook, and a lady at the convenience store in Mažeikiai says she hasn't seen a sturgeon in fifty years but when there were sturgeon they didn't want rotten food, they wanted fresh sand shrimp on big hooks.

I try deep holes behind rapids and eddies beside fields of bright yellow flowers and big, blue, shadowy troughs. I try clams and night crawlers and—once—frozen chicken thighs. I keep thinking Mrs. Sabo will pipe up, will remember, will tell me how it's done. But mostly she sits there with that long-gone look on her face. My brain gradually becomes like a map of the river bottom: gravel bars, two sunken cars with their rust-chewed rooftops just below the surface, long stretches of still water seething with trash. You'd think the surface of a river would be steady but it isn't. There are all these churnings and swirls and eddies, bubblings and blossomings, submerged stumps and plastic bags and spinning crowns of light down there, and when the sun is right sometimes you can see forty feet down.

We don't catch a sturgeon. We don't even see any. I begin to think maybe Grandpa Z is right, maybe sometimes the things we think we see aren't really what we see. But here's the surprising thing: It doesn't bother me. I like being out there with Mrs. Sabo. She seems okay with it, her son seems okay with it, and maybe I'm okay with it, too. Maybe it feels as if the wretchedness in my gut might be getting a little smaller.

When I was five I got an infection and Dr. Nasser put some drops in my eyes. Pretty soon all I could see were blurs and colors. Dad was a fog and Mom was a smudge and the world looked like it does when your eyes are completely full of tears. Four hours later, right around when Dr. Nasser said it would, my eyesight came back. I was riding in the backseat of Mom's Subaru and the world started coming back into focus. I was myself again and the trees were trees again, only the trees looked more alive than I'd ever seen them: the branches above our street were interlaced beneath an ocean of leaves, thousands and thousands of leaves scrolling past, dark on the tops and pale on the undersides, every individual leaf moving independently but still in concert with the others.

Going out on the Nemunas is sort of like that. You come down the path and step through the willows and it's like seeing the lights in the world come back on.

--------●--------

Even when there's not much of a person left, you can still learn things about her. I learn that Mrs. Sabo likes the smell of cinnamon. I learn she perks up any time we round this one particular bend in the river. Even with her little gold-capped teeth she chews food slowly and delicately, and I think maybe her mom must have been strict about that, like, Sit up straight, Chew carefully, Watch your manners. Emily Dickinson's mom was like that. Of course Emily Dickinson ended up terrified of death and wore only white clothes and would only talk to visitors through the closed door of her room.

Mid-August arrives and the nights are hot and damp. Grandpa Z keeps the windows open. I can hear Mrs. Sabo's oxygen machine wheezing and murmuring all night. In half-dreams it's a sound like the churning of the world through the universe.

Yellow, green, red runs the flag flapping in front of the post office. Sun up top, Grandpa Z says, land in the middle, blood down below. Lithuania: doormat of a thousand wars.

I miss Kansas. I miss the redbud trees, the rainstorms, how the college kids all wear purple on football Saturdays. I miss Mom walking into the grocery store and pushing her sunglasses up on her forehead, or Dad pedaling up a hill on his bicycle, me a little person in a bike trailer behind him, his maroon backpack bobbing up and down.

One day late in August Mrs. Sabo and I are drifting downstream, our lines trailing in the river, when Mrs. Sabo starts talking in Lithuanian. I've known her forty days and not heard her say so much in all of them combined. She tells me that the afterworld is a garden. She says it's on a big mountain on the other side of an ocean. This garden is always warm and there are no winters there and that's where the birds go in the fall. She waits a few minutes and then says that death is a woman named Giltine. Giltine is tall, skinny, blind, and always really, really hungry. Mrs. Sabo says when Giltine walks past, mirrors splinter, beekeepers find coffin-shaped honeycombs in the hives, and people dream of teeth being pulled. Anytime you have a dream about the dentist, she says, that means death walked past you in the night.

One of Grandpa Z's magazines says that when a young albatross first takes wing, it can stay in the air without touching the ground for fifteen years. I think when I die I'd like to be tied to ten thousand balloons, so I could go floating into the clouds, and get blown off somewhere above the cities, and then the mountains, and then the ocean, just miles and miles of blue ocean, my corpse sailing above it all.

I think when I die I'd like to be tied to ten thousand balloons, so I could go floating into the clouds, and get blown off somewhere . . .

Maybe I could last fifteen years up there. Maybe an albatross could land on me and use me for a little resting perch. Maybe that's silly. But it makes as much sense, I think, as watching your Mom and Dad get buried in boxes in the mud.

—◦—

At nights Mrs. Sabo and I start watching a show called Boy Meets Grill on Mrs. Sabo's big TV. I try cooking zucchini crisps and Pepsi-basted eggplant. I try cooking asparagus Francis and broccoli Diane. Grandpa Z screws up his eyebrows sometimes when he comes in the door but he sits through my Bless Us O Lord and he eats everything I cook and washes it all down with Juozo beer. And some weekends he drives me up the road to little towns with names like Panemunė and Pagėgiai and we buy ice cream sandwiches from Lukoil stations, and Mishap sleeps in the hatchback and at dusk the sky goes from blue to purple and purple to black.

Almost every day in August Mrs. Sabo and I fish for sturgeon. I row upriver and drift us home, dropping our cinderblock anchor now and then to fish the deep holes. I sit in the bow and Mrs. Sabo sits in the stern and Mishap sleeps under the middle bench, and I wonder about how memories can be here one minute and then gone the next. I wonder about how the sky can be a huge, blue nothingness and at the same time it can also feel like a shelter.

———— –•– ————

It's the last dawn in August. We are fishing a mile upstream from the house when Mrs. Sabo sits up and says something in Russian. The boat starts rocking back and forth. Then her reel starts screaming.

Mishap starts barking. Mrs. Sabo jams her heels against the hull and jabs the butt of her rod into her belly and holds on. The reel yowls.

Whatever is on the other end takes a lot of line. Mrs. Sabo clings to it and doesn't let go and a strange, fierce determination flows into her face. Her glasses slide down her nose. A splotch of sweat shaped like Australia blooms on the back of her blouse. She mutters to herself in Russian. Her little baggy arms quiver. Her rod is bent into an upside-down U.

What do I do? There's nobody there to answer so I say, Pray, and I pray. Mrs. Sabo's line disappears at a diagonal into the river and I can see it bending away through the water, dissolving into a coffee-colored darkness. The boat seems like it might actually be moving upriver and Mrs. Sabo's reel squeaks and it feels like what the Sunday school teacher used to tell us during choir practice when she'd say we were tapping into something larger than ourselves.

Slowly the line makes a full circuit of the boat. Mrs. Sabo pulls up on her rod and cranks her reel, gaining ground, inch by inch, little by little. Then she gets a bit of slack so she starts reeling like mad, taking in yards of line, and whatever it is on the other end tries to make a run.

Bubbles rise to the surface. The swivel and weight on Mrs. Sabo's line become visible. It holds there a minute, just below the surface of the water, as if we are about to see whatever is just below the leader, whatever is struggling there just beneath the surface, when, with a sound like a firecracker, Mrs. Sabo's line pops and the swivel and the broken leader fly up over our heads.

Mrs. Sabo staggers backward and nearly falls out of the boat. She drops the rod. Her glasses fall off. She says something like, Holy, holy, holy, holy.

Little ripples spread across the face of the river and are pulled downstream. Then there's nothing. The current laps quietly against the hull. We resume our quiet slide downriver. Mishap licks Mrs. Sabo's hands. And Mrs. Sabo gives me a little gold-toothed smile as if whatever was on the other end of her fishing line has just pulled her back into the present for a minute and in the silence I feel she's here, together with me, under the Lithuanian sunrise, both of us with decades left to live.

Grandpa Z doesn't believe me. He sits on the edge of his bed, elbows on the card table, a mildly-renowned Lithuanian tombstone maker, with droopy eyes and broken blood vessels in his cheeks, a plate of half-eaten cauliflower parmesan in front of him, and wipes his eyes and tells me I need to start thinking about school clothes. He says maybe we caught a carp or an old tire but that for us to catch a sturgeon would be pretty much like catching a dinosaur, about as likely as dredging a big hundred-million-year-old Triceratops up out of the river muck.

Mrs. Sabo hooked one, I say.

Okay, Grandpa Z says. But he doesn't even look at me.

Mažeikiai Senamiesėcio Secondary School is made of sand-colored bricks. The windows are all black. A boy in the parking lot throws a tennis ball onto the roof and waits for the ball to roll down and catches it and does this over and over.

It looks like every other school, I say.

It looks nice, Grandpa Z says.

It starts to rain. He says, You are nervous, and I say, How come you don't believe me about the fish? He looks at me and looks back at the parking lot and rolls down the window and swipes raindrops from the windshield with his palm.

There are sturgeon in the river. Or there's one. There's at least one.

They all gone, Allie, he says. You only break your heart more with this fishing. You only make yourself more lonely, more sad.

So what, Grandpa, you don't believe in anything you can't see? You believe we don't have souls? You put a cross on every headstone you make, but you think the only thing that happens to us when we die is that we turn into mud?

For a while we watch the kid throw and catch his tennis ball. He never misses. Grandpa Z says, I come to Kansas. I ride airplane. I see tops of all clouds. No people up there. No gates, no Jesus. Your mother and father are in the sky sitting on the clouds? You think this?

I look back at Mishap, who's curled up in the hatchback against the rain. Maybe, I say. Maybe I think something like that.

———————————— • ————————————

I make friends with a girl named Laima and another girl named Asta. They watch Boy Meets Grill, too. Their parents are not dead. Their mothers yell at them for shaving their legs and tell them things like, I really wish you wouldn't chew your hangnails like that, Laima, or, Your skirt is way too short, Asta.

At night I lie in bed with Grandpa Z's unpainted plaster slowly cracking all around me and no shade on the window and Mrs. Sabo's machine wheezing next door and stars creeping imperceptibly across the windowpane and reread the part in my Emily Dickinson biography when she says, "To live is so startling it leaves little time for anything else." People still remember Emily Dickinson said that but when I try to remember a sentence Mom or Dad said I can't remember a single one. They probably said a million sentences to me before they died but tonight it seems all I have are prayers and clichés. When I shut my eyes I can see Mom and Dad at church, Mom holding a little maroon church songbook, Dad's little yachting belt and penny loafers. He leans over to whisper something to me—a little girl standing in the pew beside him. But when his mouth opens, no sound comes out.

The willows along the river turn yellow. Our history teacher takes us on a field trip to the KGB museum in Vilnius. The KGB used to cram five or six prisoners into a room the size of a phone booth. They also had cells where prisoners had to stand for days in three inches of water with no place to sit or lie down. Did you know the arms of straightjackets used to be twelve or fourteen feet long? They'd knot them behind your back.

Late one night Mrs. Sabo and I watch a program about a tribe in South America. It shows a naked old guy roasting a yam on a stick. Then it shows a young guy in corduroys riding a moped. The young guy, the narrator lady tells us, is the old guy's grandson. No one wants to do the traditional tribe stuff anymore, the narrator lady says. The old people sit around on their haunches looking gloomy and the youngsters ride buses and move to the cities and listen to cassette tapes. None of the young people want to speak the original language, the narrator lady says, and no one bothers to teach it to their babies. The village used to have 150 people. All but six have moved away and are speaking Spanish now.

> The KGB used to cram five or six prisoners into a room the size of a phone booth. They also had cells where prisoners had to stand for days in three inches of water with no place to sit or lie down.

At the end the narrator says the tribe's old language has a word for standing in the rain looking at the back of a person you love. She says it has another word for shooting an arrow into an animal poorly, so that it hurts the animal more than is necessary. To call a person this word, in the old language, the lady says, is the worst sort of curse you could imagine.

Fog swirls outside the windows. Mrs. Sabo stands and disconnects herself from her machine and takes a bottle of Juozo beer from the refrigerator. Then she goes out the front door and walks into the yard and stands at the far edge of the porch light and pours some beer into her cupped hand. She holds it out for a long time, and I'm wondering if Mrs. Sabo has finally drifted off the edge until out of the mist comes a white horse and it drinks the beer right out of her cupped hand and then Mrs. Sabo presses her forehead against the horse's big face and the two of them stay like that for a long time.

That night I dream my molars come loose. My mouth fills with teeth. I know before I open my eyes that Mrs. Sabo is dead. People come over all day long. Her son leaves the windows and doors open for three days so that her soul can escape. At night I walk over to her house and sit with him and he smokes cigarettes and I watch cooking shows.

The River Nemunas, he says in Lithuanian, two nights after she's gone. He doesn't say anything else.

Two weeks later Grandpa drives me home from school and looks at me a long time and tells me he wants to go fishing.

Really? I say.

Yes, he says. He walks across the field with me; he lets me bait his hook. For three straight afternoons we fish together. He tells me that the chemical plant where Mrs. Sabo worked used to made cement and fertilizer and sulfuric acid, and under the Soviets some days the river would turn mustard yellow. He tells me that under the Soviets the farms here were collective farms, where many families worked a large area, and that's why the houses out here are in clusters and not spread out, each to its own plot, like farmhouses in Kansas.

> I count to three and try to yank my rod up. It doesn't budge. It's a feeling like I've hooked into the river bottom itself, like I'm trying to pull up the bedrock of Lithuania.

On the fourth day, I'm fishing with a chicken carcass when my line goes tight. I count to three and try to yank my rod up. It doesn't budge. It's a feeling like I've hooked into the river bottom itself, like I'm trying to pull up the bedrock of Lithuania.

Grandpa Z looks over at my line and then at me. Snagged? he says. My arms feel like they're going to tear off. The current pulls the boat slowly downstream and soon the line is so tight drops are sizzling off it. Every once in a while a little line cranks off the reel. That's all that happens. If I were to let go of my rod, it would shoot upriver.

I consider cutting the line. Something pulls at me and the boat pulls at it and we stay like that for a long time, locked in a tug-of-war, my little fishing line holding the entire boat and me and Mishap and Grandpa Z steady against the current, as if I've hooked into a big, impossible plug of sadness resting on the bottom of the river.

You pull, I whisper to myself. Then you crank. Like Mrs. Sabo did. Pull, crank, pull, crank.

I try. My arms feel like they're disappearing. The boat rocks. Mishap pants. A bright silver wind comes down the river. It smells like wet pine trees. I close my eyes. I think about Mom's raspberry bushes, Dad's filing cabinet, the new family that's moving into our house, some new Mom hanging her clothes in Mom's closet, some new Dad calling to her from Dad's office, some teenage son tacking posters to my walls. I think about how Grandpa Z says the sky is blue because it's dusty and octopuses can unscrew the tops off jars and starfish have one foot and three mouths. I think: No matter what happens, no matter how wretched and gloomy everything can get, at least Mrs. Sabo got to feel this.

It's as if I'm going to separate at the waist. But gradually, eventually, I start to gain some ground. The boat rocks as I pull it a yard upstream. I heave the rod up, crank in a couple turns of line.

Pull, then crank. Pull, then crank. We skid another yard upstream. Grandpa Z's little eyes seems about to bulge out of their sockets.

It's not a fish. I know it's not a fish. It's just a big piece of trash at the bottom of the Nemunas River. I say a prayer Dad taught me about God being in the light and the water and the rocks, about God's mercy enduring forever. I say it quickly to myself, hissing it out through my lips, and pull then crank, pull then crank, God is in the light, God is in the water, God is in the rocks, and I can feel Mishap scrabbling around the boat with his little claws and I can even feel his heart beating in his chest, a little bright fist opening and closing, and I can feel the river pulling past the boat, its tributaries like fingernails dragging through the entire country, all of Lithuania draining into this one artery, five hundred sliding miles of water, all the way to the Baltic, which Grandpa Z says is the coldest sea in Europe, and something occurs to me that will probably seem obvious to you but that I never thought about before: a river never stops. Wherever you are, whatever you're doing, forgetting, sleeping, mourning, dying—the rivers are still running.

Grandpa Z shouts. I open my eyes. Something is surfacing twenty feet away from the boat. It comes up slowly, like a submarine, as if from a dream: huge, breathtakingly huge, the size of a desk. It's a fish.

I can see four barbells under his snout, like snakes. I see his fog-colored belly. I see the big hook stuck through his jaw. He moves slowly, and eases his head back and forth, like a horse shaking off a wasp.

He is huge. He is tremendous. He is ten feet long.

Erketas, says Grandpa Z.

I can't hold it anymore, I say.

Grandpa Z says, You can.

Pull, crank. Breathe in light, breathe out color. The sturgeon comes to us upside down. His mouth sucks and opens, sucks and opens. His back is covered with armor. He looks fifty thousand years old.

For a full minute the fish floats beside the boat like a soft white railroad tie, the boat rocking gently, no Mrs. Sabo, no Mom and Dad, no tape measures or hanging scales, no photographs, my arms ablaze with pain and Mishap barking and Grandpa Z looking down as if he's been asked to witness a resurrection. The sturgeon's gills open and close. The flesh inside the gills is a brilliant, impossible crimson.

I hold him there for maybe ten more seconds. Who else sees him? The cows? The trees? Then Grandpa Z leans over, unfolds his pocketknife, and cuts the line. The fish floats beside the boat for a few seconds, stunned and sleepy. He doesn't flick his tail, doesn't flex his huge body. He simply sinks out of sight.

Mishap goes quiet. The boat wobbles and starts downriver. The river pours on and on. I think of those photos of Mom, as tall and thin as a blade of grass, a bike rider, a swimmer, a stranger, a suntanned sixth-grader who might still come pedaling up the driveway of her father's house some afternoon with a jump rope over her shoulder. I think of Mrs. Sabo, how her memories slipped away one by one into the twilight and left her here in a house in a field in the middle of Lithuania waiting for skinny, ravenous Giltine to carry her to a garden on the other side of the sky.

I feel the tiniest lightening. Like one pound out of a thousand has been lifted off my shoulders. Grandpa Z slowly dips his hands in the water and rubs them together. I can see each drop of water falling off his fingertips. I can see them dropping in perfect spheres and merging with the river.

We hardly ever talk about the fish. It's there between us, something we share. Maybe we feel like talking about it will ruin it. Grandpa Z spends his evenings etching Mrs. Sabo's face into her tombstone. Her son has offered several times to pay but Grandpa does it for free. He puts her on the granite without her glasses and her eyes look small and naked and girlish. He draws a lace-collared dress up tight around her throat and pearls around that, and he renders her hair in cotton-candy loops. It really is a very good job. It rains on the day they put it over her grave.

In November our whole school takes a bus to Plokštinė, an abandoned underground Soviet missile base where the Russians used to keep nukes. It looks like a grassy field, hemmed with birch, with an oversized pitcher's mound in each corner. There are no admission fees, no tourists, just a few signs in English and Lithuanian and a single strand of barbed wire—all that remains of seven layers of alarms, electric fences, razor cable, Dobermans, search-lights, and machine gun emplacements.

We go down a staircase in the center of the field. Electric bulbs dangle from cracked ceilings. The walls are cramped and rusty. I pass a tiny bunk room and a pair of generators with their guts torn out. Then a dripping black corridor, clotted with puddles. Eventually I reach a railing. The ceiling is belled out: one of the pitcher's mounds must be directly above me. I shine my flashlight ninety feet down. The bottom of the silo is all rust and shadows and echoes.

> Don't tell me how to grieve. Don't tell me ghosts fade away eventually, like they do in movies, waving goodbye with see-through hands.

Here, not so long ago, they kept a thermonuclear ballistic missile as big as a tractor trailer. The iron collar around the rim of the hole has the 360 degrees of a compass painted around its circumference. Easier, I suppose, to aim for a compass heading than for Frankfurt.

The urge to know scrapes against the inability to know. What was Mrs. Sabo's life like? What was my mother's? We peer at the past through murky water; all we can see are shapes and figures. How much is real? And how much is merely threads and tombstones?

On the way home Lithuanian kids jostle in the seats around me, smelling of body odor. A stork flaps across a field in the last of the daylight. The boy beside me tells me to keep my eyes out the window, that to see a white horse at dusk is the best possible kind of luck.

— ∙ —

Don't tell me how to grieve. Don't tell me ghosts fade away eventually, like they do in movies, waving goodbye with see-through hands. Lots of things fade away but ghosts like these don't, heartbreak like this doesn't. The ax blade is still as sharp and real inside me as it was six months ago.

I do my homework and feed my dog and say my prayers. Grandpa Z learns a little more English, I learn a little more Lithuanian, and soon both of us can talk in the past tense. And when I start to feel the Big Sadness cutting me up inside I try to remember Mrs. Sabo and the garden that is the afterworld and I watch the birds fly south in their flocks.

The sturgeon we caught was pale and armored and beautiful, splotched all over with age and lice. He was a big soft-boned hermit living at the bottom of a deep hole in a river that pours on and on like a green ghost through the fields of Lithuania. Is he an orphan like me? Does he spend all day every day searching for someone else he recognizes? And yet, wasn't he so gentle when I got him close to the boat? Wasn't he just as patient as a horse? Wasn't he just about as noble as anything?

Jesus, Dad used to say, is a golden boat on a long, dark river. That's one thing I can remember him saying.

It's quiet in Lithuania in November, and awful dark. I lie on my grandfather's bed and clutch Mishap and breathe in light and breathe out color. The house groans. I pray for Mom and Dad and Mrs. Sabo and Grandpa Z. I pray for those South American tribespeople on the television and their vanishing language. I pray for the lonely sturgeon, a monster, a lunker, last elder of a dying nation, drowsing in the bluest, deepest chambers of the River Nemunas.

Out the window it starts to snow. ⚜

FICTION

Jason who will be famous

Dorothy Allison

Jason is going to be famous, and the best part is that he knows he will be good at it.

He has this real clear picture of himself, of him being interviewed—not of the place or even when it happens, but of the event itself. What he sees is him and the interviewer, a recording so clear and close up, he can see the reflections sparking off his own pupils. It's hi-def or Blu-ray or something past all that, a rendering that catches the way the soft hairs just forward of his earlobe lift and shine in the light reflecting off his pale cheeks. All he has to do is close his eyes and it begins to play, crisp and crackling with energy as the microphone bumps hollowly against the button on his open collar.

"A lot of it, I can't tell you," he says, and the interviewer nods.

Jason is sitting leaning forward. His features gleam in the bright light, his expression is carefully composed, focused on the interviewer. Jason nods his head and his hair swings down over his forehead. One auburn strand just brushes across the edges of his eyebrows. The interviewer is so close their elbows are almost touching. He is an older man with gray in his hair and an expression of watchful readiness—a man Jason has seen do this kind of thing on the news before, someone to be trusted, someone serious.

That is the word. Serious. The word echoes along Jason's nervous system. He is being taken seriously. Every time he imagines it again, the thought makes him take a deep breath. A little heat flares in his neck as the camera follows his eyes. He looks away from the interviewer, and his face goes still. He looks back and his eyes go dark and sad.

"I'm sorry to have to ask you about something so painful," the interviewer says to him.

"It's all right," Jason says. "I understand." He keeps his expression a mirror of the other man's, careful and composed. He can do this. Piece of cake.

Behind the cameraman, there are other people waiting to speak to Jason, others are standing close by to hear what he has to say. Everyone has questions, questions about what happened, of course, about the kidnapping and all the months in captivity. But they also want to ask him what he thinks about other things, about people, and events. In the interview as Jason sees it, he always has answers—surprising and complicated, wonderful answers.

"That boy is extraordinary," he hears the serious man tell another.

Extraordinary. The heat in his neck moves down into his chest, circles his diaphragm, and filters out to his arms and legs. He hopes it does not show on his face. Better to remain pale and impassive, pretend he does not hear what they say about him. How extraordinary he is, that everyone says so, some kind of genius. He half-smiles and then recomposes his expression. Genius. Jason is not sure what his genius is exactly, but he trusts it. He knows it will be revealed at the right time, in the right circumstances. It is simply that those events have not happened as of yet. But they will.

He opens his eyes. He has stopped at the edge of the road. Dust, white-grey and alkaline, has drifted up from his boots, and he can taste eucalyptus and piney resin. He looks up the road toward the next hill and the curve down into the shade of the redwood stand there. Should have brought a bottle of water, he thinks. Then, extraordinary. How would you know if you were extraordinary? Or a genius? He's pretty good at math, and music—though nothing that special. If he worked more, put more of himself into the work, no telling what he might not do. His dad told him that, once, when he was still living with them. His teachers have said something of the same thing. All of them though, his dad, teachers, and his mom, they say it like it's a bad thing—his talents and his waste of them.

"If you worked more. If you worked harder."

They don't understand. No one does.

Jason wipes dust off his mouth and rocks his head from side to side. He knows the problem. It's not that he's lazy or stupid or even scared. No. The problem is that he never has had enough time or focus. There's just always so much that has to be done, and how does anyone do that kind of kung fu stuff anyway? How does anyone become extraordinary? Like Uma Thurman in the Tarantino movie? Years going up and down staircases. It's like that. You do some stupid thing over and over and over, and sometime along in there, you discover you have achieved this enormous talent.

Jason is not sure what his genius is exactly, but he trusts it. He knows it will be revealed at the right time, in the right circumstances. It is simply that those events have not happened as of yet. But they will.

He glares up the road and resumes his pace, boots kicking dust and his hands gripping the straps of his backpack. He could do extraordinary stuff. Given the right circumstances, he has everything in him to do stuff that will startle everyone. It just takes the right circumstances—getting everything out of the way. He nods to himself. He can feel that coming toward him—the opportunity, the time, and the focus.

He has dreamed it so often, he knows it is coming—though he doesn't know all of how it will happen. That too, he sees like a movie, the movie of his life going on all the time. Step in and it is already in motion. Like that. He grins and speeds up slightly. Might be, he will be walking home along the river road from Connie's on a day just like this one. He'll have something in his backpack, after working for Connie all day, doing what he does so well, little baby buds his specialty. Connie always tells him how good he is. He knows exactly how to clip and trim and harvest only what is ready to come away, leave what should be left behind. That shows talent. That shows aptitude. Bonsai killer weed work, he does that all the time. Connie knows she can trust him. Some people she strings along, but him she always pays with a ready smile and a touch along his arm or one quick knuckle push at his hip. Cash or buds, she pays him, and that's all good. Just as it is good no one knows what Jason has in his backpack. No one knows his business.

Still, he knows, the day is coming. Someone is going to snatch him up right off the road or outside the liquor store downtown—some old guy maybe, or even one of them scary old dykes from out the bay side of the Jenner beach. Those bitches are dangerous and he can barely imagine what they would do with a piece of work like him. Everyone knows they all got stuff, guns and money and stuff. Bitches like that stick together. But maybe it will be someone from nowhere nearby, some bunch of crazies with some plan he will never fully understand, that no one will understand.

He nods slowly, his hands gripping the straps tight as he imagines it— the snatch, the basement, the months alone and everything that comes after. He has been seeing it for a long time, the story in his head, the way it will happen. It was a dream the first time, a nightmare, grabby hands and the skin scraped off his knees—a nightmare of sweaty basement walls and dirt in his mouth. But by the third or fourth time he dreamed it, everything receded and it was not so nightmarish. He was fighting back and able to think. Then it was magical how he started thinking about it in the daytime, daydreaming it, planning what he would do, how he would handle things. Then what came after the snatch became more and more important. He had started imagining the person he would be afterward. He didn't think so much about the kidnapping then, or even the kidnappers. It was all about him and the basement and what he did down there, who he would become, who he was meant to become. It was set and in motion. It was coming, Jason was sure of it. Not that he thought he was psychic or anything, it was just that this big thing was coming, so big he could feel it, and he had thought it through and whatever happened, he was going to be ready.

He stumbles and stops. He is almost gasping, smelling the sweat on his neck, the dust on the road, the acrid breeze from the eucalyptus trees past the stand of old-growth stunted apple trees around the curve. He leans forward, stretching his back, and straightens to watch a turkey buzzard circling the hill to his left. No hurry. It is only half a mile to his mom's place, two twists in the road and an uphill grade. Jason shakes his head. He knows this road in its whole length, two and a half miles and every decrepit house along the way, every crumbling garage and leaning fence. Of course, everyone here also knows him, which is sometimes more than he can stand. But somewhere someone who does not know him is coming along, and they will change everything. He nods and resumes a steady pace. Everything will be made over—and he will never know when or why. It will be a mystery.

He thinks of the basement room, that dim space with the windows boarded over. Nothing much will be down there, but he won't need much. He would love a piano, of course, but a guitar is more the kind of thing you might find in a basement. Nothing fancy. Some dented old acoustic. Jason thinks about it, the throwaway object he will use. God knows what he will have to do to tune the thing. Not likely to be any help in the junk people keep in basements. But there will be paper or notebooks. The notebooks will have pages marked up, of course, but he can work around that, use the backs of pages or something. It is what he creates in the silence that will need to be written down, the songs or poems. Lyrics. He will write it all down—easy to imagine that—him singing to himself in the quiet. The pencil marks along the pages. Of course his music notation sucks. He's never been too good at that. He sighs and stops again.

Maybe there will be a recorder—some old thing probably. A little old tape recorder, not a good digital. But hey it will get the job done. He smiles and hears above him the turkey buzzard's awkward call. Ugly sound from an ugly bird. He watches a big white pickup truck drive slowly up and past him. Big metal locks clamp down on the storage bin at the front of the truck bed.

Connie's boyfriend, Grange, told Jason you could bust most of those locks with the right chisel and mallet. "It's all in the angle. Got to hit it right."

Jason has a chisel in his backpack but no mallet. He licks his lips and resumes his slow hike between the ditch and the road. You got to have the right stuff to get anything done. Unless you are lucky or have an edge.

Famous is the way to go, he thinks. You get stuff once you are famous.

Jason wipes sweat off his neck as he walks and imagines it again—the reporter, the camera, the intensity of the lights, the intensity of his genius. It will take time, but he will figure it out. Maybe it won't be music. Maybe it will be words. He's damn good with words, not like those assholes at school who talk all the time. He knows the value of words, keeps them in his head, not always spilling them out like they mean nothing. He doesn't have to tell what he knows. He just knows—lyrics and poetry and all that stuff. Good poetry, he tells himself. Not that crap they want him to read in school. Kind of stuff makes your neck go stiff, that kind of poetry, that's what he likes. He looks at the dust on his hand, sweat-darkened and spotted with little grey-green bits. Little nubbins of weeds and grass flung up with the dust as the trucks pass. He'll get on the computer tonight, look up all the words for grey-green. Emerald, olive-drab, unripe fruit, something or the other. Nothing too hard about getting the words right.

> He knows the value of words, keeps them in his head, not always spilling them out like they mean nothing. He doesn't have to tell what he knows.

Jason wipes his hands on his jeans, enjoying the feel of the fabric under his palms. Truth is more important than how you tell it, he thinks. And he knows stuff, lots of stuff, secrets and stuff. He has stories.

Maybe that will be it, the stories he tells himself to pass the time. Movie scripts, plays, dialogues between characters that come and go when he is all gaunt and feverish. In the basement, they won't feed him much, so he will get all dramatic skinny and probably have lots of fever dreams. He'll write them down, everything. His hands will cramp and he'll go on writing, get up and pace back and forth and write some more. Pages on pages will pile up. He'll bathe his face in cool water and walk some more. He'll drink so much water his skin will clear up. His mom is always telling him that if he washed his face more, drank more water and yeah, and ate more vegetables, his skin would do that right away. Maybe she has a point. Maybe in the basement that's all they will give him. Vegetables and water—lots of water, cause you know they ain't gonna waste no greasy expensive stuff on no captive. No Coke, no potato chips, no Kentucky Fried Chicken.

Pure water and rivers of words. Jason grins and lengthens his stride. Maybe after a while he won't care what he eats, or he will learn to make an apple taste like a pie. That would be the kind of thing might happen. He could learn to eat imaginary meals and taste every bite—donuts and hot barbecue wings—and stay all skinny and pure. That would be something. He could teach people how to do that afterwards maybe. Some day he might run an ashram like the one his mama used to talk about.

The turkey buzzard swoops low and arcs downhill toward the river. Jason stops to watch its flight. A moment in time and the bird disappears. Things can change that fast. Anything could happen and you can't predict what might come along. But what he knows is that there won't be any distractions down in the basement, anything to get in the way. Cold walls and dim light and maybe just a shower. Might be it will only run cold water, but he can handle that. What he hates is tub baths, sitting in dirty water. No way there is not gonna be a shower in the basement, or, all right, maybe only a hose and a drain in the floor. But he knows he will bathe himself a lot 'cause what else will there be to do? 'Cept write what he knows and use the weights set. He laughs out loud. Maybe there won't be no weights, though every shed or garage he knows has some stacked in some corner or the other. If there's nothing like that in his basement, still there will be stuff, something he can use.

He grabs his backpack straps again and begins the uphill grade. His steps slow and he focuses on the notion of making do, figuring out what he will use. Stuff like old cans of paint or bundles of rebar or bricks left lying around. He'll Tarantino it all, laying on the concrete floor and pushing up and down over and over till his arms get all muscled, and his legs too. He'll push off against the wall or doorjamb or something. He's gonna be bored out of his mind. He'll get desperate. He'll be working out, running in place and lifting heavy things—whatever he finds. Yeah, he'll get pretty well muscled. He grins. That is how it will be. He's going to come out just amazing.

Jason looks up the road, quarter of a mile to his mom's turnoff. He's right at the spot where the old firebreak cuts uphill, right up to his dad's place. He can almost see around the redwoods along the hill up to the house. He won't be like his dad, he thinks, he won't waste his chances. He'll grab what comes and run with it. When he comes out of that basement, he'll be slick. That is what it is all gonna be. Slick and sure, and he will know how to manage it, not wind up house-sitting for some crappy old guy wants you to carry stuff and keep an eye on the dogs.

Fuck it. Jason says it out loud. "Fuck it!" He's gonna come out of that basement Brad-Pitt handsome and ready for anything. He'll be ready, all soulful and quirky like that guy from the White Stripes, only he won't take himself too seriously. Everyone else will do that for him. He'll know how to behave.

Jason laughs out loud again. "Yeah," he says. Yeah.

Serious. Yes. That's the word. He is going to be seriously famous.

That's when his mom will realize how shitty she has treated him. Then his dad will hear about it, for sure—and maybe let him come back up to the house and hang out. Of course that creep that owns the property will be around too, but Jason knows it won't be scary like last time. He'll have all those muscles, and he will have gotten past being scared of small shit like grabby old guys and dads that don't give a shit.

It will be different. It will all be different. His mom and his dad will work it all out. His dad will be his manager, his mom will take over the press stuff. You got to have someone handle that stuff, and if the creepy guy comes round to stake some kind of claim, it won't be no big deal. Everyone will know how to handle him—what to believe and what to laugh at. He can almost hear his dad talking loud in his growly hoarse voice. He can hear him finally saying what he wanted him to say before.

"Jason didn't take nothing off you, old man. Look at him. What would he need off you?"

Yeah.

But maybe he will let the old guy hang around. Jason thinks about it, looking uphill and remembering. He gnaws at the nail on his left little finger.

Maybe not.

Why would he want that old bastard around?

He thinks about his dad, what he looks like now, all puffy and grey around the eyes with his hair so thin on top. His dad has this belly on him that he tries to hide under loose shirts, and he's always worried about money and stuff. That kind of old is embarrassing. After the basement though, his dad will be all different. He'll be old, but not so gross. He'll be more like Clint Eastwood old, craggy and wise. That's the notion, and his dad will have figured stuff out all that time worrying about Jason. Things will be different once he sees his son clear. Maybe he'll even own the property by then. The old guy can't live forever. Maybe he'll just give his dad the top of the hill as a kind of death tip. Might be it will turn out like that guy in Forestville a few years back, that black guy who got the thirty acres in the will of the man he worked for all that time.

That could happen. And then if his dad needs someone to help him with things, Jason will be there. That bad leg will hurt his dad a lot by then, even though he will try not to show it. Jason could do stuff—carry things for him and give him a hand. Maybe that is how they work it out—all the anger and guilt and shame and resentment. He can see that too, hear how it will go, them finally talking.

"You had no business running off like that, leaving Mom and me, I was just a little kid."

"You don't know how it was, how desperate I had gotten. I couldn't take care of you the way I wanted to, and you know your mom. She was always telling me I was lazy and the world wasn't gonna wait for me to get myself together."

That was just the kind of thing his mom said all the time. Jason nods. His mom can be a real pain in the ass. He sees himself looking at his dad and trying to imagine how he had felt when he had left. Maybe his dad had left in order to get himself together, to try and make something of himself so he could come back and take good care of them. After all that time cold and miserable and hungry in the basement, he will be able to feel stuff differently. Even standing in the dust of the road he can imagine his dad looking at him with an open face. Maybe they could talk finally, and it would shift all the anger around.

> His dad will know the story, how the kidnappers beat him, and starved him, and how Jason endured everything and stood up to them.

Maybe his dad will get to the point where he can look at him and see Jason clearly, see how he became so strong in that basement. Maybe he will finally see himself in his son. Of course, like everyone, his dad will know the story, how the kidnappers beat him, and starved him, and how Jason endured everything and stood up to them. It will make stuff in his dad shift around. He will get all wet-eyed and ashamed of himself. Jason can see that—the moment between them as real as the interviewer and the cameras, the moment burning him right through to his backbone. He almost sobs out loud, but then stops himself. His eyes are closed. The wind is picking up the way it always does as the afternoon settles toward evening. There is a birdcall somewhere up in the trees, but Jason is inside seeing into what is coming, what has to come.

They will touch each other like men do. Men. Yeah. Maybe his dad will embrace him, say his name. Jason can see that. It is as clear as anything. That is how it is in stories, how it is in his head, how it could be.

Jason sways a little there by the side of the road in the sun's heat. His ears are ringing with electric cricket sounds, the buzzard's cries, and the movement of the wind. Still, he hears a vehicle coming and the sound of its tires on the gritty tarmac. Rock and redwood debris grinding into dust and crackling as the wheels turn into the bend. Jason can see that, the wheels revolving and grinding forward. He imagines the kidnapper's truck, white and thick like one of those big Dodge Fat Boys, but one with a camper on the back—just the thing for snatching a guy off the road. Slowly Jason lets his face relax into a lazy smile. He doesn't look back. He keeps his eyes forward. His mom is always telling him to stop living in a dream, to be in the real world. But this is the real world, the road and the truck and everything that is coming toward him.

Anything can happen any time.

Everything can change, and it is going to, any time now.

Any time.

Any time.

Now.

Hummingbird

I.

Small bird, pollinating bird, impossible bird,
You are the only one that can fly in reverse.
Your heart beats 1,200 times a minute. Absurd!

But I find it more absurd to learn the Aztecs
Worshipped you as an icon of war and sex
(But not of fatherhood; males never keep nest).

So tell me, winged one, are you more afraid
  of birth or death?

2.

Hey, little man, named after the hummingbird,
You lived your whole damn life in reverse.
You shot yourself twice before you died. Absurd!

They say basketball was a deadly game for the Aztecs.
If so, then you were the point guard of war and sex
(But not of fatherhood; you never kept nest).

So tell me, cousin, what do you regret more:
  your birth or death?

Ode to Mix Tapes

These days, it's too easy to make mix tapes.
        CD burners, iPods, and iTunes
                Have taken the place
        Of vinyl and cassette. And soon
Enough, clever introverts will create
Quicker point-and-click ways to declare
        One's love, lust, friendship, and favor,
                But I miss the labor
Of making old school mix tapes—the mid-air

Acrobatics of recording one song
        At a time. It sometimes took days
                To play, choose, pause,
        Ponder, record, replay, erase,
And replace. But there was no magic wand.
It was blue-collar work. A great mix tape
Was sculpture designed to seduce
        And let the hounds loose.
A great mix tape was a three-chord parade

Led by the first song, something bold and brave,
A heat-seeker like Prince with "Cream,"
Or "Let's Get it On," by Marvin Gaye.
The next song was always Patsy Cline's "Sweet Dreams,"
or something by Hank. But, O, the last track
        Was the vessel that contained
        The most devotion and pain,
And made promises that you couldn't take back.

Militant

a Fibonacci sequence poem

"Don't

Go

To ants

For wisdom

And morality."

That's an Edward O. Wilson quote.

To illustrate his point, he speaks of a Malaysian

Soldier ant that carries poison in two large glands.
     When that ant's colony is attacked,

It will run next to an enemy ant, contract its abdomen,
     explode, and spray its deadly poison. That ant
     is a suicide bomber.

I don't mean to anthropomorphize the ants but they have
     genocidal ambition.

Without pause, they slaughter, dismember, behead, and feast.

We are not the cruelest. Ants act

With greater haste to

Create more

Gore than

We

Do.

Among

The worst ants

Are the Argentines,

Who have stowed away on airplanes,

Invaded islands, and eradicated insects

And other ants. Why are they such efficient
       killers? Because newly pregnant queens walk

Instead of fly to form new nests and quickly inundate an
       area with closely placed clusters. And since the
       Argentines produce ten times

More queens than any other ants, it's easy to
       understand why these matriarchal

Warriors are so feared. Don't be fooled
       by their small size.

Collectively, ants weigh the same

As all humans do.

That factoid

Mocks me

And

You.

Smudge

A

In nature, always reality. In art, always nature.
            If representational,
the recognizable governs technique.
If freer than figurative,
            you can feel the object
referencing a primitive system of punishment.
Beneath the bruises, *brushstroke brushstroke*, skin.
To express Expressionism, the thumb of time
smears humanity, blurring history.
Truth, too, contributes to the pain-pulse of memory
as if color, complexion and flesh-spectrum,
as if, only if, the material
is men, women and children,
all in their greasy mornings.

B

A good exhibition decomposes theory
but the dead in the work remain dead, remain swirling reminders
          of evil's palette,
pre-blister and post-burn.
The only thing surreal about weeping
are all the eyes, the absent ones lost to erasure.
The real map of mercy is here,
animated in Oil on Cotton
like the path water makes through abstract stone.
Shadow, ashcan, shadow.
Victims lined up, washed in the violence of vision.
Ghost-portraiture, shroud.

C

This is what "resilience" looks like
from a sensitive satellite.
I almost wrote "suffering" but I chose "resilience" instead,
thinking of how painting can bring blood
          back from earth.
Some sense of all of the elements is here,
depth of fear, harrowing despair.
Some sense the torturer, lost in layering, his aerial gaze.
Not being able to make out
a face or a family
          does not diminish these sacred, deformed forms.
Artifice, anonymous or mere remembrance
some smudges haunt the soul with hurt
bright as a cemetery of yellow, human flora.

D

Many of the images melt

while others appear to rumor, ghetto-fashion,

into one another.

       White is not used to brighten, only to accent

un-witnessed regions of grief.

I like it when Leica, breathing plastic and messy rainbows

       collide.

Even the self, as graphite,

seems dimensional as handwriting.

Gravediggers, too, owe something to perspective.

Art can rip the skin off of

a cherry picker

—the same way the solid, September sky

can reject both above and below.

Private collections are worse; they hide proof.

Written in response to the paintings of David Stern and read at the Yeshiva
University Museum in New York City on January 28, 2009.

THROUGH A GLASS
LIGHTLY

Francine Prose

The drugs got harder and the crime rate spiked, but still, the seventies weren't so bad.

My son drives a beautiful 1971 Lincoln Continental, navy blue with a white vinyl top, a white leather interior, and a Cartier clock on the dashboard; a rolling eco-disaster, it gets seven miles a gallon and requires two parking spaces. He plays saxophone in a seventies-style soul band, listens to James Brown, and collects vinyl LPs, which, he claims, have a "warmer" sound than CDs. In his closet hangs a pin-striped suit almost identical to the one his father wore on our first formal date, and his loft is furnished with pieces—a pedestal chair, a geometric-patterned area rug—that look as if they could have been purchased at Austin Powers's yard sale.

From time to time, I consider explaining to him that the 1970s were not exactly the funky, creative idyll that he and his friends imagine. If the sixties were a dream about a more open and equal society, a freer and more idealistic way of life, the seventies were the rude awakening—the long, tough morning after. Overnight, it seemed, the drugs got harder and the crime rate spiked; heroin replaced psychedelics as the street pharmaceuticals of choice, and the junkies waged a guerrilla turf war against the urban hippies in the East Village and Haight-Ashbury. The graffiti that, from this temporal distance, look so vibrant and colorful were a lot less pleasant to live with; the scrawled-on subways and streetscapes felt somehow lawless, threatening, dangerously out of control. But what always stops me from breaking this disenchanting news to my son is a glimmer of a certain memory, a bright shard of recollection sparkling at the far edge of my peripheral vision. What keeps me from telling him that the seventies he imagines is a fantasy, a product of his own wish for a looser and more liberated era, is an image I can't—and don't want to—forget.

It's the memory of the three drag queens, made up and dressed to the nines, in the early hours of the morning, performing in the produce aisle of a San Francisco supermarket.

It was late in the summer of 1973. I had just arrived in San Francisco, in flight from Cambridge, Massachusetts, and from everything that I had assumed that my life was going to be about. I had gotten married too young, and now that marriage was over. I had, by default and for lack of any definite idea about my professional future, gone to graduate school.

And now I had finally admitted to myself that academia was not—not by a long shot—where I wanted to be.

I knew that what I saw around me—full professors bullying hapless assistant professors and the timid wives in long peasant skirts who prepared hearty casseroles for the stiff, grimly competitive dinner parties at which I always felt I was saying the wrong thing even when I didn't utter a word—didn't remotely resemble the life I wanted to live.

But I had no idea what that more exciting and fulfilling life might be.

I'd grown up in New York, which was, I realized, far closer to the nerve center of anything vital happening in the culture. But I couldn't imagine how I could fit into that culture, nor how I could make a place for myself in the city in which my more hard-headed, single-minded, and clear-sighted college classmates were already avidly pursuing literary and art careers. I was lost, adrift. I remember, all too well,

the day that the astronauts landed on the moon: I was walking through Harvard Square and weeping in the street, because my "real life" was supposed to have begun, and it obviously hadn't.

My experience of the sixties had hardly been the groovy, flower-power, round-the-clock love-in that's become the popular perception of that era. Timothy Leary had advised our generation to turn on, tune in, and drop out. But although I'd certainly done my share of turning on and tuning in, though I'd marched on Washington and taken to the streets to protest the Vietnam War, I certainly hadn't dropped out. I'd spent my undergraduate years reading Victorian novels and hanging out with my college boyfriend, whom I married—again, for lack of a better idea—during my senior year. In graduate school, where I was studying medieval literature, a surprising number of my fellow students were, for some reason, nuns, whom my semi-sadistic Chaucer professor loved to torture by asking them to translate the dirtiest passages from *The Canterbury Tales*. On the home front, Julia Child was my domestic goddess. I prepared wildly overelaborate recipes from her cookbooks and shopped at the old-fashioned family-run supermarket where she shopped in my desperate attempt to run the graduate-student semblance of a paradoxically hip and middle-class household.

And then it all dissolved. The so-called sexual revolution took its toll on my marriage. There were betrayals, recriminations, adulterous and inappropriate love affairs. In early August, a friend called to say that he was across country. Did I want to come along? Oh, I did. I did.

School wouldn't start again until mid-September. A change of scene, I thought, would do me good.

I found a place to stay, in the spare bedroom in the apartment where my friend H— lived with his girlfriend. At that point H— was making a living by writing pornography for Maurice Girodias's legendary Olympia Press. It was, I realized with delight, a far cry from my friends back in Cambridge, dutifully laboring away on their doctoral theses on Sir Gawain and the Green Knight.

My new home, in the Sunset neighborhood, directly across Golden Gate Park from the Haight, was often filled with artists, writers, underground filmmakers, potheads, crackpot inventors, and eccentrics of all sorts. Across the bay, in Berkeley, I had friends who lived in rambling houses whose inhabitants had come together on the basis of their vocations, their sexual preferences, their hopes and dreams, their bad and good habits. I liked visiting the house populated by manically entertaining alcoholic gay men, the commune of militant lesbian folksingers, the one made up of former girlfriends and ex-wives of famous rock stars, the household whose members were plotting to run an alternative candidate for the mayor of San Francisco.

One night, our apartment in the Sunset was, as usual, full of visitors. It was after midnight, and everyone was very high and very hungry. We needed a volunteer to go to the supermarket for avocados so H— — could prepare his specialty: avocado, mayonnaise and alfalfa sprout sandwiches on sourdough bread, a snack that tasted far better than it sounds. I was glad to go. The very existence of an all-night supermarket was still a source of wonder for me, as was the miraculous abundance of the produce section. This was before the current era, of course, when every corner store, in every city and every season, features gorgeous berries, crisp apples, bright oranges. Never—not even in Julia Child's favorite supermarket—had I seen such a variety of fresh fruit and vegetables of the range and quality that you could get then in California.

I was surreptitiously pinching the avocados for ripeness when I sensed a sort of low-key hum, a disturbance in the field, almost like the initial tremor of the earthquake I had been trying not to think about. And it was than that I saw them.

There were three men—I knew because they had beards—dressed in low-cut satin evening gowns, trailing feather boas, with ostrich plumes in their hair, occasionally lifting their skirts to reveal high heels encrusted with rhinestones. Everything about them sparkled. Their eyelids were coated with glitter, costume jewelry winked from their arms and necks and earlobes. And one of them had purple angel wings fastened to his back.

Back in the apartment, the marijuana pipe hadn't entirely passed me by.

But I knew that I wasn't stoned enough to be hallucinating these creatures who

My new home . . . was often filled with artists, writers, underground filmmakers, potheads, crackpot inventors, and eccentrics of all sorts.

looked more like brilliant birds of paradise than ordinary human beings. They swooped and glided and called out to each other, raised their arms in the air and shimmied. They were hoping, it seemed, to create such a stir that no one would notice or mind what they were really doing—which was, I gradually realized, shoplifting. They were their own sleight of hand, the fascinating distraction, their dramatic grand diversionary tactic that held your attention as they grabbed mangoes, papayas and even (was I dreaming this?) pineapples and stuffed them into their beaded purses and down the fronts of their bodices.

And then, suddenly, they were gone, flying out of the market and leaving me feeling a bit like Dorothy in *The Wizard of Oz*. I wasn't in Cambridge any more, Toto.

--- ◆ ---

I ran back to the apartment to tell my friends, who seemed to think nothing of it. Maybe it was the Cockettes, they said, the already legendary drag theater troupe who had ceased performing not long before, but still sometimes appeared in the streets, in full glitter and gowned regalia. No one seemed to understand the momentousness of what I'd experienced. But I felt as

if I'd seen a vision, a glimpse of a way of life that couldn't have been more thrillingly unlike the straightlaced and proper society I'd left behind in Cambridge. I'd been shown—more clearly than I was able to see among the writers and filmmakers who frequented our apartment—the freedom, the outrageousness, the sheer fun of being an artist.

The next morning, I woke up early and typed a letter to my graduate department informing them that I was sorry, but I would not be returning for the fall semester. I walked to the corner and mailed it and felt a sensation of giddy lightness, almost weightlessness. One life had ended, another had begun. I was free; I could go home.

A few months later, I left for New York to find the seventies in full swing.

Maybe the streets and the subways weren't as safe as they used to be; maybe the city was in a fiscal crisis that eventually led to bankruptcy.

Maybe there was the occasional mugging, an undercurrent of free-floating paranoia that I can evoke even now by watching Martin Scorsese's *Taxi Driver*. But the truth was, I didn't care. I was just so happy to be part of it, to be there. In fact, I liked how vaguely dangerous and on-the-edge everything felt, how it often seemed that a heartbeat, a wrong turn—a conversation with the wrong guy in a bar—might make all the difference between a pleasant evening and a nightmare.

I looked okay in bell-bottoms; I much preferred the Hustle to the Twist, and certainly to the tranced-out, anything-goes dances that I was happy to see disappear along with the sixties. Everything seemed possible, in motion, fluid, up for grabs. If you didn't like the way things were, you could pick up and go somewhere else. Rents were cheap, space readily available.

I moved in with some friends who were sharing a nearly raw, gigantic, semi-legal loft in Soho, where—in contrast to the weekend-shoppers' paradise that the neighborhood has become—there were only a few artists' bars, a restaurant or two. My roommates were mostly documentary filmmakers and one architect-designer who'd been responsible for the practical and ingenious way that the space was divided. There were few amenities, no intercoms, certainly no doormen; when visitors came, they phoned from the Broome Street Bar, then stood beneath our window, and we threw the keys down, cushioned in an old sock.

Whatever intimations I'd drawn about the liberating, gender-bending, inspirational aspects of in-your-face cross-dressing were confirmed and taken to a whole other level by Charles Ludlam and the Ridiculous Theatrical Company. Their *Camille*, which I went to see almost as soon as I got back East, took the Cockettes'

rowdy campiness and elevated it into art. I remember laughing uproariously and then finding myself on the edge of tears as Ludlam, with his rolling eyes, his hairy chest and revealing gown, enacted the final agonies of the dying courtesan. A gay friend took me to the show, and then out dancing at the Limelight, where handsome, bare-chested men—guys who could really dance!— partied and flirted in the flashing lunar light of the disco ball.

Sometime during that period, I went to see Patti Smith perform at CBGB, on the Bowery. She wore black pants and a T-shirt striped like a French sailor's, she snarled at the audience, and, once, spat on stage. Her voice was rough, but she was magnificent, and what I remember admiring most was how clear it was that she was her own person, that she didn't give a damn, that she insisted on her freedom to do and say and think exactly what she wanted.

And all of it gave me courage, nerve, the faith and belief it took to write a novel, and then another. By the time the seventies ended, I had become a writer. And I had found that life that I longed for, without knowing what it was, as I'd sobbed my way through Harvard Square.

I thought of all this the other day, driving with my son in his Lincoln Continental, on a beautiful late summer afternoon in the country. One of the car's odd quirks—along with the fact that the headlights cut out when you make a right turn—is that the radio seems only to play music from the 1970s. It's eerie, almost supernatural, a little like *Christine*, that homicidal vintage car in the Stephen King novel. But the explanation is considerably simpler; the radio isn't in the best shape, and the local oldies station puts out the strongest signal.

In any case, the radio was playing a series of great soul classics—Wilson Pickett, Sam and Dave, Joe Tex—the music my son most loves and also performs, in the band with which he tours. They're the songs I'd loved when I was his age and still have a soft spot for in my heart. We rode without speaking for a while, and then he nodded at the radio and said, "That must have been such a fun time to be young."

I paused, about to say all sorts of things. Being young, I wanted to tell him, is never entirely fun. I almost described what it felt like to know that the sixties were over, and to realize that the wondrous transformations we'd expected weren't going to happen. I considered telling him what it was like to walk through the streets of Cambridge with tears streaming down my face because I was so afraid that I would never find what I really wanted to do, or a life I wanted to live.

But then I remembered my old Soho loft, that first time I saw Patti Smith and the Ridiculous Theatrical Company. And I saw, with utter clarity, the vision of those glittering guys in beards and evening gowns cavorting in the produce aisle. It occurred to me that things are more difficult now for my son and his friends—rents are higher, jobs scarcer, the world seems like a more threatening and unstable place; it's no longer so easy to find that sense of sheer freedom, of fluidity, of limitless possibility. No wonder they idealize, and long for, an era that seems, in retrospect, so innocent, so sweet.

Aretha Franklin sang on the radio. The fields of high corn and wildflowers streamed by outside the window of the Lincoln. I turned to my son.

"A fun time to be young?" I said. "Actually, it was."

Sunday in Windy Key

Sundays Mr. Prendergas took a few boys to the village for an hour or two of the real world, as he called it. These were all kids from Greenwich and New York, so the town of Windy Key was the real world only in its comparison to the regimented life at Coverton Academy, where we were all at school so long ago. During the week he'd tap a boy or two to see if they wanted to go "off hours," which was the Coverton term for off campus; there were a lot of terms. If you were free, meaning you didn't have three or more excuses that term and you weren't on dining hall or library, you'd jump at the chance to drive the twenty miles to the seaside village and walk the two streets and shop and lay in candy or cigarettes and other contraband. The first week in December, he asked me after sixth-form history, and I told him I wanted to go along.

FICTION

∞

Ron Carlson

Football was over and hockey didn't practice on Sundays. I had come out to Coverton as a postgraduate to play hockey. I had been an all-state defenseman in Michigan, and when I got turned down at Brown, they said to go a year to this prep school on the coast of Maine and apply again, meaning I'd get in. I'm glad I did. I liked the little place, all boys, no cars, just read, write, and walk to the rink. The classes were very small and at first when I saw everyone in coats and ties, all these guys looking like weary experts, I thought I'd have a heck of a time keeping up, but in fact, they were just high school kids, most of whom were rich, and they read right to left and down the page, as Mr. Prendergas put it, and I was fine.

Postgraduates are greeted and known as jocks, which means a kind of automatic acceptance, and I needed that. I'm a man who all my life looked different than I really am. I'm a big guy, and in high school I had a heavy brow, and the scar on my cheekbone from a skate was an angry thing that year. Guys I barely knew at school felt free about jostling me, something that happens when you're big. Inside I was a little kid, I see now, and later I went into medicine with a kind of wonder and no real hope of mastering and changing health care. I've done all right and my patients stay with me. It is said I have a good bedside manner, which is to say I can listen, which when you look at me is not apparent.

Mr. Prendergas was a popular teacher who seemed to have been made to be a prep school master. I think that year he must have been thirty-two or thirty-three, though to us he was simply permanent. He'd been at Coverton since college. His wife was a short woman with a blond ponytail and she ran the infirmary. Later that winter she would reset my nose carefully, and I liked her because when it clicked in her hand and the tears sprang out of my eyes, the way tears jump whenever anyone works your broken nose, she said, "You are going to be one handsome hockey player." Mr. Prendergas was a well-dressed, well-spoken man who sometimes smoked a cigarette conspiratorially in his office, cracking the window a bit while he went over your term paper. He carried a gentlemen's silver pocketknife with which he peeled apples in the dining hall, and he always had a pressed handkerchief in his sport coat pocket. He taught a class on the sixties that was always oversubscribed, but in such a school that only meant there were ten of us.

The day we went to Windy Key, the two other boys were Miles Kellogg and Jerome Mead, both sophisticates who lived in my house. By the time we arrived in the village along the winding coastal road, Mr. Prendergas had laid out the drill, which was that he was going to stop at the tobacconist, go to the Book Barn behind the auto body shop, and stop in at the Clinic, which was the nickname for the worst pub in all of Maine. Its real name was Klines Tavern, and Mr. Prendergas took undue pleasure in calling it the Clinic. There were two other tourist places right on the main street, pubs with gold letters and a hanging sign where they actually served real food and not something in a wrapper that came out of the greasy microwave, but he was after authentic experience. It was the place where once a month the gray state bus pulled up and two or three pale men with prison haircuts would deboard. They had been released and were dropped in Windy Key.

> When we crossed the railroad tracks at the bottom of town, Mr. Prendergas pulled off his tie and threw it with a kind of fake recklessness into our laps in the backseat.

"If any of you want to join me, I'll be there by two o'clock. Harriet has some sodas in the old fridge." He wanted us to know that he knew the owner's name. I had come from a town much bigger than Windy Key, but it was rough. My brother is a fireman, and he told me it was never a good idea to be in a place long enough to call the barkeep by name.

When we crossed the railroad tracks at the bottom of town, Mr. Prendergas pulled off his tie and threw it with a kind of fake recklessness into our laps in the backseat. "I'd advise you to do the same, gentlemen. We are about to deal with the general public. They eat preppies for dinner."

"It's lunchtime," Miles said, "and nobody's going to bite Nunley." He was referring to me, but still he and Jerome slid their ties off and stuffed them into their jacket pockets. I didn't bother with mine. The truth was I hadn't had to wear a tie once to high school and I enjoyed the things. If I looked like a big dumb guy who was late to graduate from prep school, so be it.

He parked that day in front of the little red door of the Episcopalian church, and when we stood out of the car in the cold, gray day, Mr. Prendergas said, "Oh, we need the world. Meet me here at three o'clock, gentlemen, for our return voyage. On the dot." We could hear the ocean behind the storefronts and even in the winter day I could smell the sand and salt.

Jerome and Miles disappeared. Everyone at Coverton Academy knew the charms of Windy Key, including a café by the little harbor where you could get all kinds of fresh and fried seafood, and there was Larry's Liquors, a little shed where the guy would sell to kids. The campus was riddled with half-pints of Jack Daniels and Smirnoff in kids' golf bags.

I had no agenda for the day. I had been happy to come east to school and I was going to play hockey and go to Brown, which turned out to be a good place for me in that I met my wife there and got ahold of science in pre-med, and I paid for the whole thing by skating. So, I followed Mr. Prendergas into the Windy Key General Store, the front counter of which was all tobacco. Students at Coverton were not allowed to smoke, but the campus was wall-to-wall Marlboros, which everyone kept paper-clipped inside their lampshades.

It was the first store I had been in since August, when my father had taken me into Groves in Boston to buy the last of my school clothes, and it was strange to actually see things for sale. The old wooden floor creaked and I went past the candy case and past the T-shirts and cloth kites hanging from the ceiling. I looked at the papers and the magazines and the wool jackets while Mr. Prendergas shopped and re-shopped for foreign cigarettes. I let him leave before I bought two comic books and an Almond Joy. These things gave me great pleasure. The fall had been good, but a grind.

Back on the street I walked up a ways to the little fire station, and I could see the Book Barn down on the lower street, just as I'd imagined it from Mr. Prendergas's stories. The Book Barn was an actual barn. The little front room was heated and there was a desk and a workbench where the owner stood putting together what looked to be an old clock. He nodded back and said, "Feel free." So I went into the back where the books were, thousands of old hardbacks. The space was not winterized. It smelled powerfully of old books about to turn, and I loved the place immediately. I wanted to get hardbacks of the books we were reading in school and I found some.

The owner had alphabetized all these treasures and I picked my way through the homemade shelves. I could see my breath. I was there about an hour, and the cold did gather, the seacoast cold creeping up my legs. I found several books, including *The Scarlet Letter*, from some classic press reprint, but a clean heavy book anyway, and I found *Look Homeward, Angel*, and then I found a book I still have, a first edition of *Ethan Frome*. It was a thin maroon book, the paper jacket long gone. All of these books were marked, inside the front cover in pencil, $1.00. I went out front into the tight hot office and paid the man and of course there was no bag or receipt, just me then out in the town of Windy Key with my new books. It was warmer out in the dark day than it had been in the gloomy room of books.

At the cross street I saw the gray state bus pull away from the wooden building known as the Clinic. It was a garish blue and needed painting. Of the two large windows in the front, one was fresh plywood. The streets were empty; this wasn't tourist season. I turned up the collar of my sport coat and walked down to the tavern.

I'd been in taverns. I wasn't much of a drinker in high school, but my brother had taken me to places and there were a couple of joints out of our town where we would go some weekends. My buddies in Michigan called me the designated bouncer, but I never had to intervene. This place was

The campus was riddled with half-pints of Jack Daniels and Smirnoff in kids' golf bags.

close to the bottom of the barrel as roadhouses go. The bar was a narrow room with about nine stools along the Formica bar; maybe it had been a diner at one time. Beyond that was a larger room with a pool table. This room was dark with its wooden window and I could see all of the pool cues standing in the corner; the cue rack was broken off the wall. Everything, judging by the shadows and scuff marks, had been broken off the walls. Behind the bar there was a door with a cloth curtain and I could see living quarters through the gap.

I was too big for the room and the bartender, an old woman in a green and yellow flannel shirt and Levis, looked at me with alarm. I knew she was going to call me "Sonny" and ask me what I wanted. Mr. Prendergas sat down the bar, talking to a man in a green flight jacket with a fur collar. His hair was very short. There were four beer bottles in front of them on the gray Formica counter, and I walked down and sat beside him.

"Mr. Nunley," Mr. Prendergas said. "What'd you get?"

I showed him the books. "Oh this is very fine," he said. He showed the three books as a stack to the man beside him and said, "Another young scholar." Then Mr. Prendergas lifted his hand and called to the woman. "Harriet." She came down the bar with her hands on her hips. She didn't like him using her name. She looked at me.

"Just coffee," I said.

She turned and lifted the metal percolator off the stove and poured a mug, placing it before me. The backbar was a sort of little kitchen and there was a round-shouldered fridge and a microwave. There was a red sticker on the front of the refrigerator that read *Asshole of the Month*, and the name Big Fred was written in marker below it.

"This is Mr. . ."

"Vic," the man beside Mr. Prendergas said. He nodded but his eyes stayed everywhere else.

Mr. Prendergas was speaking too loud, the way he did in class sometimes. "He's been convinced to allow me to start his library. He's been away and wants reading material. We're going back over to the Book Barn for a minute or two."

"You're going to get some books?" I said. I was lost for a minute, and then the two of them stood and Mr. Prendergas dropped a twenty on the counter and they left. It was way too much money for that place.

The only other people in the bar were two men with the same haircuts, sitting at a tiny table by the one glass window, in their coats, drinking beer and eating from a bowl of pretzels or nuts.

It was the moment for me. Luckily I had my books and I opened Edith Wharton's novel and saw the date on the flyleaf and my first thought was that it was old, and then I knew it was a first edition. I was in that tavern when I saw it.

The coffee was bitter but hot and I wanted some cream, but I wasn't going to ask. I liked Mr. Prendergas. He was a good teacher, fair most of the time, and he was encouraging. He told a lot of stories in class about his old classmates and places he had been: London and Florence, stories that I would consider again when I visited those cities. He liked Kerouac's novel *On the Road* more than I did, and he said that it was the first novel of the sixties, even though it was published years before.

I saw what he was doing with his Sundays. He'd come to the village and go back to school with a story or two. I felt it myself, the otherness of being in the terrible barroom.

I left the coffee on the counter and went out into the cold. He was going to buy the guy some books. I cut behind the buildings on Main Street, straight for the Book Barn. In the weedy alley the town showed itself to be a ratty enclave hunkering down for winter. Old willows sprang stiff and bare from behind every shed, and in the willows, trash. He was going to hand Vic some books and help him start his new life. I clutched my books and ran.

The proprietor now was sitting in a greasy wooden office chair sucking on a mug of something, which he held in both hands. "Hey," I said. "Is anybody back there?"

"One fella," he said. "I think."

I went through to the space and was stung again by the still cold. It was brown dark in there like a sepia print in an old book, and I walked the long row against the wall. You could see daylight between the barn planks, and there was Mr. Prendergas, on his hands and knees in the back corner. He was crying and when I put my hand on his shoulder he continued crying. "Mr. Prendergas?"

I'd pulled out my handkerchief and handed it to him. He took the cloth and closed it on his face and he turned over and sat on the dusty planks. His eyes were swollen and I thumbed his forehead back to see where he'd been hit. When I coached peewee hockey I'd done this twenty times to some kid flat on the ice and when he opened his eyes, I'd ask him who was the vice president. It was from the first-aid book. If they could answer, they could rest and play again. If they couldn't there was a good chance it was a concussion.

There was no mark on my teacher's face, but his eyes were wrong and I asked him, "Did he kick you?"

Mr. Prendergas nodded and closed his eyes. It was hard to see him crying there, scared and hurt.

"Are you going to vomit?" I said. "It's okay."

"No," he said. I was glad to hear him talk. He was very pale.

"Did he take your wallet?"

He shook his head. "Just the money," he said. "Eighty bucks. Ninety."

"Are you okay?"

He closed his eyes deeply and whispered to me: "Yeah."

He put his hand up on my elbow and his breathing started to level out. He pulled his knees up and leaned back. "Mr. Nunley," he said. "We won't mention this." I wasn't going to mention anything. I wasn't a person for confidants and there were plenty of stories at Coverton Academy without any of mine. We would meet Miles and Jerome at the car, their faces red and their mouths full of breath mints and their jackets smelling of cigarette smoke, and we would drive in the early dark back to campus.

"That's right," I said. "We're okay."

And I lifted him up and we were okay. We never became friends the way he did with some of the guys, but he never held it against me that I helped him that Sunday in Windy Key. 🛡

Sherman Alexie's most recent honors include the 2009 Odyssey Award for The Absolutely True Diary audio book. His most recent novels are *Flight*, released in April 2007 by Grove/Atlantic, and *The Absolutely True Diary of a Part-Time Indian*, his first young adult novel, published in September 2007 by Little, Brown. Hanging Loose Press released a new collection of his poems, *Face*, in March 2009. He lives in Seattle, Washington, with his wife and two sons.

Dorothy Allison is the acclaimed author of the nationally bestselling novel *Bastard Out of Carolina*, which was a finalist for the 1992 National Book Award. The recipient of numerous awards, she lives in Northern California.

Steve Almond is the author, most recently, of the essay collection (*Not That You Asked*). He lives outside Boston with his wife, two children, and mounting debt.

Charles Baxter is the author of *Believers*, *Through the Safety Net*, *Saul and Patsy*, and *The Feast of Love*, which was nominated for the National Book Award. His most recent novel, *The Soul Thief*, is now out in paperback. He lives in Minneapolis.

Aimee Bender is the author of three books: *The Girl in the Flammable Skirt* (1998), which was a NY Times Notable Book, *An Invisible Sign of My Own* (2000), which was a Los Angeles Times pick of the year, and *Willful Creatures* (2005), which was nominated by the *Believer* as one of the best books of the year. Her short fiction has been published in *Granta*, *GQ*, *Harper's*, *Tin House*, *McSweeney's*, the *Paris Review*, and many more.

She's received two Pushcart prizes and was nominated for the Tiptree Award in 2005. She lives in Los Angeles and teaches creative writing at the University of Southern California.

Ron Carlson has written four novels to date and four collections of short stories. He currently teaches at the University of California, Irvine.

Lydia Davis is the author of several works of fiction, including *Break it Down* and *The End of the Story*. She is also a noted translator. She teaches at Bard College and lives in Port Ewen, New York.

Olena Kalytiak Davis, whose last book was published by Tin House, has a new chapbook coming out from Hollyridge Press. She still lives in Anchorage. She has a very complicated relationship with poetry and is currently (not) writing texts about poems that don't exist.

Brian DeLeeuw is an Assistant Editor at *Tin House*. His first novel, *In This Way I Was Saved*, is forthcoming from Simon & Schuster in August. He lives in New York City.

Anthony Doerr is the author of three books, *The Shell Collector*, *About Grace*, and *Four Seasons in Rome*. Doerr's short fiction has won three O. Henry Prizes and has been anthologized in *The Best American Short Stories*, *The Anchor Book of New American Short Stories*, and *The Scribner Anthology of Contemporary Fiction*. He has won the Barnes & Noble Discover Prize, the Rome Prize, the New York Public Library's Young Lions Fiction Award, and the Ohioana Book Award twice. His books have been a New York Times Notable Book, an American Library Association Book of the Year, a 'Book of the Year' in the *Washington Post*, and a finalist for the PEN USA fiction award. In 2007, the British literary magazine *Granta* placed Doerr on its list of twenty-one Best Young American novelists.

Stuart Dybek's fiction and poetry have appeared in several issues of *Tin House*. His most recent books are the novel-in-stories, *I Sailed with Magellan*, and *Streets in Their Own Ink*, poems. He is a Distinguished Writer in Residence at Northwestern University.

Thomas Sayers Ellis co-founded The Dark Room Collective (in Cambridge, Massachusetts) and received his MFA from Brown University. He is the author of *The Maverick Room* (2005), which won the John C. Zacharis First Book Award, and a recipient of a Mrs. Giles Whiting Writers' Award. His poems and photographs have appeared in numerous journals and anthologies, including *Callaloo*, *Best American Poetry*, *Grand Street*, *Tin House*, *Poetry*, and the *Nation*. Mr. Ellis is a contributing writer to *Waxpoetics* and *Poets & Writers* and contributes to "TSE's Pick of the Week" at www.tmott-gogo.com. He is also an Assistant Professor of Writing at Sarah Lawrence College and a faculty member of the Lesley University low-residency MFA Program. *Skin, Inc.*, a new collection, is forthcoming from Graywolf Press in Fall 2010 and his *Breakfast & Black Fist: Notes for Black Poets* is forthcoming from the University of Michigan Press.

Joshua Ferris's first novel, *Then We Came to the End*, won the Hemingway Foundation/PEN Award and was a National Book Award finalist. His second novel, *The Unnamed*, will be published in January 2010.

Tom Franklin, from Dickinson, Alabama, has been a Barry Hannah fan since 1986 and once drove six hours to sneak into one of his classes at the University of Mississippi. Franklin is the author of *Poachers*, stories, and two novels, *Hell at the Breech* and *Smonk*, all published by William Morrow. A 2001 Guggenheim Fellow, he teaches in the MFA program at Ole Miss and lives in Oxford with his wife, poet Beth Ann Fennelly, and their two children.

David Gates's first novel, *Jernigan* (1991), about a dysfunctional one-parent family, was a Pulitzer Prize finalist. This was followed by a second novel, *Preston Falls* (1998), and a short story collection, *The Wonders of the Invisible World* (1999). He has published short stories in *Esquire* magazine, *Ploughshares*, *GQ*, *Grand Street*, and *TriQuarterly*, among others. Until 2008, he was a senior writer in the Arts section at *Newsweek* magazine, specializing in articles on books and music. He teaches in the graduate writing program at Bennington College in Bennington, Vermont and at The New School in Manhattan, New York.

Tom Grimes is the author of the novels *Will@epicqwest.com*, *A Stone of the Heart*, *Season's End*, and *City of God*. His fiction has twice been shortlisted for the PEN/Nelson Algren Award and has been recognized as a New York Times Notable Book of the Year, an Editor's Choice pick, and a New & Noteworthy Paperback. He directs the MFA Program in Creative Writing at Texas State University.

Barry Hannah is the author of numerous novels and story collections including his first, *Geronimo Rex* (1972), which won the William Faulkner Prize and was nominated for the National Book Award. Other books include *High Lonesome* (1996), which was nominated for the Pulitzer Prize. He has taught creative writing at the Iowa Writers' Workshop, among other programs. He resides in Oxford, Mississippi where he is the director of the MFA program in creative writing for prose fiction at the University of Mississippi.

Amy Hempel is the author of the short story collections *Reasons to Live, At the Gates of the Animal Kingdom, Tumble Home*, and *The Dog of the Marriage*, all found together in *The Collected Stories* published by Scribner. She lives in New York City.

Born in Tel Aviv in 1967, Etgar Keret is one of Israel's bestselling authors. His books were published in twenty-six languages. In 2007 Keret co-directed his first feature film, *Jellyfish* ("Meduzot"), which won three prizes in the Cannes film festival, including the prestigious Camera d'Or. In the same year *Wristcutters: A Love Story*, an American feature film based on a novella written by Keret, was nominated by the independent free spirit award for Best First Feature and Best First Screenplay.

Stephen King is the author of dozens of bestselling novels and countless stories, but not very many poems. He lives in Maine and Florida with his wife, Tabitha. His most recent books are *Just After Sunset*, a collection of thirteen stories, and *Duma Key*, a novel. His next novel, *Under the Dome*, will be published by Scribner in November 2009.

Cheston Knapp is Director of the Tin House Summer Writer's Workshop and is Associate Editor of *Tin House* magazine. He lives in Portland, Oregon, with the choices he's made.

Jeanne McCulloch was a senior editor at *Tin House* magazine and founding editorial director of Tin House Books, from 1998 to 2006. Her work has appeared in the *Paris Review, Vogue, O*

magazine, the *New York Times Book Review*, and *Tin House*, among other publications.

Rick Moody is the author of four novels, three collections of stories, and a memoir, *The Black Veil*. He's at work on a new novel, due out in Spring 2010, *The Four Fingers of Death*.

Jean Nathan's essay *The Secret Life of the Lonely Doll: The True Story of Dare Wright* went on to become a book of almost the same title and is under option to Killer Films. Her magazine work appears in *Vogue* and *Departures*, among others. She is at work on her second book and lives in New York City.

Lucia Perillo's fifth book of poems, *Inseminating the Elephant*, was just published by Copper Canyon. Her book of essays, *I've Heard the Vultures Singing*, is now out in paperback from Trinity University Press.

D. A. Powell's most recent book is *Chronic* (Graywolf, 2009). His poems have appeared in numerous anthologies, and he is the recipient of awards from the Academy of American Poets, the Poetry Society of America, *Boston Review*, the James Michener Foundation, and the National Endowment for the Arts. Powell has taught at the University of Iowa Writers' Workshop, New England College, and Columbia University. For three years, he was the Briggs-Copeland Lecturer in Poetry at Harvard University. He is currently on the faculty of the English Department at the University of San Francisco.

Francine Prose is the author of fifteen books of fiction, including *A Changed Man* and *Blue Angel*, which was a finalist for the National Book Award, and the nonfiction New York Times bestseller *Reading Like a Writer*. Her latest novel, *Goldengrove*, was published in September

2008. She is the president of PEN American Center. She lives in New York City.

Jon Raymond is the author of *The Half-Life*, a novel, and *Livability*, a collection of stories, two of which were made into the films *Old Joy* and *Wendy and Lucy*. He lives in Portland, Oregon.

Elissa Schappell is a co-founder and editor at large of *Tin House*, as well as the author of *Use Me*, a finalist for the PEN/Hemingway Award, and co-editor, with Jenny Offill, of the anthologies *The Friend Who Got Away* and *Money Changes Everything*. She is a contributing editor at *Vanity Fair* and a frequent contributor to the *New York Times Book Review*. Her essays, articles, and stories have appeared in numerous magazines and anthologies such as *The Bitch in the House*, *The KGB Bar Reader*, and *The Mrs. Dalloway Reader*. She teaches in the low-residency MFA program at Queens in Charlotte, North Carolina, and at Brooklyn College.

Jim Shepard is the author of six novels, including most recently *Project X*, and three story collections, including most recently *Like*

You'd Understand, Anyway, which was nominated for the National Book Award and won The Story Prize.

Rob Spillman is the Editor of *Tin House*.

David Foster Wallace is the author of the acclaimed novels *Infinite Jest* and *The Broom of the System*. He is also the author of three short story collections—*Girl with Curious Hair*, *Brief Interviews with Hideous Men*, and *Oblivion*. His non-fiction includes the essay collections *Consider the Lobster* and *A Supposedly Fun Thing I'll Never Do Again*, and the full-length work *Everything and More*. He died in 2008. This was his first published story and ran in the *Amherst Review* while he was still in college.

Jillian Weise is the author of *The Amputee's Guide to Sex*. Her first novel, *The Colony*, is forthcoming from Soft Skull in Winter 2010. She is living in Argentina on a Fulbright.

Colson Whitehead's most recent book is *Sag Harbor*.

CREDITS, BACK COVER PHOTOS:
Top, © Getty Images, Tim Hawley,
Bottom: © Getty Images / Image Source

the CALVINO prize

V

fabulist experimental fiction in the vein of italo calvino

new, bigger prize ~ $ 1,500.00 & publication; $ 300.00 - 2nd.

final judge for 2009 - harold bloom, sterling professor of humanities, yale university

~> deadline october, 15, 2009 <~
details: www.louisville.edu/a-s/english

TinHouse MAGAZINE

WRITERS GUIDELINES

Please submit one story or essay (10,000 word limit), or up to five poems at a time, to Tin House, PO Box 10500, Portland, OR 97210. Enclose an SASE (or IRC for international) or we cannot guarantee a response to or the return of your work. We respond within three months. Wait to hear back from us before sending more work. Please do not fax or e-mail your submission. We accept simultaneous submissions, but inform us immediately if your work is accepted for publication elsewhere. Our reading period for unsolicited work is September 1 through May 31 (postmark dates). Any unsolicited submissions received outside this period will be returned unread.

Tin House now accepts submissions online; visit www.tinhousesubmissions.com

ADVERTISING

If you want your ad to be read by the coolest, smartest people on planet earth, then advertise in Tin House magazine! Rates are $150 for a quarter page, $250 for a half page, and $400 for a full page. Frequency discounts available. Log on to tinhouse.com before calling Tonaya at 503-219-0622, ext. 13.

INTERNSHIPS

Would you like to be part of the magazine all the kids are talking about? Internships are offerred in both the New York and Portland offices on a rolling basis. Want to learn more? Visit us at tinhouse.com.

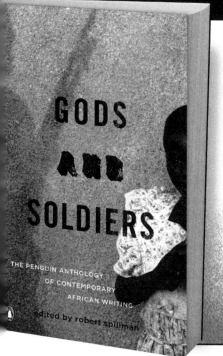